PAUL WEST

THE CORRAL, THE EARPS, AND DOC HOLLIDAY

A NOVEL

SCRIBNER
NEW YORK LONDON TORONTO SYDNEY SINGAPORE

SCRIBNER
1230 Avenue of the Americas
New York, NY 10020

SCRIBNER and design are trademarks of Jossey-Bass, Inc. used under license by Simon & Schuster, the publisher of this work.

Designed by Colin Joh

Set in Janson

Manufactured in the United States of America

1 3 5 7 9 10 8 6 4 2

Library of Congress Cataloging-in-Publication Data

West, Paul.
O.K.: the corral, the Earps, and Doc Holliday: a novel/Paul West.
p. cm.
1. Violence—Arizona—Tombstone—History—19th century—Fiction.
2. Frontier and pioneer life—Arizona—Tombstone—Fiction.
3. Holliday, John Henry, 1851–1887—Fiction. 4. Tombstone (Ariz.)—
History—Fiction. 5. Earp, Morgan, 1851–1882—Fiction. 6. Earp, Wyatt,
1848–1929—Fiction. 7. Criminals—West (U.S.)—Fiction. I. Title.
PS3573.E824702   2000
813'.54—dc21   99-089924

ISBN 978-1-4165-7750-8   ISBN 1-4165-7750-5

I mixed up with everything that came along. It was the only way in which I could forget myself.

—Doc Holliday

Doc was a dentist whom necessity had made a gambler; a gentleman whom disease had made a frontier vagabond; a philosopher whom life had made a caustic wit; a long, lean ash-blond fellow nearly dead with consumption, and at the same time the most skilful gambler and the nerviest, speediest, deadliest man with a six-gun I ever knew.

—Wyatt Earp

Portions of this novel appeared, in different form, in *Conjunctions*, *George* and *Parnassus*.

Sweet old nightshade, his mind whispered as he lurched across the saloon, bumping other drinkers but intent on leaning over the spittoon to make a vertical shot. Not for him the sleek parabola or the deadeye straight line between two points. He hardly wanted to be seen, which was never true of him in his bright seemly days back in the postbellum South before being told when he was twenty-one how sick he was. No one here saw a dull red blob fall from his lips into the mouth of the cuspidor, not even making it resound faintly, and nobody cared among that ravenous, besotted rabble. Doc was part of the scenery, alive, doomed, or dead. Now the old wonder-worry began of what was he doing there; was this all he had been born for? Poker, faro, killing, and haughty buckaroo justice meted out with an erratic hand and a good aim? Here he was, pretending to be several kinds of men, mingling with killers and desperadoes, far from chiming Chopin pressed into sound by his thick muscular fingers, and fine judicious reading, from the Bible to—well, by now he had forgotten the names of the poets he used to read. He even read some Latin. What had drawn him into the stark company of the Earps? His familiarity with death? His ability to sum up his lived life in the teeth of all the days he was going to be dead and all those days he had remained unborn? Who then had urged him to move westward in search of a better clime in which to breathe, as if breath were a tournament of hard icicles in copper-plated lungs? The Earps' closeness to death had echoed his own, he thought, as once again, many times hourly, its raw shadow limped across the buoyant outline of his heyday, one day soon to take him and dust him away as if he had never been. Or, he wondered, did he keep on playing dangerously in the hope of forestalling the reaper's knock? Ida

Pempest had urged him, that was who, she of the spoken spittle and the beefy legs.

Having advanced from sobersides good citizen to playboy, then onward into gunplay addict and glowering death-fancier, Holliday had become an incontinent figure in certain saloons whose gaming tables drew him in like fragments of some holy grail: chance writ large as mediocre heraldry. He pondered, as ever, the spectacle of himself, simply pleased but sometimes even awed that he could be going downhill, up and down Boot Hill, so completely, becoming a man who, the more his lungs wore out, the more he needed to lunge in on other lives. It was a poor bargain, he decided, worthwhile to some other man maybe, less educated than himself, less of a funereal cavalier, but skewed, shameful, almost as if he Holliday were bucking for attention from popular novelettists of the times, to whom Earps were bread and butter. He winced at being himself so much and resolved to do better, though lacking anyone to model himself after. The horrors of being unique in Trinidad and Leadville, Cheyenne and Deadwood, made him wish he had stayed a gullible boy gnawing on a toothpick in pseudo-masculinity, hoping never to be caught out in greenstick maundering, aping other boys while wondering how anyone could come into this world without a blueprint, a clear direction to go in, even a clearly defined road to hell. Was this what Earp provided, then? That old question, nagging at him daily, making him sure of himself even while he went on trembling and his mouth, like that of any dental patient, went on filling with blood? Doc Holliday shook his head at himself, trapped in the tenseless tension of his day-to-day, doing something irrevocable every second, unable ever to draw back from the vast ongoing suck of life, patron of all sweet atoms as they rose and fell.

How had it gone when he rode into Jacksboro, Texas, in '72? Right there at the edge of town had been an oldish bald man carpentering coffins, who looked up at the stranger riding in and called as if in greeting, "Five foot eleven, I'm never wrong, mister. Be seein you." At that Holliday had drawn and threatened to blow the man's brains out, miming the whole performance as he rode slowly through the uplifted fan of the other's gaze, the pair of them held hard in mutual disdain. Then he was past and he holstered his gun, thanking the gods for the reassuring smack of metal against his palm. He was not a killer yet, although a premonition of that status gnawed at him somewhere deep inside as he advanced westward toward health, noting how behavior got more and more boisterous, more final and absolute, as if the Devil had come home to roost. Doc didn't mind this gross declension, rescuing him as it did from the poor fate of becoming a fop, done up in pale blues and satin grays, nattily crafted suits and cravats tied like roses. It had not taken him long, torn as he was between the dandyism of the Southern dentist and the clinking leathers of the Western shootist, to decide how to dress for his journey and indeed all the years afterward (as he thought): in a long gray coat closed at the neck, like a clergyman gone to seed, though perhaps a gravedigger or a sexton would have dressed thus as well. Already he was Doc Holliday rather than Dentist Anyone, an unkind intervener, a confident man who, if he ever made the time, would write an autobiography entitled *Left to My Own Devices*, an epic of lordly whim. Airs and graces he had left behind him in the land of sly gentility, and now he figured on that harsh and arid landscape as of no more significance or consequence than a mosquito on a naked calf of a leg, setting up its unique filtration circus. Early on, he had developed the knack of ridiculing himself just to keep from getting too uppity with the wrong folks (such as the instantly measuring coffin crafter), and would keep things that way, mildly insinuating himself into that or this limb of society until he could bear to show himself off, sponsoring gunplay. In short, as he saw it, he was a hell of a prospect who, once he got himself launched in a dry climate, would soon become a somebody to be reckoned with, taut and stern and no huge respecter of human life. Going out to infect or infest the prairie, he reveled in the prospect of himself, born to elegance, graduand in deviltry, not so much a self-made man as one self-destroyed and ravished by the process of his own decay. How many souls he took with him on his deadly swoon he cared not, provided they did not haunt him in the after-life. He would be happy to be thought of as accursed, *maldito*, self-abused into rotting bravado.

I, he mused, am very much a man of blood, fancy as that sounds. I am at home with it and its pumps, its pomps. I am an invader, coughing disease all over the West after having polluted the South, forcing that metallic-acrid aroma of blood into the mouths of who knew how many willing patients.

He thrilled to be so decisive about himself, knowing how women recoiled from his breath and then became accustomed to its fruit-of-death bouquet as if his very saliva were the manna of orgasm and, when he came, he came red or frothy pink, splutter-ing with it as if God had first choked him on it and then told him to relieve himself. *Rougemont*, he murmured, that might be my name; sometimes, I am red's rider.

What he had learned had not been much, but he had absorbed something precious that told him an abiding truth. Early in life, he had found, the battle was with other students, with memory and manual demands, examiners and resisting teeth, all a matter of smarts and qualification. You were always sticking your head in the sand for safety's sake only to expose to the world the parts you did your thinking with. All that was behind him, kind of, at twenty-one; the battle, henceforth, was with mortality, hardly a competition like that in medical school, or for the hand of some Southern belle sans merci whose mouth prefigured, modeled, that other slimy workbench of nature he had first discovered when he was twelve. Whatever he managed to bring off from now onward would have to be ranked opposite death, compared with it, measured against it, tested against it, which ennobled whatever he did. It was like testing a burp against a tornado, all out of pro-portion of course, but huge and insolent. How many men have you killed compared with how many death had? The very idea gave him potent shivers even as he recognized the nonlogic in the thought. Death was not a competitor but, if you could bear the thought, an ally, a goal, a prize. Surely that was how to think if you happened to be, as he, spoiled, ripe for plucking, a youth dwindling into a fated man, swapping a dental tool for a six-gun in the hope of some infernal reprieve, so much death's that death spared him.

Here he came again, the overmotivated young adventurer, heading west by stagecoach and horse to save his life, confident of the outcome and thus unable to sever the expedition from green-stick notions of savorship. Something exalted preyed on him and supplied a carnal thrill that almost replaced lust or fantasy; he was not leaving the South merely to make a living, to get rich, he was en route to a resurrection that would take him to ninety and beyond, into the flaming new century. When the truth emerged, as he awoke daily or settled down to sleep, the cough always racking him, he was the young explorer gone sadly wrong, exchanging visionary milk and honey for a superlative wasteland on which nothing grew, ran, or cried. It was hard for him to come up with an attitude that responded fully to having failed to save his own life, doing that very thing each day without the faintest idea of what to do next other than go farther, taking his blight with him.

Where, oh where, were the sanatoria he had heard about, mostly in alpine climates, where sufferers lay on long chairs in leaky sunshine, wrapped in furs and quilts, inhaling the frost that (he thought) slaughtered the bacillus? They were in his mind, defunct idylls, denied him by some mishap of geography. So he would be unable, either, to fall in love on an elegant veranda facing a partly frozen lake, with another consumptive of course, forbidden to kiss, or even to breathe upon each other, but mentally enraptured while their lungs teetered.

Where had he acquired the notion that, if things went wrong, they went wrong late, in doddering dotage with a whole other generation on hand to help out? Here he was, an invalid in early manhood, uselessly trekking from one place to another in quest of some accidental angel who would purge him of disease overnight and swoop away with him, offering him career and fortune with the same glad hand, and love's delicate conflagration to boot. Not only did it not bear thinking about; it made him wonder if losing an impromptu gunfight wasn't the best way out, under the roasting sun, in the eyeteeth of a screaming blizzard. All he needed was an end, which he would then attach to his life with disconsolate brio as if brio were glue.

Hence, for him, the interchangeability of all places. One after another they came and went, or rather he came to them and left them, staying when he stayed like a trapped insect, moving on when he did so with weak-willed callowness. There was no compass to this ride, only a journey up and down like the mercury's in the thermometer with no way out, never mind how far his eyes could see over the tight-stretched drumskin of Kansas, say. After a while he began to understand that he did not need an attitude to the spiritual inanity that had overtaken him. He thought of surrendering himself to a monastery in which to spend his last few years in a rough black or brown habit, waiting for the final spasm; but he dismissed the notion in favor of what he came to call his floating fury.

How he longed for the days, not long ago, when he aimed that imitation six-gun and made explosive sounds with his mouth: *kisk*, *kisk*, after which triumphant smoke curled from the barrel commemorating accuracy's kiss. It had been the same when he rode into Jacksboro; the gun had been fully loaded, but the shots had been pretend. He wanted to head back into the gulch of the make-believe, where Wyatt Earp was only a myth and the Latin that Doc quoted was dog Latin, all fake, far from country-dentist erudition. The point-down triangle of his bandanna folded double was something else he wanted to revoke; had he actually held up the Benson stage, a masked man with sullen good manners, asking them to stand and deliver like the Dick Turpin of old, back in the old country? *English highwayman, subject of legends*, the book had said, not *Doc Holliday, American consumptive, subject of make-believe*. Had he ever shot open a strongbox and then kept the box as a spittoon, closing its lid when visitors came by? What had he done with all that scratch? All that blood? Had he really carried old dental tools in a leather bag, telling folks he kept them for torturing people with? They jangled as he lurched and formed new patterns when he jerked to cough. It was never enough to arrive in a saloon, ask for a bed and a bottle; his needs were more elaborate than that. Most of all he needed an audience, not to talk to, but to watch him as he retched and then wiped tears from his eyes, the tears he called neutral because they had no feeling behind them save that of discomfort. A tin cup perched on a chipped plate was never enough either, though he had made do in many a saloon and lean-to. "None of your beeswax," he had said a thousand times when he asked for some decent crockery, an unencrusted fork, and they had wondered none too civilly what he was being so fussy about. Had he once worn an india-rubber jacket guaranteed to keep the cold out, but not the lead slung at him by those who hated the cut of his jib, as he nautically called it?

It must have been the dentist, doctor *manqué*, in him that noticed as no one else seemed to the constant wailing of women in those Western towns, the canker sores, the cold sores, the boils and styes. Something was wrong with everybody without their ever needing to handle poisonous snakes or drink full-strength strychnine, or, more privately, inhale the noxious odors of a severed head kept in isinglass like an egg, to ward off evildoers and encourage sanctity when hung on a pulpit. He had not seen everything, but he had seen too much without, ever, managing to stitch it all together into what he might have been able to call a social code, a mode of life, a tissue of unruly habits. It was not his way to integrate, but to leave disparate phenomena be, refusing to call a million grains anything so united as sand. To him, experience was an addition, a forever ongoing process with nary a sum at the end, enabling him to live (as he wished) from incident to incident without thinking either to death.

He was a chameleon, then, and had often heard that word applied to him, even thinking back to his first train journey from Georgia, when he undressed in a sleeping car so cramped it felt like undressing under a bed. Three berths high, the overnight accommodations held all three of him (the hothead, the aesthete, the dentist) in suffocating proximity. That night in Kimball's sleeping cars, which took him only as far as Chattanooga, did little to calm him for the odyssey—Memphis, New Orleans, Galveston, Dallas—that followed. He had the paralyzing sense that America was insurmountable, actually expanding the farther he went by train and steamer. Fuming, he asked his fellow passengers why the trains were so slow (he had checked on them before leaving) only to be told that, although they could go at a good clip of 60 if the throttle puller allowed it, local by-laws restricted them to a mere 20. At this rate, he thought, the dreaded consumption would sweep him off long before he stumbled gasping into the drier climate out West. Woodburners, hell, he said, they could always burn the dead, just s'long as you could git. Once having seen a hippopotamus in the Atlanta zoo, he remembered its image of congenital slowness, with the bottom cape of its dense overcoat hanging low over its hocks as it trudged away from him. He had hoped that train travel would be swift, river travel lavish, but he soon had a sore spine and a numbed rear end. What did he hear that haunted and perplexed him as his fellow travelers speaking to or past him summed things up and wished themselves far enough? "Horsepital at the depots, they gotta have em." "Unlessen they's dead." No one had the spirit or vim to talk, but, crunched in the bone and yielding periodically to nausea, all assented to the miserable summaries that moved back and forth along the trains.

Dallas, which some of his nebulous-minded friends had assured him lay out West (what was out West was never quite clear to Southerners and Easterners anyway), was as far as the railroad went, and, to be sure, its artesian water might do an ailing dentist a power of good. Boomtown, he said, not a doom town. Who needed to go all the way to legendary Colorado? One who went that far might never get back. At Dallas he would make a stand, sinking not into tonic immobility but being a dentist all over again, plying those big hands of his at something he loved doing. Only later did it occur to him, in one of his spells of highly attuned instinct, that a man could talk himself into anything; no matter where he went, he could persuade himself he was in the right place to cure him, Vancouver or Brooklyn, Archangel or Fiji. He had not pored over maps for nothing at Valdosta Institute, where his early schooling took place. Mentally he had traveled all over the world at a speed of 60 miles an hour, hardly able to distinguish a passport from a pisspot but sucking on horizon.

Sickness, he had discovered, taught you how memory revolved around itself, disobeying time and maltreating space. Even while traveling by train across Georgia, or riding sore-eyed into Jacksboro, he was back at the Withlacoochee swimming hole, where, to clear the water for white swimmers, he had fired into the air above some blacks he found swimming there, vaguely yelling at them in a non-English imperious in tone and jagged in shape. That was the Valdosta bathing beach, purchased by Doc's uncles back in 1872 as a private facility. At first the black youths had refused, obeying some dim memory about water belonging to the planet, but cowed by his gunplay. Behind his words skulked the other words, almost *Git off mah land*, but he was never that hidebound, although about the offspring of manumitted slaves, which these youths were, he wasn't quite sure, not having thought it through. In newspapers and legend he killed several on that occasion, with others moaning on the ground even as he emptied his pistol. Odd that the mythic West toward which he headed in the sleeper or on horseback was close to the West as it was, whereas this mythicized episode from his early manhood wandered far from the truth; they wanted him a badman before he had even started, when he had only loosed off a few rounds to clear the air and the swimming hole. All the same, there were those who said he had no business shooting a gun when language would have done almost as well. He left under no cloud, though. No stigma attached.

There were those who said he had gone to Dallas to try out his meanness, though why he could not have tried it out at the Withlacoochee swim hole remained unsaid, a plausible slander suppressed. Clearly John H. Holliday was a restless, impatient sort of fellow, uncurbed by a father who, on losing his wife in 1866, had promptly remarried, thus incurring the lifelong disapproval of his assertive only son. After all, the boy had grown up fatherless, Major Holliday having been away at the war, and, to prove something, or to get something out of his system, had at the age of thirteen ridden toward the disbanding armies to pick up his uncle, en route running into plenty of hardened fellows who might have knocked him in the head for his horse. He thus proved himself by returning with both uncle and horse, having passed through the hordes of Georgia soldiers mustered out, tough veterans trudging back from as far away as Savannah and Virginia. Denied a robust diet during the war, Doc had succumbed, like so many young Southerners, to the beginnings of tuberculosis. So it would be right to think of him almost as an undernourished daisy, a mother's boy suddenly unmothered. The boy graduated without any acclamation of trumpets, ever aware of the federal garrison stationed at Valdosta to keep an eye on the vanquished. These were poor auspices, inviting clamorous display and high-handed pretension, almost as if, through some quirk in military reciprocity, he had been among the few who won the war for the South after all. Where the flag bit the dust, his ego took root, enabling him to assert himself in ways that other people secretly admired. If the war had been a means to draw the South into the Union, now the South found itself thrust out. The young Doc who fired on would-be swimmers at the Valdosta bathing beach was punishing the blacks who manned the Negro garrison there. No one had required this of him, but he had gleaned it from the smoke of postwar bickering. He grew up a rebel fully formed, having learned, so to speak, to eat scraps off buzzards' beaks and how to hold a wolf by the ears.

Victim of austerity and frustration (all natural luxuries of a well-to-do class suppressed, fastidious connoisseurs of wines now imbibing common potions made from bark yet appraised as vineyard classics), he would make his way through the social detritus of the peace, but hampered and doomed even as he began to feel outward toward a career, an unregional life. Into and two years later out of the Pennsylvania Dental College he went (not the more prestigious Baltimore College of Dental Surgery), then to Atlanta, a young man with a nameplate but also a bacillus that was going to bring him down fast. In his beginning was the malefic blueprint of his end.

So, by the time Doc reached the significant age of twenty-one, he had achieved some reputation as a killer of blacks male and female, defender of family property (much as the monarch of Britain was the emperor and protector of India), and, extrapolated into the harsh ruckus of postwar Georgia, the rightful descendant of a clever youngster with excellent manners "bred in the bone of the small fry belonging to his kind and time," witness the opinion of John Myers Myers. Wise amenders of the local social record went to the Withlacoochee property and noticed how, if you happened to be firing a Colt 1851 Navy revolver toward the broken fencing that gave the far end of the swimming hole a derelict temporary look, as if an ill-built rig had crashed there, a huge bank fifteen feet tall would accommodate any loose rounds; it was like a firing range, so there was little chance of hitting anyone beyond, even if you fired high over the grinning heads, shiny like a drowning piano.

"Shoot over they heads, boy!" John Holliday soon to be Doc had cleared that area himself to make it a commodious pond, sweating and cursing as if he was in the thick of the war itself: his peaceable contribution, he lucky to have missed joining his uncle when that worthy was mustered to the colors. Wholesale lists of revolvers could be had from John P. Moore's and Sons on receipt of a business card. You wonder, though: the holster of Doc's Colt was not so much frayed as charred-looking, having fallen into a campfire on one occasion. A keen observer of the fencework at the swimming hole would have seen the lead shot into the wood when Doc and his uncles practiced with their weapons in the terminal moraine of war, almost as if to frame an elegy in gunshot's echo. This was hardly the frontier, though, only a hormone nursery where a young whippersnapper, whose first cousin, Robert A. Holliday, had founded the first dental school in Georgia, might entertain the idea of going on to greater things.

In fits of insecure, doting adoration, young John clings, cleaves, to his mother, inhales consumption from her like any lover. The bacillus moves among them like a social climber, making the household one of muted coughs and furtively stowed smeared handkerchiefs, wadded absently down between the side of a cushion and the arm of a couch, often forgotten only to be retrieved days or even weeks later, more crisp than before, a rose in hemorrhage buried in once-fresh-ironed linen. It was a house of handkerchiefs, then, as Alice Jane his mother came to white heat in the putrid, choking summers, hoping always for a reprieve, nibbling on petals to sweeten her breath, then turning to mint like an alcoholic. She had never been well since marrying Henry B. Holliday in 1849, who had brought back with him from Mexico two years earlier a war souvenir called Francisco Hidalgo, Frank Somebody as Doc came to call him, an orphaned ten-year-old Mexican. Lieutenant Holliday had raised the boy himself, for no doubt garish and atavistic reasons that held steady even when his son John was born in 1851, the wife unequal and uncommitted to the task anyway as her strength leaked away from her, wondering as she did what the unspeakable relationship was between her unknowable husband and that young dago forever years ahead of her own boy. Just say, and leave it be, that Doc was an angry young Southerner, rebuffed, challenged, provoked, slighted, wounded, snubbed, and heaven knew what else, who cast around and around for some worthwhile outlet for his singularly graceful rage. A volatile melancholic, he prided himself on his slightness, as if not all of him was ever there, as if a phantom inhabited him, wanning and winnowing, and his pet theory—that fair-haired blue-eyed men were invisible in the South—proved itself again and again; he was never seen where he was supposed to have been seen, shooting or wrecking, shouting or threatening with the raffish audacity of a person mostly wounded.

So, although a successful product of refined education, he grew up part refined, another part posing crude. Did he even answer "I already et" or claim something "shriveled mah pod" or boast about shoveling horse-poop or claim he felt like a bump or ask a friend to "quit pullin on that jug afore our damn lives end"? He did more, angling his mouth to say "thang" for "thing" and claiming in select company that he was actually a "spa," as it sounded, when he meant a spy. This baroque exfoliation of his already firm accent must have been a throw-forward to his frontier days when speech cheapened by everything else cheapened itself by becoming not a lingua franca but a stuffy barrier between ranting egos. There was something theatric in him that endeared him to some, his strategy having always been never to try it out on those who couldn't stand it. This called for some subtlety in figuring folk out as soon as met, which he did while almost playing possum: a sly, quizzical fellow while he summed you up, which gave him a reputation for being a cold fish in black, which he never wore, preferring various grays. He had never dreamed actively of the West, but sometimes his malingering imagination conjured up gaunt cowpokes with bushy mustaches riding through rainstorms in long white mackinaws, dread bearers of death and famine. He never suspected he would one day be among them, a sophisticated changeling sent out to grass; for some reason he thought of Colorado, and not even of Arizona; his version of the promised land had silk and gentility within it.

Ever hearing his father arrive home from the Mexican War and dismiss him, he tried to abolish the talk he overheard and transform it into golden reunions of the heart. Instead, however, he heard the old barrage line for line, with his father becoming irate merely because the damned exchange went on and on, his mother weakening and yet, in bursts of well-spoken frenzy, reading the riot act to herself in private disgust.

"You found him where?"

"I did not say. He's kin, come home."

"A Mexican."

"Them's human."

"Your own chile not enough."

"I'll raise him by myself."

"To be like *you*."

Instead of answering he smiled his military smile, clapped Francisco Hidalgo on the back, and hauled him off to the kitchen for a lemonade, leaving one final remark to pollute the air behind him: "This boy got a bit of bull in him."

That was it, the declaration of dependency, hopeless as a knife fight in a sentry box; Doc felt ousted and failed, wishing he too had a Mexican name. His absent missing father had come home to remain absent: it was as simple, crude, and lethal as that, and Doc winced at his sheer sensitivity, amazed that any fifteen-year-old could feel anything so devilish, so vast, within the natty confines of home sweet home.

He soon became familiar with the wearisome apparition of himself burning midnight oil, studying with a beaker of bourbon at hand, marking important places in his dental texts with a spreading dab of liquor in the margin, made by his left-hand little finger being oh so delicate. Or, if drinking at the time, he incised the same marginal place with his thumbnail, sometimes making two little parallel lines, yet haunted by not the most important of phrases: *abrasion of the vermilion border* or *heavy metals (e.g., lead and bismuth) may cause gingivitis.* Most of this sank in as if he had prepared a bed for it; he was amazed by his receptivity to learning, which shows he had already forgotten what a ready student he had always been. To become an expert on people's mouths while his own seeped and purged appealed to his ironic sense of travesty, and the maybe banal concept of the injured surgeon nibbled away at the heroic side of his mind, urging him on, holding him back, assuring him that there had to be another way, another career beyond this, at which he was bound to fail, not for lack of zeal, charm, skill, none of that, but because he was already one of the walking wounded. Was he the forerunner of the man he kept seeing (his mind's eye monopolized)? Alone on a rickety chair, not a dentist's one, in an empty room, this man crouched where he sat, trying to bring a drink to his lips yet somehow always stopping short, unable to raise the glass the last few inches. Saddle trash he may have been, but mythically thirsty he squirmed and writhed, prisoner of invisible bonds perhaps in seven places, even trying to push his lips lower and lower by simple Yoruba-type extrusion until they reached the low-held glass, but to no avail. He was permanently in check, a man bent out of shape by a bad dream, implacable arthritis, a weird notion that he was not dead yet.

Such was the least palatable, least comprehensible, of his daydream follies, nowhere near as stirring and comfy as his lascivious meditation on women, on the secret that made them half-smile, which, he was convinced, was the remembrance they had of their first yielding to male importunity, when the big expressive blood-choked bulb blundered its way past the famous lips, and forward. No woman ever forgot it, and women in a group looked at one another in almost choral unanimity of memory, each knowing what the others were remembering, as if the first time, like the first time Homer spoke aloud his *Iliad*, never died, could never be replaced, became the sole witness, the experience of experiences. This proved, he thought, his openness to women and their experience; he understood that conspiratorial feline smile as it fondled first memory after, just perhaps, the long agitated wait. His women patients loved him, the huge unyielding hands that skimmed their upper bodies as he adjusted their position in the chair, but they flinched from his boyish cough, the cough he coughed instead of coughing outright.

What was the brogue he lapsed into in flagrante when he mumble-blustered his own way in, half smirking at how it was all mouths? What on earth would he have done with a vagina dentata in the chair? Occupied it, he told himself. No, don't you flinch, he'd say, you gotta have it, you bin waiting your best years for this, don't you shrink now. You lit it all relax, honey, like you lost control, an I'll do the rest. No cocksman (he drank too much for that), he nonetheless cut his swath among the girls and ladies of Griffin, Georgia, to which he had moved after a brief stint of dental practice in Atlanta with Dr. Arthur C. Ford on the corner of Alabama and Whitehall streets. He needed a more private office, beginning in spite of himself to develop a circular rather than a straightline notion of his career, putting the most recent thing first, and vice versa, as if tucking time's aberrant tail back into its mouth and canceling all cause-and-effect explanations of why, so early on, he was going downhill though with cheerful fatality, his debonair demeanor the core of his livelihood. Where would he move to next? Someplace he had already been? His career was a carousel, he thought, created to entertain a distant somebody with a passion for the ridiculous, like setting a man with asthma to work among lions, a blind man to lead an expedition to the North Pole. Oh for something more sweeping, he said, like a mustache.

Certainly he possessed a sense of humor although uncertain what having it entailed. Did it mean that, in his heart of hearts, nothing mattered, that all was ridiculous? If so, why try for any career at all? It would be better to float along for seventy years ridiculing everyone else: the sardonic passenger. Why bother taking train or stagecoach to anywhere? Why trouble to keep trespassers away from your own private swimming hole? Why fight a Civil War, so-called? When this mood came upon him, like darkness absorbing light, he turned to drink, though even that struck him as too rational a response. Practicing with knife and revolver, just to protect himself against men more powerful than he in the gambling saloons he frequented, he caught himself asking a series of whys, his mind circling like a dog trying to sit. Why learn to be a son of thunder when, already, he was doomed? The upshot of all these worries was that he decided to live absurdly in an absurd world as best he could, dimly aware of how passionately the mind clung to old ways of making sense of things. So Julian Bogel's saloon in Dallas became the venue for Doc's display; it was here that he rolled the easily moving barrel of a six-gun along the naked arm of Hester Osiris, an only too willing prostitute, just to show that he could do it and how familiar he was with guns. Soon famous for his gentle admonition to "play poker, hombre," a stage line learned, its meaning *don't cheat*, Doc worked on his persona, sometimes setting his knife on the gaming table as an earnest of his good intentions; he had heard that, at Navy courts martial, the accused found a knife on the table at which the presiding officers sat. If the point was toward him, he had been found guilty. So Doc took to pointing his sheath knife at the Ed Baileys of this world, at least until he lost patience and slashed Ed Bailey, the one and only, in the brisket, ensuring his departure from a game corroded by his constant monkeying with the deadwood or the discards. Bailey had offered to pull a gun on Doc, maybe to intimidate him, but Doc was faster. Then they all wanted his blood because Ed Bailey was a popular man in town, but Big Nose Kate got him out of there, tethering a horse for him out in the alley and then setting fire to the small shed in which the horse had been stabled. Peering at Doc through a back window, she had liked the look of him and decided he had little chance of getting out alive. So she found him a six-shooter too. Her cry of "Fire!" got them outside, all except the marshal and his constables, who had the drop on Doc.

"Come on, Doc," he heard as she handed him the gun, "time to go." The marshal and his men made not a move. Rescue by loose woman, Doc was thinking, unable to cure himself of the bad habit of ironic thoughts at dangerous moments. They spent that night in the willows down by a creek and next day she dressed herself in male duds of Doc's brought by a woman friend and the two of them rode the four hundred miles to Dodge City still unintroduced but comrades in arms, always in their mind's eye backing out of that saloon, she in a filmy pink dress, her hair in a carefully arranged upward tousle. Having come together through the rough-and-tumble attending a poker game, they almost wanted their time together to replicate their debut: informal, hectic, no time to think. It could not be, but their impetuous lifestyle guaranteed a dearth of dual thought; they were always involved in some scuffle or skirmish there in the gaming rooms, and often on the move, leaving behind them a gaggle of frustrated lawmen and cardsharps. They expected to be trusted and admired, she the altruistic guide, he the walking dead man sent to sober them up. Bighearted and bumptious, she had the slightly blown looks of the woman who drinks, with her tiniest capillaries (the nose; beneath the eyes) beginning to show like finest spiderwebbing. At some point, the nose would deviate, bloat and begin to wander, changing from dainty upcurl to tuber, but she still had years to squander and her complexion would not achieve that crushed-coral look until she was long past it as a whore. Doctor Holliday, she made sure, would continue as a dentist—"Office at room no. 24, Dodge House. Where satisfaction is not given money refunded"—no matter how much he made from gambling; she wanted a respectable professional man offering her his arm, a role into which he could slip whenever a more ribald, frontier lifestyle threatened to let them down, coaxing them nearer to debt and death.

"You need to see a doctor," Big Nose Kate told him, her hand gripping his forearm as if trying to arrest him.

"I a doctor am," he answered. "Some who are doctors can consult themselves, at their own risk. Some who are doctors don't suffer. Most of the people who do suffer are not doctors at all, yet they go on consulting themselves. I have seen doctors. They all tell me the same thing. What I need is a doctor who tells me a different thing, who says my nose keeps on bleeding and the blood pools in my throat, not coming from my lungs at all. Now *that's* what I'd call doctoring." He envied those people who knew everything, answering all questions, confounding miscellaneous interrogators with templefuls of data culled from the sciences, the history of ideas, summaries of world literature, distillations of economic records. He was not a learned man but one with a narrow, fixed emotional stand from which he never budged, never mind how much Kate pushed him, urging this or that upon him only to recognize in the end that he had long ago made up his mind about his fate and had gotten used to it, gambling always, surrendering prematurely so as to have a smooth decline into deathliness. Was that fair to himself? She thought not, but she could see how much he needed to be firm about things, as if it would be effeminate of him to keep on hoping; it was braver, more heroic to take the death sentence on the chin and tough it out.

"You need a doctor," she insisted. "*I care.*"

"Maybe," he said, locking his big hands together and cracking the knuckles to some unknown rhythm, "I need Colorado. If I really cared, I would try to go to Switzerland. You might say, and here I quote as only a boy who attended grammar school at Valdosta Institute can, I am half in love with easeful death."

She had not heard the phrase before, and she found it repulsive, fresh-raised from some sewer; romantic dalliance with morbid melodies was not her forte.

"I was quotin," he said.

"Nothing new."

"Oh, I don't know," he joshed. "I sometimes go a whole month without that. I remember stuff but I don't say it 'loud."

He was looking into the oily sheen of a certain swimming hole as if, a mirror to futurity, it contained his fate, the exact length of his days, the manners of his final cough, the last words he would utter, a far cry from her humdrum daily talk about sloshing milk, choking on a pepper, possum pie and whupping storms, stogies smoked and men contemptuously addressed by other men as "girls, you girls." Above all he didn't want the black of a high school band uniform; that was too much and a rending nostalgia to everyone. He was not a mere cowpoke craving a poke, but a doctor denying his own sickness, then going along with it as his own special impresario, proud of the manner of his going, although always choosing the wrong words when talking about consumption to those who did not have it. He yawned the gape of a man not getting enough oxygen, murmuring to her, "It don't have to be this way, I shouldn't have to talk about the thing at all. I'm my own man, with all my old speeches rammed back inside me to wait for the last trumpet. Honest."

She blotted her tears with something silky and bulky, not altogether fresh, but salty from an earlier use; when had she last cried? Oh, five minutes ago, in her cups maybe, when she failed to manage the spontaneous sympathy that had sent her to him in the first place with a horse and six-shooter just to get him out of an impossible standoff. Had she been weeping then? She had not, but how she felt about him, *on sight*, had been the internal form of grief, seeing how he was fixed and not backing down, a doomed man standing his ground. Now, how had she known from the back of his head, the set of his shoulders, that he was doomed? It was something that came off him, diluted lightning or dispersed blackness, she could not say exactly what, but it had been there hung over him like a miserable, grave canopy shielding him from livid rain. She sometimes thought she was a mystery woman, all visions and hunches, maybe a long-distant ancestor getting

Paul West

through to her across the ocean of time to acquaint her with truths as bizarre as peach trees wrapped in goatskin gloves. Doomed men were entitled to marry whores; that was the truth of the moment, though she had not told him and never would, she never, *nivver*, a pleader once her mad was up, and it was up now.

·2·

She could hardly believe the degree of her dedication. Here was a man who had knifed another in a brawl over cards and she had helped him escape the local law, bringing to the event the kind of intense resourcefulness people came up with when they were shocked to the core. Because she wouldn't do any such thing, she did it with aplomb and so impressed Doc that he was still with her, on the run, hoping to settle somewhere, even though, as the days went by, he felt his life had careened beyond his control. Irrevocable bets had been placed; final acts had happened. He was no longer that nebulous fusion of dentist, gambler and boozer but an equally cloudy fusion of criminal, pessimist and fancyman. He could so easily have been someone else with a different partner; he felt all his options slipping away because untended, unregarded. And, though erotically partnered, he felt more and more alone, cut off from the culture whose familiar irritants had sustained him. He missed most of all the delicious embarrassment of having too many things to choose from, which was no doubt another way of saying he had left early young manhood for a maturer state, glancing back, shrinking forward. Impulse, he told himself, guard against impulse, it takes you to the country of no reprieve. One knife slash and your entire life changed. One Ed Bailey, coming toward you from who knew what point of the compass, could make a new and unworthy man of you in seconds, even if his own life had changed permanently because, willy-nilly, you had laid his foolish stomach open in a fit of temper. Then why go a-gambling at all? To stay away from such places would save you, if you made the resolve in time, protecting the life to come with a velvet prudence. Doc knew that thinking it over would get him nowhere, but his tendency was to ponder things anyway, suddenly aware that you didn't so much learn from experience as experience learning, which was never of any use. He had discovered, in the wake of so many frontiersmen, the farce of the impromptu, which occupied you for seconds only but shaped you for years. You lived from impulsive act to impulsive act, filling the in-between time with liquor, cards and women. That was the way of it: none of your sublime, calculating dentist with a diploma on the wall and a swelling clientele who loved his conversation. Now his diploma was in the scabbard of his knife, would soon be in the dark holster of his gun; wherever that line had been between aspiration and finality, he had crossed it, walking hand in hand with Big Nose Kate into the Wild West.

Was it a pandemonium then? Not quite: it had its sedater lulls, its pauses for payment and civil greetings, for fried food and purchase of clothing and paraffin; but mostly it was a roaring plenty, Dallas or Leadville, Fort Griffin or Dodge, improvised by cowboy drovers fresh off the long cattle drive and those lurking there to curb them for a week at most.

He soon discovered she was one of those women who kept insisting he apologize for this or that half-forgotten thing: a lost temper, a sardonic word, as if he had always to be mouth-perfect. He wished he had never left the South, where they were more hospitable to outbursts of rhetoric. "I would no more apologize for losing my temper," he told her after she had stood there grinding her parasol into the dust, "than I would try to suck back a fired bullet. My temper is mine to lose. That is what it's for. Not to be kept in, bridled, but to be lost and lost again. Tempers are for nothing else, certainly not to be kept." This infuriated her, but she ascribed his orneriness to consumption, making excuses as always for the man she could not fathom. It should vividly be explained to women that losing one's temper is part of the male badge, and, in Doc's case, using a gun to reinforce it was a must. In the right fit of rage he would plug anything that moved and see nothing amiss in so doing. Often enough he had heard his mother refer to his father as a bear with a sore head or as a moon man, lunatic at certain times of the month, and he knew their rows came from their being utterly different, from the ancient rift between male and female. He was happy to be how he was, volatile and trigger-happy; he wanted to be sincere rather than decorous, and that got him into all kinds of trouble in saloons and stagecoaches, on trains and porches: born irritable, as the poet said of poets, but meaning men in general.

So here he was, clad in gray suit, derby hat, accustomed to coughing it up with the best into spittoon or chamberpot, pulling iron whenever he wanted to and beating all to the draw—though by no means a perfect shot. Many, having seen him outdraw them, chose to short-circuit the battle by dropping their weapon to keep him from firing, but to do this they had to get their weapon out in time to drop it before his trigger finger tightened. Ironically, this meant that those few who got away with it, making him hold off as they disarmed themselves, were the very ones who might have winged him, after he had winged them of course, but winged him all the same. What mechanics went into surviving and winning. He improved slowly, eventually coached by killers as if he were some music-hall performer, in the end good enough to hold his own in their company. Yet he was always better with cards than with guns, preferring faro (he loved the echo of *pharaoh* in the name) to poker, but willing to take on all comers at all games. He enjoyed the reasoning, the bluff, the guesswork, the feat of memory involved. Less ponderous than dentistry. You sat down to it. You made more money. And you met a lower class of people, which gratified you if you weren't a snob. Most of all he liked the mix of women, booze, suspense and suspicion that attended the tables. You could enjoy these things all at once, and whoever you shot was right in front of you, waiting a table's width away, ready to die.

How he got to this state from being an amiable roustabout he never knew, attributing all his changes to what made him cough, but he suspected that having to cut a figure for the women, out of vanity, had something to do with it; not quite a show-off, he nonetheless wanted to produce credentials when required to. He could no longer be anonymous, and he soon was not. Once his head had begun to buzz, his brain took off and fed him images that changed his whereabouts to something more exotic, the saloon girls into houris and odalisques, the gunmen at the tables into knights; and the words uttered took on a nobler cast:

"What you starin at, mister?"

"I ain't starin, I'm prayin for a better hand."

That sort of stuff came out nobler, tainted with derivative magnificence. Then, when he sometimes had to fall flat as a pancake on the floor, Doc would make sure he landed right, able to do his twist draw because the butt faced forward, for speed. And whatever had been shouted—"Balance all to the bar!" meaning drinks all round—went on repeating itself like the gunfire that broke out right at a table devoted to Spanish monte or whatever. That he was doing something undignified never occurred to him, perhaps because the etiquette accompanying consumption did not have to be civil or gracious, only the merest concession to a force beyond a shootist's control.

Was it the landscape that was harshening him? No buildup, no plumes, no fronds, no arbors, no gardens meant for sauntering in? Where he had moved to was all practical, bare, too much horizon perhaps, not enough social clutter that, seeming to get in your way, gave you delicious dilemmas to think about. The South had been edible, he thought, amused at his own turn of phrase, not so much created for human convenience as the outpouring of some doodling divinity intent on thickening up the region until it needed a hairdresser, a manicurist, a masseur, certainly a trimmer to keep it all within acceptable limits. The West needed no such thing: a man or a woman was isolated on the vast plateau under a punitive sky with uninterrupted wind, much more alone with his or her thoughts than in the South. Thrown back on your perhaps incomplete desire to be yourself, in the West you began to weary of self-assertion, yearning for the old hypocrisies, the curlicues and deviations of everyday hypocritical behavior. If he had a frontier streak in him, and his shooting spree at the Withlacoochee waterhole proved he had, it required full development to pass muster here as an acceptable trait. The towns throbbed with bumptious, drunken shootists, the barren plains gave them somewhere to practice in, an art form between gratuitous offensiveness and vengeful monomania. Here, pushy as he was, he had to push even more, and hard, even to be noticed, and, God help him, he did want that, he hardly knew why, but perhaps because on the way down you want to have people's attention, especially if you don't scream or complain. So they would remember him, if at all, as the gunman who spat blood, a picturesque cameo they probably needed if they were to have a complete pantheon.

Bare tough lands made bare tough men. It surely could not be as simple as that, he mused. How about: bare tough lands bred bare tough dentists—it could be true. And then bare toughness invaded the dentistry as they plowed and yanked in people's mouths. Suddenly he saw it: if he gave up dentistry and whatever minimal physical satisfaction it brought him, he would depend more on gun and cards. It was the beginning of a wobbly theory, not to be tried out on Big Nose Kate, who loathed all such frippery, but to be pondered nightly as he fell asleep, unless, as was likelier, he had stayed up until dawn and the huge brass ball in the sky had loomed to greet him as he staggered back to his lodgings. For insufficient reasons, Doc liked to hang around until sunup, certain then that he had survived into another day, snatching one back from the Furies, better than losing one (as he saw it) by dying in his sleep a few hours before dawn, as would have been the normal way. He resented sleep as a mindless deduction, at the same time forgetting to resent drunken stupor as yet another. Between the swings of sleep and the roundabouts of inebriation he came out even, little pondering that equation as a man hectically on the go, bound to win.

His very name concerned him, which was to say his nickname, the name that eked him out. When he had been a straight dentist, "Doc" had seemed almost an overcompliment, whereas now it suggested something criminal and underhand, as in "doctoring the books." Still qualified, indeed still practicing, he wondered how many colonels there were left over from the Civil War, no longer colonel-ing yet reluctant to drop the rank. Some lawyers called themselves Esquire, which amused him no end, and he wondered how far other obsolete titles—Sheriff, Special Agent, Ranger, if these were titles—carried on, tagged eternally to the names of their owners. It was clear that, confronted with eternity or merely a lapse into the petty humdrum of civilian life, a man needed some supplement, a one-second prelude that announced a person of consequence. People by and large, he decided, did not like names, preferring descriptive prefixes, which suggested to him they enjoyed thinking in categories such as the Reverend or the Reverend Mister (this the correct form, he dimly remembered). So: "Doc" had overtones of professional usefulness, but had fast acquired a new, extra tone of perversion: the doctor who both cured and killed you. Behind the relative amenity of the sound lurked a morbid joke about the doc who cured you with a bullet, and all your medical troubles were over forever. Was *that* how people saw him? No wonder they fondled their holsters in his presence.

His mind played truant, meaning it rewrote history for him without warning. This time around, at the Withlacoochee swimming hole, he killed everyone in sight, and that included the little Mexican parasite Francisco Hidalgo wished upon them by his father. Down at the swim hole, with rubber gloves impeding his hands, he strangled and drowned the twenty-three-year-old Rachel Martin his widowed father had espoused, murmuring to her lightly floating corpse, "You don't belong, honey, you don't belong." He even stationed an armed guard, with orders to shoot to kill, at the water's edge, equipped with a bucket of lime to dump on any corpses that happened to float to the brink. When he finally met his uncle at war's end, instead of returning home they set off on an odyssey through the South to sample its abundant gorgeous poetry, all the way across to California. Best of all, he went for treatment to Salzburg, where for an entire month he inhaled a special gas of peppermint and methane, dispatching the bacillus and returning home in flawless health. He became the only Southerner to wear his six-gun butt forward and eventually became a special marshal in Atlanta, rounding up Mexicans. This revised life came and went in his mind, neither dream nor reverie, but an assemblage of torn restitutions, patches of an honorable flag, bits of physically endured nostalgia begging to be jigsawn back into the perfect pattern of his life before consumption. His mother was cured too, which meant she never infected him.

·3·

Big Nose Kate, as Doc kept reminding her, was actually Hungarian, her childhood having been spent in the Pest section of Budapest. Her name, Mary Katherine Haroney, which Doc in his provocative way told her rhymed with baloney, transferred easily to Davenport, Iowa, where Katherine's parents finally settled, sounding Irish until they opened their mouths. Kate, as she came to be called, never lost her Hungarian sarcastic cast of mind, eager always to make something sting if it could be tender, a gadfly to Doc's Southern hot temper. Something of a wanderlust fanatic, she ran away from a series of guardians, who took her on after her parents died in the same year, when she was fifteen, and took the steamboat south, soon to begin work in a charitably dubbed "sporting" establishment run by a James and Bessie Earp. Baldizar, her mother's maiden name, degenerated into Elder, and Kate Elder then showed up in Tom Sherman's dance hall in Dodge City. Kate had one of those finely sculptured European foreheads sloping back not a bit, a perfect rounded rectangle with the thinnest of skins draped over the mild bulge. It was a shape loaded, one presumed, with exquisite motives and noble impulses, very much the forehead (the beforehead) of a scrupulous and fastidious lady, bony in its delicate austerity, smooth in its sheath. To contemplate it reassured you that she came from the finest, almost ethereal stock and would never allow a hair, never mind a lock, to dangle over it, impeding the view of that chaste curvature. It was a high, honed forehead, pleasing Doc because he had never seen one quite like it, and her nose sloped gently down from it in a minor inward curve to the bold philtrum and the sharply chiseled mouth. In later life she combed her abundant hair forward into bangs, which Doc disliked, but she refused to change it, convinced that it was unladylike to reveal too much forehead lest she be thought much too brainy. Most of all, Doc loved to lift her bangs and kiss her all over it, omitting not a fraction, until the whole area felt cooled and moist, in the course of which process he tugged her hair back hard so as to expose her forehead. He fastened her hair back with saliva sometimes pink, an act she found repulsive at first until she recognized he could do no better with the materials at his command. Had she really, as Doc had heard, come from a posh St. Louis finishing school? Or had it been Switzerland—Davos—where she had been awaiting Doc's arrival to consummate a meeting generated in myth? If only he had gone where his intuition had prompted him. Whence that pervasive dream of her saying, "We'll go to the Crimea and gather flowers"? That was all she said; he never answered, and they never went, in the dream or otherwise. She sometimes stirred in him the oddest feelings of here-before or, worse, the sense that this was not their scheduled life together, but an unsavory dry run.

"Romany" he would incorrectly sometimes call her, or even Gypsy, making a gesture in the direction of European nomads. In a sense they had both become wanderers, congenital drifters eager to shed names and reputations and happy to have become part of a lifestyle that depended on guns, cards, and liquor. She was not the only gun-toting woman he knew, but she was the least inhibited and therefore the most likely, in a quarrel, to shoot him dead out of pique. "Yeah," she told him several times (it was one of her things to say), "when a woman takes offense, you call it pique, a little bit of a flash, but when a man does it's the end of the world. You fellows take yourselves so seriously. It all has to do with getting it up or not getting it up. The strain shows over a lifetime, doesn't it, my daisy?" He knew better than to protest, but he added all such comments to the big sum of grievance he kept mentally, something to get back at her for in the fulness of time. Now, to a man with consumption, what the hell was the fulness of time?

Life as they knew it never began before afternoon, when they took the air strolling; but that was a mere prelude to the resumption of busyness around five o'clock, when things really began to hum until well past dawn. This inverted life suited him well, he who had trembled on the brink of bourgeois respectability without falling in. Life at its most intractable had converted him, he said, had switched him from tentative respectability to heroic grandeur, going up in flames without ever whining, but initiating from that extreme stance actions of desperate caliber that got him into newspapers and on the lips of gamblers far away. He would not have liked it otherwise, delighted to have settled in somewhere, at the innocuous-sounding address of c/o Deacon Cox's boardinghouse: Dr. and Mrs. John H. Holliday; not that they ever married, but they often availed themselves of the pious formula, though also going out of their way to scrap it, she heading back for bawdy night life, dancing and carousing, he finally removing his dentist's nameplate—a man could not draw teeth after a night on the town. Besides, as he became better known in the cow towns, the desk clerks in the hotels began holding rooms for him until at least three in the afternoon, lest he showed up demanding. This irritated other travelers, but it soothed Doc, who liked his mounting reputation: Do not cross him or he'll start shooting. It wasn't much of a name to end up with after all that education, but it was a tangible something, much as to his Kate a five-minute row with him was worth a month of married bliss. Combustible both, they were a potent alliance when they focused their energies, but usually they wasted them on each other, magnifying tiffs into melodramas with six-guns waving. Any day he might plug her, she worried, but that was what added the piquancy to life. And he may well have, especially when in his cups, only vaguely aware of what he was doing and she had become just one more mannequin in the array of dummies who encircled him at a distance, all part of the not-him, there to be shot to pieces or ignored as the mood seized him. All he remembered day to day was that she had saved him, maybe from a lynching, and that in his primitive system of debts and payments ranked both high and permanent; he was always, he felt, paying her off without quite discharging the debt. Perhaps he loved the bond it created, attaching him to her through thick and thin, whatever either of them said when their dander was up. This link survived any number of wounding remarks by either party; it was his responsibility to save her, and there was no way in which he could since she was too fearless, too self-reliant, too much of an individual. Now and then she craved his affection or his tributes. That was it. When he refused to court her, she would go on a public toot denouncing him like the dynamic tart she was, miscellaneously calling him liar and cheat, criminal and rustler, but also whoremaster and deviant, daisy and poof. Once she had let off steam, she tanked up again on liquor and repeated the volley, varying and trimming it until as far as rhetoric went it had a certain offensive shape. No slapper of women, Doc would arrive and march her out heedless of her screams, privately thinking it was only a marital spat. And that was the way of their evenings, dawns.

Gifted always with a keen nose, he preferred women heavily perfumed, not to mask whatever natural aroma they gave off, but because the artificial appealed to him—the multiple tang of tar, eucalyptus and camphor coming together where rank sweat might have been before. He never tried to pin smells down, defining them at best in terms of other smells, but he was minutely responsive to them. Big Nose Kate, his concubine, perfumed herself distinctly, maybe cheaply (he wasn't quite sure), but it was not woodsy, not herbal. Fruity perhaps? He thought not, always resolving to ask and then backing down. Something acrid and metallic came off her, almost as if she had sweetened a vinegar and mingled it with ammonia. In his mind's eye he saw her decocting vials in her private room in Deacon Cox's boardinghouse, almost—he grinned at his formerly learned self—a Lady Faust at her laboratory, making herself fragrant before trolloping out for the evening in a swirl of undulant loose flesh that had the doodaddled-up cowboys goggling. She was some picture in the evenings, a woman become her own bouquet, her scent preceding her by yards especially on one of those dusty windy Dodge evenings when the wranglers came outside to refresh their lungs before diving in for another bunch of hours. Some of them had spent three months on the trail, anticipating the Big Nose Kates all the way, whereas Doc had been there inhaling her daily, fascinated by the little rubber bulb of the atomiser she squeezed in loving patrol over her entire body.

Coming to know her body intimately, he developed an intenser relish for its less private places, eyeing her forehead most of all, wondering at its convexity, asking the dentist in himself if there wasn't just a touch of hydrocephaly to it, and did that account for her explosive behavior? Cupping that curve, he both took pride in it and minutely flattened it, wanting it less outward, perhaps indented slightly inward, he had little idea why, but that was what he wanted in a perfect world. The idea of perfection, however, soon left him; he was making the best of a bad job, attuning himself to conditions he'd never anticipated, not for a man with his background. Much the same was true for Kate, the transplanted European aristocrat, earning a coarse and vulgar living on the edge of hell. Noting once the amazing width of her tongue when she opened her mouth wide in extreme pleasure of all kinds, he made nothing of it, merely reminding himself she had a wide face, so all was proportionate and dainty. She *was* an unusual-looking beauty, that was certain, and many envied him who watched her on his arm even when she was chiding him.

"Doc, you shouldn't, you really mustn't."

"I sure as hell will," he'd answer. "I'm my own man."

Sometimes, of an evening, they had to push hard through the throng milling about on Front Street, cowboys airing their lungs, after years of months in the heartless open, unaccustomed to being cooped up in saloons full of smoke and other fumes. For a fair number of dollars they could watch a lady's limbs flicker atop an ancient matt-veneered grand piano, two teasers in red garters, but they had come from a long siege by thunder and lightning, rustlers, swollen rivers, hurtling winds, tornadoes, Indians, and sundry gross acts assignable to God. So they jammed outside and did not walk, just stood steaming in the chill of evening and got in Doc's and Kate's way, yelling and swaggering, drawing without shooting, throwing up and falling over, clapping one another on the back in manly affection, shoving shoulder against shoulder as if involved in some arcane heaving heavyswing contest whose prize was—what? Inhaling deep the perfume of the lady trying to get by, her long nose aimed downward at the straw, dung and dust beneath their feet? Yes, Doc thought, these are the world's outriders, come all that way from Texas to see the elephant, as they say, and here they are at the elephant, ready to buck the tiger, whatever they mean by that. Truth told, they are like the Bedouin of Africa, hardened by savage landscapes into professional receivers of suffering. They don't even notice the pain of it all, the discomfort, knowing they have Dodge or Abilene to come at the end, like saints going to heaven. When they drive the herd through town in a kind of celebration, that's the end, that's the last ritual, and then they go hog-wild. I can understand.

·4·

Up the Chisholm and Western trails they had come, aimed at the region where heaps of hides and bones, debris left by buffalo hunters, adorned the snaking rail tracks. This was where herds of buffalo impeded the trains, delaying them for hours, and a cowhand might die of astonishment. Who here rode night watch on the buffalo? It was a different life, from which eventually they were glad to ride away, their minds haunted nonetheless by the smells of the raucous cattle town: straw and manure floated over by the wholesome aromas of baking bread; coalsmoke and woodsmoke mingled with brutal perfume from brothels whose open doors brought them the sounds of piano and fiddle, an occasional banjo. This was the oasis their minds ferried back to where they were semi-respectable citizens in bunkhouse or home, here only to gape at the train whistles and admire the trains as they lumbered in. Pistols were as thick as blackberries in these towns, and the tanned young men, crop after crop, were centaurs, more than half horse, but squandering their pay on new white hats and furry chaps, having their photo taken as if this was their last day on earth, tophands and wranglers and punchers, the rough army of the Texas breeders come to blow out and then smuggle home the image of a violent paradise open only to cowhands.

Doc caught himself envying them their uncritical, wild approach to the Dodges of this world, and then realized the riot was all theirs: without them, Dodge would fast become a pious haven, and Gospel Ridge would gradually extend itself deep into town and respectable lawyers and bankers would sun themselves in little gardens fenced off from where the orgies used to roar. No more redlight district, no more shootings. Prophetic nostalgia made a lump in his throat as he saw that he was here for carnival too, verbally correct as he tried to muster his *farewell* to his own *flesh*. Here in the heart of buffalo country, the educated side of him labored to annihilate itself, forgetting what it knew, murdering its vocabulary, restricting life to a few shudders in the loins and many more in the liver and the kidneys. Drunk enough, he would pass muster as a no-count ruffian, hard-assed and arrogant, ideal fodder for the Prairie Grove Cemetery and the improvised oral obituaries of some Hambone Jen or Squirrel Tooth Alice, alive in repute only, a hero of Babylon who had volunteered to mark himself down like a hat gathering dust and mousedirt in a storefront window. Sometimes Doc was hard on himself, setting up the old South as some huge slab of confectionery, creamy and tricked out with icing, sweetened with cachous and lemon peel, candied fruits and Jamaican brown sugar. That was where he belonged, or rather where his healthy counterpart did. Here among the con men and the shootists, he was like Macbeth striding past the midpoint in that river, lucky not to be among the night's leftover dead wheeled away each morning with other refuse.

Was he liked, this pasty-faced rather thin blond with the blue eyes? Some said he was dead from the eyes down while others found him a witty, unpredictable companion. In spite of having a rowdy, overweening slut on his hands, Doc managed to gain a reputation as having several degrees from European universities and having completed his education at Heidelberg. According to this version, Doc spoke several languages, was well versed in the stock market, and sojourned in the homes of the well-to-do. He had been an excellent shot since his grammar-school days and had spent time as a United States marshal. Far from being the sourpuss that some said he was, Doc was a man of elated vitality and spiritual poise. He was everything—a banker, an inventor, a judge, an attorney, a sea captain, a naval officer, a doctor, a dentist, a university professor in Philadelphia—and a great seducer of highborn women. Roaming around on a buckboard with an entourage that included a professional heavyweight boxer, a racehorse, a fighting bulldog, several gamecocks, and a couple of overbearing whores, he had won a name for being a ready man, a man of parts, a man of insoluble but fascinating complexity, an affable misanthrope who, if he did not like you, told you so. He had even, some said, a collection of scalps taken not by himself but by Indian hangers-on. "You the man who's been ev'where and done it all," Big Nose Kate told him only to hear, "Don't you believe it, honey. Shucks, I'm just a gentleman out of his depth."

Whatever might have been said against Doc—that he was as cold-blooded as a snake, liked his own company only, turned into a user of people—it had to be conceded that he became more and more observant, watching life in detail as it receded from him, not least Big Nose Kate's face, over which he pored and pored, even when she was talking a blue streak at him as if the specimen had come to agitated life under his anatomist's gaze. Her nose, that famous nose, for instance, attracted him because, starting at a sharp point, it curved down away from her face because her septum, instead of going more or less horizontally backward, described a convex curve, showing up in profile as a major portion. It was every bit as noticeable as the rest of the nose, and this fascinated him, making him wonder what Hungarian quirk it embodied, from whom; but, when he asked her about it, she dismissed the whole thing, being nothing of the scrutineer that he was, especially of herself. She did not look back, and she spent little time peering into mirrors, the tenor of her life being self-assertion so that others would do the looking, pushed into an almost passive attitude while she blazed away. Her standard answer to his probing, semi-learned questions was a bluff, hearty "Well, I'd better be gettin a hitch in my getalong," or some such frontier formula that meant I'm exasperated, shut up, leave me alone, don't fuss, act more like a man less like a dentist. There was no annulling the inspectorial side of his nature, though, the side that should have gone on with speculum and probe, "doing people some good," as he referred to it. It was strange when those who got to know him found the temperate examiner of phenomena in this consumptive hothead, as if another personality had completely taken over, but this was the cold-as-a-snake side as they called it: not so much an attitude to people as an affinity with them as ailing samples, like himself, what the dying Doc had in common with them as their livers, hearts, lungs, and eyes gradually gave out under the pressure of pell-mell debauchery. Of the few calm folk in the vicinity—the scribes, the weighers, the record-keepers, the accountants—he knew little, but he would have appreciated their impassive skills.

Of course he made Kate uncomfortable, forever quizzing her about matters she'd forgotten. Trying to be precise, he became aware only of myth's nonstop hyperbole as it worked even on their own lives: she had rescued him from a gaggle of deputies by setting fire to a saloon, and several had been injured in the fire. On the tale went, deviously embellished, until, he thought, a mere blink of his in the morning (if they could so much as catch him alive then) would return elaborated to him in the evening as a dirty look preceding gunplay during which he actually closed his eyes while firing. Kate hardly noticed such quivers in public attention, such trespasses upon finitude, but he never forgot how, being quite active in his daily life, he underwent their sea changes unconsulted. They created the Doc they wanted, prey in that rowdy cow town to plunges of zealous necromancy.

When he saw forward, as he often did, disregarding the imminence of death by tuberculosis, Doc saw himself as a respectable citizen penned in behind a garden gate festooned with barbed wire to keep the rabble out, yearning to go watch the trains come in opposite a blocked-up culvert full of boulders and broken staves with misbehaving cowhands gallivanting on the tracks, almost caressing the locomotive as having come from the land of heart's delight, somewhere north of here, Montana perhaps, where the sweet snow of Texas in winter became the spiked snow of nearly-in-Canada. Would he ever last that long, until the red lights of the railmen all found their way back on to the locomotives, the brothels having closed after railroad tracks wormed their way to Texas and beyond? Was he going to last until civilization even of a deep Southern kind found its way to these droning prairies? Everyone but he had no regard for the future, confident they would live to see it, yet sure they would not need it, whereas he, under siege, forever correcting his demeanor lest it seem hangdog or fickle, needed it like a cure and knew in his heart of hearts, his lung of lungs, he would not live to see the day. Never mind, he told himself. Grab the now, do it all at once, three days in one. Never come just once; make the lady wait, sluice off, then go at it again until not a jet, a spot, was left and he was spunked out. That was how. He was a man who, denied his private swimming hole, made swimming his entire mode of life, becoming a water-baby, a water moccasin, when he might have become a casual swimmer who took his daily swim without fuss or formality. Now, what he longed for was too far away and he was obliged to craft a lifestyle from crude and violent elements more appropriate to the Civil War than to a qualified dentist. Thus made over, he cheered up at the rumor of bullfighters coming from Mexico to enliven the local circus; Eddie Foy, strutting about onstage at the Dodge Comique in a convict suit and a tinhorn's monocle was not enough diversion. He had heard of people who had arrived in Dodge only to become recluses while reading or rereading the whole of Shakespeare's works, shot dead, however, before reaching *Macbeth* after only one rash excursion into gambling with the likes of him. How he had done it, he wasn't sure, but he was fast acquiring the reputation of a badman, a callous gunslinger to whom his fellow men were optional targets. Nobody out here killed half as many as he was supposed to have, but the legend went out, the entire township fed on extremes and lies, munching myth before the incident ever took place, if it ever did. This was a town whose inhabitants wanted to live hugely, bringing to events an attention that enlarged even before it managed to get anything in focus: premature grandiosity, he said, the disease of Dodge. All cows were buffaloes.

Throughout his wanderings in the West, Doc had developed an acute sympathy for other wanderers, not just young girls transplanted from Hungary into buffalo country, but any human catapulted from, say, India into Atlanta, who ended up so bewildered they thought they were looking with the wrong pair of eyes. It was an old trait of eyes that they looked comprehendingly only at what they were accustomed to, all else being barbarous rebuff. Familiar as he had become with Dodge and all those unkempt places in between, he retained his outsider's amazement, though nowadays he doubted if even Atlanta would suit him. Just possibly, no place was now his, giving off for him the comfortable harmony of an old girlfriend. Here, in the wild and monotonous prairie, in the big flats, you never cozied down but stayed on the alert, ever ready for some tumble that would send you crazy for keeps. Born far too early to know what a displaced person was, he identified himself as such, with the way wide open for him to change his name, the color of his hair, his profession, his mode of dress, his way of talking. Here a man might start all over again, reassembling himself from the ground up even as others drew a bead on his heart or his brainpan, heedless of the crisis in identity hidden behind all that skin and bone. Whoever you might be when the bullet struck, you were shot as him or her; it didn't bear thinking about. Here the random met the accidental and left it cold.

In the domain of the slickshooter, he decided, a man's faults were hidden by the dazzle of his finest moments. Something like that. Or vice versa. Habituated to people-watching, he came to the weird conclusion that, of all those he gambled with, he hadn't seen a single one stand up. They somehow arrived in sitting position and left in the same way. So he didn't know who was short and who was tall, so he guessed from such things as one man's having a tall man's stoop in the set of his shoulder blades, another's being too thick in the neck to be one of those long drinks of water. What he went by, mostly, he called doxology, Doc's Ology, which was to say hunches regarded as doctrines, with a medical man's mind applied to unworthy subjects, like Charles Darwin playing darts. He was astounded by some of the things he'd heard about that not a soul in Dodge regarded as even competent fiction. Too much thinking about where he had landed himself, and with whom—Hungarian termagant and devourer of the flesh—and he would be done for; but a man had to have somebody, it was no use drifting around in a long shiny coat waiting for the next challenge. In Dodge, as elsewhere in the West, you had to combine the ordinary fart-trapping of everyday with pure high-flown moments of sheer terror. There were old gunmen, there were bold gunmen, but no old bold gunmen. If he had made that up, he was improving, no longer the slave of what ailed him, whether it galloped or seeped. Some days he was strong and could take deep breaths without a coughing spasm; others he crouched over as if above the source of bliss, campfire or vapor rising from a pot of stew, but the crouch was a pose of surrender, an acrid lean that said he was packing up if it went on like this, and he wondered which poets in an unknown language had made final and permanent their own doxology even while coughing their last. The only one he remembered was Keats, but there must have been more than him, even in the deep South after the war. A ravaging sense of loss came over him again and again because he half-knew what his life might have been like if only the bacillus had not invaded him and his mother. He might not even have been a dentist, but maybe a soldier or a teacher, a maker of speeches, a judge. Did all men, he wondered, spend their days revolving inside a miasma of the omitted and the unattained, wailing for a life never had, unable to manage the one that came their way? It seemed to him that most commitments to career were playacting, nothing but deliberate assumptions of a petrifying mask behind which the indecisive man choked and bled. To spend even a short life thus was murder of some kind, a slow-boat suicide not worth praising even for its transcendent obstinacy, fine phrase for cussed drive. He no sooner lost hope than he found it again. Let that be said for him in his dither.

The serious, compassionate man summarily buried inside the miscreant and ruffian managed to see that his Kate had problems almost matching his, but he found it hard to think of her difficulty as she moved in a cloud of cheap scent whose war cry was Come and get me, I'm available. She made no bones about her lecherous and commercial side, and he realized that, although he was the biggest rock on her beach, he was not the only one. Something ravenous in her abolished the amenities of a love affair. Too attractive to her sexy father, she had suffered his nightly incursions, half-interested, half-revolted, wondering why men remained so implacable about their organs, unable to say them nay. Sexually precocious, then, she soon became past mistress of the diddling arts, almost as if Daddy were grooming her for the oldest profession, getting her ready to oust her competitors. She had told Doc a little of this, subject in which he interested himself little (the war was over, the battle lost), but he could not make up his mind if girls who had been interfered with by their fathers came out any worse than girls left to their own catastrophic endeavors. Whatever their initiation, it was all bad, all good; that was what nature wanted for them on earth, nothing else mattered. So when she came to him in a reflective, nostalgic mood, eager for solace, he contented himself with the notion that, had her father not jumped her, she would never have smelled so good as she did now. Blousy, bosomy, filmy, frilly, drenched in the aroma of violets, she incited men to cheap, lascivious dawdling, fragrant always with soap or shampoo. As Doc saw it, they came to her for a good sniff; unwilling to wash themselves with any degree of vigor, they would retreat from her after getting their money's worth to her cries of "learn to scrub, buy some soap!" She was a reformist at heart, wanting them all as fastidious as Doc himself, who didn't so much want a monopoly of her as never to see her other customers. Besides, because of his illness, he could not always perform, and on such occasions he told himself he needed nobody at all; the mere sensation of being alive was enough, which was, perhaps, to assume the outlook of the puma or the roadrunner. Nothing human about it: just the quiet seepages, the rub-a-dub-dub of the heart, the indeterminate rhythm of the brain's silk suet. To be in proprietorial touch with such miracles was almost enough, sometimes; but he could see how such self-denial affronted her, who dwelled on personalities and encounters, puzzled by his ability to shrink back from people into his well-tempered abstract delirium. There were times he didn't want to be anybody at all: just a cougher and a bleeder, harnessed to nature by misfortune, but filling his part of the bargain nonetheless. If nature made you bleed, there was a way of doing it; you did not have to invent it for yourself. The blood vessels were always there, to guide or spill, it didn't matter to them.

Thus, sometimes feeling at several removes from the affable, jaunty life the rest of humanity lived, he became hypervigilant, having nothing to do save monitor the sponges and jellies within him squooshing away. He missed nothing, might indeed have made a splendid gossip reporter, as alert to nuance as to major ruction. A born watcher, with all the character defects traditionally associated with such a person, he relished the human pageant: here, the gambling, drinking, shooting, the whole spectrum of brawling, not as entertainment but as an index to vitality he did not share in. He husbanded his energy for those instants when his life depended on his being fast, wily and brave, as when, right there in Dodge, a little time after he first met Wyatt Earp, Doc saw Crawley Grove draw on Earp behind his back, apropos of nothing. Doc's pistol came out before his warning did, and his bullet passed clean through the assailant before he could even pull the trigger. Watching this event, a bunch of wild and woolly Texans cheered and stamped their feet while Earp mustered a strained, wide smile. This same person that Doc had shot had tried to get behind the Comique bar and run things, free, from there, and that had started things off. There had been some headbashing with gun handles, and then intervention by Earp with city marshal, ready but not premature. Only Doc was going at the speed of the drunken cowboy, and there he was in the shadow, a sleek, sartorial figure with a white shirt that rose to a ruff around his neck, wide-brimmed grayish hat, sleeves if anything rather too long, no cuff showing, his feet wide apart like those of an athlete prepared to lift. One knee was forward, bent, making a distinct bulge inside his silk-faced long coat, his big hand dwarfing the sixgun, his sometimes almost invisible eyes aimed at where the bullet was going to go. He could gear himself for such instant action by being, much of the time, passive and aloof. He knew this, calling it the arithmetic of readiness. Now he and Earp had met for a second time, on this occasion through the techniques of their métier; no brief nod, no handshake, no mutual civil growl, but a detonation of gunpowder, a squirt of blood. And still Earp seemed distant, even more distant than Doc estimated he himself could be on certain days. Here was a case of the calm exterior promoted into statuary, he thought; you would have to kill more, make more noise, get wounded yourself, to extort from this paragon any kind of gush. Yet, as Earp later told it, on that occasion he was surrounded by desperadoes, all with revolvers drawn, and seconds behind them, only to have this shiny phantom in the shadows do it all so fast it seemed a trick of the light. When at last that version reached Doc, after running around Dodge for a week, he felt appeased: Earp had really noticed after all how Doc had saved his bacon.

"You bin shootin again," Kate chided him.

"I always was. It's my way."

She then launched into a recital about how a stray bullet had struck one of her friends in the arm, but he showed no interest, instead extolling the virtues of the soft-leather gunbelt. He was occupied with matters of style, noting how Wyatt Earp wore the kind of shirt that had a detachable collar: no ruff, like Doc. When he wore a necktie, he attached his collar on two studs.

Kate leaped upon this as soon as he mentioned it. "You men," she said, "always thinking up ways to get an extra few days' wear out of a filthy shirt. I wouldn't be surprised if they didn't come out with a half-and-half shirt, so's you could launder one half while wearing the other." Doc's only response was to wave a clutching hand in the air as if giving up hope. He had saved the man of the hour, it was as banal as that, and he felt his presence in Dodge begin to slide into the orbit of myth, already knowing how he would figure in all the other versions of the shooting in the Comique. If Earp ever smiled, he thought, you'd never see it because his muttonchop mustache hid his mouth completely. He could have been smiling for a month, just so glad to be still alive, and Dodge would never have known. "Dreamin about Earp again," she said. "You men don't dream about women anymore."

·5·

How that chiaroscuro from the Comique plagued him, as if he
had been photographed and the image burned into his brain, dim
as the light had been, crowded the venue. Something about it
appealed to him, reassuring him that he had gone beyond being
merely useful or sensible into almost a perfect stance, becoming a
paragon of loyal zeal. The entire sequence was a homily to all
men, and he, Doc, had shone in it, thinking quick and shooting
sharp. It is perhaps a sad day when a man begins to believe in his
own glory, or when he suspects there may be more to him than
commonplace humanity. Nobody else defended Earp, who would
surely have been killed or maimed. Was there enough light? No.
Was anyone backing Doc, from behind or at some other angle?
No. Was Kate lurking, as before, with gun in hand, rescue in her
Hungarian heart? No. If Doc had seen his own photograph, taken
by no one, he would have observed an oddly contorted fellow
with a droopy mustache, both his legs foreshortened because one
leg was bent in the direction of his target, though why he had to
crouch in order to aim at a shoulder cannot be known. Oddly
natty in his shiny-faced long saddle coat and frilly-topped shirt,
Doc seemed wholly out of place: an import from the deep South
to be sure, almost posed as if he had stepped right off a river
steamer without his bags. There he semi-kneeled, taking aim
even as the other's trigger finger tightened and Wyatt Earp
almost stopped breathing. A blaze of light fell upon his boots and
spats, but the rest of him was in gloom, the barrel of his revolver
parallel to the beading that ran across a panel to his left. Earp
looked surrounded, by watchers and the man with the gun. His
hands were low, his left almost over his crotch, his right frozen in
the upward grope toward the forward-facing butt of his pistol.
His face had a look of indignant bafflement, almost as if to say

O.K.: The Corral, the Earps, and Doc Holliday

Let's begin again and see who comes out on top. You can't possibly start this way, not with me in my clean striped shirt and the red scroll on my chest that signifies my role with the Dodge City police. You have drawn on an officer of the law, mister. Not a word escaped him even though he had the psychological upper hand, being the genius of the tawdry place. Doc was an irregular appendage, that was all, while the Texas cowboys, looped and mouthing off, looked unfit to draw on anyone. The true contest was between Doc and Crawley Grove, man whose grave never even bore his name. Above the hats of the Texans three globes of light shed an oval of yellow in front of their feet. The entire event detonated and collapsed with the sound of one shot, and spurs clinked again as boots trod the boards; people were walking around, even promenading, out of sheer relief; it was as if Dodge had never had a shooting or a stand-off before, or perhaps never a deadeye dick of a dentist restoring order by means of an extraction of the highest caliber.

After that shooting, Doc had more than an inkling of the way his mind was going to behave in the future. The thought began that, because any reasonable man hated a person's illness, he might grow to hate the sick man too. Hating his own sickness, he hated himself for being so. Was there a catch in this? He thought not; the transition was logical and sensitive, even if its results were severe. Certainly someone could be something other than his sickness, but the basic fact about him would be the one that all civilized folk detested. Why, he had seen it in people's eyes when, after a cordial first meeting, they had heard and seen him cough, smuggle a bit of blood out into a handkerchief or even his cupped hand. They had looked away, all the light going out of their faces, the ready warm affability draining from their postures. If he was like that, then they wanted no part of him—he might even get some of that stuff on them, and who knew where it would end. They might finish up in the same sanatorium together, each cursing the other. Along these lines his most intimate thinking went back and forth, determined to indulge in nothing rash, but preoccupied with woundedness and retaliation. It had not hurt him at all to shoot that Texas cowboy; Doc's standpoint was the view from the grave, a tad premature maybe but invincible.

There was something else gnawing away at Doc, something related to this business of sickness and hatred. To prevail in the face of death, in other words to maintain your dignity and pride, it helped not to have an attitude toward it. You did not respond emotionally to such an unemotional thing. He kept trying to reach this attitude, convinced that being no more worked up about death than death was about you was exactly the way to go: not so much the Almighty's view of you as death's. Once you had attained this view, however, and in this he was imagining, it might just happen that you adopted the same view of people, receding from them emotionally on the grounds that, doomed by disease, they might be hateful to contemplate. In a short time, he suspected, he could be hating the entire human race, willing to kill or not to kill, it didn't matter. Having no attitude at all save marksmanship and speed on the draw struck him as a possibly evil point of view, but justifiable if you had a bacillus taking you over, converting you into sponges and jellies, dribbles and spasms, spit and ghoulish. No amount of joking or good humor changed this fact because from day to day its hold on him increased fractionally, so he was obliged to hold the line at impassive passivity, talking to people as if he still cared, but at bottom having despaired so much of his own recovery that he would sooner end it all for him and them than hang around for the miserable finale. So he was working out as best he could a strategy and tactics for moribundity, like someone trying to invent radio or photography, the like of which had never been heard or seen, least of all in the interior temple of private being where pain met shame.

Don't make too much of your affliction, she kept telling him. Don't put people off. People included her, by the way. It didn't take much to get them moving away from him, and he wondered how he would seem, twisted up upon himself with his vocal cords tied in a knot, trying not to cough or clear his throat of frogs. He would have loved to be that kind of person who had a bell-clear voice, was always ready to speak with the cleanest, clearest enunciation, an operatic filament ablaze with light. The impression he gave, he thought, was always hesitant, nervous, especially to people who did not know what was wrong with him. How could he be so keen with a pistol and so diffident with his mouth? He was not always diffident with it, though, and had found suitable occupation for someone such as himself, oddly pertinent, he decided. One day, stark naked, she wound herself up in a huge sheet, not a winding sheet by any means, and told him to do what he could to please her. She loosened the sheet. Up he climbed, from her ankles to her groin, inside the sheet, like a cat burglar on daytime assignment, even as she gurgled Hungarian belly laughs at his initiative. When he emerged, after a while, knowing he had given pleasure and offense at the same time, his mouth was stained red, and they cackled with laughter wondering whose blood it happened to be. Their memory of this encounter kept them from any repetition, mostly because he felt some double taboo had been broken, some fell fate had been invited down to do its worst with them. Trouble had already arrived, it was no use inviting it in, or asking the Furies to come feast on your short hairs. I know what it amounts to, he explained to himself, telling her none of it: I am suffering from that unique side effect of the liberal conscience—guilt. Well, if not guilt, then superstitious remorse, at the back of my mind the ancient theory that all the bad things that happen to you come because, way back, you asked for them or consciously dared them to take you on. Blaspheme, and then ask God to strike me dead if he cares. All those taunts could add up to a dose of consumption, brought into being to teach him a lesson. Pleasuring her at the wrong time of the month could bring pagan ambivalences upon him, when he was not sure what kind of life he should be living other than this: oh, perhaps still in the part of Dodge called the Devil's Addition, wrong side of the tracks of course, in redlight Valhalla; he wanted something extreme and racy, violent and scandalous, but at the same time he wanted a few bourgeois comforts, not as if he were a gunrunner in Africa or a bomb-thrower in Mecca, but just maybe a dentist in the Middle West, marooned in soft furniture in the landscape that had seen the deaths of twenty-five million buffalo. Not for him a one-week spin in a trail town, but some quiet immersion in Florida plantations or a fortnight of that bracing pollen-free Prince Edward Island weather. He could not resist the feeling that he had chosen his lifestyle from too few options, now self-condemned to life in a series of towns where vice paid the salaries of the police. He could have been a banker here, or a successful dentist, having children and helping finance the local church, but it was too late for that. Several times a week, arriving cowboys wretched from months on the trail shot up the town, bashed in the windows, uptipped the stores, helped themselves in the saloons, perforated signs (Try Prickly Ash Bitters in Front Street a chronic favorite) and in general raised so much hell it became part of the background to a good game of cards. Few people came out to see; it wasn't safe to do so, and the residents of Dodge had better things to do indoors. After a year in Dodge you bore your own semi-monastic quiet about within you, incapable of being disturbed by whoopee gunplay, or by wind, rain or quaking earth. So, briefly, the externals belonged to the invaders, from James H. Kelley's two-story opera house, the Occident and Old House saloons, Hungerford's Meat Market, the York, Hadder & Draper Mercantile store, to Samuel Marshall's Land Office, Mary Goudy's Bakery and John Mueller's Boot Shop. The amazing thing was that so barbaric a town had stores of any kind and not just a billiard hall. Had it been so, Doc would not have been able to tolerate living there; the hidden bourgeois in him would have revolted, crying out in his bones for Atlanta, Valdosta even, and he would have lit out, not just southward in winter, as he often did, but hugely outward in search of civilized amenity.

As day succeeded day, Doc felt he should have had a bigger response to it: he was a day nearer death, and it would never come back. An irrevocable fraction of his life he had squandered away and had not paid it the least heed, riding his idiot's treadmill in pink-eyed oblivion. How could a man, even one with "galloping" consumption, do something so drastic with so little heed? Perhaps it was because a day was a mere splinter, hardly worth worrying himself to death over; perhaps it was because he had already given up the ghost and was spending his last days in a fatuous charade. Maybe, he thought, someone with strong enough imagination could bring days back, stroking them home from near-oblivion with a lover's hand. If so, he did not have enough imagination, or enough longing, he who was still in his early twenties and unlikely to enter his late ones.

Then there was Earp, whose woman Mattie had joked about her teeth, offering Doc a loose wisdom, but getting in return only a hostile look and a few quick unmedical words: "Keep your baby teeth in your mouth, ma'm, where they belong. I've no use for them." She took it well, but privately wondered what he thought she had been offering him. One look at her and Doc was convinced he would have to deal with Wyatt on a bachelor basis. And deal he did, for some reason swearing to himself loyalty and usefulness to Wyatt, not out of the goodness of his heart but because he sensed in Wyatt a man with a design for Dodge, for Kansas, that he intended to force the township, the state, into, whether it wanted to go that way or not. That was the pragmatic side of him, related perhaps to his hero-worshiping one, that saw Wyatt as a clever colossus in a feat of exaggeration open only to a sick man yearning for grandeur and achieving it only by proxy. He had twice already been of use to Wyatt—had actually saved him on another occasion by intervening in a highly unorthodox way, racing from the gambling table and Cockeyed Frank Loving to where his gunbelt hung on a rack alongside another. Snatching up both, Doc hurried to the door—how could he ever forget it? If Wyatt had not been a hero before, he was one now, yet only because his gratitude had been overt and complete; if he had acknowledged Doc's help only slightly, Doc might have gone far astray, reluctant ever to help again, indeed going so far as to assist those, of whom there were always plenty, aiming to gun Wyatt down. Beyond the practical and the hero-worshiping sides of him, Doc felt a true, transcendent call to greatness of his own, the only career left open to him, to be written in gunsmoke as Keats's was in water. Only with an Earp at his side, though, would he succeed in this, or so he thought, waiting there in the anteroom of virile ambition, wanting to assert himself with ironclad authority. What had he called out to those Texans on the night in question? "Throw em up!" Had he really, to the amusement of the cornered Earp, added ballocks, bloodsuckers, assholes, buffalo fuckers and other profanity to his pure command? He hardly remembered, granting only that, if he had, he had shown more presence of mind than he'd ever known himself for, more gift for cursing than a Union soldier. All this with a Georgia accent, somewhat effeminate to the wide-open-mouthed Texans, who nonetheless did as they were told, all but one. "What will we do with em, Wyatt?" At that moment, Wyatt had buffaloed Ed Morrison with the long-barreled Colt given him by Ned Buntline, laying him low with a single smack. Then Earp spoke, in a voice just as cool and baritone as Doc's: "Throw em up!" Then Doc and Wyatt had stripped them all of their guns, rammed these into a sack, and marched the Texans, still with hands up, across the deadline and the tracks to spend the night in jail. That walk back from the jail to the saloon had been Doc's coming of age, resplendent in office without a badge, hearing Wyatt utter those magic words: "Withouten you, Doc, I'd a been cashing them in, this time. Mean guys, all. You didn't have to do nothing so fierce, so—forgive me—foolhardy. How you came not to be shot, I can't rightly tell. You *must* be fast." From that day on, Doc became one of the local elect, avenging angel on Wyatt's right hand, a man with a destiny cobbled out of a rowdy night.

Doc conceded he *was* fast (he always had been, from his teens), but he was something else: he was brave, and this not in the I-can-take-it mode of the blustering invalid, but in the other mode of the visible hero, acting it out in front of hostile men. It was like the conversion of penmanship to print: the brave man seen to be brave, and therefore expected to be brave thereafter, wearing a star or not, using few or no words, neither dressing the part nor trading on it. He was just a man called to hectic service, no longer outlaw-in-waiting but a local celebrity to be dreaded and answered to. A slow spiral chill invaded Doc whenever he thought about what he had done that night: his moment had come and he had met it handsomely. He could retire now from peacekeeping and he might remain a legend of the West, even if he did nothing more beyond drink himself to a premature death. He would leave no letters, no widow, but hand good report of him to be accomplished by the Earps, the Foys, the mahogany-skinned old-timers who dined out on him time and again, memorializing their sickly paladin. No one would recall his table talk, for he said little while gambling or carousing, having committed himself to the silence of blood, bone and skin. Silent, he was alone with his body and in the best of company. Son of a patrician society, he went off to die among the surviving buffalo and be ever remembered as a transplant, a stranger.

"You're somethin now" was Kate's verdict.

"I was before," he told her with his best Georgia accent, staring her down in a highfalutin manner.

"In Dodge, I mean."

"What I did," he slyly insisted, "was spontaneous. I had nothing else in mind."

"I like my Doc bein the nice guy," she whispered. "He never does anything for hisself." The rest was Hungarian and inaccessible.

"Some help to Wyatt," he said. Voice of smashed velvet.

"Your star is right now bein hammered out," she told him, "with all the silversmiths in Kansas. Soon you won't be speakin to the likes of me, poor soiled doves of need."

"You and whose angels?" He scoffed and shoved her backward on the bed, where she actually bounced, more down than up, so soft and sundered was the mattress.

"Well then," he said, murmuring from a distance, "I am going to renounce my profession as a dentist, as well as that of consumptive. I am going to be a gunman. It didn't take much. A man might just as easily become a banker or a goldminer."

She was humming some unrhythmic tune, her gaze on the ceiling so as not to meet those cold quizzical doomed eyes.

"Yes," he resumed, "a new destiny, to put it fancily. No money in it, strictly an amateur, that's me. But worth a bit of effort. I haven't shot anybody through the head yet, not that I know. The day will come, and then no turning back."

·6·

If he sounded impressed with himself, he thought, it was only because, for the first time, his name had been joined with the names of the good guys like the Earps and Charlie Bassett, and the bad ones like Ed Morrison and Tobe Driskill, even Pat Garrett, said to be among the motley Texan crew, years before becoming the sheriff who killed Billy the Kid. The only name he did not recall in his roundup of a daydream was that of Crawley Grove, the punctured.

"You're big guns now," she said, both taunting and idling. "You the big gun."

"No," he said, "I am the big blood. That's me. I have little going for me in this world. Nothing in the next. Maybe my lousy destiny is to kill off a few badmen before I go. I could do worse, Kate my bonny." His voice, blurred by mucus, rose and fell, as if searching for the ideal pitch to match what was being uttered, but he never found it, and settled for a wobbling, warbling kind of delivery that quarreled with the firm tenor of his thinking.

"You big-man," she hissed, half-envious.

He told her to quit it afore he welted her one with the barrel of his six-gun, not so much feeling his oats as sending her out to play, do whatever she wanted, even seek a new client in Front Street. He was bigger today than being possessive; the only thing he cared about right now was living up to the role fate had offered him even as he gambled and the house was losing.

He would not truly have arrived as a peacemaker until, like Wyatt, he had an emergency arsenal stashed in some easy-to-reach place like the Long Branch, where Wyatt had his. It was a matter of knowing the chances. Four or five double-barreled shotguns would suffice, he thought, wishing with all his heart he had had one such when confronting cowboys. What damage he would have done, although with such a weapon in hand he might not have needed to fire. How did you evaluate the imposingness of a shotgun against the hotheadedness of any given cowboy? Frighten them to death, he thought, cough on them and teach them the truth about the bacillus. When you pistol-whipped someone with a shotgun, you terminally smashed their skull; you were serious, you would rather maim than kill. He was learning, gradually. Twenty-five whiskeyed cowhands was almost a war situation, which led him to the thought that any such assembly in town had best be scrutinized and not allowed to plague the streets. One at a time, these cowhands didn't amount to much, but as a mob they could work untold damage. There was a philosophy among the leading lawmen that said exploit *the dead man's moment*, when you had one second before the other's bullet thudded into you and you had, at least, to avenge your own murder by taking one of them out with you, knowing you had this choice only: be shot unavenged or be shot avenged. When there was no hope of escape, this was the best you could strive for, murderous in the finale, balancing the mortal books. Pondering this crude philosophy, Doc almost wished he were still a dentist, thinking what a mean little cobra a man had to be to even sign the showdown with his signature. Always to be thinking of such last things, on top of fretting about consumption, would surely be too much, never mind how fancy and potent was the badge you wore. Why, men breaking their foot shackles with an ice hammer had better odds. Then he saw: these were not odds at all, only the stylistic difference between two different ways of dying.

He tried to tell Kate, but she went all Hungarian on him, giggled, dismissed the topic as foolish, and tried to tease him into an erection. Meretricide, he mused in a fury, is murder of a whore. How come this woman can never tell when I am thinking, or join in to *what* I'm thinking and provide me with compatible notions? How different, he decided, from his confidante at a distance, Miss Mattie Holliday, his cousin, to whom he wrote some candid letters even after she took the veil not long after his departure, becoming a Sister of Charity in an Atlanta convent. How good it felt to have someone uninvolved out on the periphery of his shambles, unjudging him and urging him to concern himself with the afterlife. Anyone preoccupied with the dead man's moment, as Doc was, would do well, she argued, to envision as best he could the successive plateaus on which the soul might rest, especially after being evicted from the riddled body.

A soul may be worn, worn out, she wrote him in 1878, *but it must remain symmetrical, it must have a dignified shape, not be some impromptu ragbag of pious tatters but possessed of grave integrity, knowing where it had come from and how it must now appear, called home from earthly horrors.*

He had no idea how to counter her absolute zeal, her penchant for visually apprehending the most abstract entities. It would be simpler to agree with her in all matters, trusting that her care for him would work in his behalf among the crystal lattices of heaven crowded with angels and caulked with prayers. So he never quibbled, seeking always to adjust his rhetoric, his gunman's doxology. The contrast between the two of them was almost criminal, yet they had in common a preoccupation with death and how to approach it, she seeing it as a blessed reunion with all-embracing spirit, he more crassly as what was, with polite crudity, called a hog ranch, meaning a brothel. Of killing she said nothing, although he had told her in rather stilted sentences about Crawley Grove. She eased herself away from the nub of this violence by assuming he shot at men to save others; it was always a feat of altruistic self-defense.

Not the details, she wrote him, *but the tenor of your days.* He answered (or retaliated) by resorting to wit, as when he asked her if there was an Irish equivalent of *mañana*, making her wait until his next letter for the answer: *Yes, but it lacks the urgency of the Spanish.* This kind of witticism proved to her he was on the *qui vive*, but what with her averting her mystical gaze from his gunplay and his debauchery and him suppressing his increasing devotion to frontier life, all they had in common was soft eloquent moribundity like cream cheese between wafers of charcoal. He was a dime novel confiding in a rosary, something such, a ruffian blessing himself with a postulant's prostrations. Who was that Younger, he tried to recall, shot in the face so badly he could never again take solid food, who killed himself rather than live out his days a cross between a bagpipe and a colander?

Are you praying? She asked him this in each letter.

No, I am not, he wrote in each of his. *Are you praying for me?*

Weeks of waiting. Then:

It has to come, she instructed him, *from a profound sense of unworthiness, you have to plumb the abject in order to do it.*

The usual month or three weeks ensued even while other letters went off and arrived. How could they remember except through insatiable obsession?

Never, he told her. *How can a bacillus from Mama make you abject? Angry, indignant, maybe. Nothing else.*

Wish yourself worse, she responded. *Speak to God from the lowest rung, down in the mud of your killings and your Kate.*

He could not, confessing that his mind surged up within him, asking him to mend his ways by killing more and more evildoers. What a virtuous obsession.

Then apologize to the Almighty, she hectored him with slashing pen strokes, *on the occasion of each one: before and after. Be contrite as a dog that has bitten.*

Doc was not up to this, yet he needed her nominal succor, blaming himself without retreating, asking her to intercede with the deity that had created nature and allowed it to go wrong.

Francisco Hidalgo, he steams, *get thee behind me, I have enough troubles here in Dodge without acid memories.*

I remember Francisco, she wrote, *your Dadda's peace trophy, his blood money for Mexico.*

Then please forget him, he told her weeks later, the mail seeming to take longer as they peered aurally at each other over the ravine of consecrated time, each wondering why the other needed to be in touch. *Clammy, fevered,* he told her, *wake up in a headsweat, watery most of the time with little scraps of free-floated tissue, always a tightening in the lungs, I am an oil light going out. Did your divine one want me this way?*

Her reply invoked weakness of the flesh, its perishability, the prime virtue of the soul as rising above all despicable phenomena, and her hope that he would avert his gaze from the destructive element this world was and waft clean away, ultimately wholesome and renewed.

He had even told her how Jim Kennedy, no marksman but a blusterer with a gun, had been trying to kill Mayor Dog Kelley, whom he had not even hit. His shot, however, had ended the life of Dora Hand, who once had a passable stage career as Fannie Keenan before inevitably sliding into the displaced-person universe of the red light. Jim Kennedy had been fond of her, as many others had, and it seemed to him hardly kind when Charlie Bassett, Wyatt Earp, Bat Masterson and Bill Tilghman galloped after him, an eminent posse.

But, *had Miss Kate been killed just as accidentally,* she wrote to him, *you would as you say have been charged with the crime, and no doubt not let off as Jim Kennedy was for having been shot once by Masterson. What an odd ricocheting kind of life you lead there. You have to be careful whom you befriend lest their accidental death convict you. Don't be there. Come home to the South. In any case, Dora Hand seems to me a better stage name than Fannie Keenan, which sounds common and undignified. Yet what do I know of such things, marooned in a nunnery, by choice?*

He told her nonetheless he was glad of her views, which gave him some perspective. Their exchanges, sometimes taking the form of pellets or mere phrases, had to endure long times in between. Saying something lengthy, he would pause in order to send it off to her, and she would respond just as tersely, rather enjoying their taciturn concision, knowing an exchange such as this might occupy a full year, embedded as their phrases were in lengthier, more self-explanatory splurges:

Can I ever forgive myself? he would ask in January.

Not up to you, she'd tell him in February, wondering if he remembered his question only to be asked in April if Wyatt Earp would do.

No, she told him in May.

Then you do it, he wrote her in June.

I am not qualified, he heard from her in July.

Oh God, he wrote in August.

She let that stand as both an appeal and as a cosmic summary of this predicament, so her silence on the point arrived in October and he wondered what her silence was about, he who had posed so many questions to the abstraction of her person, as trapped back in Atlanta as he in Dodge. It was amazing that they both retained the thread for several months, relishing their pithy give-and-take as if seated in a room together with a vase of tulips to focus on. She would urge him toward the Church, one kind or another, whether she was being long-winded or concise, and he would parry her suggestions with almost breathless austerity. She was only too aware that she was dealing with a man on life's edge, and this very peril was what attracted her to him, unsensual as their friendship had been. There he was floundering and hunting for reasons to be violent, and here she was, as profane as sacred, masterminding him from a distance, wondering what he actually did and saw from day to day, and exactly how Miss Kate seemed when he reported her as having been in a scrape, so much so that she looked as if an ore wagon had rolled over her. In her delicate but highly structured imagination, she saw Doc at his limit, blundering his way toward eternity, deliberately truncating his remarks so as to sow up the process of her rebukes. It was not so much a correspondence as a ballet of impulsive mutuality curbed by distance from becoming too responsive. There was not so much a bridge between them as a neutralizing void.

Some enterprising editor would squeeze them closer together, abolishing the dates and making their shortest lines come closer together as in an isobar, closer together for wind and riot. If the metaphor holds good, that should be a way into their juxtaposed personalities. It was just possible that, had he stayed put in the South, she would not have entered the convent but would have fixated her heart upon him out of pity and familial affection; if anyone needed succor, it was Doc, doomed by his twenty-first and willing to take just about anybody down with him, a cousin or a whore, preferably a Francisco Hidalgo or someone from the swimming hole.

Leave them all to their depravities, she told him, *you have been dipped in acid.*

Too late, he answered. *I am scalded.*

Reculer pour mieux sauter.

I have lost my French, he said, *'cept for kissin.*

We'll get it back for you, John.

Best write me off, Mattie. I am fading away.

Not in God's eyes.

It went on like this, geographically prolonged, retarded by penmanship, the consumptive and the assumptive exchanging devout trophies, withered without falling apart from each other, and, just perhaps, through some inscrutable twist of eagerness, even more firmly entwined together than buxom, neighbor lovers. Something grew between them, even if only a palsied plant, an unconducting strand of wire. The more they felt apart, and mutually at odds, the more they teamed up, spurred into genius by the presence of the impossible, always the Almighty's specialty, or so they had both been told in orthodox catechisms. Merely to write to her was to honor her mind, merely to answer him was to check his trigger finger. They were two parallel people saying goodbye to this world in utterly contrasting ways, she by transcending the flesh, he by immersing himself in it. Polar lattices. Remote Bermudas.

Their longer exchanges, meaning when they spread themselves out a bit, were chattier, less occupied with raw decisions. They had frolicked together as children and now they capered in their letters, neither a fanatic about dignity, both relieved to have this outlet severed from the scrutiny of others. Of course, with a little effort, and some mighty scene-changing, he could head back South. Of course she could leave the convent and come nurse him. But returning would kill him sooner than staying put (though he was not far enough westward to profit much from climate), and she would never countenance that. Like some preposterous balancing feat of high-wire artists, their tryst had to be done in midair via stagecoach and train, moldy mailbags and sore-eyed postal clerks. How they needed airmail, whose very risks would have fanned the cool emerald flame of their canceled passion. They wanted to be colder to each other, verbally luscious but, behind that façade, as cool as siblings cut in stone. Where there was no hope, the only possible romance was scriptural. While she trained her soul to enter regions that kept no record of her presence, he worked at degrading himself into a redlight shootist. It was almost as if two mystics had got their imagery wrong, not trying to couch transcendental experience in erotic tropes, but delineating their affinity in melodramatic duets, almost as if they should really have been singing to each other across those hundreds of miles, achieving a synchrony no one could check until after their deaths. Something elegiac prevailed between them, a cry of despair last heard in the Middle Ages from lovers cruelly separated in distant towers. No, they were not lovers, but carnal twins.

What you tell me, she wrote on one occasion, *about the joint owner of the Alhambra Saloon's ejecting a young cowboy and using too much force doing it makes me wonder what kind of place you yourself live in. Do they push you around because of your cough? I marvel that Mayor Kelley had rented out his shack to Fannie Keenan and Fanny Garrettson, both of the Dodge City dance halls. Then there is this Jim Kennedy, son of someone who owned a huge cattle ranch, standing in his stirrups and firing two or four shots into the shack, through the front door, several thicknesses of bedclothing, through the plaster wall, and the bedclothes on the second bed, hitting Dora Hand or Fannie Keenan under the right arm. How peaceful we are here. She was a vocalist, you say, in the Varieties and Comique shows, and had sought divorce from Theodore Hand. I think of all the night walkers and loungers there outside the Alhambra at three o'clock in the morning, and people gyrating in the dank shadows outside the only place open in all that mist. It is a scene from Hell. Now you tell me that a Deputy Sheriff Duffy was with the posse too and that they traveled seventy-five miles the first day, but the next day found themselves ahead of the killer and so waited for him in the blinding sunlight with their horses unsaddled and grazing, and here he came, now he comes, slow as slow can be, suspicious, making as if to thrash his horse with his quirt. They shoot him in the shoulder and three shots kill the horse. It is like going with you to the theater. An outing! It has been so long. You would not make up something such, would you, just to please me in my tedious little regimen? I wonder at what you tell me, that he went free as air, having failed to hit his target, having killed a mere woman by accident, and already ridden home with his father, but only after serious surgery to remove the half-inch ball from his shoulder. His father waited in town for a whole week, just to get him out of there. Would there otherwise have been a lynching, a necktie party as they call it? This whole life of yours might be taking place underwater for all I know of it. And, in case I took you seriously when you identified your friend Wyatt Earp as a deputy United States marshal, you now inform me, rather late in the day, that he was an assistant city marshal. Well, I was crushed when you told me that. I had been building an image in my head, so what a comedown. Forgive me, dear John, Sister Mary Josephine has given me her cold and I am sneezing my chin off. Must you live in such an accidental place, among the Fannie Keenans and the Fanny Garrettsons and the Dora Hands and the Jim Kennedys? Imagine the Mayor renting out his shack to two floozies, one of whom is to be cut down in full bloom without knowing about it. All this in her sleep. Perhaps that would be the best way to go. An impact. You wouldn't even be, as you say they say it, "scairt an' figity." I will add to this later. Can there be mist in Hell?*

He had learned to call Kate a plainswoman, term that almost seemed to imply a plainspoken woman too, except she was outrageously profane and lurid with it. Mattie, at a distance, was an alchemist of souls, having explained to him how the soul, almost like a gas intended for condensation, passed through hundreds of curly, coiled-up tubes which, defeating its desire to get somewhere, allowed it to get by in only its purest form; what reached the end of the crystal line was uncontaminated, the dregs having been left as a coating on the walls of all that convoluted glass. This struck him as a miracle to begin with, this envisioning of the soul as some experiment in chemistry, but she had the knack of peopling abstract ideas, at least until he got the drift and could allow metaphor to fall away, in other words when, if ever, he was ready to deal with the soul undiluted, which was just about never. He could see why she prodded and squeezed it in this way, sometimes having wanted to burn away the dross of his own being, but he felt unable to turn metaphors into gold as she did, shedding the mystic's good-natured approximations at long last for the translucent core of eternity. She saw the life beyond this with prodigious energy, almost as if, without her to envision it, it would not exist; she was important to it in a unique way, and he knew this was arrant egotism, just the sort of thing fanned on by zealots. It was no use arguing with her, though, not when a letter took ages to come and go, not when she, installed in a convent like a knight in a tent at a tournament, was ready to do battle with a host of special weapons. He liked hearing her prate of ineffable wonders that opened themselves up to a believer; in a way, reading her vivid exaltations helped him to a gentler view of himself as a piece of experimental matter being worked by prankish furies. The answer, she explained to him in several different versions, was to apply the mind to the crudest events, somehow snapping them up from the level of crudery and purging them of their own history. He never understood quite how to do this, suspecting he would fool himself if he tried it, but he tried it on several occasions, which was no doubt why people remembered him for his cold bisecting eyes—when he was intent upon a mental shift he could hardly talk about.

I can see that Hell never closes in Dodge, she wrote to him on one occasion, and when at last he mustered the grace and courage to reply he could tell her only that his mind had become a penal colony whose prisoners thought only standard thoughts, unable to dream themselves into freedom.

Oh, you are a bother, she at length replied.

To which he retorted, in their de rigueur at-length, *What then might a God-botherer be? Isn't that a word for a chaplain?*

That was true, she conceded, and he was right in another way, having implied (she thought) that an anchorite should take upon herself the worries of the worldly. From then on she discouraged herself from rebuking him, suddenly recognizing that he was almost like Pico della Mirandola, dreaming of divinity with his feet in the mud. Her letter saying this arrived after he saved Wyatt Earp, only a day after, and it somehow confirmed him in his own privately arrived-at doctrine of savage rectitude. He would stay in the mud, just to test the nobler side of his being. The bacillus was already testing him, so now he would test the bacillus—which he now regarded as part of himself, suffering the sneers, relishing the praise—in another element, becoming the man informally appointed to clean up Dodge. All of a sudden he had the reputation of a Crusader, and he wanted to live up to it, fortified at a distance by a woman married to Jesus. It made him blink to be so distantly sustained, but was she farther from him than from God? He abandoned the question to ponder what Kate had lately told him about Lottie Deno, a pert and mobile-faced slut who had said, "If I should step in soft cow manure, I would not even clean my foot on that bastard!" He knew not of whom this had been said, but he took sardonic pleasure in her euphemism, wondering if in the end it were not fouler than what it avoided. How tell Mattie this kind of thing? Would she dismiss it as dirt of the universe and have done, or dig up old Pico della Mirandola again to make her point? Who am I and what? A neat dresser with not many true friends, always ready to back off until he rushed in, he aspired to daredevil courage and justifiable battery. A lunger, as they said in Dodge, threatening contagion wherever he went. What would Mattie make of the women locally called doves of the roost, tid bits, fallen frails, Cyprians? Eating his bread and bacon and mopping up the grease, he tried to compose an uplifted letter.

Do you remember me as I was? Picture me, your holiness, in double-breasted jacket with four rows of buttons, slight shapeliness to the waist. In me, the eyes seem farther back from the glasses than in other folk, an effect of perspective, I guess. Ears still come out generously at an angle. I see myself reflected in a bacon fat, or rather on a shiny plate. The hair I used to carry across my forehead down to my right ear is now trimmed short to rest curtailed on my right temple so it doesn't droop forward and wag about in the wind. Mustache's neat, like everyone else's, exposing only the bottom of my bottom lip. I have aged, or so you would think. All in all I remain your dapper, notorious, coughing cousin. I must send a photograph if the lord above wouldn't mind.

Imagining her response to this, he quailed, almost ripped it up, then fell to thinking about the James Kennedy trial, rigged by his father who founded the King ranch. "Paid them off, off, off," Earp had said. "This beats lawin." It certainly beat the gentle art of letter-writing. As Earp would put it, there was lawin, jawin, and pawin, all a waste of time when big money ruled the roost.

"Hell," Earp had told him, "times I think I'll quit and get me to Arizona Territory. Better'n goin in circles around here."

"That's where I'm supposed to go anyway," Doc said. "I got a feeling I should be moving on. You just let me know, and I'll fix myself up for a long ride."

Earp had taken to wandering around Dodge without a weapon, no doubt counting on his reputation to keep marauders at bay, but with caches of arms and ammunition in his favorite haunts. Doc could not understand this, thought it foolhardy, reposing too much on good fortune and the power of a name in the dark. All the more reason, he thought, to haunt the sixty or so saloons with both guns loaded, just in case, not so much trailing Earp on his rounds as keeping an ear open for trouble: gunfire above the click of playing cards or the supposedly snappy repartee of Eddie Foy in his four-hour blackface and Irish comedy shows with Miss Belle Lamont.

"Belle, you are my dearest duck."

"Foy," she answered, "you are trying to stuff me."

"You got to be in a hell of a good humor," Earp groaned, "to find anythin funny in that. Stuff and nonsense."

Drier climes, he wrote to her in exasperation. *I am headed for drier climes, if they exist, but I'll never get out of here. It holds you down. The wind alone cripples anyone accustomed to walking upright, but all they ever say about it is yep it blows a mite don't it? They must be used to something fierce. Sorry, I don't mean to complain, but of course I do it all the time, my mind haunted by those drier climes, surely many thousand miles from here.*

He gave up. Some days she seemed already closer to God than to him. What, he wondered, about the drier climes nearer to heaven. What was up there? Legions of the coughing? His view of divinity was that it was not a humid act or state, but, rather, arid and brittle. No sloppy wet kisses, no dank armpits from Hungary, but the tyranny of the toenail, goading your shin in the night. Who was to know? Mattie, for all her ingenious theology, stepped aside from such thoughts: God was all climates, she told him, not subject to the whims of a plains gunman. So he bided his time, asking her only questions that gave her a rhetorical lift, sent her spinning skyward in inventive joy. Not matters of fact, but matters of consummate fabrication. No, he mused, her theology was orthodox, but the imagery that accompanied it was bizarre, revealing what was unique in her and therefore to be admired by any quality-loving deity. Dared he tell her this? No more than he told the truth to Kate about her Stygian breath.

Several times he caught himself in the act of hero-worshiping Earp, which was not to say he had abandoned his former social status back in Georgia, but that, here in Kansas, a different order prevailed and it was plain loco to insist on anything else, on the superiority of the refined, the exquisite, the manicured, the dainty, the flawlessly produced, whether a bouquet or an accent. Prince of darkness that he may have been, Earp had almost a glamour, matt finish, cat-burglar moves, the taciturnity of onyx. It took some getting used to, a combination like that, especially when you were accustomed to a more highfalutin society. It was gorgeous to read the menu, outrageously suave, in a couple of the hotels, soaring high above the No Dogs notice into the svelte realm, as it sounded anyway, of

Columbia River Salmon, au Beurre et Noir
Fillet a bouef, a la Financier
Russian River Bacon
Pinionsa Poulett, aux Champignons

Casserole d'Ritz au Oufs, al la Chinoise
Sucking Pig, with Jelly
English Plum Pudding, Hard Sauce

This dinner is served for 50 cents.

He took inordinate and repeated pleasure in the *boue* (mud) misspelled into *Bouef,* in the missing accents, and the Oafs not far from Oufs intended for fresh-laid Oeufs. His French would never desert him, he concluded, not with solecisms leaping to the eye like disemboweled frogs. Where else in this drastic land of sharpies and muckers, bipeds and wenchers, saddlers and boomers (a lingo all on its own), could he find amusement, if not in her lapses into Hungarian, which became rarer and rarer as she became more established in her profession, which waxed and waned as her relationship with Doc prospered and declined. She was never exclusively his, though she pretended they had married awhile back, and he sometimes wished her far enough, out in that roistering wind. She reeked of onions and plum duff, mothballs and cauliflower, a woman who had arisen from the earth like a vegetable, of the earth earthy.

"What you scowlin at now?" she would ask with truculent finality.

"Get yourself some pippermint," he told her, relishing his mispronunciation. "Or get yourself some dead men's baccy and chew on that. Take a chaw, Kate."

"And have me throw up all across Dodge? No fear."

"Then just breathe the other way," he said, weary of her cantankerousness. "I'm tryin to get my breath back."

"I seen you injoyin my breath sometimes."

Not recently, he told her; she smelled of old sperm and new sweat, insignia of her off-and-on trade, and her personality sometimes was like nettles. A man in his position, forever arranging his posture the better to disguise a cough, or even a bout of it, wanted things just so, without having all the time to adjust to sudden new smells that made him retch. The slightest variation in familiar aromas and he was off, pounding his fist against his chest, slapping his thigh, his rear, his head, anything to make it cease. How he endured the stench and smoke in the saloons he gambled in, he never knew, deciding that sheer concentration weakened the impact of all else, even the sounds and bangs. The more intent he became, the more he became sealed within himself, a closed superior system until, as the gunfire became intolerable, he came back to himself and launched his energies in a wholly different direction, leaping up to protect Earp.

He wanted to be left alone to rot, that was all. What a mob. Wenchers were womanizers, muckers had lowly jobs in the mines, sharpies were hangers-on trying to be swells, boomers were opportunists and saddlers were itinerant bums always looking for a handout or a free meal. Earp, his local god, was at least three of these: wencher, sharpie and boomer, an epic arriviste whom Doc would have cut dead back in Valdosta and paid miserable wages to defend the swimming hole. Here, though, a ruffian among the rough was a gem to be extolled and cultivated. Where else, Doc wondered, would the waiters in a restaurant wear a smock from midriff to boots, and suspenders over a semi-clean shirt with no collar? He sometimes felt the mustache did duty for a collar, black ruff getting above itself to be dipped in tea, whiskey, any devil's ambrosia.

So, as again many times, he summed it all up—his expatriation—in a phrase or two and sent it stumbling over the landscape toward Mattie, who would understand. *I almost had a cow*, he wrote, to indicate indignant astonishment, calling like everyone else in Dodge on ludicrous obstetrics for turn of speech. Say a month later, he was still fingering the same emotion, but saying *Well I never*, not as effective by far, and then, oh a whole season later, as he guessed, still tinkering with the old astonishment in *Lan sakes*. The more exported he felt, the more he unearthed Georgia idioms, baffling the citizens of Dodge but cheering himself with old home remedies.

If language was for people, he thought, then what was the way to talk to God? If ever? God read minds, that was likely. So, when

Mattie prayed, which was often, she uttered nothing, just thought her thoughts, *thot her thots*, and up they flew, light and airy, ascendant orisons he envied. She had urged him to pray, especially after a shooting; even killings she downplayed to shootings, which could always have missed, especially when couched in the tolerant language as shootings off. You shot off a gun, didn't you? In this way she managed to create and nourish her harmless image of him as a lost soul in an opera, doing his best to survive an alien culture that was merely a way station for him en route to heavenly Colorado, whose name meant colored or tinted, maybe even hued.

Suddenly Doc had the sense that his life was rich, full of opportunity, not the barren nest it had seemed. For conventional chances of happiness he didn't give a hoot in a rainbarrel, he had given all that up—wife, children, fruitful career, courtly and sensitive male friends—but he was still willing to enjoy something on the level of will exerted, other lives made to suit his preference, admiration without love. Was this because the trio—Mattie and Kate and Wyatt—had lifted and widened his horizons? Imagine: until last year he had contemplated a future, cozy and mindless, quite devoid of mystery, lust and heroic self-assertion, an almost chemical formula for disaster. Yet the disaster, in the form of the bacillus, had already come to be; nothing he did now could be worse than that. This ghastly thought occupied him daily, attuning him to the skeleton on his present life, whose bones he labored almost in vain to combine, wishing he possessed a blueprint, a diagram, always ending up with improvisation yet never giving up his idea that a lively man, shoved to the edge, would come up with a unique life unlike the one he had envisioned for himself, unlike even lives he had heard about. Was Earp more unique than he? A distant echo of a Latin class told him there were no degrees of uniqueness, any more than there were degrees of extraction for a tooth. He wanted to make sense of how he was going to live; he did not want to find himself living impromptu and ending up with a reputation, a record, that ill-suited him.

Uncanny misgivings, these, unlikely in someone as impetuous as he, but understandable by anyone who went and stood outside Dodge for five minutes, beyond the perimeter of that seething jamboree. Mattie had taught him to pray, Kate to fuck and Earp to kill. What was there left to learn? He had so far failed to teach himself how to bleed without getting embarrassed, how to stop wishing the bacillus had waited until he was forty-one, say, with all manner of bright catastrophes under his belt. The irony, as he now called it, was having to learn so soon what he would never need in his maturer years. All these temporary things were final too, and that was the muddle he could not abide. In the circumstances, then, he kept wondering how much he owed to the copybooks of good behavior, to bourgeois maxims, genteel traditions brought with him from the South because he had no idea how to rid himself of them. Clearly, he could sit back and do nothing; all would happen by default, but happen it would. Or he could busy himself to create a new, compressed life devoid of standard pleasures but crammed with weird sensation. It would be an experiment in growing within a condemned garden: something like that, a last orgasm that he knew was final.

Contrariwise, he addressed himself to Mattie, the farthest away of his faraways, intimating something. *I am coming to it,* he told her, *got an idea how to get through my next year. Will it be the last? If so, how do you choose what goes into it? How do you develop even the faintest notion of which last things to do, and how many, with whom? I give up on all that, will assemble it all mighty loosely and hope to see January 1, 1879, in spite of everything. Then it will start again, and I will have to solve the problem.*

Always the dust vexed him, the dust on the wind, as if some malign overseer had decided to reduce the world to its smallest components—*pulverize* it—to humiliate the occupants, reminding them of the old formula dust to dust. Dust and spit, he thought, luckily blown together to make a race. He was not in the mood for dust, or for any other signs of the Creator's omnipotence. He envisioned a kit in a cardboard box, within it ten pounds of dust, instructions saying fashion a human from this and mail it in for the next larger kit, which will reach you in six days. August 14 frightened him more than December 31 because that was *his* day, meaning his years ended and began sooner than the planet's did, and he could never quite bury the sense of victimization in the worldwide splurge of seasonal merriment. For birthdays he had never been ready, certainly not for those after the fifteenth, when he sensed something uncouth and grotesque looming, dripping slime and bulging to draw attention to itself. He trembled all through the thirteenth. *Don't have many to boast of,* he wrote to Mattie, wondering if the future held a cure he would never see. It always paid to last as long as possible, even in wretched condition; there was a design in human affairs that took care of everyone in the long run, even if they never prayed.

Lord God of the universe, he began, *maker and breaker of forms,* and could go no farther, unable to summon up a face to pray to, not even an exact stained-glass window or a cliché beneath a halo. You couldn't address a prayer to an utter abstraction. That was why Mattie considered herself wedded to Christ and wore a gold ring to prove it, though it troubled him that she needed the physical symbol at all—or her convent needed her to wear it. Surely, he thought, the invisible should be dealt with invisibly. It was clear that he had no gift for this kind of chop logic, dimly aware of the heroes he had read about in grammar school back in Valdosta, Georgia, men who stayed in touch with the huge forces that propelled them and humbly communicated with them direct. Because the forces had faces.

If I stay here, he wrote her, *I am likely to kill or be killed,* which is O.K., *but I need to know how much I need a face to pray to, as in the illustrated prayerbooks.* In the long run she told him to keep a space in his mind for the Lord, who would one day in His own time appear. Yes, but which Lord, he wondered. Who does what? It's all too remote for me. He doubted if Earp prayed. He sometimes doubted if Earp breathed or ate or broke wind. Earp was a walking grandeur of prosaic disposition. It was no use asking him things; he rarely spoke and never answered, consecrated to his role as evenhanded colossus, dominating the night and the day with other people's whisper of his name. If Earp came, they either left or tried to kill him, heedless of the scores who had attempted it already and had not even come near. Not only was Earp too fast, he was too astute; he could see them coming and had an almost preternatural ability with angles and perspectives, a killer who was also a surveyor. Doc's problem was fast becoming the choice between Earp and some divinity: nothing parasitic, simply a matter of where did he go from here, he who was unwilling to be a man alone on the plains, without a vocation save gambling and drinking. Having once saved Earp, at least as he, Doc, saw it, he had put Wyatt in that peculiar position beloved of the Chinese: the man whose life you save belongs to you, owes himself to you, even if the question never comes up.

Lordy, Doc thought, what a swap.

It could happen. He is much more likely to save me for the first time than I am to save him a second one. Therefore I need not worry so long as I stay close to him. In this town they arrest only the really dangerous shootists; the rest of them keep the economy going, and, besides, there aren't enough jail cells for all the badmen.

Was he deluded? Was it all starting to come clearer as he puzzled away at the fix he was in, over glass after glass, as hands were dealt and evaporated like gussied-up mirages? Those who saw his pensive look assumed he was planning their downfall at faro, but only one part of his brain attended to cards, tucked away in the recesses of all that glistening gray suet like a tiny factory devoted to the calibration of barometers. Go back to Georgia and ask the lady's hand? And so become a nun-snatcher! No, she was sweet on Christ and would never prostrate herself before an ex-dentist turned gunfighter and cardsharp. Whenever he saw Earp, always without his weapons in insolent-looking bravado though never far from his cache, Doc saw the personification of the world he lived in: obtuse and sharp, bloody and debauched, to which—his unique offering—he brought the morbid emanations of a spitting man whom they could not save and who, even if they killed him, would not be much of a kill anyway, at best a wounded buffalo just standing there, tatterdemalion hulk, waiting for it. It dawned on Doc that no man had ever been as free as he, to decide himself according to the givens, no longer shilly-shallying but playing with heroic brio the card that was himself. He laughed at such a universe, so stale and carnal.

Now came another chance to take part in something virtually

legal, almost on the side of the angels. The call had gone out for volunteers to defend the Santa Fe railroad workers against men hired by the Denver and Rio Grande. This was a track war, officially to become known as the Royal Gorge War fought, on the Santa Fe side, by Sheriff Bat Masterson (no particular friend of Doc's), John Joshua Webb, the unpredictable violent Englishman Ben Thompson, and Deputy Fuffey. Invited to join them, Doc first did his bit by going around recruiting, even to the extent of accosting comedian Eddie Foy with an overlong explanation that sounded like a parody but wasn't. "Sure, Doc," Eddie told him, "I can see as how the Atchison, Topeka, and the Santa Fe is kind of like our 'own' railroad, I sure can. But who am I? Not a gunman, to be sure. Would you ask a flamingo to box? I have heard about all the good pay, but, hell be swelped, look what I am. No fighter. I couldn't hit a man even if I shot at him and he held still. I couldn't hit a mesa."

"Eddie, that's all right," Doc then told him. "The old Santy Fee won't know the difference. You kin use a shotgun, see, if that's your likin. I dare say you stage gintlemen likes a scattershot effect, quite destroying the countenance. *We* are the gintlemen of Dodge and we want to make a good showin in this here affair. You'd help swell the crowd, you sure would and you'd keep us clever and cheerful while we was about our killin. You just shoot away at anythin that attracts your attintion and you'll git yore pay."

Eddie informed him that he was just joshing, trying to steal his trade, and they left without him, thirty-three pseudo-desperadoes armed to the teeth clambering aboard the morning train, soon to take on a detachment of United States soldiers, only to discover as the shooting heated up and the Dodge–Santa Fe contingent began to prevail that the two railroads had come to an agreement. "Too soon," Doc said, by now entrenched in his military role. "I was jist gittin int'rested, from an impartial view of course."

"See," Eddie Foy told him, "you didn't need me after all. I'd have killed some of *you* off for sure. I'd best stick to wisecracks, Mister Holliday. You can keep the Royal Gorge, the Atchison, Topeka, and the Santa Fe and the Denver *and* the Rio Grande and shove them up your rear end. I don't hold with railroads hiring gunmen."

This really killed off Dodge for Doc, whose long fruitless meditations on his fate had buffaloed him quite, supplying neither motive nor a rock to stand on. He had nothing in Dodge to hold him, with the Earps gone and Kate gone her own way, considering Arizona. Doc had come to know everybody's conversation by now. "Let them build their damned line into Leadville," he shouted at the table, "I don't need silver at my stage of life. I need good cards. I went and I came back. I should never have gone and never come back. This town is turnin respectable." He should, he thought, have made his way to Trinidad, Colorado, out past Coolidge and Springfield, but yet another journey daunted him, who depended on his mail and wanted to set up his address with Mattie before leaving. Why did she never reel him in while all he did was wait? Now he would be heading west, away from her, not even a cowpoke but a motley gentleman, a tragic version of Eddie Foy the goggling funster.

Before leaving, Doc asked the Dodge worthies about the best route to take, and they counseled him to take the northern pass into Arizona, going in a straight line through New Mexico; Apaches, they told him, oversaw the southern pass. Besides, the northern trail was even and level whereas the other one, over which Doc had just galloped, would have sent him too much uphill: a hard and unnecessary chore. "This will soon be a ghost town," they told him in Dodge. "Without Wyatt Earp, this here town will shoot itself in the head." Somewhat miffed, Doc rode away at punitive speed in case anyone was watching; he had done his own share at keeping the peace in Dodge and, after all, had become Wyatt's unofficial deputy. Doc raced after the dawdling Earps, who in fact took two weeks to head south as far as Trail City in the Indian Territory.

Hearing a rider coming up after them, Wyatt kept on staring forward as they put Trail City behind them, a ghost town's ghost masquerading as a crossroads settlement and no doubt inspiring in his failing ears the sounds of a phantom pursuer who never caught up with them, push his horse as he might. On they plodded, heedless of noises, like Wyatt, surrounded by impenitent ghosts from the good old days.

Where *was* Wyatt headed? Doc would soon find out. Like a provident madman, he had brought with him in his saddlebags paper, pen and ink, determined to write down something of the trip, but with no hope of mailing the result, not until they re-entered, intact or not, so-called civilization. Here, he told himself, men had cut the ears off their mules and sucked the blood from them because there was no water. There was little grass, so the only fuel was buffalo chips on which to boil a kettle, if water they had. Some profound, ancient excitement stirred in Doc; for once he was doing something worthy of him, even if all he noticed was the tall undulating prairie grass giving way to shorter stuff that had little or no motion—an index of movement forward, if nothing else. Here the bison had been, the drums of Indians, the rustle and thud of arrows, and wagons on fire encircled by marauding tribes.

Inspired, and curiously lifted from his former surroundings into something distinctly moving, he made every effort to intrude into her nunnery with the details of travel along the pioneer trail, conscious for perhaps the first time of his ancestors, evident only in scraps of canvas, smashed wagon wheels marooned in the quicksands, and skeletons breaking up, as anonymous and stark as teething rings. Without fudging, could he get across to her what lingered here on these fabled plateaus of chrome yellow sunflowers graced with dust? Alone among the forgotten, or so he felt, he wondered at the planet's capacity to devour those who puzzled their way across its rind, first blackening their tongues with thirst, then swelling their eyes red with dust storms and crippling their minds with mirages. Only the curious disinfectant aroma of sage and sodden grass endured their passing, and the teeming flocks of prairie chickens so that all Virgil, the provider, had to do in the dewladen mornings was go out with a ramrod and kill them where they milled about. No one lived out here, except Indians and wild horses, which came after the mares of their wagon train. His heart lifted when it should have sunk; the whole place was a living, mindless memorial to those who had endured and prevailed, sometimes the first explorers to break the virgin surface of the land with their wagon wheels and the bison-mumble of the silence with their clanging pans and pots as the wagons lurched over the bumps of bunch grass and settled only to heave upward again, like a retreating army. It was not his turf, but it was certainly his memory, and he, a civilized Southerner uninitiated in primitive things, felt awed by all that the land lacked. It was not God he sensed out here, though he might pretend differently when he wrote to Mattie, it was time the voracious and unheeding, heedless of the grand oranges of sunrise or sunset, but flooding like an infection through and beyond them, hauling them along and dragging them down, enacting their ration of days for them. As intimidated as awed, Doc tried to raise a smile in that dwarfing place. Here was something vaster than gunplay or even death, where the blood he still spat at intervals had a written chemical destiny among the dust and along the sod. It was appropriate to spit here, or even to deposit other pieces of your being as you made your way, urinating and defecating along with the buffalo into the knee-high grass. How soon it swallowed you up. You might be tracked going through it, but the thoughts you had while doing so, pell-mell befitting the latter-day atavist, fell away bleeding, gone in a trice as having no consequence compared with alkali water and incessant fever. In a way, all this was the traveler's reward, this litter of bones and wheels and pans and canvas shrouds, the detritus of forebears softening the land a touch for the next comer, domesticating it with death and triumph as if death and triumph were unknown languages until you set foot full of hope on that brutal lawn tamed only by maps.

He sighed and, settling down on the buckboard, began to scratch away with his pen, using a board as a desk, elongated and shaggy. *Buffalo grass*, he told her, *seems a poor and scanty thing, a khaki color, tight-leaved and wiry, not worth lowering your jaws for, if you're a buffalo. Yet it is sweet and sustaining if you can get at it. Picture the grazing human kneeling to take some in! I am here in the middle of nowhere, or rather this is the middle of the middle of it, which goes all the way to the Rockies. I feel better already, as if nature has relented, yet only so far, giving me a more distinct sense of my disease and so of what I am going to lose. You cannot mourn losing this until you have seen it. It is not just an idea in the mind, but a huge playground for animals, once more so than now. Seen from afar, the buffalo might be low trees, a mess of black walnuts scattered in the same place, moving apart then merging again even as, from some other direction, somebody begins to shoot, maybe riding alongside the herd as they panic and run. What a grue-some sight. They cannot miss. Down go the buffalo, legs spread wide, their huge shoulders humped forward in a death dive, their lives ending with a series of little convulsive kicks. Who wants them then? The skin gatherers do. The skinners, who show up in wagons and bull-wains. They come fully equipped to live out here, with cooks and pony-minders, all paid a wage to wipe out what begins by not being in the least afraid of them. They find a Y-shaped stick to rest their Sharps rifles on and just pepper away at the outside of the herd, and those in the middle just don't seem to get the point for long enough. Then they do and the stampede begins, Mattie. Sometimes the shooters get trampled, when they don't get back to their ponies fast enough, and you feel somehow glad. It is here that the railroad workers paused to watch the Buffalo Bills using their hot insatiable rifles as God's redundance dwindled and the smell of cordite mingled with the saline one of fresh blood.*

Sensing he was beginning to flourish a little too much, he made a conscious effort to sober up, adding only, still a bit stagey, *The Earps and I are one. I have caught up.* Now he held back, tautly smiling to himself as he remembered someone who used to say "unre-quieted love." It almost made sense. You could puff into language, he thought, as into a balloon, almost as if your ardor was all that mattered, not the meaning. He was responding to something almost beyond his powers to express, to Mattie or to himself; it was real, nonetheless, as real as the salt the cattle barons fed their cows to make them drink before selling them.

A much more devastating thought followed, even as he helped

Virgil with just-killed fowl. "You was writin home, Doc." Virgil was an observant inhibitor of talk. "They do say," he added, astonishingly, "that the more they hears from you when you's off and away, the more they wants you to come on home so's they doesn't have to go on reading it." Snubbed, Doc swung down and started plucking.

The devastating thought had to do with buffalo. Instead of getting shot in a duel, he would lie down among the buffalo, on his side maybe, which was how he slept, and go to sleep among them, dreaming of how hunters despised skinners, how a hunter never laid hand on a hide, how they used horses to drag the hide off a carcass, then cut off the tongue and hump to cook, leaving the rest for wolves. He would lie down among them and be pounded to pulp, then gradually make his way lower and lower into the soil, bit by bit, rotting and disintegrating like everything else, his blood no longer an expectorant, his ribs a birdcage briefly, his brain an unusable mush devoid of all the memories that made it unique. Perhaps they would crush him with a few well-aimed kicks, and that would be that, or torment him with little taps and cornadas that pecked him to death. Whichever way, he would be taking his medicine, as folk said, like a man, neither whining nor joshing. Had it taken a trip out here, in a wagon train of eleven wagons, to get his mind to this point? Where reason and justice had failed, atmosphere had worked. He was amazed, most of all by how little he envisioned or resented pain. What had really hurt him all these years was the delay, the frustration of not knowing when. On the trek, it was a different mode of life, quite uncivilized: salt pork, wild turkey, and antelope out of which the hair pulled easily, peaches, dried apples, molasses and sugar, with coffee. Not a bad diet, he thought, he no expert on food, but willing to share with the Earps and give them his Cuban cigars. He felt almost like a Texas Ranger, innocent young outdoorsman hoping to win this or that badge of prowess, yet not doing much to help other than mentally encouraging the Earp families, falling in love with the evening ritual that had each family huddling around its own fire, and then, as the fires died out, the last rendezvous at a big new fire where they talked and smoked. This *repair* to the ultimate campfire moved him a good deal and supplied a sedate, formulaic end to his day, about which he could write her at length on the morrow.

How can I be dreaming things? he wrote. *I am not a dreamy person, but out here you get this odd sense that you are living a hundred years ago, or just a dozen. I should think in tens or dozens, not both, shouldn't I? Some days I think we are surrounded by buffalo, then others they have all gone. They do have a right to move about, I guess, but you come to depend on them. There aren't enough of them to make a steady impression, so you couldn't just lie down and wait for them to come along and pound you, you'd have to figure out where they are, congregating, and take it from there. It's easier to deal with the buffalo than with certain people, that's for sure. The Indians come and go, asking a dollar or two, look clean through you to their ancestors, I guess, and then vanish like smoke. You'd think we'd be having picnics, which sounds a bit grand, but we do better, deploying a huge red tablecloth scarlet to vermilion, taking china out of its wrapping, and when you lie down like a Roman to eat, you get a better sense of the horizon and what is against it. No tin plates on this expedition. At night I lie out there and think the stars are fuzzy and soft, almost murmuring and getting blurred. They seem so close, just dangling there, their purpose unstated, their composition unknown. I watch them until I fall asleep and can hear only the horses tethered on long ropes near the camp. It is all mighty soothing, especially when you carry around inside you something like a cuckoo clock that longs for the South all the time, the view of the stars from there, the picnics of my boyhood, the swimming hole. You will remember all that, of course, and I wonder which of us is more cut off from civilization, you in your convent or me out in the middle distance. Perhaps it is good for the soul (oh we must talk of the soul) to be so severed, so marooned, with only the stars and, in my case, the Earps and a couple of newlyweds the Edwardses for company. Life among the buffalo might be better than life in Dodge. We are making a dozen miles a day, not too bad, but hardly a riot. So I fall to thinking, as we bounce and rattle along, how busy it used to be out here, buffalo and Indians, hunters and skinners, whereas now it seems to have passed into the orbit of America, ready for new towns such as East Las Vegas, of which we spoke, and hosts of different people all the way from Europe, seeding the wilderness with hope and bustle. It is like witnessing all over again the birth of America.*

What he never knew was that she lived in a damp, cold room that even in summer needed a fire, and into this as she read it she slid each page, needing no evidence on the premises. So his correspondence with her depended on her memory, crisp and decisive without being wholly retentive, and this made for lacunae in their already disjointed exchanges. Right into the flames went his best, most candid thoughts, almost as if she had taken them from his very hand, perused them, and sent them to God. He, on the other hand, rolled up all her letters, with tender hand, and kept them in an oilskin, treasured and authoritative. Here, of course, he received none at all, nor mailed any, which gave their epistolary career an abeyant, obsolete quality he rather enjoyed, knowing that when he could mail off to her it was all congealed, and that when he at last received a letter from her it had a tincture in it of Gibbon's history of Rome, born ancient. Because of these delays he despised conventional letter-writing, with its quick changes and exchanges, its almost telegraphic quality, its approximation to chatter. Here, instead, was something heroic, not unlike the letters children addressed to Santa Claus at the North Pole, or to their friends with the address expanded to include the Western Hemisphere, the World, the Milky Way, as if location were elastic. In her dingy room there was no sign of his existence two thousand miles away, and he did not even have a dingy room, only this measureless gazebo with no roof that had somehow lifted a weight from his scalp, not merely the burden of habitation (or cohabitation), but what he might have called housedness: timbers, planks, walls, beams, the rest. Suddenly he had discovered the joys of the al fresco, not so dangerous as it used to be; Indians only stole horses nowadays whereas the whole world seemed to have been stealing beeves from Mexico to drive northward into profit and invisibility. Now he understood how vital it was to experience, if you could, a country without the people in it, so that your love of the land might shine through all your relationships with both the quick and the dead.

Like a toy gyroscope atop its mount, the Hanging Windmill on the Las Vegas Plaza had served vigilantes as a scaffold for years, at least until local residents complained about blood in the water supply, not to mention other substances become the noxious by-product of necktie parties. Men could have been hanged from a point within the skeletal steeple of the structure, plunging down into the square framework below, releasing all beneath them into the sand. Usually, though, the lower structure served, giving them a shorter drop, indeed more a strangling than anything else. Complaints had no effect, so one night in 1880 incensed and disgusted citizens tore the windmill down. Doc Holliday arrived in Las Vegas in time to see it serve its purpose, at first setting himself up as a dentist again in some vain lunge at renewed professional life, hating to see his qualifications go to ruin, after which he opened his own saloon on Centre Street, East Las Vegas, in July of 1879.

So it was in Las Vegas that Doc witnessed his first public hanging: Comb Harris, rustler and itinerant badman, set to dangle from the bottom of the windmill steeple, one of his executioners toppling from the frame and catching hold of Comb on the way down, almost an act of mercy as the extra body jerked the rope and converted a sure strangulation into an episode of broken neck. Cheers and jeers accompanied this double act; only Eddie Foy was missing, doing commentary in his accomplished parody of Doc's Southern accent. Through the opera glasses Doc had brought to the event in a spirit of disabused curiosity, he remarked a sameness of face in Comb Harris, no discernible change as he exchanged this life for another, no twitching or jerking. The fallen executioner climbed off and down, or down and off, spreadeagled with a sheepish grin, while Comb swung and swung in the town square, only the first of six whose names had been printed on a handbill as if this were a show at the Comique. Here, Doc told himself, was more than frontier justice; it was a sermon in last things, one that might apply to him only too soon if he continued to carry six-guns and get into trouble gambling. Did he feel nausea or disgust at the spectacle? He thought not, but resolved to tell Mattie nothing of it. There were limits. A lifetime, a *young* lifetime, devoted to one atrocity (the Crucifixion) was already more than enough, he decided; there was no need to rub her nose in the unseemly life and death of Comb Harris, so called because his lank hair was always falling in front of his eyes. No, this would go under the catch-all heading of local color, an event stylized into a jumping contest from an old windmill if at all.

Delighted at having time to meditate (and indeed in being free, not doomed to go the way of Comb Harris), Doc tried to pull the sting out of his days. Dodge was behind him, a big scab left oozing; Kate, who had first left Dodge out of boredom, then returned on hearing news of huge cattle drives in the offing, was ahead of him somewhere; and Earp, in whose shadow he vacillated, had gone on to Arizona to clear the ground, although no doubt stopping en route to clean out a few nests of shootists. I am virtually alone, Doc thought, at liberty to view the hangings, watch the new town of East Las Vegas grow into another Dodge. Do I go on, or do I stay? His very atoms seemed to urge him forward, but his weight kept him back, even if only to write letters full of a new town, new faces, new gamblers. He had to be careful what he told Mattie as, at any moment, she might succumb to righteousness and end their correspondence. He tried to picture her settling in Las Vegas, but almost choked; it would annul so much of her being, and goad her into becoming a zealous reformer. On the other hand, from what he knew of Catholicism, she might forgive them all, having built sin into her universe with the welcoming generosity of a mother whose child had erred. If, he mused, you created a universe, then surely there was room for things to go badly wrong: the miscellaneous complexity of things would guarantee badmen, even good people going wrong. So, as he saw it, the universe was just another mode of gambling, full-blooded faro. He wondered how she would respond to such an idea. Into a brawling saloon he went, found a semi-quiet table, and composed a small pale blue page to her on flimsy paper, writing with a dreadful pen whose nib had opened like a bird's beak. This chore accomplished, he folded the missive and hiked back to his boardinghouse, for once missing Kate the indiscriminate lusty.

Still, the final image of Comb Harris, with the others—Blinky Welch, Norm Dudek, and three more—lingered and bothered him, fixing his mind on mankind's ability to end someone's awareness, forever, at this point or that, never to bring them back. It was not a sentence of twenty years' oblivion, it was one of eternal blankness, in terms of time an unthinkable uncountable epic of vastness, all done with a hemp rope, the benign lariat that collared straying cows. What a staggering world it was, full of dread and bliss, and you never knew what was coming your way next. Thoughts for Mattie, these, and he spared a passing glance at how young she and he still were, yet both committed in contrasting ways to last things, working with a huge degree of doomladen anticipation, she by choice, he through bacillus. Unwilling to pursue the matter further (where could it lead except to the needle point of the unknown?), Doc drowned his dream in the Kentucky whiskey of the lonely man caught between Dodge and Arizona (or Colorado), and wishing with all his heart he could find it within him to head back East to an accelerated end. Tears formed in the gray-blue ice of his eyes. The dentist in him craved business with probes and extractors. The village philosopher in him went into abeyance, miserable at ever coming up with nothing fresh—an idea that would save him and transplant him. It looked as if he was going to have to go on with his via dolorosa (phrase from Mattie) as far as the West Coast, where life was easier and calmer. By the ocean, surely that would be true. Visions of an improved life came and went, almost demoralizing him, teaching him that his range of choices narrowed daily, and that the only adjustment he might ever make was on the level of ideas, where geniuses lived and failed. He wanted to be beautiful again, casually shooting over their heads at the swimming hole, and first learning to probe and extract in Baltimore, far away as Atlantis.

He realized that millions sang to heaven, achieving poignant and exquisite effects, which proved surely that the beauty of their orisons came from the gods. From where else? Surely, even in a freakish world, humans would not achieve a beauty of sound that the gods could not have created in the first place? He wondered, though; could humans, in their superlative choruses, be chanting to gods who weren't there, who weren't anywhere? Could it be that, just as mind was a tribute to the subtlety of matter, the beauty of art was a forlorn, gorgeous thing entirely on its own in the universe? A ravishing delusion? Such problems afflicted few gunslingers, who snapped at interrogators with some such phrase as "None of your mix, stranger." There were millions of things he would like to know, but he'd settle for two or three really huge ones, or even one, about the existence of God. How could he ask Mattie about such things, as he once had in their teens? Perhaps Comb Harris had found out, dangling broken, or the rest of them hanged that sunny morning, sensing that if the afterlife did not exist it would hardly disappoint them. He was not sentimental enough to think that the men he and Wyatt shot at, or shot dead, became their emissaries to the unknown region, but it impressed him that untold numbers of men had already been stilled, numbed, without ever a sign of interest from anywhere in the world. A flame of radiant plumage did not rise from the breast of the man shot; he just stayed still. Never seen since. *That* was the phrase for it.

As the hanging scene replayed itself, something in it nagged at him, something he had seen before but not understood. On his way to the tower, Comb Harris had had a thumb in his mouth, baby-sucking; for some reason he had not been pinioned, though he was surrounded by eager captors. Something awry in this image made Doc wince: had they deliberately made him look, or feel, pathetic beforehand? What was to be gained by such dumb-play? Maybe he had been a baby-killer; but, when you have only just arrived in a town, and you ride by (intercepting the coffin-maker, noting the execution in the square) you don't take everything in, and you certainly don't know who is who and what they've done. Monkeying with kids, someone told him: the final taboo, even here in the hardly extant town of East Las Vegas. Doc was right to wince, but a wince is a temporary response, and clearly the other condemned men were not baby-killers but authentic he-men, bandits, murderers, rustlers, stagecoach holdup men, worthy of the commonplace style. But the sheer appropriateness of the doomed man with his thumb in his mouth struck home to Doc; that was what execution reduced all men to, a babbling nonentity terminally without hope. They had had five-hundred-dollar prices on their heads, but now were worth nothing at all, bags of garbage in the final showdown. Somehow, Doc felt, East Las Vegas was to be only a way station on the trail of tears that led from Valdosta, Georgia, to—where? Arizona? Colorado? Anywhere westward would do, but the getting there was painful slow, although the mind could think it fast, go there in a trice and heal the body in an afternoon of golden dry air thin enough to make a cricket gasp.

Having left Dodge behind him, he was now again an outlaw, no longer a lawman, no sooner having arrived someplace than he lived up to his status, putting a bullet through some spook who bothered him in the small hours with a two-pistoled threat. Scuffles, these, at least as far as he was concerned: a bullet put through a certain Kid Colton, who recovered; a fine of twenty-five dollars for maintaining an illegal gaming table in East Las Vegas. He attained immortality in the court records of Las Animas and other counties, yet without achieving flagrant local status. He was marking time, his mind intent on how Old Las Vegas had a name as a health resort, just the place for him except he lived in the new development, East, next to the railroad. In Old Town, for a while anyway, next to a jeweler named Bill Leonard, he did teeth, while in the New Town he ran his saloon, straddling his new location, at least until dentistry gave out, Doc responding keenly as always to the lure of his Dodge City cronies, now established in Las Vegas as the Dodge City Gang, unrecorded in the records of San Miguel County. Doc had gone gunfighting with these men on the Santa Fe Expedition—Josh Webb and Dave Rudabaugh among others—and he felt at home with them, in their company managing to keep alive in him the old plague of gun-toting virility, and never mind Hoodoo Brown the tough local lawman, a gambler himself, a desperado elected to office by other desperadoes. His most famous utterance, perhaps his only claim to fame, was the way he opened court: pointing to the huge double-barreled Winchester lying beside him on the desk, he'd say, "Myself and my partner will now open court. Take it easy, folks. Hoodoo Brown is here." A doting, gloating judge, he was also a swindler and a blackmailer, someone Doc would have preferred to shoot right at the get-go to ease social life in the new town.

By the time Kate caught up with Doc in East Las Vegas, having failed to find sufficient venery among the newly arrived cowboys in Dodge, Doc had moved to a higher plane of mayhem, provoked by a mere falling-out into a challenge: out of his saloon into Centre Street, where he shot Mike Gordon dead. No rumors about this one. Knowing that Hoodoo Brown would as soon dangle him from the windmill tower as look at him, Doc took his leave, abandoning both saloon and woman to ride the lower fork of the Santa Fe trail, taking him off in a circular evasion not entirely to his liking, but the best way out of there, his mind in a dither, haunted by the notion that he had to settle down and stop investing in saloons.

Any port in a storm, he decided. I'd gladly go as far as Mexico just to get clear, and I wouldn't care how many came after me. It had all been so automatic: the quarrel, the confrontation, the slightly slewed series of shots, the man crumbling into disregarded marionette, the shakiness in Doc's knees, the rivulet of moisture along his back, the flushed, burnt, copper-smelling taint of his face. Then impetuous flight, leaving his memory behind for coyotes to rend. Seeing death one more time made him resolve to head for Arizona. Vegas was doldrum now the fever of the kill had raced through his blood and left him quivering. It was to Arizona that he should have gone ages ago, there to turn his wretched lungs inside out and air them in that stoked aridity. It was easy to rejoin Wyatt, trekking westward in a buckboard tailed by a number of saddle horses; Wyatt was in no hurry, though some of his siblings were. The entire Earp clan was on the move: Jim and Wyatt together, Wyatt traveling by buckboard so as to match his speed to that of Jim and his wife. Virgil was out in Prescott, Arizona, and they would collect him there, while Morgan would be coming in from Butte, Montana, to join them all in Tombstone. Warren, the baby, would be joining up with them too. Doc felt suddenly more alone than in years, contrasting his self-sufficiency with the tribe of Earps, who could not only, being first-class gunmen, look after one another, but spread their influence over a wide area, drenching it with their peculiar philosophy of law. Jim, wounded in the War between the States, was not the gunslinger he used to be, but he could still tote and use a weapon. Doc had the extraordinary feeling that, if he ever got into deep trouble, these would be the men he wanted to be with: not fearless, but heroically disciplined, not selfless but impartial to a point, and, while not exceptionally calculating, ingenious enough for the Wild West.

"Where you headed, Wyatt?" Doc already knew, but a breathless man needs something to say, whether his mind is working or not.

No greeting, no howdy-do. Sometimes, above the art-form known as taciturnity, Wyatt Earp ascended to the holy grail of rudeness. Tombstone, he told Doc, who at once declared his intention to come along, uninvited, unrebuffed, unencouraged even while humping his saddle into the buckboard and jumping up beside Wyatt as if he belonged there alongside the congenitally lonely man whose life he had saved. "I'm on the run," he said, but Wyatt did not even grunt. "I'm out of Vegas like a leper," Doc said. "I shot and killed Mike Gordon."

Still not a sound from Wyatt, whose thumb however came cautiously up. Lord God in heaven, Doc thought, surely he isn't going to suck on it and then be hanged.

"On the lam," Wyatt suddenly said. "'Bout time you dun some runnin. Good for yore wind, Doc. Yore kind git awful helpless in them saloons, just a-suppin and whorin and all that dumb stuff. Guy like you needs where we are right now. Frish and lively's best. A man kin breathe up, most of all a man like you." Doc was overwhelmed by this outpouring and hoped for more, but Wyatt was done, his word-hoard emptied, his place in myth already half-secure, his destiny so definite he could slow-motion his way to it in a buckboard loaded down with who knew how many hangers-on. It was a sentimental rendezvous that lovers might have planned upon a map, saying, rather, let's meet in Santa Fe, that palace of romance, and to hell with everywhere else. But Doc had dropped in on Wyatt like a piece of mail, good or bad news depending on how Wyatt felt.

Up yonder, out there, far from here, he began, but was unable to complete the thought, vastness having invaded and then sealed his mind. Yes, he decided, the mind is a sewing machine at best, one of those noiseless Wilcox and Gibbs ones, and the world is a fabric without edges. That was all he could come up with, but this idea like all his nighttime ideas failed to get written down and disappeared with dawn. He was not sleeping enough, having been roused and made insomniac by the great poem of the plains, soon yielding to the roasting Jornada, between the Cimarron and the Arkansas: a true desert, bound to make the traveler yearn for prairie grass left behind. It was hardly letter-writing country, but a zone of swollen tongues and pristine-looking sand, a waterless watershed where the Wrights' sickly little son, with whom Doc had felt some sympathy, seemed to go downhill even more, becoming a pasty-faced relic with black-ringed hypnotic eyes. There was, sad to say, a useless freemasonry of the tubercular based on empathy and torment, all of its members tempted into something illicit in order to defy the natural regime that had punished them for no good reason save some fluke in body chemistry. Drifting away from some moral norm, they made a pirouette of death.

Next they endured dreams of cold water sluicing them while they tore at their clothing to make a draft. The Jornada baked them alive even as they slowed down, the horses too dry to whinny, what water there was in the holes brackish and full of tad-poles. Smelling water, the horses tried to leap ahead to it and had to be restrained by major force, except that they broke away and then had to undergo a restless wait while the waterhole filled up again. Doc told himself he would be glad to go no farther; even Dodge was better than this. What saved him and them, as it had saved thousands before, was the radiational cooling at night as the ground's heat spread itself outward into the near-vacuum of space, able to go away endlessly into nowhere, leaving an accept-able temperature behind as if the heat had been some pestilential visitation. You needed faith to get through the days, though, and Doc now knew he was not a born traveler, trying to fix his mind on the etiquette of letter-writing, from a letter composed and sent while waiting for the other's reply, a letter that repeated the previ-ous letter, to letters that ignored all questions posed and letters that were all questions. Surely, he thought, somebody had written on this, an epistolary guide for amateurs, putting them wise to genteel technique, even a technique for literary gunmen whose hands trembled when they held a pen with bird-beaked nib. Would she ever visit him? Would she ever be allowed to? Would he ever visit her, crouching in the little anteroom with its puce upholstery and guillotine-like hatch through which all blessings and refusals flowed? Could you be admitted to nunneries? Would she come out of the darkness like Ida Pempest, almost forgotten, whom he had once gone to see in the asylum and she had appeared at the stumble, her face swathed in jelly and bread crumbs, even a smudge of butter, her eyes bloodshot and her hair greasy-lank and confettied with dandruff. It was always better to avoid places that *contained* people: pens, jails, convents, asylums, not so much places where they were inviolable as places where they slowly receded from the human race, almost like Doc, whose breath sometimes lapsed into being a pink fizzy drink.

Then the benediction came as the sand ended, the cropped dry grass lengthened and greened up, mutated into scrub, and another universe appeared, puny to burly, of piñon and scrub cedar and, at long last, pine trees. He had done this journey in his mind many times over, always wondering why he had never made it, what impetus had been missing. Aimed at distant Santa Fe, the royal and ancient city of St. Francis, they peered down at the huge plateau beneath them, that ample and commodious reward exacted from geography not by prayer but by grit, and the Rio Grande shimmered for them alone, the slate-blue Sangre de Cristo Mountains to the north reminded Doc of elephant hide seen in a traveling circus. They had reached an oasis.

Doc sensed a dividing line had begun to spoil even his own wretched life. In his first two attempts at being a dentist again, he had behaved in the usual way, hardly distinguishable from any one of a thousand other practitioners. In Las Vegas, however, for a brief time he had got into things he had never anticipated, first of all, with elegant civility asking the patient to bear with him as he blindfolded them with a bandanna, explaining the risk to sight as tiny pieces of pulp or bone sped through the immediate work area. This done, he opened the patient's mouth wide and slid the barrel of his right-hand six-gun, secreted under a crisp white towel, in among the mucous membranes and actually tapped the tips of the teeth with the gunsight, tempted to pull the trigger and explode the entire head. Why he did this, he could not tell, but he speculated about it, deciding it was just a morbid prank, far from being executed. It would certainly not accompany him to—where he went next, Prescott or Tombstone, as he had decided to give up dentistry. Sliding the barrel into the patient's mouth had therefore been a farewell to his profession. No? Then it was audienceless bravado, for him only, one of those I-dare-to-do-it performances that enliven a man's maturity. In no sense was it a dress rehearsal for some future feat, or even an obbligato to an actual killing in the street. Perhaps he was trying to scare himself with the prospect of an up-close shooting that sprayed him with slush and fragments: nothing as clinical as the bullet from fifteen yards away or the tooth hauled out with might and main. He was teaching himself the difference between the remote and the immediate, something best not ignored if he proposed for himself a career between outlaw and lawman. What if the patient dragged the bandanna down and saw? What then? The gesture's only charm for him was its silent, invisible inefficacy, a gesture in the corroded night, addressed to God or the plains. There, but for the grace of the Almighty, he would go, a surgical monster instead of a sometime shootist. Doc felt burgeoning in him things beyond suspicion; parts of him were opening up into twisted dimensions. Six or seven times he had played his game with the gun barrel, each time soothing the patient with groomed phrases, imagining the red crescendo and just as swiftly having to clean up afterward. Something else not to write to Mattie about, or to tell Kate when she reappeared, worn out from pleasuring scores of cowboys. He confessed only to himself, and hardly even that in full, casting himself as a satanic actor on a bloody stage: no more than that, certainly not becoming anyone else irrevocably.

It bore thinking about nevertheless. Just as the bacillus had made him familiar with the imminence of death, the rot within the body's daily aurora display of sweet cells, so did his time as a gunfighter habituate him to killing. Death, not insult or infamy or shame, had become his familiar, with whom he was grudgingly at home. It was lucky that he had not become as some had a grave-visitor, a coffin-peerer, a corpse-fancier, a wound-prober, a blood-supper. So easy to go that way, especially if a good education had primed you for the variety of human roles, telling you to despise nothing, find nothing alien. I am only, he reassured himself, adapting myself to the business I find myself in; dreadful images prepare me for the worst, and, whatever I end up doing, or having to undergo, I will not flinch. It sounded pat, but it was probably the truth, garnished a bit and cleverly embellished. A man does not live his sweetest moments sweetly, he lectured himself, if his experience of the dreadful is inadequate; you need the shocking background in order to succumb to bliss. It was not much of a discovery, but it would serve him, who until the bacillus had been slow to look forward, always trusting that life would bring him, unbidden, the next delicious slice.

Now, he discovered, the mind took care of itself and put itself through exercises designed to protect, infect and calm. This was the way to the unthinkable, whose presence in the civilized mind, at least on the level of tutorial images, guaranteed a happy life.

Learning to discern behind the most exquisite scene or face the gorgon-head of things at their worst was a saving grace. To live otherwise was to invite insolent catastrophe to do its worst with you, rending and destroying just when you thought you were in clover. The notion of acid-burned clover appealed to him because, in the midst of his gruesome maunderings, he sensed a logic that said: If life is absurd, live absurdly; if it confronts you all the time with the hateful, then add to the amount of it, hating the hateful all the more, and with personal animus, because some of it happens to be your own work. He could not have defended such thoughts in a rigorous argument—he never got into such arguments—but was nonetheless willing to live by such a code, knowing that somewhere between Dallas and Las Vegas his heart had found its final rhythm, nothing chipper but a more or less survivable fumble among the grave discords. No one else, presumably, thought any such thing or needed such boosting, though maybe the famous silences of Wyatt Earp betokened some profoundly inward inability to get horror into speech. Wyatt survived only because he kept trying to eliminate the unthinkable; he always needed the gunshot of tomorrow, the affront of next week, otherwise doomed to decline into the benign stoicism of the chronic dotard.

Of all the explanations Doc offered himself of why he had begun to turn lethal there was the unusual one of soft flesh versus steel. It was flesh that had let him down, steel that had sustained him, in early pistols and dentist's tools. Not that steel could save a man; it would ignore his very passing, but was always something to hold on to, neither ambiguous nor vacillating, neither rotten nor morbid. Other men had found comfort in other pieces of equipment, from trousers press to Bowie knife, from guillotine to golf club. All Doc wanted was something that would not fail him, that would bear his weight and, when all was slithering away from him in a deluge of rancid sponges green or scarlet, give him the illusion of a rail, a banister, a certainty that sat there cooling in the night at his beck and call, his useful badge. Where such thinking ended, he did not know, but where it began was clear, and the next few stages remained clear to him even as he contemplated how bad the life of a badman was going to be, going to the dogs because the dogs had sunk fang into him in his tender years, before he even got launched. What had he told himself about living absurdly? Well, in a cruel world, be cruel. Was his conduct to be as obvious and reciprocal as that?

I am getting severer, he wrote to Mattie, *quite unsparing with myself as I resolve no longer to settle for soft options such as owning saloons, racing to catch up with friends traversing barren plains. I have reached a sticking point. I find it hard to remember my own bad deeds. People come up to me murmuring "Kid Colton, Charley White, Mike Gordon," as if the names have an abiding allure, but I never recall who these men were, part of the flux flowing past me. Even the brother of Ed Bailey is looking for me, they say, but I can be found, so I attribute all these reminders to active imaginations having too little to do. Everything makes sense. The Santa Fe has bypassed Las Vegas, so East Las Vegas springs up next to the tracks. It's the law of human development. I heard that Wyatt Earp is on the track of some silver, a strike in the Southeastern Arizona Territory—Tombstone; he was never paid enough, which may have been all right when you consider how often he paraded himself without arms, hoping to quell nightly brawls through sheer force of personality. It was I who pulled iron for him, it was I whom they got to see when they entered town. I was the watchman. But I can see why money whispers to him, as it whispers to me on the faro tables. I try to rise before noon and then take a twenty-yard walk for my health; farther and I am coughing. Not for me to go around town lassoing cigar-store Indians; I leave that sort of thing to the cowpokes as they come into town, raising hell and shooting out the lamps. Did you ever consider the expression "raising hell"? Is it sacrilegious? Are believers forbidden to badmouth hell? I wonder about these matters, having no strict orientation, of which I guess I could use a buckboardful.*

When answer came, after following him around, back to where he started from, and then outbound again, he wondered if they should communicate only by telegram. Everyone would read their letters, true, but they could always write in highfalutin language, the theologian addressing the doctor. *John,* she wrote in her reply, *Not everything makes sense. Remember that. Even the most devoutly revered entities and events have mystery within them and have to be considered not only under the aspect of eternity but as subject to unfathomable divine will. It is almost like your Santa Fe railroad, bypassing human understanding so much that, in our very frustration, we build East Las Vegas out of the dust of revulsed understanding. I mean, East Las Vegas is the town of all the books and sermons that try to understand. Where you choose to live is a personal matter, in town proper so as to take in the teeth the full brunt of baffling divine ways, or in the railroad town, to make life a mite easier. I hope the comparison does not offend you; here, we have to watch our similes and metaphors like mad lest they infect holy subject-matter. They too work on behalf of understanding, and sometimes the mind actually needs a smile or metaphor which, known to be wrong or inaccurate, it cannot do without* (sometimes, in haste, or fervor, she would write *smile* instead of *simile*). *Such is imperfection, John. So: you have become the watchman. Good. Watchman, what of the night? The dark night of the soul of which we always think though we do not speak. "Raising hell," since you inquire, is in no way sacrilegious, but does it not go back to John Milton the poet? I may be wrong in this, not having read his work for ages. It would help your raising of yourself above the common ruck, as Pico might have said, if you did not resort too often to foul and profane expressions, which corrupt the soul from the skin inwards. You are right to ask if something might be sacrilegious; to some sisters, nearly everything is.*

Here she had paused, gone to do some pious chore, gratify some bodily need, and then returned with the thought not quite in its original position in her mind, having let it rutch (as she said) or slip a little from pre-eminent warning to, well, this: *Orientation, I think, is basically a Muslim idea, such as facing Mecca. I never heard of occidentation, if such a word exists. The chore is not geographical, not really, but more like being faced with an intended void you wish were fuller. Our discipline consists in allowing God's presence to fill that void without ever deceiving ourselves.*

Although we may be, sometimes.

How can we tell?

O.K.: The Corral, the Earps, and Doc Holliday

There is no authority outside the one whose authority we try to prove exists.

Rather than getting too deep, I am getting too shallow. Forgive me until my next round. Your Mattie in Christ.

When he read that ending, he winced, aware that she had gone far beyond him in soul-searching; he did not so much search his soul as hold it up, bandit-style, and rob it of its riches. He was his own life's boldest desperado, having won his reputation against drunks. Was that true? It was a far cry from Mattie's convoluted lariat of devotional thought to Kate's "Take me back, Doc, I didn't mean to do it" and "I don't know what got into me." What got into her, he knew, was lechery; she couldn't get enough, so she followed the herds, returning to Dodge only to ply more business as the drovers rode into town and shot it up. She was a herd follower, eager not for money but for frequent, coarse attention such as Doc, with the best will in the world and the weakest libido, could rarely provide. She needed a lot, she once told him, and she needed it fast; it was such need that had driven her into the profession in the first place, not money-lust. At derisive times, she called him to his face "the little deputy," but he shrugged that off; what bothered him much more was a Hungarian expression (she claimed it was such) that sounded like *serethetelek*, or *secret heartache* (as he named it), which according to her meant *I may have loved you*, which formula she claimed was just a mess of bits added on (suffixes, he said). So she would at her worst seem to be saying "secret heartache" only to utter an ambiguity meaning *in the past I did* or *I otherwise would have*, the upshot being that either she no longer did or she never had. It was a poor prospect and, in a foreign language, more wounding than he would have thought; surely something in an alien tongue was remoter, but that brought it closer to the unsayable awful, and he could not abide it.

Talking to the on-again, off-again Kate was no kind of preparation for writing to Mattie. Doc had once known exactly what his sexual needs were, before he attained the age of twenty-one: above average, but hardly towering or insensate. The disease had weakened him in all ways, so much so that, now, writing to a nun was in some ways more exciting than fondling an exotic trollop. It was more of a trespass, he thought, and, anyway, how much of a trespass was it to grope a woman felt at by most of the cowhands in Kansas? In any event, a woman who kept saying the wrong thing was more than he could cope with. "Why don't you put the rope around my neck," she had said in reference to some hanging, "and pull on it when you want me?" He would, he thought, having her dangle from the windmill in the Las Vegas Plaza. On the other hand, asking Mattie what she thought heaven was like was an astounding expedition into the uncluttered unknown. Turrets and pinnacles, he thought, belvederes and dazzling promontories. No, *she* thought, it was mostly a soft carpet of moss with only the faintest light, and you felt your way, caressing the memory of this or that creature, murmuring the dearest names you knew until a vibration in the strangely acidic air made you aware of their presence. They had been there all the time, reticent witnesses of your initial bewilderment. *You're so clever,* he wrote her, *I don't know why I open my mouth. It is right to lock you up with your mind. I can't see black anymore. I do not deal in silhouettes. If there is ever darkness, I am lost. I ask you too many questions without ever once asking if you would prefer me to call you Sister Mary Melanie as I do on the envelopes. If I could only be in Savannah, not with you, I know how wrong that'd be, but close by, near to family. I'd hear the singing maybe, and quiet my mind listening to it every time it told me Wyatt's brothers resented my influence over him, who was really a preacher and always telling folk how to behave. Left to them, I'd be the leper chosen to scrub the toilets. Forgive me, I am not mainly a man of coarse allusions. They see me in deerskin gloves and derby, and they say what's* he *doing with Wyatt? Where did a flower like that spring from? Be assured, I think reverently of Saint Vincent's Convent, the monotonous illustrious grind of the pipe organ; I sometimes feel like such an organ being played on by the universe, and with heavy hands.*

Oh well, it is late, meaning almost dawn.

In only a week, I surmise, your reply to my last letter but two will be here, rustling like a new twig. I have heard of communication, even if not quite epistolary, by telepathy, but I imagine that radiant energy from the holy cross would interfere with our concepts and my own timid, classically groomed mind would baulk at the criss, never mind the +. Yours eternally, JHH

Only a day later, behind a door blocked by a dresser shoved against it (his paranoia talking loud today), Doc is writing to her again as if this, and not gunplay, were his only vocation and future. He has just written *Then they say it's quiet, and I, instead of giving the time-honored response, give them a taste of what I am really like. "Yes," I answer, "some frailty in the inexorable stars has bent the crook of life." They ask me who the crook is.* He answers for her, whispering his version of a king's noise: *Naughty.*

Then back into the everyday he tumbled, trying her with a tale dear to his heart, how Mrs. Edna Mumby, who taught him English, one day had him think about a line in *A Midsummer Night's Dream. I think it went "Why, Bottom, thou art translated." I puzzled a bit at that, because I couldn't see how a man, even a Bottom, got translated. Then she said, "John, you know Latin. Think about trans-late." I still didn't twig it, then she reminded me of the verb* ferro, *and I completed what she said with* tuli, latum. Ferro, tuli, latum: *to carry. Right, she told me. Bottom had been carried across into another species because he's wearing an ass's head. I guess the translation did not endure. But my mind was already moving ahead to how strange language is, that those frisky old Romans would come up with words so unlike one another to express related concepts. Imagine, going from* ferro *to* tuli *and* latum. *What a jape!*

Not that he knew it, Doc had graduated into the league-to-come of fighter pilots, supposed to be single men with no firm obligations to anything save the colors: available for death at short notice and relatively unmourned in that heartless fashion of the military, to whom cannon fodder was almost anonymous. Doc sensed his role was that of front man, but without the perilous glamour of a later generation that included the lads of the American Eagle Squadron in the Battle of Britain. He was never to know, of course, but ever since being saved by Kate and his own saving of Wyatt, he had felt more exposed, more in demand, both expendable and ephemeral. Wyatt was a family man, indeed a

107

man of many families, a man of tribal family moving around the planet with siblings surrounding him and all their hangers-on. Doc, on the other hand, was not just a lone wolf but a condemned one, knowing already in his bones the fate that awaited those who shot it out with him. They said of him that he did not care, that he had made his peace with death long before any gunfight began, and he stayed that way, never allowing experience to deter him. The more he took gunslingers on, the more he knuckled down to fatality, seeing it as a gruesome bauble, almost a reward, a piece of palatable eternity available to those who went into battle without the slightest misgiving. Did he achieve all this without a trace of vanity? Perhaps so. Men with chronic fatal disease can develop bizarre traits of involuntary selflessness, never quite becoming laudable altruists—the ones who save the nation, say, from Cincinnatus to Jim Bowie—but freeing the family men, the tribally afflicted, to get on with other jobs. Doc had an inkling of this privilege and celebrated it in moments of quiet rhetoric almost akin to the sendup he liked to utter, or to phrase in his mind, when someone said, "Gee, it's quiet," this time saying, "Yair, the decorum of infinity's a bit blurred today." A small victory, no doubt, but his alone amidst the millions of simple-minded agree-ers to whom the automatic rejoinder "Yair, too quiet" was an act of faith, a communal bond.

There was too his sense that he did all his important work on foot, though he rode well, as his skill in evading pursuers proved. There was something noble and statuesque in the way riders pulled their mounts up, making the heads rear a little, themselves jolting back in the saddle as if awaiting transfer to some eminent prow. He had never aspired to epic look, but he was aware of how, in the most unguarded moment, merely because they had reined back, the unlikeliest and least noble of men assumed a transient grandeur, mounted there and swaying back as if having almost collided with the godhead. Good God, he thought, you can muster *some* dignity when on foot, but never the same. Isn't that what the Indians found when the Spanish conquistadors first appeared, mounted, an unknown breed of men riding high on huge machines? His knowledge of history was spotty, but for a moment he became an Inca, awed by the invader, even if the end of that ravishing line degenerated into someone such as the cattle baron Shanghai Pearce. Doc did not wish to be ennobled or embellished, but he did want to think that, somewhere within his assumed frontier role, having swapped southern comfort for Western rough-and-tumble, there thrived a smidgen of honor. He had given up so much, had been cheated of how many years, so he deserved to feel he added up to more than a mere deputy to Wyatt Earp, a mopper-up of Dodge City, gambler, sot, occasional cocksman. Perhaps he was groping for a pyramid amid a handful of sand, but the urge was there, even in his decorum of dress, his courtesy to women encountered on the Front Streets of the Western world. The problem was that he had become an outlaw, known to be such, and his reputation was beyond denial. Here he was, in the flesh, the one and only, as accustomed to shabby lodgings that reeked of damp and rot, ancient vomit and recent estrus; he took all that for granted, able to bear it so long as he could admire from close up the figure he sometimes cut, the heroic *in parvo*, he smiled, the hero in little, going nowhere but marking time with imperious dignity.

There, not bad. A little touch of honor discerned, he scribbled to her, *in the mix. Nothing grand, just a touch. I am working on it. More later. Always trying for the big improvement.*

"Where headed now, Wyatt?" The echo, completing the lariat loop from when he first asked, sounded more hopeful, like one of those questions he dimly recalled from Greek that presupposed the answer yes, but of course not what Wyatt actually said: "Mogollon Rim, then down to Prescott." Now, Wyatt did not answer "hell," or "perdition," or, as sometimes when he was feeling ornery and taciturn, "down the road a piece, Doc, you ain't comin I trust." Not like that at all, but serenely civil as if travel alone by buckboard in a convoy had mellowed him, and, after weeks of it, he had become the man they all wanted him to be, rushing him through the preliminaries of hero worship toward premature divinity.

Pumped up toward godhood. Times were, Doc resented Wyatt not for what and who he was, but for what and who he would never be. Oh, he might become the famousest lawman, church deacon, real estate pundit in the world, but just maybe never the fastest gun, the biggest threat to a badman, the loyalest spouse. To know him was to want to reform him, Doc knew, whereas to know Doc was to want to be sure you got invited to his funeral. So now Wyatt's answer was geographical, almost as if he were an eagle surveying from on high and not an ant perusing his way across barren tracts unmarred by human settlement. Wyatt had perspective.

Doc worried that, about shooting other members of the human race, he did not worry quite enough, but he reassured himself that men in extremis were not bound by ordinary laws. The old legal chestnut about shooting dead a person falling from a high building did not apply to him; he was the man falling, with a perfect right to shoot into the window of the person looking out to shoot the man falling. It was that kind of madness, valid no doubt in the patchwork quilt of frontier life where, as the clumsy cowboys' regimen had it, men were men, which was to say radical killers. To say that life was cheap was not savage enough; it was worth nothing at all, whereas gun skills, maybe in some belated tribute to Vulcan and his smithy, mattered most, as if some force akin to the old Greek *anangke*, that told the gods themselves what to do, had challenged the primitive technology of the region—Smith & Wesson Russian revolver such as Wyatt Earp was to give to Sam Brown in Alaska twenty years hence; Doc's 1851 Colt Navy revolver; the 10-gauge Richard's shotgun with short barrel; the derringer, like that given to Doc by Kate—to do its worst. It did. Perhaps the most exaggerated version of the gun was Wyatt's long-barreled Colt .45, special ordered, whose barrel according to who beheld it varied from ten to twelve inches and made a fine crowbar with which to break open someone's head. With toys such as these, easily available though nominally forbidden in saloons and theaters, the men of Dodge, for example, could indulge in a lethal art-form whose stances and sounds became more famous than the discovery of gunpowder. The streets teemed with imitators, Doc-ets and Earp-ets, few of them equipped with Doc's shotgun or Wyatt's Buntline special, who shot at one another with ritual regularity. It was a slapdash merchandising of death, responded to by those watching as merely a context rather than an act of curt savagery. Soon over, the gunfight entertained, made them all thirsty, and provided a magic carpet of smoke upon which a certain few sailed to a glory that outlasted the century and lived all through the next. What a later author was to call the gift of death was everyone's holy grail, hardly an echo or forerunner of military massacre, but a democratic assertion of power that implied how gallant were the men to whom killing and being killed ennobled survivors, marking them as men who knew a greater truth than any vouchsafed to others, who had seen the fire and felt it sear them. To be thus among the elect among the doomed, some of whom had not long to live, was a special bargain almost matching the lavender hedonism that, across the ocean, was stirring up the chaste quadrangles of Oxford University where Walter Pater and others preached the doctrine of burning with a hard gem-like flame. This cruder version of Pater's pansified sensualism had seized hold of all men who wore a ten-gallon hat: a promise of an unprosaic life, never mind how short, and the inestimable illicit pleasure of shooting someone almost made the price of admission worth it.

Doc knew nothing of Pater, or world movements in intenser living, but he invented such things for himself, given the gift of moribundity in order to give the other gift of gunshot. If this dueling paralleled some cosmic arrangement he had heard rumors about, he never said, but it was beyond even the Kate who had the derringer she gave him inscribed on the back of the butt with *To Doc from Kate*. That far she was willing to join in the mayhem, but she was more lascivious than bloodthirsty, eager to see Doc survive from week to week while others bit the dirt. So, although he was sometimes a lily-livered bastard, he was also the gaunt, striding hero whom Dodge obeyed, and he who didn't got planted. This should have appalled her more than it did, or so she thought. She had become blasé, as calm about the big floral fistful of money Doc came home with from a long night's gambling as about the men he had plugged en route.

"We can have us some fun with all that," she'd say, goggling.

"We kin parley it into even more," he'd tell her. "Leave it alone, you bitch-trollop. Earn your own."

There is no need to sample the profane rage this answer brought forth, but she had energy and ingenuity, calling him *fodyahstash* or consumption. He never asked her what the word meant and she soon slurred it into *fuddystash*, which he did not understand either, rebuking her from time to time with the kind of doggerel he had rejoiced in as a child:

> Tall Doc Holliday,
> He likes to have a girl a day;
> Stuffs them raw, then hot,
> Then sits them on a chamberpot.

Usually she slapped him for such effrontery, not that she cared; Doc was many things; an ardent lover was not one. He let the libido build up, like rheumatism or his own special pain of the lung tissue, then sought her out, but not finding her (sometimes they cohabited, sometimes not, needing to be kept apart) he forgot the stone-ache as he called it and transferred the impetus to faro. There at the table, among the reek of Havana cigars, the coughs of them all, the Miss Laura Denbos and the Clells (truncated from Clelland), the drooping pistoleros and the beautiful dreamers from the open range in long white gleaming raincoats, among the burpers and the vomiters, the greedy and the humble, the dead-tomorrow and the victors, he entered his skillful trance and fleeced them all, nobody knew how, but it had something to do with a photographic memory, a knowledge of (he claimed, jesting) ancient Greek, and a gift for bluff raised almost to the point of prophecy. He quietly ran riot until he had more than enough to buy a saloon or an angel.

One of Doc's worst worries was that, with his days numbered, he tended, after a while, to kill men before their time: not before they had drawn, of course, but before they had achieved the status of full-blown nuisance. Was it right to take them in the midst of a petulant fit when a harsh word or two would have served? He wasn't sure, but he did tend to rush into things, at first hanging back to create the illusion of the reluctant inhibited greenhorn, then producing out from behind it the fine calibration of the killer, aiming with sundial certainty. He was faster than Wyatt, he knew, but it looked as if he wasn't—spectators added his preamble time to his shooting time whereas, of course, it did not belong, it just seemed to melt into what followed it. Maybe this preamble was the snake hypnotizing the victim, making him attend to what he did not need to watch: a frill, a furbelow, a twitch, when both of those eyes should have been on the gun. Doc had his own sultry ways, famous for what they called his foreplay and he, privately, named his *introit*. Indeed, just as he took aim with his eyes without moving his hands, he seemed a shy man on the verge of asking to borrow your newspaper or even your comb, and then you were dead, not knowing that you had not known. Earp, with his long barrel, was slower, but he took longer to holster his pistol, deliberately prolonging his afterplay so much that watchers wondered if they had really seen what they had seen and only now was he beginning. Whatever would happen if Doc shot it out with Wyatt?

·11·

God help me, Mattie told herself, I am properly Sister Mary Melanie. Why go on pretending to be Mattie? Sometimes her outward yearning was so great that the moths and feathers Doc had mentioned floated about in her own room, not theirs, sign of moldy linen and busted upholstery. Why, they even seemed a luxury compared to teak and stark mahogany, the featherless mattress, the only too receptive, sagging bedstead. She knew that she was preparing for the Life, but she had never suspected there needed to be a rehearsal for the preparation. She was far from ready, had not yet developed the narrowed view essential to an anchorite, and here she was with letters from a gunman-dentist smuggled to her by an aunt. One of her few consolations was a prayer-poem she had written when much younger, a short thing she had worked on until it almost made her sick; but it soothed her during her utmost privations, relating the child in her to the postulant. "High star," it began, "I hold a bit of you in one hand and think I like you, but my other hand is empty." She winced and turned away from the little, crumpled text, once a square of cream-laid Chesterford paper. "Will you please make like a house call as when we get very sick, and touch my brow? If you touch me, I touch you." It no longer seemed so easy. Neither touched either. "Then I can get on with things." It sounded too much a bustle, quite unprayerlike, in fact. Who hurried through prayer? Well, all religious did, come to think of it, afflicted with terminal impatience. What kind of a religion was it that you had no time for, when you had given up everything else for it? To her credit, she thought, she did all things slowly, prizing them as leftovers from another life or majestic discoveries of another dimension altogether: licking a curl of dry toast or saying a prayer. To do things slowly, she thought, made your life last longer. On went the prayer she had composed and kept: "I hold back from prayer as I do from bones, crusts and fire. Please stir my soul for me, to make me better at denying myself. I do not like to ask, but I will need you for almost always."

That last line moved her still, loaded with gravity, and she considered how good a poet she had been: budding, no doubt, but with—what had someone called it?—a feisty, almost lapidary sprightliness; visual, enameled, sometimes blisteringly sardonic, which was the other face of her crescendo piety. She had shown Doc her first poems and he had nodded at them agreeably in the bluff manner of a premature man of the world, only to find them haunting him all through dental school. He should have gone back to her instead of heading off to Dallas; in those days too full of himself and his blooming fresh career. He didn't need her then, not even for the chaste kisses he had planted in innocuous places. The most intimate kisses had been bestowed by fingertip in the oval dimple either side of each knee, his hand grazing his lips and then touching her with circumspect intensity. It had been a delicate, standoffish period, he not so much shy as preoccupied by the banter and commotion of another city, she lady in waiting but resolved never to lead (or egg) him on. They stalled in each other's presence, daunted perhaps by a perfection they sensed in the air around them, but which they could never achieve. And so they became replicas of Palamon and Emily, medieval lovers howling for each other from matching towers. Doc and Mattie did not howl, but something gravid sucked them down, kept them low, made them lose faith in each other, though she gloried in his dental tools, he marveled at her skill with short lines. Something that was due to happen, and would have done, given only nearness and boredom, never did, and here they were, hewing massive careers of indirection from unpromising materials: gunplay from consumption, chastity from excessive calm. Surely some importunate intervening pander would have pulled it off, but none such had appeared, both parties given to a certain degree of saturated solitariness. So now they paired by postman, as racked with longing and deficiency as could be, determined to make steel out of sand.

Tempted to write him what, in childhood, she had called "a budget," a huge voluminous eyewitness album, she decided not to, but wondered if, at such a distance, and plagued by the jerky caesuras of time, she might not go back to poetry and send him the results: acrid, stinging, acerbic poems designed to fit his frontier moods. She would send them anyway, she resolved, and count the labor as a form of prayer, relying on her memory for topics, faces, names, scandals, plagues, whole epics of rot and rage, as it were to shake him loose from his doomed mania. It might be done with words, she thought, where love, handkerchiefs, and pleading had failed. All she wanted was for Doc to turn around and, somehow curbing the bacillus, come home healthy and sweep her off to Zanzibar; failing that, to the Withlacoochee swimming hole. It was no harder for him, she thought, than touching God was for her. She had heard that God's apparent absence was the finest goad to pious perfection ever devised, but she did not buy the sop, preferring (she reassured herself) the blatant visibility of some Asiatic deities. The Christian God and His mutilated son struck her as too easygoing and, for easygoing figures, not lenient enough. She and Doc had discussed these matters for hours in their ponderous teens without getting anywhere, and establishing only that, of the two, she had the keener sense of the divine, about which he had always felt vague, thinking that if humans, at terrible cost, could be precise, then so could gods—at least they could show their faces.

"Well, John," she retorted, "they do—in all those old masters. There is no shortage of icons."

He saw at once how right and converted she was, willing to accept an imagined physiognomy, someone else's vision of the deity and His son, as factual. Only a believer worked on that trusting, humble plane. It was like accepting a police artist's drawing of your own mother, all guesswork and scratches.

"Not for me, honey," he said slowly, thinking much more than he could say, and thinking it off-handedly as if the thoughts were not his.

"On that we differ," she said, eyes moistening.

"It's not really a difference," he told her, "it's just an opinion."

"You've heard of an *aide-mémoire*," she said. "Well, my fine beau, it's an *aide-pietas*. It helps you to remember what you didn't know you'd forgotten."

Chop logic, he told her. This was the rock on which they would founder; yet he could foresee a life with her during which they never discussed the matter again, they would suppress it in the interests of passion and pride, union and loyalty.

She was saying nothing, sensing defeat between them, yet not sure who had prevailed. Let's both be pagans, she wanted to say, but she said nothing of the kind while he hummed, buzzed, grimaced in mock-solicitude, dumbfounded by what had begun as cosmology and ended as a spat. Could religious art have forced them apart? He couldn't believe it. "Isn't imagination," he began, but ended the inquiry. She stared at him hard, as gentle a gaze as he had seen, but he did not touch her until, cupping her elbow, he left her alone to cry in the hot light-cone of a reading lamp.

Staring at her few possessions, Sister Mary Melanie wondered how much longer she could spend adjusting their sit in the drawers and cupboards, arranging lines in strict parallel, removing them to polish off nonexistent dust, weighing them in her hands as if cradling some rare Aegean vase. Comb, brush, spectacles, small sewing kit, nail file, portraits of her parents, writing pad and envelopes, a roll of stamps intended for faraway (she almost regarded him as overseas), a shoe brush and Kiwi polish, a little red glass box for coins, a few clothes—this was her life's hoard with her life, she grimaced, put away in penultimate storage. Each day she tended her stuff, slightly changing its places, but no more able to relocate things than an author can change the places of sentences in a printed book to defy the index. She speculated what the presence in her room of certain foreign intrusive objects would do: a wheel from a carriage, say, the head of a giraffe, a bottle of bourbon, and she warmed to the idea, thinking that, if her last day came, one way or the other, she would arrange to have the room transmogrified. Of course her last day would come; what had she meant? Oh, if she ever intended to leave, quit the religious vocation and become a full-time poet doing journalism on the side. Fat hope. The sheer energy required to undertake such a feat had already gone into the moving in, the weeding out of her life in preparation for entry. Where could she find the energy for anything? The regimen of the convent was hardly Draconian, but it took her best, sucked her dry, leaving only a remnant vivacity for a monthly letter increasingly written to express herself rather than respond to his many questions. How did that other woman, that Kate the Hungarian, "do" for him? Did she take good care or leave him to his own devices? It was hard to tell because he told only one variant of the truth, the one that would not offend her yet would get across his lack of true comfort, his nowhere to put his legs up, his lack of clean handkerchiefs. She envisioned herself, as her piety bloomed, moving into an even smaller room, then into one smaller still, until she had to be almost shoehorned into a closet that only just exceeded the dimensions of a coffin. She had heard of religious mania, as well as of theological euthanasia, and was not alarmed; she had not come here to spread herself, and her Wordsworth had come with her: "Nuns fret not at their convents' narrow rooms." She fretted a little but did not make a profession of it, recognizing that the truly emancipated soul requires no plinth. She was a smuggler, really, whisking things out, having them brought in, but putting all letters to the flame and pounding the ashes with the poker lest anyone come to peer and have her expelled.

As for Doc, or John, her first duty, as with someone bereaved, was to weep, not to argue or cajole, but just to let him know she was there, hurled into eternity with him. Then, after the weeping, nothing; he would not have survived. She was glad, in a way, she had her faith to fall back on; dealing with his affliction without a spiritual basis would have been wretched, and she would have tormented herself to death with undisciplined empathy. Clearly, one had to learn how to give understanding: there were proportions to be observed, an etiquette of the identifying heart, and these things she would teach herself as the years went by and, slowly, the vision of a radiant universe outside began to pale and shrink. Soon she would be gliding along the beam of light that denuded you of everything: poetry, comb, toothpaste. Perhaps the day would come when even furniture insulted the purity of space and she would inhabit a bare tank on whose floor she slept, in the leak from whose ceiling she washed, in the sow bugs of whose floor she rejoiced, having at last identified her true companions. Poetry would be consumed and sent up in fire long before that, but there was still room for poetry now, cunningly sent to Dodge or Las Vegas, New Mexico, for posterity to claim from the estate of a tubercular dentist. She shook her head at the vicissitudes of fate and resolved to be a good sister, not rushing things, but not dawdling either on her way to the complex radiance promised her.

A letter would more than vent how she felt; it would do her good to tell him what life had become like: *We are always being told to bless ourselves, keep our eyes and hands raised, to be on our knees on the bed or floor, to keep our mouths filled with holy words mostly Latin, to keep holy water by us always, to fall toward an altar, to say the five greetings, the seven this, the nine that, to beat our breast, kiss the earth, cross the mouth with the thumb, fall to the ground on workdays, bow toward it on holy days, to draw two fingers from above the forehead down to the breast, to say the hours too soon rather than late, always to stand in honor of Our Lady, to say the psalms sitting or kneeling, and never, never to open a window, peer out, show ourselves at it, since the double black curtain signifies to the world we are black, the sun has burned us, and those outside, the men, want to see the pit of the young anchoresses, whose words are a pit too, as well as her beautiful face and white neck and light eyes, all a pit for filth whose stench we stop with a wooden lid as with a toilet hole where the jackdaw devil lurks with his heathen army, whereas hope is a sweet spice, which she who jabbers tends to spit out even as those from without bring news of mill and market, smithy and tavern, all of those rotten places. O alas, alas, how has the gold become dark, how has the fairest color turned and faded! We should keep silent, as does someone deaf and dumb, we would better hang on a gibbet than commit sin, even holding out a hand or touching one. We should grovel on the ground and scrape up the earth of our graves in which we will rot.*

My God, Doc told himself, they do boss them about, ramming all kinds of disgusting stuff into their minds until they don't have a normal response left in them. Remember thy last end and thou will never sin. That, writ large. It is really telling them that to be alive is sinful, even though they did not choose to come into this world. In a long reach of his mind, he filled the convents with feather-clad girls from the local hotels and the lewd stages with simpering nuns, just to gladden his heart. Could this taut fanatic, telling all, be the girl who had once said to him, "I am going out for something sweet. Back soon"? To which he had replied, "You, lady, are the sweetness you're going in search of." How could this groveling servitor be the same woman? What had he said in belated and distant answer when he wrote back to her?

Is there ever a spare second in your day? Do you eat? It must be hard to believe in all you say. Do you inflict punishment on yourself for supposed shortcomings? Is the whole thing one of trust? I am astounded, really, that those who guide and counsel you find God's universe a thing so vile, to be turned away from. Much as when somebody with bad breath always attributes it to the person he is kissing, but decades later smells himself and undergoes agonies of guilt. Do you see what I mean, you who used to be so open-minded?

Yet in an odd way he sensed that all he wanted was his Mattie at a distance, rather than anyone else nearby, no woman certainly. He wanted to see the South Seas and the glaciers, but they would keep; he did not need to go anywhere so long as he had her at a distance, communicable with and sedate. It was as much intimacy as he could stand. She never answered his carping questions, but reassured him of her piety and her advisers' warm punctilio— why, they had even worked out, she said, the exact placing of the elbows during the singing of "Ave Maria": to the ground, then on a step or bench. Such provision for motion and repose strengthened her no end, but made Doc wonder if prayer and holy incantation were that much different from gunfighting. Now he read on, trembling somewhat as if doomed to fail: *Her head turns sideways in aloof anxiety, shrouded in a wimple. She has been walled inside her window with a corrugated blue roof over her, as in a kennel, but she has no body to speak of, her mouth rather shriveled, moving toward her nose as if unable to breathe. On her right there stands a bishop or some such figure with two joined fingers outstretched, giving her a benediction. At some point his hand and arm vanish back into his dark blue velvet cloak and the apparition that his ring is retreats from her. She remains in her cell, which indeed becomes her tomb, and it remains sealed forever so that she rots in peace.*

He was almost gagging at this recital, not, as he now grasped, of her own life and fate, but of a nun in a painting, nonetheless intended to reassure in the most devastating way, as always with religious propaganda. Clearly, she doted on such pictures for their prophetic and everyday value; it was not difficult for her to see herself, a better-looking woman, in place of this nun. The entire idea of being walled up both sickened and excited him. Just so long, he mused, as there was a bottle of bourbon buried with you—he had read Poe, and the imp of the perverse had seen him through many a frontier crisis, encouraging him to take things to extremes at which he could function and others could not. He would shoot or walk away, as decisive in the latter as in the former.

If he had thought that was all and that she would revert to matters more humdrum, he was mistaken; now she spoke of some rough pelt around the heart, of being soft and mild within, sweet and fragrant-hearted in the presence of injury, the pelican as the type of the passionate anchoress—all of it like some inherited formula that only had to be said, or written, to be powerful. Now she was into blood that had to be cooled before it could be tested, anger as the shape-changer, mankind as naturally mild. He wondered if he would ever subscribe to such beliefs, especially living where and how he lived. Instances galore she gave him, from St. Andrew on his cross to St. Lawrence on the gridiron and St. Stephen being stoned. Could he endure what these men had? He doubted it, wondering though how they would have responded to a bacillus making them cough incessant blood. *Ponens in thesauris abyssos*, she wrote, and that was God in the act of (he thought) putting into His treasury the worst of people, for reasons he found obscure, unless God was given to colossal charity. On she went: *Be always thin, if you can manage it. Nuns must not hoard, or live easefully. Better to keep by them in their nests a gemstone such as an agate, which no vile thing dares approach. You see how much of an allegory life is. Even to the extent, with some, of wrong etymology, making out certain names in Hebrew to have meant this or that appropriate thing, all based on Isidore of Saville's* Etymologies *and a* Book of Names *supposed to have been written by St. Jerome. What piffle we live by, John, as if life and death had to be made more meaningful than they are, just because God made them.*

He recoiled and laughed. The old devil was not dead in her yet, but she was giving him a dreadful ride for his money. There was in her way of putting things a disobedient sprightliness that argued she might one day blow the coop, leaving behind her all their hair-splitting, weird exaggerations. It was there in her, but who nourished it? He alone perhaps. When she referred to herself as just possibly being "the night-raven in the house" or "the pelican of the wilderness," or even referred him, in the land of stagecoach and hold-up, to St. Gregory discoursing on one who carried treasure openly on a road known for thieves and robbers ("hell's pilferers," she told him), she seemed bulging with self-esteem, reveling in her virtuosity: a poet, after all, perhaps only now coming into her own after a preliminary career of pamphlets and slimmer-than-slim selections. It was not often, but it was often enough, that she told him *I am alone in a solitary space. Hilarion and Benedict, Syncletia and Sarah, Paul and Antony, these have gone afield into the desert or up the mountain, and rejoiced in the isolated life. God was their only company, which, when you come right down to it, is an extraordinary economy, not making the most of little, but recognizing how huge a human being is. Each time you kill—well, no, drop that. I did not say it but I will not waste time, ink and paper scratching it out. We would-be nuns are carrying a costly fluid, such as balsam, in a fragile container; the prelates who teach us call us "linctus in a brittle glass," which phrase I do not especially care for as they intend a tribute to virginity, but* linctus *unless all of my Latin has gone from me means* licked, *and that is hardly the image we desire. They split hairs. Not that. They argue about virginity gone and irreparable and another kind of break that, through chastity, can be mended, I wonder with whose thread and needle. Imagine it if you will. Only they who live sterile lives can prate thus about what they do not understand. Women are as distant from them as the stars. For myself, and this is something you more than any will understand, what is lost is lost, but only its physical integer, so to speak, so it may be possible to be virginally-minded and no longer a virgin. How? Through confession and repentance. I just wonder, John, how many of the women in here are virgins, how many came here in order to be chaste. And what has touching yourself, or having another do it, have to do with virginity? Some of the most depraved women in the world are lascivious virgins.*

He was beginning to weary of her obsessions, at least until he realized she had gone there to nourish them, watch them grow and turn into delicious hymnody. Had he been in that instant writing reply, seeking in vain some flash-of-light reciprocity, he would have told her that saints regard the world as a footstool to stand on while their hands grope for heaven, clothing themselves on the way with the true sun. That was all right: he had done his share of groping, all kinds, in his day. So now she seemed to want him out in the desert, murmuring *civitatem non ingredior,* which was commonplace Latin ("I will not enter the city") for the far better known bit of Horace that went *odi vulgus profanum.* Sharing Latin as they sometimes did, they belonged to an ancient order of alchemists or scholars designed to be understood worldwide: atavistic pedantry, coming up with unidiomatic American such as "the throng is hateful to me," when they meant they hated crowds.

What else had she said? Visit the widows and the fatherless. Arsenius (d. 450) was a senator, learned and august, appointed tutor to the sons of Theodosius the Great; after ten years' teaching, he left the Constantinople court for Alexandria and finally entered the desert. Am I supposed to do the same, Doc asked himself plaintively. Paul (d. 342) was supposed to have been the first Christian hermit in the Egyptian deserts, and much good may it have done him. Good breathing, pure lungs. Was there a connection between the bacillus and the hermit? He would love to know. He had asked, but that, like so many of his questions, having been carried all the way to Georgia in conveyances initially protected by the Earps of the world in their role as U.S. marshals, had vanished into the wind unanswered, not even spurned: just lost, gone, puffed upward.

And what were the fifteen Gradual Psalms of which she wrote? Why *Gradual?*

All those old prelates dispensing advice to young nuns expected a lot. Did this mean that in the old days, as even now, nuns knew at least *three* languages and therefore came only from well-to-do families that could afford to educate them?

The sun was Christ. He knew better than that. Zeus too, and Buddha, Krishna, the list was endless, at least if you had an open mind and were not a nun. Then there were her runes, utterances he never fathomed, ask her as he did: "We are seven foals, God's thieves, investing our sins in God through devotion and insistent piety." You, my precious, and *who else?*

On the letter went, he feeling her correspondence was all one, fused into a permanent train and explained glory. All she had to do and watch out for seemed a trial, yet it also exalted her, lifting her somewhat above the tribulations of the species, certainly above the daily things that afflicted *him.* Why, she even talked of gold and how to purify it as if gold were a soul. The worse the sickness, she reported, the better the goldsmith. He felt ambushed by metaphor, whose finer implications had passed him by.

It is all a ball game, John. A mere drop of dew. Sickness is your goldsmith, both a purge and a lenity. Better the quiet workings of the divine goldsmith than a beating with devil's mallets. Who would want to be bashed? Temptation by the flesh may be likened to a foot wound, but temptation of the heart, the soul, the spirit, we liken to a breast wound.

Then she was off, mentally dancing (as he saw it) toward the cubs sired by the lion of pride, its stink worse than that of any rotting dog, followed by a litany of don'ts pertaining to minor demeanor, the only omission being that of licking the lips:

Beware, we learn, of carrying the head too high, looking sideways where temptation is bound to lurk, arching the neck, contemptuously peering, blinking to attract attention to our eyes, pursing the mouth as if in judgment or appeal, making derisive gestures with hand or head (tossing it), or even walking stiffly as if made of mahogany, or lisping. We never lithp. Then there is affectation of the veil, the head-cloth, always culpable if too much, or anything else—girdles and pleats. Away, we learn, with all ointments, dyes, foul flauntings, eyebrow pluckings or shaping them with a wet finger. Some wet their eyebrow finger I will not tell you where, but old nostalgic memory may reveal it. So we are ever on the qui vive, *trying not to get into trouble but mostly in it because, if you try too hard, you always miss something. I myself have to guard against* Pusillanimitas, *when the heart is too poor and cowardly to undertake any high thing or to trust in God's infinite grace. Never do good with a heavy dead heart or you will rue it. That is what we are taught. What on earth would happen if you tried to teach any such thing in one of the saloons you frequent? What would happen in heaven? Grumbling is bad too and false tears. I feel like a young soldier with too much equipment, too long a list of it to remain in charge of myself, ever on guard against so many natural things—a girl's giddy laughter, flighty whorelike eyes, indecent touching coupled with enticing words, not to mention blunt bold outright lewd ones, all toward not filthying myself up with devil snot. There are even those who squat in the cold white ash of yesterday's fire and draw designs in it with their finger. The ashbum. Gold and silver are merely earthly ashes, though, so perhaps that is why they sit and doodle. They know. Do you know? Have you learned by now?*

Doc flinched as if burned. His thoughts about gold and silver were quite different, and here she was trashing the magical aspect, dumping all alchemists in the can. She would even poison them with molten brass to drink, reminding him that stench rose upward: *Under thee shall the moth be strewed and worms shall be thy covering. Isaiah 14:11.* She seemed to develop a stronger wind as she rambled on, all the more capable of rebuking and accusing him from her position of—what was it? Tentative severity? Apprentice bliss? So much steam came out of her; she was a steam-press of the heart, whether citing Isaiah or quoting her mentors direct. It was in the Lord's interest, she told him, to spare the young and the feeble and draw them out of the world sweetly and pleasurably. To begin with, anyway. In later years ("after years," she called them), things were not as gentle or pleasurable, as he already knew. She kept writing about childhood and the various rules children were supposed to heed, so perhaps she saw a relationship between the spontaneous innocence of children and the worked-at one of nuns. An anchoress was not a housewife, after all. On she cantered, sure of her audience's rapt incredulity.

Ille hodie, ego cras.

What on earth was she getting at? He today, I tomorrow, yes; but *what* was the implication? That he too would follow in her steps? Ridiculous.

As soon as anyone uncements herself, John, she is quickly swept away unless her sisters hold her down. It is often seen. You can just as easily end up in a herd of swine, many swine feeding, offending the pigs so much they would cast around for some ready way of suicide rather than inhale the stink of her pit. I am going to leave you with something profound I have discovered in the writings of St. Augustine that goes as follows: "Better is he who tracks down and seeks out thoroughly his own feebleness than he who measures how high the heaven is and how deep the earth." I send a loving kiss from the old Mattie.

Seek out, he thought, your ancient old mother. *Exquirite antiquam matrem.* Or rather unearth your old flames and rekindle them with a lewd word, a salacious tap. Have a nun oil your holster (or hers) with jissom. Ah, he sighed without a sound, never rebuke what you have been; rather, praise it for having endured.

He could see now that she would never use certain words such as (his pronunciation) the newfangled *cigareet* or the renowned *electric doorbell* to be found in Denver's top-drawer homes. Like some suckers in the local saloons, she had allowed herself to be tied to the bar and would never break free, would never hightail it out of Savannah. He had read in some newspaper filler about the composer Orlando di Lasso, who in his day sported a Latin name, told that his parents in faraway Belgium were failing. Off he set at once from Rome, where he had gone to make his name and fortune, only to find them dead on his arrival, so long the journey had been. Now *that* was the kind of world he and Mattie lived in, too far from each other for the processes of life and death, dead in a devastated interim, either one a lost soul at the end of a pointless trip, tethered, if at all, by stumblebum letters that made it only to be obsolete, her thoughts having moved on to some form of flouncing, his to the necessity or otherwise of gunplay in frontier towns. So long as he felt able to sum up their nonlife together, he felt stronger, but it was a reductive, heathen strength. True, he decided, in our different ways, we are both stammering.

In his mind's eye, Doc saw her neat, dark, pretty, compact features, mobile mouth, understated chin; she had always seemed to totter when she walked as if her ankles were giving sideways, but she was certainly svelte, an affable introvert whose pithy remarks he had always enjoyed. She was almost a wit. Kate on the other hand was a woman who started talking to you in the distance, many seconds before she arrived, and she had the face that went with it—somehow all aimed forward and outward, the physiognomical equivalent of the pushiness in her oral style. Most of what she said she delivered while walking, or even striding, and she never hesitated, as if speaking from a script well learned. Perhaps the reason for this was that she peppered her speech with profanities, so giving herself extra opportunities to think. Nothing diffident about her; she had spent much of her time (he could never forget this) holding or accommodating the male organ or trussing it up with ribbons and string. No tottering; her locomotive calf muscles moved her across the surface of the earth with coarse agility, and she had in her word locker those odd words of Hungarian attuned to a special pitch of disdain or rebuke, so that the tone she used offended him even when he had no idea what the words meant. He complained, but she was as much of an intimate whore as he wanted; indeed, too much, which no doubt explained her pell-mell promiscuity—she mixed her men, their secretions, and thus became an anthology of (he shrugged, put off as the phrase completed itself) bad taste.

Yes, he said with urgent fervor, as if her face would never come back to him: pliant mouth, thin lips, she is almost bird-like, with big round eyes, her hair lank even when clipped short; huge brow,

all of this a million years of evolution beyond that Hungarian wal-
rus with the commanding voice and the thickly featured face. The
choice was clear to him: neither, but maintain relationships with
both just in case. In case of what? He had heard some rumor, no
doubt started by a visionary miner with prophetic leanings, that
gold dust was the cure for consumption, that all you had to do was
mix the dust (if you had any by you) into your porridge and lie
down all day. Or could it be silver? What a disease to have in this
region of gold-and-silver strikes! It sounded like poetic con-
traries, making him toy with the idea of a complementary universe in which each disease had, someplace, its cure; there was no
cure without a disease, and vice versa, ideal by-product of a
sentient god with a developed sense of symmetry. He paused,
deploring his own zeal. A sick man would credit anything, any
rumor, just for the verbal pleasure of matching an illness with a
remedy. Were there, then, no wealthy men with consumption?
Had the bacillus choked on pulverized nuggets of local gold?
Resolving never to ask, Doc decided to write to Mattie and tell
her about the journey from Dodge to here, repeating himself no
doubt, but getting the utter majesty across.

The part of Doc's mind that forever disobeyed him, objecting
and slide-slipping even when his mind had been "made up," now
began to haunt him with the idea of gold dust inhaled mainly, but
also swallowed, producing sneezy pepper effects and pains in the
stomach. Of course he would engage in no such dosing, but at
night he did, seeking out in remote shacks on the edge of town the
area's obtuse alchemists, who slid rods down his throat and into his
abdomen, then flexible wires into his lungs seeking samples and
making furtive deposits. At once he began to feel worse, waking in
dream-induced pain, then abruptly recovering, in his befuddled
state vaguely recalling stories about gold's poisonous qualities, silver's too perhaps. Or was it brass that really laid you low? He
had heard of other remedies, from overeating to regular doses of
red wine, to raw eggs swallowed whole to incessant bed rest until
bed sores made you miserable. All that had remained for him on
the level of optional pipe dream until now, when he began to

detect in his waking self a desire to mend after all, to go through rigorous and degrading exercises, whatever, just to be able to go on and survive until fifty or sixty, and, having gone that far, maybe to ninety. Living was its own reward; there need be no huge promise of an ample, blossomed life, merely the benign trudge from day to day was enough. Perhaps Sister Mary Melanie's praying had had some effect, not that he knew any of the details. Prayer, she had once demonstrated to him, before her departure into holy orders, was like a geometrical proof with one stage missing and unfeasible. You had to leap over and beyond it, taking for granted whatever property the gap might have. He hadn't followed this at the time, though her diagram, blurred by the intrusion of prayer into its tidy design, had endured in his memory, a puzzle, an epiphany of sorts, bound sooner or later to explain itself. It never had, and now, whenever he thought about it, he saw how the entire universe shook when it became impossible to say whether a certain angle was a right angle or not. Into these realms, at least until the phantom of gold dust arrived, he had been reluctant to tread, always the former dentist; but once a man advances beyond dentistry and Southern gentility into gunslinging, not to mention whiskey-guzzling and other debauchery, his spiritual potential changes: he becomes more open to alternative solutions even though denied them day-to-day. Doc sensed a reprieve in the offing, if only he would rejoice in nature as he had during the wagon train journey, be less himself than a mote flickering past other phenomena.

Enough of that, he decided. Such thinking was for weaker moments, as when his head swam after a fit of violent, painful coughing. Life, he suspected, was going to go on as before. Kate was going to catch up with him, as she always did, and Mattie-Melanie was going to hover over his future like some devious albatross, fanning and shading him while he tried to work out how many months, or years (if those), he had to come. The open-endedness of his predicament made him tremble. Who out there was going to advise him? Truth told, he himself was the most qualified person to administer the verdict, pitting a dentist's expedient medical know-how against the ravaging bacillus, evoking that old tedious conundrum the educated guess, which had taken many to destruction even while they believed in the value of half-baked ideas. As time went by, more and more areas of his lung tissue would cease to function; it was that simple, and breathing would become more and more difficult. How might a man in that state even imagine returning to the South to make a pious woman abandon her faith and re-enter the world to hold his hand during the Calvary in store? It was all too late, and he was left with the grand but almost untenable notion that all he could do was live intensely what was left, either through killing or taking mortal risks, occupying his mind all the time with trivial details, from the dandruff on his comb to the scurf that fell from his eyelashes.

Mattie-Melanie, an empathetic imaginer, knew much of this, having always been able to work him out; she had amazed him with her readings of his condition and this ability had always drawn him to her. She smiled on him. She made him glow. It must have been, he long ago decided, the divine in her that gave her such acuity, and there she was wasted in a nunnery, addressing her subtlety to God, who had no need of it. One of their old teenage games together, of the more intellectual sort, had been to invent nicknames for the deity, from Sir, Frank and Tall Star (hers) to Boss, Monsieur and Lee (his). The game had petered out, not only because difficult, but because she had sensed in it some sacrilege—God's name was not supposed to be said, or messed about with. She lowered the boom on the game but went on privately adding to it, trying to come up with something better than old routine appellations such as Lord, God, Almighty and the rest. Very difficult, she told herself, because we have no idea what we're describing or referring to. It was not a game but an exploit in densest knowing, and she knew how mystics, at a loss for the right idiom, turned to erotics for metaphor. Should she do the same, she who had virtually no experience of anything such save at second hand? She asked Doc, who counseled her not to indulge in sexual experiments for the sake of an image. Make up a nonsense word, he said. Call him Gloops.

"Meaning?" She was impressed, but dumbfounded.

He had no idea, it had just come to him, he said, in a moment of transient stupidity that he hoped was now over. God's name was no doubt mathematical, he added, a formula that never ended.

Coming up with names for God, he felt crude, almost like the barber-surgeons who preceded the *dentators* of the fourteenth century in France: the first dentists, really, and he wondered why the French were ahead of everybody else in this. A more advanced person than himself would have no trouble in concocting names for someone otherwise called Yahweh or Jehovah, but all he could think of were Indian names—Shawnee, Lakota, Apache, Pima, Shoshonee, Arapaho, almost tolerable names for an entity of unthinkable massiveness and scope. His thoughts twisted away to dentistry again, wishing for a later century's tools. It was all very well to drill teeth with something you worked by treadle like a sewing machine, and he had heard of electrical devices just invented, but where there was no electricity there was no high-speed drill. A lumbering artisan, he wished he had been schooled in some other discipline than dentistry: classical literature, say, or philosophy, or even physics and biology, something he could get his teeth into and feel proud about. Then he would not be thinking God might be otherwise named "He Who Yawns" or "When Dogs Could Speak." She, on the other hand, being a poet, could devise long serenades to the deity, in whom after all, she had a vested interest. His own view was that, after journeying through the center of the nation, he would rather arrive at a name for God after reviewing the superlative landscapes he had passed through: the deity as *dentator,* perhaps whereas she was content to leave God's works out of it and focus on his essence. Why not? None was more qualified than she, and he wished with all his heart that they had more in common religiously, so that their letters could be more glancing, more allusive, less frontal. If there had to be long, awkward lacunae created by the creaky postal system, then one way of cheating them would be the letter that took oceans for granted and implied a vast amount, almost a tangential code. It was not a matter of concealing things (he hoped), but of controlled ricochet, letters not so much of explanation as of casual disclosure, as if he were to open up a bird's egg, something duck-egg blue without being a duck's, and reveal the mother-of-pearl interior without a word, or as if she, intent as ever on liturgical routines, were to proffer him a glimpse of her open prayer book without indicating any specific passage. He knew little of nunneries or churches, but he knew that Protestants such as his own people set more store by the printed word than Catholics did, hence his inclination to see her page.

I wish we could talk instead of write, he wrote to her, *much as an elephant would like to tap-dance.* He never got an answer to that; she knew it was hopeless and that by the scrawled word they would live or perish. Eventually she would inform him of the true telepathy that dispensed with correspondence altogether, but she knew the argot of angels was more readily available, and she wondered at herself, exchanging letters with someone who, judged by his own admissions, was going to mortal seed in the West, wedded to his six-gun and and a certain Mister Earp. Death, she decided, was their tender bond: that and only that, but billions joined together under death's banner, so was it the prematurity of death that drew them to each other, holy vows construable as a form of death, at least to the uninitiated? Was a nunnery yet another calaboose? Were vows akin to six-gun law? Was he really a deputy or had he just invented the role to sound important? She would make up her own mind about such things without any help from him, preferring him as a creature of inordinate myth, beloved from childhood, altering himself at will like Proteus, becoming all things to all men, and, because his time on earth was foreshortened, living several lives at once, all of them suicidal. It was a poor conclusion to fuel letters to a distant frontier town; she might have been writing to a ghost, a werewolf, a vampire, the modification of his elegant being having gone so far already. If there was no pulling him back from the thorny brink, what could she do but fortify him in his impostures, the lies he told himself and lived by, the rumors he relayed to her so as to achieve fame among the nuns of Georgia? She was no go-between but a terminal source, beyond whom his reputation would not move.

Santa Fe stupefied both Doc and the Earps, a humble town, the
first they had seen since Dodge, full of apparently happy tanned
and wrinkled peasants, many of them puffing on brown-paper
cigarettes. What was their secret, Doc wondered. Would they
tell? "Don't you ask me," Allie Earp told him, "nobody dies. They
all just dry up and blow away. The sun keeps them happy while
they chew on poverty." Perhaps, Doc thought, this was the place
for him to roost in, like them wearing a gaudy blanket and a bell-
trimmed wide sombrero, owner of nothing but a wooden plow
and an undersized ox. He would live in one of these flat-topped
adobe huts in the shadow of the cathedral and yet, in a way,
marooned in the enormous plaza. It might not be so bad, having
Kate walk past him with a big water jug balanced on her head
(that would slow her down, to be sure). No cowboys, no brothels,
no dance halls, only the domesticated wilderness held captive by a
shrunken-looking pueblo like something brought to life out of a
child's picture album: the image of the perfect, pious place. He
hastened to tell Mattie all about it, lest it fade with the sun, but
he knew better, reassured now that he was not obliged to spend
the rest of his days in raucous cow towns. Yet how long could he
go without gambling, swilling whiskey, even rowing with Kate or
a Kate? Was he good enough, modest enough and humbled
enough for life in such a benign bubble? No Earps, no riot?
Somewhere, he told himself, he would have to train for life in
Santa Fe, but he saw how his options had opened up again.

This was in spite of what Wyatt had told him before they even
arrived, puffing and cursing until they saw the town. It was based
on crystal, Wyatt said, not like some towns founded on granite or
limestone, but on millions and millions of broken chandeliers, so
to speak, or vast icebergs crystalline as salt. Why, the inhabitants

walked around poor as roaches, but each with a piece of crystal in his pocket, just to ward off bad spirits or prevent some avalanche from the sky landing on them and dumping them all into the bowels of the crystal. Doc pictured it: caves upon caves of shimmering mineral, not that he could see through it, but it reflected some, and the entire understructure was a maze of stalactites and stalagmites newly polished and, in a way, similar to the lattices he sometimes envisioned as the downtown of heaven, where he and Mattie would be reunited once they had discharged their earthly duties. Nowhere else was founded on water, he knew, though he'd heard of places set on sand, clay and mud. Anyway, he decided, a holy place had best be situated on something winsome; there were standards and they had to be met—even the notepaper he wrote on, smooth to the touch as tile, had to have an outdoor toughness to it, a resilient quality that reminded him of how, once, they would not have been able to advance for herds of buffalo. So, then, the divine rested on unmelting heavenly icicles.

"Where you hidded next, Wyatt?" It was still one of the things he enjoyed saying to him, in even that phony redneck accent (accinct, he'd have said), half in jest, half rebuke. Wyatt enjoyed the business of being on the road; he was a gadabout, and he relished the fripperies that went with it. "*Now,* I mean," Doc added with the insouciant air of a scholar interrogating a well-trained macaw.

"A fur piece," Wyatt told him, seeming to intend something sexual, but it was a taciturn man's version of an outburst. "Not here," he said, "but somewhere in Arizona."

"Like Prescott."

"Yep. You knew all the time."

Doc told him he was just making sure, half of a mind to go with him, half to stay in Santa Fe—the sunbaked altar of affable poverty—and come together within himself, no longer drinking and shooting, but becoming a bit the retired dentist, the professional man *hors de combat.* Even with Wyatt giving him that granite gaze from a yard away as they returned the stares of black-eyed Indian women, Doc was able to think of other matters, most of all how life would be different if, for instance, some visiting savant were to examine him and pronounce him healed. How many spiked horrors would then back away from his tortured life. Each evening he would settle into a book over a cup of coffee and a pipe, then sleep the sleep of the uninjured innocent. Whole arrays of blessed serenity passed through his mind in that instant as he looked through the glass of history and found his own role no longer beleaguered, but mellow, complacent, sedate. He would not go back to dentistry but perhaps essay a career in writing or public speaking, politics even, making capital out of the sentimental idea that he too, like the Cherokee nation, had trodden the Trail of Tears from Georgia to the Midwest. He had been as badly done by as they. Something would come of so wounding an analogy; he could see it now, dancing in the gray button of Wyatt's eye.

"Maybe stay," Doc said with hesitant finality.

"You *kin* stay," Wyatt told him, "but Ah'm goin on. I got family, my folks is on my back." Sometimes Wyatt, almost a master of English, most of all when he wrote things down, laid it on thick, especially when dealing with someone as educated as Doc, pretending to be a rube, a duffer, all spittle an' shucks, git and goin. This primitive front endeared him to many, even those whom he dispatched in the next few seconds; at least they had been killed by a man of low pretensions, one of the common folks. Doc knew this and never let it vex him; Wyatt and he had room in their relationship for horseplay, high jinks, and oblique repartee. Sometimes Doc himself played the redneck and they had a loutish gossip almost incomprehensible to bystanders, who thought they were talking smartass lingo from the empyrean where gunslingers met with dentists and peace officers, judges and attorneys all in the interests of obfuscating the law.

"If I lingered," Doc proposed, "I might go to the dogs real fast."

"They wouldn't lit you," Wyatt said. "They ain't got the means, no liquor, no whores, no yellerbellies to shoot to smithereens. You'd die of boredom here, Doc, even if your soul curtseyed on the outskirts of heaven. Don't you lit that purified dream of yours git you balloxed out of a lifetime's debauchery. You come with us. They ain't no crime in this town worth shakin a stick at."

"They would," Doc parodied, "iffen I was around here for long. Like flies to a rotting corpse, they'd find a way to me, the badmen would."

"Esshole bullshit," Wyatt said. "No way."

"You mean I got no drawing power?"

"I mean you got it but it won't work here. They's too heavenly, take it from me. They hasn't come through those goddamned mountains, not like we have."

Doc agreed, suddenly feeling orphaned by the image of Wyatt's wagon train drawing away without him, heading west and southwest for silver, gold and mayhem. Doc knew he would have to go along, having no other constituency to dignify his life by. He was an Earpian through and through and would remain so until his imminent end. Someone, perhaps Earp himself (it was his kind of history), had told him about the mountain men of old who, if they failed to arrive at an agreed-upon rendezvous, were considered dead, never mind that their trek to the meeting point was through blizzards, ice fields and haunts of wolves. He had a similar feeling about himself, sensing that if he failed to meet up with Wyatt in Prescott, Tombstone or wherever, he should be considered dead and gone. It was no doubt a mawkish idea predicated on some obsolete idea of heroism, but Doc believed in such things, actually using in his daily talk such expressions as A man's word is his bond. He tried to keep his promises, aware perhaps that there were so many ways in which he had betrayed himself. The cactus of self-pity had scarred him until he brought to his every act the same unsparing scrutiny, almost always failing himself for a less than flawless performance. Honor was a word he used little, but a concept he revered, and this included of course returning fire with a revolver, or rather initiating fire while the other gunman was slapping leather or making up his mind. Still staring at Wyatt's bronzed, seamed face, Doc began to assemble in his mind's eye, on something like a hymnal board, the killings he had done, whether with good reason or not, separating them from the context of human cordiality and as it were exposing them to the light to see if they leaked:

> A card game in Dallas. A supreme gunman made less supreme. A quarrel had led to shooting. Obliged to leave town, in which the deceased had many friends. Went to Jacksborough, to no avail.
> There, not far from the Fort Richardson military reservation, shot a soldier dead after an untidy one-sided quarrel with himself in the minority.
> Infernal camps: Several mal hombres. On run again.
> Learned the trade of shooting to kill in the camps. Quarrel after quarrel, leading me to suppose I have a quarrelsome nature. Became a master shootist, ever-ready to draw. What a life. On to Fort Griffin, Texas.

This staccato, muddled version of his life until 1877 delighted him not. It left out all the motivation and the subtleties of being fierce. If you are ever going to know yourself, he reasoned, you have to be understanding, not fixed on the externals of things—what happened—but in what way and what was the mental accompaniment of it all. He wanted not to justify himself but to think the shootings and knifings were not the work of an automaton; rather, of a man who hesitated often, wondered about the figure he cut in semi-civilized society (thin trim frail ferocity) and wondered if his practicing with a Colt hour after hour showed. Haggard always, with wavy hair, he looked a walking paradox, almost a fop, but one with red-hot teeth.

Long before he became a gunman, Doc had heard about the practice of cutting notches on the butt of your six-gun, thinking it flagrant fetishism, waste of a file. Now he had begun to think differently, half-inclined to keep score, but just as inclined to put it all behind him even as it happened. Was he going to soothe himself to sleep by counting notches? When he felt low, which was often enough, was he going to cheer himself up by fitting his fingertip (he had small, petal-soft hands, which told you he never did much dentistry) into the filed notches? He never bothered, telling himself he needed only to keep in mind the stupefied, anonymous faces of the men he'd killed, the way they twigged it at the very last: they were going to lose, to die, and their fate was in the hands of the clock. The look of abject surrender, invaded by the faintest smile, was one he had become familiar with; some mustered it better than others, but it was always nonoral, nonverbal, more of a gape than anything, a last fruitless attempt to take in enough air to get through the next thirty seconds, which of course only provided for a decent death rattle. Doc was far from callous, but he was no sentimentalist either; when he put his mind to it, his mind closed, and he kept it closed until the man had keeled over and gone down for the last time. Then he relented, enough to walk away, not even checking to see if the man were dead or not. He never troubled himself with points of protocol, seeing the victorious shot as a labor of physical prowess. Once done, and its effects made plain, the deed was sufficient; he said no words, made no gesture, smiled no scowl, but holstered his weapon and began the walk that said I wish I didn't have to do this, but I'm willing to do it again.

Such was the deportment of the killer, drilling them one after another (as he liked to think, with an incongruous curl of his expressive lip). Wyatt was impassive in a different way, more bureaucratic and boorish; something of the gambler leaked into Doc's gunplay, something of the winner's euphoria—discernible to him but to no one else: tender current of triumphant menace running through him, revivifying and consoling. If he had to live among killers, then he had to learn to kill, and he had. When in Rome . . . Fortunately for him, nobody else had taken shooting half as seriously as he, except, according to Wyatt Earp, Buckskin Frank Leslie, who however lacked Doc's "fatalistic courage," as Wyatt put it. When Doc went into battle, he was dead already, had surrendered his doomed life; from that point on, it was all gain. According to Earp, the worst gunman ever was the melodrama actor Charles Chapin, who, incensed with Eddie Foy for putting the moves on Charlie's girl, went so far as to buy a gun and go after him. Twenty feet away, one dark and placid night, he fired several times at Eddie's outline, then ran away without checking the damage, to become a celebrated newspaper editor in New York and Chicago. "He was the worst gun thrower of record," Earp said, and Doc the best. But Earp's word was far from the only criterion. In Dodge and other cow towns, the population shifted all the time, and cowhands were gone for long months, but out there, on the trail and back at the ranches, word got around as to whom to avoid in the Dodges, and the name was always Doc, who killed when Wyatt curbed. Like all surreal reputations, Doc's was partly in response to something relevant but not blatant: his illness, which added steel and satanic efficiency to his renown; he was one of the walking dead, and anyone who took him on was dealing not only with a six-gun but with the force that ran the universe. Rumor had it that, much as Wyatt Earp was unscathed and had never been so much as grazed by a bullet, Doc was unkillable and would remain so until the Almighty took him off. It was therefore hopeless to go up against him. Once Doc divined that this was being said of him, he almost believed it; he might deny that he believed in such stuff, but a superstitious piece of him took heart from it, gradually subscribing to Doc myth.

So do certain persons of extraordinary bent make quiet love to their reputations, lolling in froth of their own making, fearing the worst yet knowing the best. When a man who is not perfect believes nonetheless he is unbeatable, he has made the sinister transit from paragon to genius, and this was what Doc detected himself doing inch by inch as his life dribbled away from him. He almost credited the wild supposition that he had been put on earth to demonstrate the art of the six-gun, and perhaps he actually went looking for trouble in order to find shootists. Perhaps, carding, he looked for cheaters harder than he needed to, or, when out with Wyatt on the town as sub-pro-vice unofficial deputy sheriff, he scanned the shadows too particularly, responded a little too sharply to grimace and grin, took too much notice of itchy hands down by holsters, men who walked funny because they had weapons secreted on them in awkward places. Doc was the pre-

eminent vigilante in Dodge, but he was also the best-known badman, outlaw, pleasure killer. Such a reputation was hardly fair to
him, but he had no control over bunkhouse bunkum or what
cowhands in their cups concocted so as to seem important or
scare themselves to death with. All his days, in Dodge or similar
towns, Doc was always performing in front of a grandiose silhou-
ette he could not see, being judged and evaluated, an Achilles in
the open being vetted for something superhuman.

Yes, he thought, or I am like those cows that run themselves to
death across open prairie only to end up poisoned with alkali
water. They didn't know, they never will. In that sense I am truly
helpless. I may be able to clean somebody's clock with a six-gun,
but I have a poor sense of navigation. One day I must make a map
of my comings and goings across these states—the impetuous
mindless movements of a random animal. If you are driven, must
you therefore have a drover? My bacillus drives me and will until,
thanks to inhalation, I have gold-plated lungs and merely by
breathing hard upon things as if intending to polish I gild them in
a flash. That will be the day. Odd, how I have always been drawn
to metals, from the cold bolt of the dental tool to the butt of the
six-gun. Perhaps I would achieve an even greater reputation than
Wyatt's if I sported a gold-plated Colt that caught the sun as I
drew it, blinding those whom I would never need to kill. Those,
they would say, are Doc's blind ones, groping their way, lucky not
to have been shot. That would begin for me an entire new phase I
will never see. I hate the foreshortening of all my hopes, even my
yearning for answered letters. I live like someone suffocated by
the future tense.

He had always meant to mention it to Mattie, but he never had:
the frontier truncation of current usage, certainly the way things
got said in the South. Take some everyday sample of the conditional—If I pull the trigger, the gun fires—and see what they
make of it here: I pull the trigger, the gun fires. I mourn the death
of *if*. Its domain becomes that of two juxtaposed statements, no
doubt pithier and more succinct than the conditional form, but at
the same time staccato and, in an odd way, more urban. You do

not expect this kind of change in speech to come about in the Wild West, home of the voluble Texan and the lyrical Kansan. Perhaps the change combined the tough no-nonsense of Missouri with the abrupt laconics of a Wyatt Earp. What bothered him most was the way a cause-and-effect formula had given way to mere next-doorness, the whole notion of effect having gone out the window. It made the world less of a sensible place in which one damn thing followed another and that was all. You were no longer encouraged to inquire into what linked things together. Things were flying apart, made social only by an almost lost convention called the sentence. Doc resolved never to drop an *if*; if he did, he told himself with grim fervor, his head would begin to shrink and his most plausible excuses would go for naught. He never wanted to be somebody who somebody else had been; he was not Wyatt Earp's deputy, alias, taskmaster, dragoon, double, slave, heir or grammar teacher. Doc had been taught enough grammar to make his own explanations of his own conduct yield savage sense, no matter when he died, and that was that.

·13·

Deciding against gambling in Santa Fe that would have been a gambol in the unceasing sun, Wyatt and Doc climbed up to the driver's seat of the buckboard and aimed for the west edge of the Mogollon Rim, through resplendent uplands, then descended into Prescott, where Virgil Earp lived, previously a peace officer there but now consecrated to mining, a man hectically in pursuit of a fortune, like Wyatt.

"No you ain't, Doc," Wyatt said, moving his jaw in symbolic dissent. "You comin with us all."

"No I'm not," Doc told him. "I was mighty tempted by Santa Fe, but this Prescott tempts me even more. A man can mine here and gamble to his heart's content." It also happened to be the Arizona territorial capital and Doc gleaned from this fact a sense of election; for once, since Atlanta, he was in a central, salient place, and he coveted the feeling of conferred importance, soon to be increased by his taking lodgings on North Montezuma Street with the acting governor, John J. Gosper, a restrained, bearded, consoled man. What am I doing, Doc thought, rooming with a politician who has not heard of me? Neither had the other roomer, Richard Elliott, an old friend of Virgil. So, he told himself, I am still in the family. I can't get over this weird sense of being among the ancients; *our* Virgil evokes that other one, the mellow poet obsessed with piety. The roominghouse itself was functional to the point of idiocy: flat front with five windows, a stoop to stand on. Nothing more. Pale gray hutch.

For a day or two, Doc toyed with the idea of a grafted respectability that would gobble up an educated man such as himself and install him in some doughty government office, so as not to waste him, and before his murderous reputation came flying in behind him like a plague. But Gosper was only the secretary of state, in office while the governor, Fremont, was away on one of his long absences; Gosper had no power to appoint anyone to anything, but merely to conserve the status quo, keep things quiet until Fremont, if ever, returned. Even the local census scooped Doc up, making him respectable without his doing anything, although less so when Kate arrived, having pursued him from Dodge in another wagon train and having ignored the melodramatic, gorgeous landscape of the long interval. Prescott was a bald, rudimentary town almost without texture, but Doc took to it, to its Whiskey Row especially, where he made a killing that convinced him to stay on and, again and again, buck the tiger. He eventually helped himself to forty thousand dollars, more than he would ever have earned in years of dentistry. Trouble was, with Kate come after him, he had no secrets, and, besides, a man winning so big got talked about until he had to leave, unless he wanted to invest and make a career of living in Prescott, at the thought of which Doc shuddered. Had he known more of Governor Fremont, he might have stayed, being just the kind of man the governor liked for his gang of pragmatic, bent politicos and murderous outlaws.

With a rueful grin, Doc caught himself speaking Wyatt-speak, not Earp's usual everyday brand of taciturnity but what he said to badmen when confronting them at their worst: "Don't you run your mouth kind of reckless, hombre?" and "Now you just go ahead and skin that smoke wagon of yourn and see how fast I make your head into a canoe." Indeed, there must exist, Doc thought, a mode of address so punitive, so acid, that it worked the trick every time, making even the most churlish gunman step down, surrender his weapon, and go to jail like a scalded rabbit. That was it: rhetoric that scalded. Doc had tried it, but he was better with a gun, and he thus avoided exhaustion by speech. Of course he stole Wyatt's best lines, although lacking his war face and his ability to pierce with the eyes. What he could do and did was use Latin, a sophisticated form of humiliation; he never got over the severe discomfiture of the first outlaw to whom he said, improvising as he had been taught to do at Valdosta High: "*Cur bellicosus, homo? Pax est pax,"* which may have sounded offensive and terminal to the desperado and certainly clamped his gob shut for the evening. Wyatt speaking Latin would have been deadlier than ever, Doc thought, and resolved to instruct him in it; the Kansas Law Dog could at least have a smattering of dog Latin. Or they could hold spelling bees right there in the open, sentencing the loser to extra calaboose for even the slightest error: barbicue for barbecue, which brought him something else from those Valdosta days: good old Shakespeare had never known how to spell because in those times there was no agreed-on spelling for many words, for even his own name. Doc preferred there to be a consensus, otherwise you couldn't use your knowledge as a cudgel against the destroyers of law and order.

The ultimate finesse he dreamed of, he who excelled at shooting a man and returning the gun to its holster before he even began that final crumple or began to bleed, was the trick of reaching forward and drawing an opponent's weapon before *he* did, actually beating him to the draw across the intervening space, and then shooting him with it. Doc had never done this sublime feat, but he was building up to it, and one day, almost like the fabled Texan in front of the whorehouse mirror, would actually beat himself to the draw, faster than his own decrepit reflection. Some gunslingers excelled at spinning the weapon by its trigger guard, which Doc regarded as mere byplay, not worth watching or applauding. With such a maneuver, you could sometimes change the mood of a badman coming to the boil, hell-bent on a shootout, turning ire to mirth with a vacant ploy. He had never seen Wyatt do it, and he had done it himself maybe three or four times, wondering in the act why he had no children to amuse, why he seemed destined for the lonely march from lodging house to lodging house, rooming with the deputy governor of Arizona or Big Nose Kate, or indeed with both Kate and the deputy governor. Never had he had such luck at gambling as in Prescott; he could do no wrong, even when for variety he tried to play badly. Other men dug for gold, panned or robbed, but all he did was sit and think, and Kate was already talking of giving up the oldest profession, which, he told her, would merely make of her an amateur whore. She could no more give up behaving whorishly than she could eschew breathing. Or so he said, lumping her future into one sleazy ball and dropping it into the spit can of rotten prophecy. Face ever speckled with sweat, headache lolling just out of sight, he felt under enormous strain, unable to live casually like other men, doomed to own only a duffel bag and have his face shaved and ministered to by barbers. Perhaps, like some of the gunmen he fought with, he wanted revenge for being born, for not having been asked about it; had he known he was going to be a lunger, he might have elected to go back into the womb like a returned parcel from the estate of someone dead. A million things might distract him, but not for long; the preying bacillus was always there, on the *qui vive*, wearing him down day after day, turning good healthy lung tissue to the condition of rotten knicker elastic. I see a red sash, someone said, possibly Wyatt, I see a man wearing it, the corollary to which must run: I see a young man perspiring, hear his frothy cough, and I see the bearer of a tubercular condition putting off the mountains month after month, never eating wholesome food, hoping in vain for the golden cure. I see a fool.

He was harsh on himself, he thought, but never harsh enough, always deflected by money, whiskey, and women, a trite enough trio hardly worthy of a man's life. Now he saw the word for him, filched from some ancient, spine-smashed Latin grammar. In Rome, because they no doubt needed it, they had a verb for the eyes' watering (maybe the winds from Terracina were strong) and another for being sick: *aegrotare*, an easy first-conjugation verb. In some ancient universities, when you were too sick to take the final exams, you got the degree anyway, and they called it an *aegrotat*, word that carried a cachet of the *mutilé de guerre*, someone who had been to the wars and come home broken, or just someone whose nerves were not up to the strain of final anything. All day he was an *aegrotat*, then, and should be wearing the regalia of that rank or condition, holding his breath on the first syllable—*ae-ae-ae-g*, until death could hold itself no longer and it all came out in a spiral of sweet atoms. It was not revenge he wanted (upon whom?), but a reckoning, an evaluation of all that went into his coming out stunted or deprived of a chance to grow full straight. Was there favoritism in heaven, or wherever he had come from? How blame his exquisite mother? Even his renegade father with his passion for moist young thighs.

Doc was beginning to see the light, at least as far as gunfighting went. Let the wicked kill the wicked wasn't so bad a maxim, he thought; but was he wicked when he began? No, he was impulsive, determined, and well-trained. It had not been as difficult as he had imagined, provided he walk away, not be detained, not surrender to the morbid fascinations of corpse-viewing. Besides, he had knifed some of them only, and some of them—both the shot and the knifed—had survived. It wasn't death through and through, but he soon found he was being blamed for various anonymous killings up and down the universe. Give a dog a bad name, he recited, and it will bite without command. Perhaps life in Prescott was going to be different, though he doubted it; if you did enough gambling, the criminal side of things caught up with you soon enough, like the smell of fish. The one led to the other. Was it forty thousand or four? In his hands, money came and went with demoralizing speed, almost a pliable malleable substance ephemerally imprinted. What counted was the apparent surrender to chance, one whose purchase upon you you had reduced through sheer skill. Was there, he wondered, a religious analogy? Did Mattie, for instance, in her dealings with the deity, make her own opportunity? Were there more successful and less successful ways of dealing with godhead? For example, was the deity predisposed to favor articulate prayer over fumbling prayer? Or prayers of homage over prayers of asking? It was a region little known to him, though Mattie had urged him, more in the spirit of one who needed to keep alive a worthwhile attitude than of one who expected to prevail. Some mystics called it the unknown region, almost patting themselves on the back because, although no one else entered it, *they* did, like alchemists invading chaos.

As Doc saw things, without patting himself on the back, he

had turned gunplay into something less than brutal, less despicable than usual, promoting it in his soul's eye into almost an art-form, its cost high in human wastage of course, but somehow estimable—for dispatch, speed, accuracy, lack of fuss and frippery, usefulness to the community, impact on watchers and, last, its curative influence on the shooter himself. It all ended if he lost, but that demise was part of the glorious pattern: put your life on the line (he smirked, remembering how good he was) and try to do your best, never wasting bullets on a good guy merely having a tantrum. The ones he killed were the dyed-in-the-wool demons, bound to lose out to the Earps or Bat Masterson and so, if killed early, spared the agony of long waiting for the inevitable final shot. It almost made sense, to him as much sense as using a shotgun technique to find God, aiming this way and that in the hope of striking gold. How pathetic humans were, he thought, always hunting something in the firmament, always assuming a gunfighter was a brainless hired hand with only one trick in his repertoire. Sometimes pleased with himself, which also meant continuing to be alive, Doc wondered if any other life would have suited him half as well. True, there were gamblers who didn't get into gunfights or quarrels, just one or two; mostly, though, they drank too much while playing, especially during daylong, nightlong sessions when fatigue became a monster in its own right, lurking in the foul corners of temperament, ready to make trouble. He himself knew when he was too weary to continue, which was when he took an extra-firm hold on himself, inventing the discipline of the appointed peacemaker, even putting his guns in a secure cache when he knew the impulse to use them was warming up. Yes, he decided, he didn't make too bad a job of that self-control thing; indeed, when he drew and fired he did so only because there was nothing else to do. He was a fatalist in this, having had the bacillus school him in what could not be changed, except by the bullet, except by the final coughing spasm in which lungs and heart finally quit. He saw himself inhaling forty thousand dollars' worth of gold dust, just to cheat the future, spitting it out and eating it, throwing it up and devouring even that. Somewhere in his body, the gold dust would take, starting the cure, but surely in his lungs most of all. They didn't call people with heart trouble "hearters" or those with teeth trouble "teethers," so what was the problem with consumption? The coughing spit? It must be so. People liked handy handles on others, hence the terms gunslinger and outlaw, when they were in fact dealing with complex individuals such as himself. Wyatt was complex because there were many parts of him quite unrecognized, such as the investor and profiteer, the womanizer and the egoist, whom nobody thought to mention because one facet dominated his local and regional reputation: one flaw, blown up, occupied all places in his personality, much as cold-bloodedness and poise did for Doc.

People had little patience with the ogive windows of identity, at least in others, with the hidden cupboards, the trellises that coiled in upon themselves, the cunning fretwork that admitted dark light only and shed it, far in the interior, on a few discarded envelopes brown with neglect. Astonishing, Doc thought, how little you knew of those you killed; it was all a matter of outlines and bad temper; you killed so-and-so as a pipe rack, so-and-so as a letter holder, so-and-so as a cigar box, heedless of their bodies' future fate, buried, burned, left for wolves and birds of prey. What he disliked about life was its peremptoriness, the lack of attention required from you in order to get through, happy to have a name to call a dog up with, heedless of personal minutiae so exquisite they made the angels weep. So much of people, he thought, he who put a goodly number underground each month, stayed underground from the first, ingeniously evolved but mostly wasted because cruder emblems blotted them out. Were those the lowest common denominators? He wasn't sure they weren't the highest common factors either. So shit on all arithmetic. It was almost as bad as counting up the men you'd slain; he made no such attempt, being no adept with numbers except in some abstruse modes peculiar to gambling. Well-schooled swell that he was, or had been, he preferred the attitudes of the ancients who had surrounded his schooldays, venerable stoics who contented themselves with an occasional *Yair*, the only comment worth making on just about any situation, the good or the bad, and could rarely be provoked into anything beyond that one word, not even *I guess* or *Shucks*. Such mastery of one-word sophistication had never been his, though he could see the beginnings of it in Wyatt. To say too much implied you knew too much and were willing to waste, on redundant frills of response, energy that you needed for the building of a mature, rounded, silent attitude. So it was to the tongue-biters of Valdosta and Atlanta that he homed in his imagination, to rustic porch-squatters and street-corner dawdlers, at heart an unresponsive undemonstrative man with emotions buttoned up to the neck.

This was the small-town curmudgeon, legendary and coarse, who said the same to all comers ("Get fucked") and chawed on in a seethe of dung-brown baccy juice. Such, wryly speaking, had been Doc's dentist silence, in the main because talking made him cough and curtly choke, so he probed and pulled as if afflicted with a vow, and left the good impression, mostly with the ladies, of a ladies' man who needed some leading or teasing out.

"Think, Wyatt," said this ladies' man, "of a brown frunt. You ever seen a brown frunt?"

Smooth in repartee (which is what he assumed Doc's question was), Wyatt said, "I'm a pink man myself, they oils up faster."

It might have been an exchange at the chuckwagon between two cowboys comparing six-shooters, youths who only once endured the three-month trail, herding surplus cattle from Texas to Dodge, say, trying to live down at long last the notion of a cowboy as somebody bowlegged who stank of horses. Who knew? One of them might soon be struck by lightning on the trail or die of the wind sickness that afflicted all who lived on the plains. Both Doc and Wyatt liked women, but they rarely discussed or compared them, part of the trouble being that, when Doc was at his drunken most voluble, Wyatt was most closemouthed, and, since Wyatt was hardly ever the worse for liquor, Doc never felt free to talk in front of him. Who felt at ease with a man who never laid an egg? Times were when Doc would have relished complaining to Wyatt about Kate, whose bumptious profligacy wore him out, but that was not the way of his relationship with this taut and silent widower who, sometimes, impressed Doc as a man fresh-born, never having had a childhood, never having suffered the pains of growing up. Like a crag, Wyatt arrived full-formed, stretching his mother prodigiously, yet without the gift of ready speech. Indeed, his being this way made Doc less open of manner, turning him into a reticent and cautious cohort; and perhaps this explained Doc's odd preamble to a gunfight, when he appeared to shrink from the act, looked away, hovered, seemed to fold minutely sideways, licked his lip, rocked some on his heels, and then recovered in a savage burst of action, shooting and (sometimes) fanning the hammer into a blur while he put one shot after another into much the same hole in the victim, after having seemed such a diffident milquetoast. Those who discerned this oddity in Doc's behavior never got a chance to pass on their knowledge. Get him while he's dithering, or pretending to be so, was the message nobody ever passed on. Would it have been the equivalent of heckling a speaker while he was clearing his throat? There were no exact equivalents in the Old West: everything seemed unique, as if some insane magician had wanded it so, allowing nothing to bear on anything else, which meant that a day there became a bumpy ride from shock to shock as disparate phenomena took their toll of those who hoped to prosper by testing one thing against another. What happened happened so fast, and so finally, there was no advice around except for negatives. Don't be there was the best advice. If you are, don't be visible was the next. Everyone, even respectable long-term residents of Dodge and Abilene, was fair game, all targets for gunslingers, cardsharps, whores, con men, and predatory journalists eager to send word eastward of the harsh exotica to be found elsewhere.

Doc had a keen sense of the figure he cut on entering a saloon or hotel, especially in winter, which added to his rigid demeanor something palsied: frozen jaw, streaming eyes, lips bloodless, cheeks on the way to concavity. He knew all this without ever having looked, having worked it out backward from the expressions of those who saw him. To have so fine a sense of one's deportment and demeanor is a rare thing; it can lead to hyperesthesia of manner, but it need not, requiring only the balance to be maintained between crippling self-awareness and oblivious unconcern. The dentist, looming at the interior door of his establishment, was always a snowman of sorts: august in white, crisp with disinfectant, tangy with mouth-peppermint, effusive but at the same time clinically cautious. He knew all that, and his technique of self-presentation had something in it of professional grandeur. Behold me where I stand, the master doctor of teeth, as willing to clean you out both dentally and financially as leave you alone to your gum-rot and halitosis. That peculiar selflessness of the savant had never left him, and, even when he showed up to gamble and they all momentarily lifted their heads in exasperated distraction, he knew that briefly they were his. He'd pause, exhale, muffle his cough, straighten his shoulders, abolish the weather left outside behind him (even if brought in with him as cold or fug), and stride slow-motion to the bar like some clockwork doll with stiff joints and iced frown. So he would arrive, order a drink, toss it back, order another and the bottle, then turn through 180 degrees to face the room, eyeing nobody but somehow assimilating all their furtiveness into one sweep executed without glass or aim, knowing he had superior eyes, capable of staring them down or looking right through them like somebody with the scotoma of a migraine attack. "Dude," someone would call him, especially when he looked extra-fancy, which in the West meant Victorian, but he would never take offense, knowing he had the edge over all of them, even if some of them, previous gambling victims, wanted to kill him then and there. They would not dare draw on him while his back was turned, having seen him perform wonders of blind aiming, and they certainly did not mess with him when he confronted them in this bland but haughty fashion, very much the man of men, not even with (like Wyatt) one hand dangling low ready for trouble. Doc went for his guns only from customary height, disdaining the extra leverage to be gained by having that hand lower than the other so as to draw the gun faster than ever—but not too far, not that fast, but just, as he thought of it, to get a good start if you needed one.

He didn't, but he had hindrances of a special kind.

First there was his cough, sometimes minor and delicate, sometimes bubbly and volcanic, which was when he found it hard to unbuckle his belt, the cough shaking his thorax and his hands enough to hold him up and make him start again, as sometimes with his collar, unpeeling it from twin studs and in the end letting the two front ends swing free like thin shields of bone escaping the skin. So, he tried to time things, letting the cough run its course, divining its rhythm and the span of its advance, and then doing buck or collar at speed, half-amused by his eagerness but weary of not being his own master in things so trivial. He kept trying to remember what the poet Byron had said about buttoning and unbuttoning, buckling and unbuckling (*that* poet had done plenty of both, he reckoned), but he remembered his Keats better than his Byron as Keats had always had the cough whereas Byron had always had the hard-on. The summer of—something, he murmured, swigging away at the bar. What could it have been that the notorious lord had said? Some animal. Doc never fussed about memory; it was memory's nature to fail and let you down, or you would go mad with the chances missed and the love disdained. "You sound like bad people," Wyatt had said to him on first meeting, and Doc had wondered if he meant bad in the sense of rotting, going off, or just morally imperfect. Wyatt never glossed what he muttered, but Doc always construed it with fine diligence, never leaving an ambiguity to dangle like a mandrake in the groin. Watching the brothers Earp wrestle was one thing; it simplified everything around it, ridding watchers' minds of extraneous commitment. Hearing Wyatt out was quite different, requiring sly contribution and generous flair. Wyatt said little, but that little had to be pondered, almost edited, then fed back into the mainstream of life, given air before it asphyxiated in the cramp it was delivered in. Being, when he spoke, somewhat voluble, Doc heard Wyatt only against the waterfall of all the things he thought but did not utter, forever therefore bound to hear others like a man in a daze, to which he added a whiskey daze, the result being talk heard like distant music on unidentifiable instruments torn from some other street by the incessant acrid plains wind.

The motion that people noticed most when Doc sprang into life was that made with his handkerchief, beginning with a wipe from left to right, often removing the thin scale of dead skin from his lower lip, then patting the tip of his tongue, which he always imagined scarlet, and finally mopping at his teeth although nobody had ever seen them stained red as Doc had in the mirror. After the ablution was done, he would continue patting as if to discourage his cough, warning it to stay down, not one of your genteel after-soup maneuvers but more definite, a fabric bung that was a solid warning. By this time, of course, if his cough had been productive, the clump of handkerchief would be almost a ball, well on the way to approximating a floret of cauliflower, too smeared to mop up but big enough, Doc jested to himself, to use as a gob-stopper should some force begin to soar from beneath and threaten those standing near. With a smile, Doc gagged himself, masking the procedure with a fully opened hand, his emaciated fingers the tines of a splayed fork. Curbing his cough was almost like learning to shoot, remembering to stick his arm out in front as much as possible to achieve a visible line to aim along, the nearer the target the better, and schooling himself not to fan the hammer because fanning was not accurate, much as he loved to do it in order to show off, firing all six shots with mind-numbing speed and a huge flourish of the digits. The anesthesia of whiskey troubled him: sometimes there was a scald in its bite that, with one sup, both numbed and slowed; other times, the liquor mixed with the waiting blood, the fuzz-ball of foam and clots lurking at the brink of his throat, and put him into suspension, neither coughing nor choking, neither swallowing nor heaving, but a sad sack of a man (Doc felt) with boiled ballocks in his mouth, wondering what to do next. Sometimes, because of the tumult in his lungs, he felt his voice was buried down there, his heart was sliding down past his liver, and pulmonary tissue in dribs and drabs was blocking his bloodstream. How he managed to maintain his sangfroid amid so many distortions of the gentlemanly demeanor learned in the South, he never knew, trusting to honor and magic most of the time, hoping he did not appear a monster under the inaccurate, fumbled yellow light of hurricane lamps that swung slowly amid the bronze smoke of the saloons.

As best he could, Doc tried to look the part of the still-young man he was, all bacillus denied.

In this windy place, he belonged with the trash that blew in from California and blew out into New Mexico, much as he belonged with the trash that had blown in from Colorado and away again into Iowa. Most of America was on the move for one reason or another, propelled by the wind machine the sun drove. He would count as lightweight, easy to topple and uproot, easy to intercept, a thousand miles away, his hair awry, his eyes blistered shut, his lungs derelict bladders lined with blood that looked like jam. That was how he felt when he and Kate had "had some words," an oddly vague expression, and she had launched into her standard tirade about becoming a nester's wife. Better, then, to head for some Chinaman's opium den, where pipe dreams of garish intimacy both roused and soothed him and he wanted to, but didn't, call, Watchman, what of the night? The trouble with life was that it required so much recovery, demanding of you time and again a rehabilitation spell of incongruous length; you spent so much time getting over things, you almost had no time to live. He tried to formulate this concisely, but could only arrive at short joy, long repine, quietly noting that it would sound better in Latin, as everything did. *Felicitas brevis*, he began, but gave up, the memory of opium wiping him out quite. A cigar would help him more, he thought, so long as the acrid tannic taste made his lungs behave and did not provoke good old-fashioned retching. The trick, he had found, was to suck the smoke into your mouth and blow it right out again along the contours of the cigar, inhaling nothing, so the cigar seemed wreathed in a cylinder of its own fume. You could at least, Wyatt-like, stroll around with a cigar, or cigarillo, hoping to appear at peace, sophisticated, astute, always managing not to have to touch the beastly thing with your hand (mark of the novice). To talk thus impeded was another *hombre* feat he cherished, if and when he brought it off, the point being to talk along the shank of it, inserting an *O* into each word as it formed.

Not bad, he thought, if you practiced it for thirty years.

Or if you never lit the damned thing, used it as a prosthesis without which your jaws would clamp shut for ever.

To Kate, the aroma of a cigar connoted luxury, and he despised her for thinking so.

Luxury was nowhere to be found, not even in tissue-paper-lined boxes packed with the sheerest lingerie or bedshirts. Luxury was suave, casual and eternal.

Luxury was definitely not in a convent, and he wondered why he and Mattie had chosen the haven of barren places, creating almost by disappointed misadventure a lifestyle of deprivation out of which to construct—well, something that nobody else knew about: austerity for both, and loneliness, and pain. Together, he thought, they would have both been worse, twice as badly off, no doubt from merely talking about what made them feel apart from the human race, fallen short of it, self-demoted. Where had he read it, or had Sister Mary Mattie told him? *Mary Melanie*, he corrected himself. Be formal. A man who takes an unusual interest in the universe—no. Try again. Anyone who joins himself to the universe has nowhere better to go. Was that it, true for woman as for man? Was the universe the last resort of the badman, then, of even the good woman? Those who looked him in the eye felt seen into, seen through; he was like that, bland-penetrant, eager to get his probe among the brain-matter as if it were a vanilla pudding. Always a dentist.

Mail mailed from Prescott would be a long time arriving. He knew this, and those who received it at the other end became accustomed to the postmark, observing how long he had stayed in one unpredicted place, yet thankful he was finally in the right part of the country for a lunger—where he should have been all along. The pleasure of winning did him good, not least because he had heard Wyatt Earp's new salary was something close to forty thousand dollars, the same sum that Doc had already won at the gaming tables, mostly at poker and faro. Bless him, Sister Mary Melanie kept thinking, he has begun to look after himself; I hope he is breathing deeply at high altitudes. She went on burning his effusions after she had read them, as if she were a lens to the sun.

·14·

How the scarlet stamp on each letter moved them; long before airmail it might have been a wing, a gash, a stigma. Obliterated, it was wounded, marred, but it had something of magic in it: the recipient sat stock still in a nunnery, in a lodging house in Tombstone, just awaiting the letter's arrival: no need to pray for it, ride down the trail to guide it. Here it came, from the beloved hand of an aunt (muslin or goat leather), from the horny hand of an official, shoved beneath an iron grille that kept thieves out. A letter was a moving piece of the main, in which Mattie resumed her faint castigations, hoping to reform him at a distance, and Doc explained that, if he gave up the six-gun and faro, he would probably become an expert on tumbleweed, structure and size, speed and direction, degree of artistic caliber—they had come in from Russia or Mexico, he'd heard, not homegrown at all. Anything so innocuous from him was manna to her; she knew him only too well, and would no more misconstrue him than she would lion-sounds from an empty stomach. Their disjointed correspondence, though, enabled both of them to propose lines of action never quite carried through, each counting on the other to lose, amid the unraveling of time and the free-associative tangents of memory, the thread: what had been promised, urged, deplored, queried. Their letters were like broken pottery, and only in some exquisitely perfect place (not Dodge or Tombstone, nor Prescott but perhaps Santa Fe) would either have a chance to put all the pieces together again. Dismantled lives bred disjunctive letters whose main drive was to encourage the other with gentle emotion rather than exact schemes. Into their exchanges the vast emptiness of the plains, indeed of the Western continent itself, entered as if with natural right, reminding them how lonely the human antic could be compared to the largely empty heavens. Both had come from a society whose prime character had been to have everything on top of everything else, people and stuff crammed together in joyous, more or less joyous, plenty. You felt hemmed in, sustained by predictable manners, a mote among other motes amid the to and fro, as if all creation were fizzing. Now, however, they were testing themselves in empty places, beside the point that other nuns promenaded (sworn to silence, looking inward), other gunslingers oiled their holsters in paranoid privacy.

The editor of the local newspaper, he wrote, *is Clum. Now, what kind of a name is that?* He longed to hear her say anything regarding it, or by some extra-epistolary magic to read *Literary, perhaps, or a contraction of* Column (she would slash out the *o*, the *n*). *He is not Clum-footed, or, of course clumsy. He must have heard that too many times already.*

All he could hear was blood flushing in his ears as in a seashell; Savannah, Georgia, was too far away even for a monosyllable such as Clum to get through, never mind how hard he willed it. Tempted to tell her that, as Dr. and Mrs. Holliday, so demure-sounding, he and Kate had to spend the night in the Gillette mine superintendent's office, parting the next day as he went on to Tombstone, she to Globe, he decided against it. He resolved against any further news of Kate, the no-sooner-gone-than-returned Kate, the no-sooner-returned-than-gone-again. To hell with all that juggling, he resolved. If I put her in the abstract, then she can be a permanent presence, no need to mention her again; it looks untidy, but not mentioning her makes me look awful lonely.

Wyatt Earp, he scrawled, *has been deputized to find six missing mules. Now located at ranch of Frank and Tom McLowery, local demonology's twin claws. Earp now appointed deputy sheriff for Tombstone district of Pima County. Am I not a hotbed of world-shaking news? It goes on like this all the time. I should have stayed in Prescott. Wyatt has now given up his job as Wells Fargo messenger guard, 125 monthly. Gave up his idea of creating his own stage line. Earp women have been, like those Norns in Greek myth, sewing canvas tents for pin money, and Virgil is a U.S. deputy marshal. As you can see, we are all wrapped up in the dreadful penny-pinching minutiae of life. If it is all going to be like this from now on, I'll pray for premature death. Well, a Miss Pauline Markham, a belle of the époque no doubt, is here with her troupe, Pinafore on Wheels, the star turn of which is one Josephine Sarah Marcus, a girl of ripe and radiant beauty such as to make yours truly come back to life, not a blood-fleck in sight.*

So, Wyatt was going to flay him with sarcasm.

"Yew hid tahm to grow you a beard long as the Chisholm Trail, Doc. You bin gone so long." This was deputy twang.

Without answering, Doc fingered the silk of his imaginary white beard.

"Yew and Kate both, yew bin goin at it so long you did not come apart for ten months. Now, if that ain't the longest piece of frunt I ever." Wyatt stopped, deflated; Kate was back in town again, glaring at him not for his raciness but because of his accent, which she thought degraded Doc. Or was it his feeble Hungarian that incensed her? She screamed at him in a tongue he couldn't understand.

"She's only tellin you what a honey yew are," Doc said, punctilious as ever with his assumed accent: that of a suave city gent among rubes of the barbed-wire frontier. "Honest."

Wyatt gave him a sinister, amused-resentful look that actually seemed to change his eyes to oily green. "A man who makes light of ten months has an ugly view of tahm."

"Or," Doc scolded him, "a nervous one. Havin too little of it, he dares to squander it so the fates will give him a fresh helpin, a frish one."

It didn't work like that, Wyatt told him.

Only deputies knew, Doc said, needling him and blowing cigar smoke back on him like one of those chubby-cheeked cherubs on old maps.

The gorgeous Jewish Miss Marcus apart, all glistening browns and pulpy symmetry, he wanted to truncate his deformed account of Tombstone life and deprive the beings of personal pronouns, the things of definite or indefinite articles, ending up with a revenge telegraphese akin to Russian, which he knew not, though his Hungarian was bound to improve. Earp women *sewing*, for example, would have been enough. Like *Wyatt Dpty Sh'f,* Virgil *dpty M'sh'l.* Something that pithy so as not to disrupt the prayerful tenor of the convent. When life became so much a matter of tiny graduations, it was not worth living or reporting. He had seen Wyatt kick someone in the face while he, Wyatt, sat on a horse, a remarkable feat of balance and aiming. Had Doc Holliday come all this way to watch such a performance? He longed for something even more spectacular than Miss Marcus or Miss Markham, whom in the old days he would have fancied in the same bed with him, teasing riot to the point of disaster. Not now, however, though Miss Marcus had that—what should he call it—sleek lasciviousness, no, lascivious flexibility, no, flexible wantonness, whatever it was he wanted it, even if only to extract its teeth. He, he realized, was not fit for human company; he had spent almost a year in Prescott accumulating money, while the Earps had been feathering their nests in Tombstone all that time, and still nothing there for him, no official position.

Having spent so long in the trim little mining town of Prescott, once more the state capital even though it had no railroad, Doc kept looking at Tombstone with Prescott eyes, Prescott where eggs cost seventy-five cents a dozen and calico twenty-five cents a yard, Tombstone where, explicably, children went to school with six-guns in their belts, drenched in premature finality. Prescott had not even had a church, which suggested to Doc that the town had no believers, or believers whose piety was so private, so firm, they had no need of a shrine needing the deity to haunt it. Prescott, where he had lingered so profitably, had always struck him as a halfway place, he the halfway man, stranded between moribundity and death, looking at Tombstone through Prescott and looking at them both with eyes that could never forget the South, where men who owned mansions set Negro slaves to wrestle one another in evacuated pigsties deep in sludge, thus having them supplement the mud they had daubed themselves with to keep off the mosquitoes. In the moonlight (why was it always nighttime?) they looked like clay figurines, commanded to life by some Chinese emperor, not shiny but matt, huge earthenware embryos letting out a slow visceral yell of the soil. He was swathed in vision still, able to come and go with passable elegance, afflicted by some palsy only when he carried a cane with which to tap offending objects as he passed them by in the gloomy light given by the oil lamps of the street. The cane gave him an urban air, he thought, especially when he wore a long top coat and a derby, a pearl in his mercury cravat. Visually he remained a prisoner of the South, his mind a pandemonium of plantations, mansions, racing deer and blunt-eyed hunters, buzz-sawing insects, mumbling serfs, rhetorical dissimulators possessed by the highest degree of guilt and determined to talk it away, never mind who was not listening, it was always a matter of vocal will. You could rip a man out of the South, but you could never rip the South out of—he paused, fearing an epitaph, then reattended the thought, telling himself that, because nothing in the West was serious, nothing mattered—whether you killed or got killed, whether you found love or not, whether you ate well or lived stylishly. The old way was a matter of ripeness, *foison* that old word, whereas the West was pragmatic, as unaddicted to blather as a fencepost. He registered what lay around him, but it hardly etched its way into his core, being (as he thought) provisional, hardly as incisive as what Mattie told him about the St. Vincent's convent, which shone through to him precisely because she told him only about its bare bones, such as the lonely tall chimneys culminating in an abstemious curl of smoke, only one of them signaling (as she never said) a pope had been elected instead of him. He dreamed a dream of chimneys from which, unless engaged in gunplay, he never woke. He pictured her scraping crumbs and rejected crusts into the embers, making a slight glow at the end of a feeble meal designed not to energize her but merely to fuel her next few prayers, as if devotions needed a refill en route in order to make it all the way. She, as she had insisted, was merely a conduit for thoroughgoing piety, was already in a way a sacrificial being; he could understand what she meant, but he hated all modes of the premature, all talk of a calf bought for five dollars, sold as a heifer for fifty. He preferred, in language and numbers, formulations that went backward, so that, even while winning, while fleecing suckers at the card tables, he doted on what had been the beginnings of things: card games, careers, quarrels, love affairs, speeches, shoot-outs even. This is to say he preferred initiation to anything else, even to the extent of always being able to move on to a new place, unless (and here his love of the start came clear) he wanted to stay in the one place, a Prescott, a Dodge, until he could no longer stomach the illusion that he was again and again just beginning there, learning the ropes, registering to vote (always registering as dentist), finding lodgings, choosing a saloon to roost in or to buy. He understood himself, but never gave himself a bad time when he caught himself out with a shameful motive; it was the nature of the beast he was, he who had coughed his conscience up with his lungs, as he sometimes said.

Lovely things warmed him, as when someone told him how Allie Earp's name had been seen cut into an aspen up in the mountains, with a heart bearing Virgil's name. This was the same Allie who told everyone trying to help her bake not to pat the bread for her, she liked to do that herself. And then that bizarre conversation after the mixing of dough, the time-honored shaping of it into loaves, work of the Old English loaf-shaper who etymologically became lady.

"Allie, don't you pat that bread, there's a honey. You don't have to. I never need to pat mine." This was Jennie, wife of Wyatt's elder half brother Newton (a competitive disgruntled fellow), she weary of God's own country, yearning for bathtubs, sewing machines, floral wallpaper, neighbors and disciplined pets (actually, Tombstone should have suited her quite).

"*My* bread," Allie told her. "Mine to pat or not."

"Bakers never do."

"I'm no baker, Jennie. I pat my bread and have survived so far on it. So has my man. Bake your own, pat it."

"No, *you* bake it, you're good."

"Then leave me and my bread alone."

Not long after this, Newton and Jennie reversed course and

headed back to Kansas, home to sweetness and light. They had not even seen a dead man, a newly dead one, slumped in the bracken, his lit cigarette still fuming as his two six-shooters did the same, fired too late.

Overdue for a fracas, Doc soon got into one, in the Oriental Saloon, losing his temper with Johnny Tyler, who had already had a run-in with Wyatt in the previous month. "Shoot me then," Doc said, "go ahead and do it, then see how fast I turn your head into skunk cabbage."

"Leave him alone, Doc," said Milt Joyce the saloon's owner, "you's jest showin off. He won't draw against a man who wants to die, he's got more sense." It was true; Tyler made no move until, with slow irreverence, he walked out and Milt Joyce began to harangue Doc for being so bloodthirsty. Weary of the other's tirade, Doc handed over his six-gun and left, only to return in a foaming swivet, a fresh gun in his holster (his stash of weapons he had already set up). Fast toward the bar he came, muttering and gesturing, quite unlike the svelte and elegant Doc who strolled the evening streets, and told Joyce to shut his frunt of a mouth. He then swung a punch that missed and Joyce hit him over the head with the barrel of his six-shooter. Down Doc went, Joyce on top of him, spoiling for more and emitting guttural, feral sounds no doubt intended to scare Doc to death. Now officers Bennett and White grappled with the pair to separate them and found Joyce had been shot in the hand, his partner Parker through the toe of his left foot. Doc had been rambunctious again, ending up the worse for wear, headachy and bleeding, due to appear before Justice of the Peace James Reilly. How on earth could it not be an Earp, Doc wondered. Was there actually a part of the peace machinery they had not invaded? That was one thing. Another was the poor marksmanship on view in Tombstone, his own included. Was it the water? Too much silver in it? Or the air? Too many farts in the wind? Doc paid his twenty-dollar fine in addition to court costs of eleven. Or he said he would, waiting two months before he did so. His word is good, Marshall White said, he was just being cussed, like all these assault and battery cases. Doc had been losing, but he had also been missing. It was not like him to hit the hand and the foot. His agitation must have been prophetic: only two weeks after he went to court, a mild cacophony of cowboys shooting at the moon was heard from an arroyo off Allen Street at about half past midnight. Confronting the ringleader shooter, Curly Bill Brocius, the marshal (White) whom Doc had begun to think of as *his* marshal demanded his six-gun, intending to run him in in the normal Tombstone way, wishing he were doing this in his sleep, as he well knew he could. Tiptoeing up behind Curly Bill, Wyatt Earp grabbed him around the middle while Marshal White in a deteriorating mood gave his best vocal blast, glad of something to do, but pissed off to have to be doing it: "Now you give me that goddamned gun, you son of a bitch asshole punk" and the gun went off, perhaps jarred by Wyatt's grip, the bullet hitting White, as they found, in the left testicle. Wyatt buffaloed Curly Bill, had the remaining cowboys pressed into the twelve-foot-by-twelve-foot hoosegow made of planks (a Tombstone compromise), and decided that was all for one night.

"We're all missing," Doc said. "Nothing's plumb anymore, Wyatt."

"You ain't obleeged to shoot straight, Doc. It's you, two times out of three, that's doin the missin. Maybe you was aimin at hand and toe. Hell, Marshal White damn near shot hisself, or Curly Bill did. There was nothin in it, not for the small distance in between them. Myself, I'd a bin shot just as easy in the nuts, bein behind him."

"Hayul," Doc answered in his best distorted frontier brogue, "we gotta watch it, Wyatt. It ain't right to say we shot somebody through the hand, the toe, the balls, because that kind of wahdens the scope of the inquiry and sends folk's mind on beyond as the bullet travels on into infinity wherever the bisected fuck that is. We should say, shot in the hand, the toe, the barls. Few get mah drift." He could never forget he was a Southerner, passionately being not merely someone else, but some*thing* else too: a shootist.

O.K.: The Corral, the Earps, and Doc Holliday

"Doc," Wyatt answered, unusually communicative for this hour, "we sure gone *substuited* the schoolmarm's paddy stick for the bullet of death. The day will soon come when these boys will be takin no risks at all, jest shootin the bejesus out of the town. We ain't never had this fashion of conversation in Dodge. Ah wish I was there, I truly dew."

Doc would never have admitted it, but he missed the sound of Southern speech, its languid, seductive, almost effete cadence; had he not, he wouldn't have lingered around to hear the occasional English accent, as yet uncontaminated by Dodge or Tombstone. The brusque clatter of Midwestern speech jangled on his ear, made him long for silence, for a world in which the only chatter was that of six-guns. Poor City Marshall White, balloxed, issued a statement exonerating Curly Bill: it had been an accident. A lynch mob was ready, though, so off to Tucson went Curly Bill Brocius with Wyatt, riding a buggy together, Wyatt just hoping he would try it. Sadder than ever, Fred White died of his wound, replaced by Ben Sippy right on the brink of an election for Pima County Sheriff. By now, in order to support Bob Paul, Wyatt quit his job as deputy sheriff and Johnny Behan, former flame of Josephine Sarah Marcus, replaced him. As Wyatt had once told Doc, his love life was too damned complicated, what with two common-law wives squirreled away, and a Marcus on the front burner; but Doc only told him, yes, he understood—his true love was back in Savannah, Georgia, and his common-law wife was a whore on the lam. Usually, when they stood together at the doorway to the Oriental, they stood with their hands clasped behind their backs, but this time they both had both hands on their shoulders, just knowing trouble was afoot. They scanned the street, but trouble was inside out of the wind. "Truth told," Wyatt said, "you can get real riled and randy if you has a coarse, lewd woman with a coarse, lewd face, but what gets me all heated up is the lewd woman with the beautiful, innocent face, and you are *aghast* when she wants to do this ugly thang with you. Then I get a hard-on like the guy coming naked out of the pond, it won't go down, and they has to look. They powders it and sprays it, saying why is it so huge? I tell em for a joke that's my Buntline Special, would they like for me to fire it, like a stoker shovelin coals. Well, that does it, y'know, they's inspired with it, the pretty, demure ones."

Doc was dumbfounded, but tried a new tack. "What you make, Wyatt, of they little clattermouse, as they call it? You ivver had much truck with that, lickin and like?"

"Gosh darn, Doc, Ah'm too unworldly for that stuff, Ah gotta have my meat in taters on the plate where I kin git at em. Now, no fancies fer me."

Doc persisted. "Yair, but them crypillows, then, and the hairless pear that grows anywhere."

"Huh?" Wyatt was looking hard down Allen Street at a group of cowboys taunting while frogmarching some whores. "You sees how *they* gits *their* jollies, then?" He grumped and took out a six-gun, rubbing his groin with the front sight until ease recurred and he could slap the gun away, sighing a vowel of dark brown phlegm full of trail dust and virility. He sounded quite Doc-like for the moment. "Upsy daisy and thank you, ma'am, that's me," he said, and nudged Doc on the elbow, one ruffian to another during the eclipse of shyness.

"I was wonderin," Doc went on, "when we come out of the tall circuitous grass and all the chips is down, what you think them Jewish women's used to. I mean, their fellers has their plum rubbin and chafin raw, permanently unpeeled again the nap of their pants, see, which must make them mighty fidgety an twitchy. It would me, either mighty sensitive or jest plain scratchy."

"Wears off," Wyatt suggested, bored.

"Yair," Doc added, "but think of their women, they gets used to the thing without its hood. They's a world of difference between one that's slit up and one that's peeled back just for business. I reckon them that's peeled has the wider circumference, and remember I'm a dentist."

"Only when they's usin their mouths, you mean." Wyatt had come back to life with this, sensing some novel obscenity fresh from green-walled hospitals.

"Nah," Doc said, "I reckon they never snip it off, they just tack it underneath, they don't throw it away for some Philistine to collect up and take home to King Solomon to be counted. That's sort of mixed up, but you get mah drift."

"Ah do not, Doc. No snippity fer me. Do you know, sometimes, when Ah'm upstairs in my fancy room, there's two or three comes up in their suspenders just to look at it."

"So as to tell their kids."

"So as to tell their kids." Wyatt cooed, amazed.

"Well, Doc," he went on, "Are you gittin yer greens? Are you gittin enough?"

"Ah'm not gittin any, Ah'm spittin too much blood. I guess Ah ain't got long to go, Wyatt."

"Then you should thrump it more," Wyatt instructed him, "with a handful of halibut oil before you inters, and hang a big rock from it when you walk around, it makes an inch a year."

Doc confessed he hadn't tried these maneuvers; he'd never heard of halibut oil, and he'd never found the right rock.

"Cod liver oil, then, and a lump of iron," which he said as Ireron. "You has to work it, Doc, and you a doctor not know that. Why, you's joshin me, for sure."

Doc allowed as how he still looked, with lechery in his heart. Many a nice piece up and down Allen Street, but the hottest snatch, he said, had been in Santa Fe, where the underground crystal reflected the women's lust back to them and made them swagger with desire.

Wyatt dismissed all stories of Santa Fe, where he had hardly paused, instead suggesting to Doc how they stand facing each other and have their (naturally huge) erections tied together with a yellow ribbon. What then, he wondered.

"Common-law husband," Doc sneered. "None of that stuff."

"You," Wyatt blustered, "you need that ixtra inch, Doc. You gotta ply it if you want to stuff em all. I got a harem, yessir, I do, and it stinks like a hoosegow full of bison piss."

·15·

It was a comfort to Doc to have these racy exchanges with Wyatt; how often did a monolith tell a dirty story or mention its common-law wives? He got the impression that Wyatt gave his women a tough time, not because he had anything against women as such, but because he was who he was, oddly stranded in human inter-course, loaded with foibles yet obliged to pose as paragon, to become always *that* Wyatt Earp: savior, peacemaker, pillar of all communities. Doc was grateful for his own spotty, indeterminate role, for the chance to go on being the eccentric he was. Why, if things were otherwise, he would be obliged to see the virtues of Curly Bill and John Ringold, two of his least favorite people. Curly Bill's middle name, Brocius, made Doc think of Boeotia, a district in ancient Greece to the west of Attica, proverbial for its dullness, the tedium of its inhabitants. Curly Bill Brocius belonged there, whereas Ringo, who had been to college, and actually made a fetish of lugging around in his duffel Greek and Roman texts to be pored over, was a rustler through and through, a hold-up artist, a compulsive drinker with romantic pretensions. He overlapped too much with Doc, he was receiving catastrophic letters done in a flawless feminine hand that sent him into epic depressions lasting weeks. His auburn hair was wavy, his manner either savage or benign, and his face ever contorted with indiscriminate loathing. Son of well-to-do parents, he had run afoul of something early on, maybe during his college days, and had never recovered. He was a moody, testy fellow, proud of himself, for what he was, and given to bouts of violent self-esteem. Only once had he killed, when one Louis Hancock, rashly opting for beer after Ringo had offered him whiskey in some Allen Street saloon, took a bullet in the gizzard for being an uncooperative drinking buddy. It never took much with Ringo, but he almost managed self-control on other occasions, expressing himself mainly through sulk and sarcasm, violent attitudinizing and sly ingratiation. Of local psychopaths, he was the best looking, and he had his pick of the local tramps. Whereas Curly Bill was a cheerful, hefty person, almost likable in the role of leader, Ringo hovered brutally on the edge of emaciation, a prey to black moods that erupted without warning. Perhaps a viable human, quoting Greek while taking charge, might have been made by combining the two, but Doc kept his distance when he could, sensing permanent trouble. One day soon, Curly Bill would really be lynched, long before a Wyatt Earp could spirit him away to Tucson, and there were few marshals as forgiving as Fred White had been.

Before 1880 was out, Curly Bill had reappeared in yet another role, still on bail, riding into town with the votes from the San Simon district; not only that, Johnny Ringo had served as precinct judge and the notorious Ike Clanton as voting inspector. What a bizarre tapestry local politics was; Doc was glad he was much less involved than Wyatt, who had resigned to back the loser, Bob Paul, and Virgil, who lost the election for Tombstone city marshall and resigned as assistant marshal in disgust. It was ironic to watch those worthy, industrious, ambitious Earps, slaving away to achieve local standing and being voted out by a bunch of cow thieves and holdup men who dominated the area. There was Wyatt, with his small mind and huge member, trying to screw the world and unable to find even the place to put it in. No, not quite, Doc, he told himself: he's found the place, by feel and guesswork, but he's too big for it, the organ of his ambition is fit only for the governorship of Arizona. Preserve me, Doc thought, from lofty, corrupt, officious men whose only goal in life, apart from greed, is power over others; that's how they get their jollies. Thank goodness my own life is more informal than theirs, my condition more humbling, my history more sophisticated. I still wouldn't take a Ringo over an Earp, the brainsick hoodlum over the priapic conniver, but I never liked having to make that kind of choice anyway. To hell with their fidgety local voting system; this is only Tombstone, barely a village; the Earps will surely tire of running for office in this dog-kennel of an enclave, and then we can fix on what really matters here: those lumbering wagons of ore, rumbling down Toughnut in a private whirlwind of putrid dust, all those down-at-heel pianos jangling out of tune in a travesty of universal harmony, the one-room adobes with insect-infested dirt floors, all counterpointed, if that's the right word in view of those uncoordinated pianos, by shelves loaded with satins and silks, rolls and rolls of gingham and calico, Brussels carpets to tread upon in the stores like trial runs for heaven, every liquor known to mankind, the click of ivory balls, the tinkle of glasses, the effusive cackle of drunken women. Why, in Tombstone, the most natural thing in the world was to move into your adobe shack and put your expensive Brussels rug right down there on the hard-packed dirt, pauper and king in one. The only sewing machine in Tombstone was Allie's, so she and Mattie went into business stitching awnings at a penny a yard, all the time trying to persuade Wyatt and his brothers to chop some wood instead of stroking and honing their long fingers, kneading their knuckles and shuffling their cards, in readiness for the next game of faro.

Doc sighed with contentment at having no family, at being a floater on the surface of Tombstone life, not wanting to be recognized, but noticed everywhere he went and not so much feared as wondered about, certainly never gossiped about like Wyatt, whose Mattie, it was being said, was not only common-law wife number two, but actually the stepdaughter of Jim Earp by a previous wife, née Blaylock. The facts of incest were missing, but its rumor tainted the air around Wyatt and made the back of his neck prickle.

No wonder. Not only was this doughty man of the law living a double life; he was living multiply as well, as he eventually confessed to Doc, having strolled with him to Mattie's Place (as where he lived was known) by moonlight, just to show him something weird. The women were asleep. All sewing had stopped. With the grand air of a prophet opening sacred books, Wyatt motioned at a closet whose door he gently opened by dragging on the knob. Doc saw, on the floor, a new-looking suitcase that seemed never to have traveled, which Wyatt carefully extracted from the closet and, whispering something about Kate's having fallen into the closet once not long ago, carried outside into the light of the full moon. Now he opened it, revealing, at least as best as Doc could see, crudely made beards and mustaches, some separate, some sewn onto black papier-mâché masks. There was also what seemed a clergyman's frock coat, a small bamboo cane, a check suit cut for a large man. Then he saw wigs, grease paint, monocles, spectacles with what he assumed were plain glass lenses, eyepatches, various collapsed hats, several bandannas, and a whole array of bloodstained bandages.

"My disguises," Wyatt said caressingly.

"For when you hold up stages."

"For when I go under cover for evidence."

"Or play cards?" Suddenly Doc thought he had seen the disguised Wyatt opposite him, playing a hand, not so much gathering information as daring anyone to identify him amid all those whiskers, with his head rammed deep into an uncollapsed hat, a big swollen ruddy bandage on one wrist, the spectacles sliding to the middle of his nose as he played and one hand perpetually cuffing them back into place. "It *was* you then, once," Doc said. "Why bother? What difference would it have made if I'd identified you?"

Sometimes, Wyatt told him, he thought that if he disguised himself enough the Almighty might pass him over, might miss him out of the roll call of death. He wanted to be overlooked until the last trumpet, and then some. Doc could not believe his eyes, viewing this heroic, randy, ambitious man by moonlight and discovering how, sometimes, he cowered away from life. If he were telling the truth. Who, now, was Wyatt Earp? Was he using disguises because he liked deception for its own sake, a born dissembler? Or were there good reasons? Why should not Doc himself make an occasional foray in false whiskers and eyepatch, merely to astound whomever he gunslung with by the speed of his draw? Ah, he thought, the pleasures of incognito. You need to be a public figure to enjoy disguise, otherwise it has no allure. Would women go for it, delighted to drag it all away from the face to find whoever they thought it was? Or were these not Wyatt's at all but Mattie's? Did disguises explain his marital secretiveness, his way of keeping two common-law wives under wraps while pursuing a third woman of extraordinary beauty? Perhaps he went to assignations thus, donning the disguise on the way out of town, pausing his buckboard, or donning it just before the romantic rendezvous? Doc's mind roamed through possibilities while Wyatt kept silent, savoring the other man's amazement. Every man, someone had told Doc in Atlanta, has a little cupboard door into his being; open that and you learn things you never suspected. Always find that door. Was this Wyatt's door, then, the true way to the full-fleshed, samite-thighed, ripe Josephine, most of all the wiggle staged by her hips, keeping her copious skirts at the bounce? She talked funny, everyone said, but perhaps that faintly anglophone twang was a disguise too, designed to get her into places where she would never be allowed to say, as came naturally, *cawfee*. Was there a voice behind the voice, a second set of breasts behind her voluminous *balcon*, as the French said, a third set of labia prancing in the interior, polka-dotted and hypersensitive? Doc wondered if the two of them came face-to-face only by courtesy of twin aliases, backing away from each other in the end so as never to feel embarrassed socially. It would never have worked, but Doc felt for the first time in months a tremor in his virile member as it asked to be restored to its former privileges under the sign of Wyatt Earp.

·16·

Ennui is the nest of regret, however; Doc felt as much impatience on looking back as he felt relief on looking forward to the mindless kingdom of incessant erection. Nothing was going to be that simple, and he wanted more than merely to join the crew of Wyatt and his horny brothers. He wanted his correspondence to go right; he wanted Kate to leave him alone; he wanted to play faro for a week without sleeping. He wanted the South, the swimming hole, to be able to quote Latin in the presence of Johnny Ringo without the least chance of being corrected. When he felt insecure in this way, he smoothed his lapels, adjusted his hair into a flawless sweep behind his ears (nothing twisting forward), patted his cravat and pearl pin, hitched the sit of his pants, remaneuvered his toes in his boots, and blinked his eyes until they seemed clear of all dust and slime. He wanted to be as perfect as the stars and stripes laid on Lincoln's cadaver, as private as all those unlabeled drawers in a Chinese apothecary shop. He was a ravenous eclectic on the millennium's rim, and his yearnings were legion. Somehow the prospect of life with a disguised Earp cheered him no end; no longer was Wyatt the immaculate icon, he was a man of deceits and foibles, hiding this or that in order to fill his pockets, plant his yard, confirm his fabulous repute. Sometimes all that Wyatt seemed to care about was having a starched white shirt across the front of him, with which to breast the world. He would go into a rage if the slightest speck showed on it after Mattie laid it in a drawer with all the reverence due a dead child. One day, Doc saw Mattie outside, flogging a fence post with a freshly laundered white shirt, tearing it to tatters because Wyatt had made a scene about flyspecks on the frill and had ripped it off him and stomped on it.

What, Doc wondered, made Wyatt such a perfectionist? Did

he have ambitions beyond the resources of his personality? Doubtful. Was he cripplingly self-conscious? Perhaps. Or did he believe in tantrum as an art-form, there to be admired and imitated? He and Doc were far apart, Doc being the sloppier of the two, the one more obviously moved by the poem Allie had shown him, the poem written by Virgil on a card fringed with forget-me-nots and roses:

> 'Ere breaks the drowsy morning
> There starts to my surprise
> A light the dusk's adorning
> From thy beloved eyes.
>
> I awake to find 'twas dreaming
> That mocked my long sleep
> And cheated by the sunning
> I long for thee and weep.

Doc didn't think Virgil had much future as a poet, but he could detect the raw devotion in the appalling words, glad he would never have to say them aloud. Why Allie had given him this card, he had no idea, but he suspected she had heard about Kate's infidelities and wanted to solace him, though when you have been betrayed and your inamorata (a whore) has gone bustling off to find new clients, do you have a legitimate grievance or not? Certainly not enough to merit a maudlin ditty with a tender posy. Down at the sewer level he thought he existed at, Doc knew he had no grievance at all; she had never pretended to be other than she was, and promiscuity was not only her goddess but her bank as well. What if he read Virgil's poem to her? She would detonate in raucous laughter, thereafter to mock Virgil whenever she saw him and call after him in the street, "I long for thee and weep! Wipe my ass and wipe my eyes, Virgil's a softie." She was a hard-boiled harridan all right, but oddly peripheral to Doc's life, more of a sample on the premises than a sweetheart or a common-law wife. Indeed, she was his common-law occasional whore, that was all, with a vile tongue and a continual lubrication. No prepping for her, she said, Hungarian women were always ready, hence their lovely Irish skin. He had never made anything of this, either the Hungarian or the Irish facet, but he had sometimes defended her when Allie or some other member of the Earp clan had denounced her as acquisitive, high-handed, foul-mouthed, all of it, saying she was a professional with professional standards, following cows and cowboys as plants tracked the sun. Somebody had to defend her, let her sink rightly back into the mumbled boozy ways of the corps de phallus that lived in the town's saloons and flounced half-naked through its filthy, ore-streaked streets.

All his life, Wyatt had sensed that, whenever he tried to amaze people, the surprise he concocted was never enough, and this presumed shortcoming led him into strained behavior. Afraid that Doc had not responded fully to the suitcase, which perhaps should have contained stars or a tiny buffalo, he debated with himself whether or not to reveal to him a second suitcase, kept nowhere near the first one, where the visiting Long Nose Kate might blunder into it and knock it open with her Hungarian fist or knee. What would Doc think when he saw the contents? Maybe he would smile and ask to join with him in the enterprise. One way or the other, Doc had to be convinced that Wyatt was a monolith of a man, not some optional person but a fellow whom everyone had to know. Wyatt did not know how much Doc looked up to him, even if Doc's knowledge of Wyatt's intimate life lacked something; Doc had a loyal streak, a bit naive perhaps, but out of something unrequited in his harrowed nature since young manhood. Doc was not exactly gullible, but he opened up to the possibility of belief and trust like a well-positioned flower; otherwise he would never have begun and continued his correspondence with his Mattie, isolated in her holy fastness.

When Doc next came around, firming up his habit of calling on Wyatt and Mattie, much less frequently on Allie and Virgil (whom one referred to in that order), Wyatt had everything ready, his glad beckoning hand appropriated from some dim echo of Open Sesame and Ali Baba.

"This'll tame you," he said, clapping Doc on the back and starting a cough that would not cease, even when Doc blocked his mouth with a gloved hand so as not to wake Mattie Earp. These midnight visits, combined with a desultory patrol of Tombstone's raunchy streets, were becoming a private fetish, and Doc wondered if the odds would increase on there being always, with each visit, something else revealed: a secretive man in the act of exposing his inmost being and ultimately opened up like a wax figure with a dozen cupboard doors swung wide on hinges fused with his rib cage, his flanks, his groin. Once Wyatt Earp had shown what he was made of, and so become a known quantity, Doc would have to entertain himself in some other way, maybe doing faro and poker at the same time at different tables.

"This here," Wyatt told him, "is smaller, more costly."

"What is it?"

Wyatt suggested they go outside, which was going to become the normal ritual; Doc could see that.

Outside, they commented on how much cooler the air was than last time, and Doc made to flip open the hasps, but Wyatt beat him to it, fanning the lid back in the gloom for Doc the doctor to see what looked like outsize pepper shakers, wood and brass, drably gleaming in the spilled light from the house. Then he saw a painted teapot with an oddly robust spout, which would surely deluge a medium-size cup. Next he noticed some metal balls and what seemed a pink model pig, almost glistening and with vestigial feet.

"What you think, Doc? You see any lahk these afore? These is mah own spisshul collection from all kindsa furrin parts. Yurrup, see, and Chahna. All over the world."

Dildoes, Doc voiced to his quaking mind. Diddledoes. What need had Wyatt for these?

"You'd be surprised, Doc, how many womens likes the feel of one or two of these. Youngs and olds, they allis goes for the warm teapot, maybe with some heated whiskey in there, see. Ah hev seen them a little team of womens pour a whole potful into some lucky gal while she lahs back, injoyin it. Them other things, they's cruder, see, but popular nintheless."

"Surely," Doc was saying, "somebody as well endowed as Wyatt Earp doesn't need this sort of stuff, brothel paraphernalia."

"Just in case," Wyatt said. "Ah get all heated just handlin em sometimes, and then I kin go for hours."

"Oh," Doc said, "I can understand that. Unnerstand you mighty well. I hasn't been exactly nowhere in my travels. I have seen the pink money perform and the whip curl, the pool balls disappear, and the lard melt. There's not much I haven't seen in between spits, I'll tell you." Life with Wyatt was now, he could tell, going to become a series of interlocked surprises introduced with grunts and gentle inquiries about his state of health—Wyatt the mellow foil, hoping to enlist his zeal and his courage. It was odd, Doc thought, to find a man so potent and decisive appearing to recruit approval from someone whose private life he did not know too well, especially when showing him sex toys from cheaply jeweled pommels of crudely stitched leather to warm-water pistols pink with black spots. What was Wyatt looking for? Someone he only half-knew, to say it was all right to run a couple of mistresses as secret common-law wives while hunting another woman whose tastes might just be extravagant enough for his bag of erotic tricks? Why should he care what someone else thought? Had it been Doc, apart from a moment or two of self-doubting indolence, he would have gone ahead with whatever deviance he had intended, and hang what onlookers or gossipers thought; but that, he told himself, was because he came from the South, where departures from the norm were encouraged so long as they remained in camera, like rotting goldfish.

Display, he told himself: that was what Wyatt cared about. He had an urge to be seen, to have his need recognized, not wishing it to be overlooked. Unseen, unwitnessed, it would have no resonance for him. In this man, Doc thought, there came together elements of circus, confessional, and braggart; it was perhaps less simple than that, especially when you were in his presence and you submitted to the heavy features, the brazen eyes, the capacious-looking hands. If Wyatt had been only someone he'd read about, he would have forgotten him just as easily as he forgot some of the men he'd quarreled and shot it out with. One day, surely, Wyatt would invite him to come see him in flagrante, much as he had seen him use his six-gun. He was too young, too early, to know of the U.S. president who gave interviews to reporters while squatted on the toilet, but to a brain as restless and twisted as Doc's such a possibility would never have been daunting. Doc was partly a formula too, mingling self-denial, other-worldliness and sadism in about equal measure—a mix more erratic than Wyatt's, more combustible, maybe, but also capable of being quieted, which is exactly what Doc did in late 1880, after the Milty Joyce affair, when Doc settled down to a peaceful life of letter-writing and meditation, gambling and afternoon walks, not even picking up his mail or his telegrams (ignoring a note about them in the *Nugget*). Generally speaking, he stayed out of things, not even helping Wyatt (for once) when rounding up belligerent cowboys. Doc seceded so much they all asked after his health, already knowing, having swiftly assimilated the one and only answer: he was always getting worse and, when he failed to put in an appearance, it was either because he was heading downhill or, because feeling a little better, staying close to home to relish and cherish the miraculous sensation, like somebody with a bowl of milk afraid to walk and spill it. How many gave him credit for hugging a moment of good health to his bosom will never be known, but he did sometimes curl up in a blanket, shrouding himself in warmed-up delight, wondering if a reprieve had at last come and how to make certain of it. He was practicing being well, or better, and he had not had much experience of that, so he tried, hoping not to exaggerate, imagining all kinds of ravishing events, from reunion with Mattie (he almost assumed that one of the rewards of recovered health was having her come join him) to resumption of his dental practice, from cessation of gunslinging to steering away from the Earps or at least cooling the bond with

Wyatt. Then, of course, the remission ended (it had only been a dash among so many dots) and he had to practice stoicism all over again, at which he was better than he was at ecstasy. One day, there would be no more improvements and his steady downhill course would be clear, and he would languorously sink with it, begging it to take him lower than ever, not to fool him, not to go back on its deadly word. Merely to think this was to hasten it. One of his theories about life was that both the happy and the sad drove you crazy, that human response per se was lethal, and the best way to survive was to have no response at all and to live like a scavenger, neither killing nor taking risks. He maintained a good, poised front, behind which thrived a bevy of Docs, each primed for action, doomed to settle everything by arguing with the others. Now, what had that last line of Mattie's prayer been, and why had she written to him apologizing that it must have seemed sacrilege? Surely she took his religious susceptibilities more seriously than he did. Sacrilege? *I'll need you for almost always,* which was more or less how she couched it, seemed to imply that the soul after death might not need God at all, having as it were made the big jump. He could see that, but surely God knew all about this and would never hold it against anyone that, having travailed all the way through dying and death, of the body anyway, they had at last assumed they were in the clear, serene in that golden upland of redeemed eternity. Something such: pious metaphor chilled him, but at the same time it promised another zone clear of gunfighting, impotence, rough-and-tumble, blood and cough. He had his own notion of heaven, different from Mattie's yet comparable in that both expected it to be solid, firm, as per guarantee. Why that last line harrowed her so much, he could not tell; surely second-guessing God earned you some latitude, you were not bound to get it right or to forgo all liberties. Briefly, for the time a firefly flashes its green signal to the ground, he thrilled to the notion of the soul in the end emancipated from God, given over to some altogether sloppier, more available organization, like transferring from a doctor to a nurse, say, or from a sheriff to his deputy. He had never told her of his cosmology (it was poorly organized and lacked a coherent set of concepts), but he believed in something such as divine honor. Skulking away from the Tombstone throng, he began to study the reformed image of himself, no longer the shootist or gambler, but the grave survivor who sang at funerals and went from door to door warning them of grief's implacable advance upon them.

Then he laughed to find his pagan self so mealy-mouthed while, outside, elections were in full swing and Curly Bill's trial for killing Marshal White was postponed. Wyatt had gone to see Curly Bill and had offered him a deal: if he would identify those who had stuffed the ballot boxes, he and Morgan Earp would swear that White's killing had been accidental. "Yair," Curly Bill murmured, "it was Ike Clanton," which started a whole new ball rolling even while Wyatt and a Doc newly out of hiding went in search of Wyatt's stolen horse, "Nick Naylor," finding it being ridden by a certain Billy Clanton. They celebrated this coup by entering horses in the Yuletide Trotter Race, gambling men to the end and bristlingly proud of having rescued anything from the mess that Tombstone had become.

"We should ride em ourselves," Wyatt said.

"Only in hell." Doc was willing to be a passenger on a horse, and not so bad at it, but the notion of being a goading competitor put him off: too specialized, too plebeian.

"There, then," Wyatt retorted. "Samazin what you kin git done once you git down to it. I ain't no jockey, but once I wasn't no lawman neither. Just look."

"Wyatt, you're out of office. You quit. Don't you remember?" Wyatt had been in and out of office so many times in so many towns he couldn't always tell if, while running Tombstone, he wasn't still in charge of Dodge. In his dreams he occupied the power seat in dozens of towns, drew all those wages, and continued looking for more, his mind set on monopoly, with Earp-justice available in every state. He felt responsible for everything everywhere, almost like someone dragooned into pruning the garden of Eden on pain of death.

They won some money anyhow, not enough to spring a full-scale celebration with drinks all round, though in their well-meaning heart of hearts they thought they had, such was the cordiality of their good cheer as they mingled among the town's denizens, laid-back but a little hearty too. All was forgiven. Besides, the votes had been fixed; nobody knew who had voted for whom, nobody ever would. Looking at those who milled around him, Wyatt could not believe he didn't have their utter support and trust, he was such a likable, wholesome man's man. Doc had no such illusions, drenched in self-knowledge as he was. He used to like the man he used to be, a mercurial dandy who wished the Civil War had never ended, but not now; he understood why he was the way he was, but he was no longer the man he wanted to have made of himself. Too many accidents had intervened and dictated to him a lifestyle some part of him still found unbearable. He was a sinking swimmer, a waving drowner, like a man with a mission whose mission had suddenly become a building in the desert, laudable but final.

"We could be racin dogs," Wyatt told him. "They does that in some countries."

"How come, Wyatt," Doc said, "you talk wrong? You know better. I have seen your writing. How come that, around you, *I* slide back several grades and jabber like some spavined redneck afraid of the English language and of his own shadow?"

"Camouflage, Doc."

Doc smiled, almost willing to concede the point. "It makes them think I'm more like them." Wyatt spread his hands as if to embrace the whole bustling scene of the street, the scruffy panorama that was his war zone. "I gotta."

"Well, I don't gotta, but I still do it."

"Then don't, you don't gotta."

"I won't. I sure peeled that apple."

"Watch yourself, Doc. I hafta be goin."

He went, with that lax, swilling walk of his, something between a swagger and a saunter, the walk of a man pleased with himself and his destiny, fully able to withstand and exploit the next trick that fate handed him. Wyatt oozed competence and command; he hardly needed guns, and the mere sight of those two empty holsters would work wonders. All knew what had rested snugly there and could do so again. An odd role had descended upon him, of seeming the most consequential person in all the places that handed him no official title, as if the only person eligible to rule the roost was an amateur, a self-elected vigilante as expert at dealing with dry-gulchers as with con men and rustlers. What you *dreamed*, you could do, Wyatt thought as he strolled down Allen Street, right in the middle; it showed, it shone through, and you needed never to talk about it, show it off. In a back alley, he paused at a building that might once have been a saloon but looked more garish, and entered, thinking how one day he would reveal this too to Doc, who showed some interest in his marginal good causes. In and out he walked, tipping his cowboy hat, waving his hand, just checking that nothing was amiss, then out into the sunlight again (he walked this beat day and night, counting his inhalations and exhalations on each street just for something to do, for the illusion of command that gave him). Wyatt was never really on the rampage, not yet anyway, but even he knew he was explosive, a tiger who only needed to be tweaked. So long as things remained quiet, or if not quiet then manageable, Wyatt was in tune with the universe. Only a combination of things would unhinge him, and they would all have to affect him at the same time. Then people would really see Wyatt Earp. He knew such things about himself, even when not looking at them directly; he suspected himself of not being quite as he should be, but had no idea of how to change, or how far to go. Doc had become his best listener, the educated man willing to slum a little, although Wyatt knew neither of them was a wordy man. In theory, taciturn men made good listeners, but never as good as voluble men, who somehow swept up what others said into their own gladsome torrent. Once, he thought, Doc had been a real talker, whereas now he coughed more than he talked, for good reasons, and was not to be argued with. On the level of discourse he sustained nothing, and all his voluntaries and ripostes ended the same way, in a coughing bout that stopped him in a trice. It was frustrating, even more so when you realized that Doc, aware of how soon chatter was going to break down, held back, closed his lip, unwilling to start what he couldn't finish and therefore self-censoring, self-sealed, his mind (Wyatt guessed, knowingly) on a young woman undulant and comely coming toward them, her child's palms as soft as her cunt.

It seemed years since he had dealt with his last ruffian in Dodge, leading him to his horse by trapping earlobe between thumb and forefinger. They were not years of time but wide expansive ranges full of solid dismay. When had a whole succession of letters arrived from Virgil, half-owner of a Prescott mine, urging him and Jim to come to Tombstone, the boom town of boom towns, and quit their holdings in Dodge, forget their dream of a ranch in the Texas Panhandle? Had there been a whole series of conversations about such swollen exotica as the future, silver, gold, the law, the profitability of stage lines between town and railhead, and coaches guarded by expert gunmen such as Wyatt and Morgan? The vision was there: magic carpet between silver-rich Tombstone and Tucson, with whole squadrons of bandits in between, but Wyatt had never considered becoming a peaceman again; his future would be in bullion and mail. He was tired of being a target. The epic, ravishing journey from Prescott to Tombstone, especially the final stretch between Tucson and Tombstone, had not yet left his mind, nor the resonant names of the physical features he and his party encountered, from the Santa Rita and the Whetstone Mountains to the Barbacomari and the San Pedro. Poetry seemed to have come after him and made an inroad into his prosaic soul. All he had needed to put the iron into him was Charles Shibell, sheriff of Pima County, saying there was no need of a third stage in Tombstone; it wouldn't pay. The dream had died.

Now he became a lawman again he widened his clipped mustache into one more in fashion, adding sweep on both sides, forlorn not to be intimately linked to a silver industry that would yield over thirty million dollars. Why, in the middle of Toughnut

Street sat a holy forty-foot hole that had given up a fortune to relentless miners with crude implements. Just as, half in jest, Santa Fe had been based on crystal, Tombstone was perched, one mile high, on solid silver. In time, the mine owners cast their bullion in three-hundred-pound alloy bricks to thwart the outlaws of the Clanton gang; but Clanton's boys fought back by using wagons as part of the hold-up. From then on, it was hard for Wyatt not to subscribe to his own myth of the man who, in spite of repeated refusals, always became a lawman because fated to be so, most of all in such a region as that around Tombstone. Whenever an Earp was riding shotgun, no stagecoach robberies took place or were even attempted. Tombstone like Dodge held Wyatt in thrall, denying him his Wells, Fargo longings, but making him famous (a Cincinnatus) even while emotionally he began to crumble, more so even than the doomed Doc, who was plagued with only one common-law wife, and she most often absent while playing the harlot.

Slowly, as his holdings in real estate increased, Wyatt became the focus of the McLowery gang's hatred: the man who, when you stole his horse, wanted it back; who protected the bullion in the stage, and helped out the army when the McLowerys rustled their mules. They would shoot him on sight, they sent word; he would do likewise, he sent word back, wondering if he were marooned (as Doc said) in some quotation from *The Iliad*. When he encountered the McLowerys in Charleston one morning, they asked if he had received the threat that was a promise, and he said he had and were they ready right now to shoot it out? Far from ready for him, and the worse for alcohol, they rode away, Frank McLowery vowing "If you ever follow us again, your friends'll find what the coyotes leave of you in the sagebrush." Wyatt wondered which of the desperadoes so patently offering themselves up for punishment would sooner or later receive it, and which for one reason or another would escape. The puzzle pleased him, prompting him to brood on the faces of badmen, most of all the sometimes jovial, high-colored but ugly Curly Bill and the ascetic-looking, sullen schoolteacher type Johnny Ringo. Nothing in a man's features told you anything, he decided; Doc's view, one of ecumenical uniformity, was better. Only kill first. Essentially, Wyatt was a businessman made to do duty as an Achilles and eventually making love to the role, not least because he made good money, never less than seven hundred a month plus all the taxes he could rope in.

Over at the Oriental Saloon and Gambling Palace, that brilliantly lit purring wonder of the Tombstone world, Doc lay on a couch by a well-equipped writing table, contemplating not outlaws but, to the erratic tune of piano and violin, the nature of the infinite, hard to pin down, impossible to ignore. Should he write to Mattie, making extensive mention of the setting, or rather the setting within his mind, with, out there in the desert, the gangs gradually coming together against the Earps and, in here, hard-earned mining money changing hands at sickening speed (to him intoxicating and gratifying)? Once the already allied Clantons, McLowerys and the Curly Bill lot had decided jointly to remove the Earps, there was going to be some trouble, and he would join in, being very much of the Earp faction, not to mention the angels. Why tell her that? It would be more appropriate to describe the hotel, as if he were the latest reincarnation of Clara S. Brown, who first put the Oriental on the map in August 1880 with a high-flown piece about mahogany, carpets, classical music, awnings, weatherboard and adobe, Mexican dance halls and honky-tonks, almost catching the split spirit of the place, of Allen Street at least. Doc read the papers, would otherwise not know about his telegrams, and took note of how a phenomenon, such as the Oriental's mahogany bar, was made to sound in an Eastern newspaper even while he, in a bit of a pickle, stared at it, waiting for it to disappear out of modesty. Sitting up and momentarily feeling dizzy, he reached for writing paper and pen, dipped, then began, more to complete his gesture than to set anything down that had just occurred unbidden. *Mattie, this is a scene of almost expert calm, good taste, and serenity, where the weary bankers come to play monte and faro. I rarely join in, but when I do I prosper.* Then, unable to restrain himself any longer from voicing a memory that plagued him, he wrote

I told you about how Marshal Fred White had been accidentally shot and killed. He had seized the barrel of Curly Bill Brocius's six-gun and kind of pulled it toward him, causing it to go off. The slug hit Fred in the abdomen and he dropped. In the meantime, Wyatt Earp had slammed Curly Bill on the head (we call it buffaloing) with his gun-barrel, and he too went down. The most awful thing was that Fred White's clothes were on fire from the closeness of the shooting, and Wyatt told somebody to put the fire out, even while slugs were whizzing all around. It was a terrible time.

So did memory haunt him, no obedient lickspittle but an inner tyrant letting him control the first, second, and third events he wrote her about, but quite snowing him with the fourth, plucked into sight by the sheer dynamic of the process itself and just about a law unto itself. He did not relish having a mind nearly out of control in this way since the whole strategy of his writing to her, whether amid the tinsel violin and untuned piano of the Oriental or back in his lodging on Sly Street, was one of careful sifting and consideration. It was almost the same as telling her, "The man you once knew is no more, he has lost control of his memory and may even be telling lies. He shrinks from the truth and then a truth he had not known he knew comes walloping out of the blue, dominating the page where he had hoped to spare his Mattie any such recollection." He might have whispered this to himself, or just mouthed it, like someone murmuring a prayer. At all costs, he told himself, he would have to exercise more control over what he set down. There would be the pages he sent and those he didn't. Yet trying to rid himself of undesired memory (Fred White's coat sizzling and smoking with the ragged hole) would be like coming out of the barber's shop reeking of honeysuckle blossom, the coup de grâce, and trying to lose it, especially when those standing by observed the aroma with pleasure, commenting on the early spring, the late summer, if such terms meant the same thing in torridest Arizona (he still hadn't quite figured out the local weather or the seasons). Once baptized with a squirt of honeysuckle, you smelled of it for days. Once baptized with a squirt of the unbidden and horrific memory, you winced under its lash for years.

So Doc abandoned this letter, little knowing (yet) that an abandoned letter has a fair chance of haunting you, completing itself without authorial assistance in accordance with the principle, loosely stated, that the unfinished is a specter doomed to pester you with amputated hand, truncated leg. The horrors were only just beginning, perhaps; the thought put him off his next three drinks, and the bits of his mind energized by the onset of letter-writing continued to bedevil him from one drinking bout to the next, from cough to cough, from one visit to the Tonsorial Parlor of the Oriental to the next. I know, he told himself: it's like trying not to think of a yellow elephant smoking a cigar. It won't go away. Only when memory had faded enough would he be able to restart and finish the letter, in the meantime filling her in on inconsequential matters she never needed to hear about and in scant time committed to the flames (not that he knew yet how all his epistles went up in smoke the day she got them). So, in his best lighthearted vein, he told her about the new man in the barber-shop who told him "I'm all the way from Chicago," come to Tombstone to lick the lip of the boom. "What kind of a town is this, anyway?" When he asked Doc this, Doc answered in kind about Chicago, where he had never been, and never been told to go. Chicago languished among the unbidden and undesired memories, never mind how far the barber had trekked in his yearning for silver and its profits.

Always a dead man for breakfast, he wrote, now back in the Fly lodgings he supposedly shared with Kate, after first inhabiting a scruffy crib at the far end of Allen Street. Best delete that; she didn't need to know. What had happened to his brain? Well-behaved as when he and Wyatt sat side by side at the barber's, like two hirsute senators reviewing recent history with monosyllabic poise, it was all over the place now and frisky as a puppy. What was dragging him into telling her the very things he used to censor? Was he aching to terminate the correspondence with some classic obscenity worthy of Wyatt? A little sermon on his penis, say, not even limp ones being excused when you were writing to nuns. Of course, however, nuns took a medical view of the loins. He could report whatever he wanted, and she was bound to regard the stone-ache as a mode of cancer.

For some time now, relations between Big Nose Kate and Doc had been strained; it was not so much that he required fidelity, or that she required a marriage beyond the common-law kind. Doc liked to keep up appearances, but, lying down with Kate, he picked up moral and reputational fleas; Kate liked to play the field, but she also liked to time her sojourns with Doc for when he was flush, having done well at faro. Their relationship was not notorious for scruple or tact, and there had been times when it got in the way of both of them. Too, there was his notorious bad temper, which conflicting with hers, could make a howling row out of nothing in seconds, the abuse stacking up so high that nobody could remember the cause—a callow word, maybe, or a moment of stinginess. Quarreling had been their standard fare, a fact they hardly seemed to notice, never arriving at an armistice or thinking they needed one: each was so self-engrossed that there was no negotiation. It was inevitable that, one day, Doc would give Kate the order of the boot, cursing her greed, or that, another day, she would walk out on him and never come back; she would find too much else to do, too many others to oblige. A man more prudent, more calculating, than Doc might have played safe with her, fobbing her off with small dollar amounts just to keep her sweet, just in case since she was the more dependent member of the pair. Doc was not that way, however, and he soon—because of TB, faro, shooting and Wyatt Earp—had her demoted to the status of fifth-rate acquaintance, not so much jilted as jolted out of her skin.

·17·

Doc had been living the quiet life so long now that he hoped it would go on forever, although now and then he had gone to Wyatt's aid, reasoning that a man who subdues killers by clamping their earlobes between thumb and hefty forefinger (before booting them into the street or the calaboose or buffaloing them with a long barrel) merited assistance from the dying at least. So he would draw on those who intended blowing Wyatt to smithereens and leave them with their hands in the air until Wyatt said his familiar clipped "Much obleeged, Doc. Herd em outside, pliz, with their frayund." On March 15, 1881, Wyatt was dealing faro in the Oriental when a telegram arrived from Bob Paul, riding shotgun for Wells, Fargo, announcing an attempt on the stage that had left Tombstone at six in the evening with a bullion shipment of some eighty thousand dollars. The bullion had survived, but Bud Philpot, the driver, and a passenger, Peter Roerig, had been killed. Wyatt at once deputized both Virgil and Morgan, Bat Masterson and Marshall Williams, and started out, headed for Drew's ranch, where the attack had taken place. This event marked the end of Doc's sweet withdrawal from the tumult of Tombstone life.

Wearing kerchiefs over their lower faces, the highwaymen had been skimpily masked and were easily identified by the stranded passengers; it had been the Clanton gang again, callously shooting Bud Philpot through the heart and Roerig in the back. The six horses had bolted, taking the bullion away with them, beyond the bandits' reach, and Bob Paul had grabbed the reins after a mile of struggling and slowed the stagecoach down—it might well have broken up, being thirty years old, worn out in California before Sandy Bob Crouch brought it to little Tombstone in 1880. The night of the holdup was cold and dank, with much radiational cooling after an early-morning snow. Up in the dickey seat on top, Roerig must have been frozen soon after leaving town.

"Damn them all," Doc told Wyatt. "If I had pulled that job, I'd have got the eighty thousand. Whoever shot Eli Philpot, born in an emigrant wagon on another cold blustery day in 1859, was a rank amateur. If he had downed a horse, he'd have got the bullion." It was the acerbic, overinformed critique of a master craftsman appraising the work of some bunglers, which was always how Doc thought, conveniently occupying both sides of any question. Rumors now began to spread that he himself had been involved, merely for having rented a horse at the Tombstone livery stable about four o'clock, warning the liverymen that he might be gone a week, but he might be back that same night. It was a typical Doc assertion, the truth being that he had heard about a game in Charleston; but when he got there the game was over, so back he came in a foul humor, his horse hitched behind Old Man Fuller's water wagon, riding with Fuller for company. Then he spent the night at the tables of the Alhambra.

"Hold!" said a voice out of the darkness as the stage lumbered up a steep slope from a dry wash.

"By God," Bob Paul yelled back, "I stop for nobody."

It was one of the great Tombstone exchanges, passed from mouth to mouth like a playing card and getting garbled in the process. People loved to hear it, as well as the fateful nonfate of the bullion, almost disregarding the deaths of two men. *Two more for breakfast*, the wags said, adopting the usual Tombstone belief in replaceability. A man's replacement had often arrived, they said, before a man died with his boots on; it was one of the reassuring features of the town, and Doc Holliday called it previous debirth, hoping the phrase might catch on with its faint medical flavor. It never did, nor did it do him much good when the rumor mill began to whirl. A better explanation of Doc's supposed part in the Benson stage holdup, better than malice anyway, was that Bill Leonard, an old Las Vegas, N.M., friend had come to Tombstone, there to ply his skills as a jeweler of a special kind. Here too, as in Las Vegas, he melted down stolen jewelry for his outlaw friends;

now he had joined the bullion thieves. Doc had always liked him, whatever association with him might seem to imply to overinterpretive brains; after all, Bill Leonard was another consumptive and therefore a soul-brother to Doc, even if Doc disapproved of such of his friends as Luther King and Jim Crane. In the event, King was the only Benson stage bandit arrested. The event deflated itself, even more so when Doc let it be known that he would shoot the next person to utter a slander about his part in any such thing. A threat from Doc usually worked; some thought he was the real leader of the Earp gang whereas, more truly, he was its spiritual personification, hiring a second horse that night in case Wyatt needed him, ever willing to serve.

Wyatt had noticed how Doc, whenever something bloody or severe happened, seemed to suck up from his surroundings all kinds of unknown details, and then incorporate them into utterances of a high-flown rhetorical kind, as if exalting the occasion, as if he connected extreme happenings with fancy prose. This was nothing Wyatt could explain, or care about; he noticed it, though, as an observant lawman would, wondering if there were some link between Doc and such events as the Benson stage holdup. In fact there was, though Wyatt did not twig it. Doc wrote letters ceaselessly, and received them too, although fewer. As well as bullion, the Benson stage had been carrying mail, which was the only reason Wyatt, as a deputy United States marshal, could get involved in the pursuit and investigation. The stage, Doc deduced, might just have been carrying a letter of Doc's, starting it on the long flutter to Savannah, Georgia. In retrospect, as Doc established, Eli Bud Philpot, born on the march like Victor Hugo, and R. H. Paul had been guarding the letter of the spirit, something begun in the Oriental and finished off at Fly's: hardly a masterpiece, but an effusion from within a tortured mind. Not only that, as Doc also found out from a diligent reading of the *Phoenix Herald* (March 16, 1881), the bandits had carried wigs and beards made of rope yarn and these remained at the site along with fifteen shells. A letter to the newspaper said so. How epistolary it had all become.

Consumptive alcoholics do not often retain exact habits of mind, whether they have been trained as dentists or not. Doc, however, perhaps in some final blaze of exactitude, stayed able to pin things down, and, because he knew he was in a special position vis-à-vis last things, felt an appetite whetted: the sharper, the more pervasive the detail noted, the more *stationed* he was—at a precise spot observing flawlessly. So he gathered up trivia, whether having to do with him or not. Then he drew his conclusions, peacefully sifting the evidence as if he, and not Wyatt, were the inspector-general of Tombstone. He was almost tempted to go along with the general persuasion that he was involved in the holdup of the Benson stage; why disappoint people? It was, he admitted to himself, just the sort of thing he liked to do, but he would never have killed Bud Philpot, he would have shot a *horse*, as he had told everyone. What intrigued him most of all was the disguises. Now he knew where Wyatt's collection came from. He collected disguises and perhaps used them, though the vision of Wyatt as a stage robber (touted by some) struck Doc as fatuous— he made too much money already unless he was insatiably greedy. Well, maybe he was. Different people knew different Wyatts, he decided, and hardly anybody knew them all. He could see clearly now why he and Wyatt were unpopular with the gangster element: three Earps plus one Holliday were really getting in the way, obstructing the shakedown rackets to which the various outlaw clans, combined or individually, devoted their best energies. The four of them controlled the little town, village even, that had bloomed beyond all civilized control at least until they had set their stamp on it, officially or not. Out on the highways, riding shotgun for such enterprises as the Kinnear and Co. Line, they got in the way superbly, cutting the holdup rate to almost nought. Small wonder the outlaws hated them and wanted to get them out. It was a lovely thought, warming him, reviving the part of him that long ago had wanted to do something constructive in the world, fostering and healing. Corrupt sheriffs, unworthy deputies, psychopathic officials and rigged elections had all helped Tombstone become a wen of the worst order, a town full of pus, apt for squeezing and poultice. Lord God, Doc thought, all a man needs is the convenient farcicality of a village plentifully supplied with idiots and he's made.

For instance, what had he said to Behan, former lover of the gorgeous Josephine, whom Wyatt now courted and, it was said, hid in his bedroll? Quarrelsome Behan, especially at faro, began showing off in the saloon Doc ran, who stopped him in his tracks and told him never to play there anymore. With plenty of witnesses, Doc told him he was gambling with money Doc had given to his woman. That stopped him cold. Then, more idiocy, there was the row with Frank McLowery over the food at Nellie Cashman's Russ House, the barrel of Doc's six-gun aimed right at his mouth, daring him to throw up.

Doc tried to run a tight, orderly ship, with as much respect for gamblers, drinkers and diners as the unbuilt Tombstone church implied for the deity (doing duty for a carillon, the tall skeletal pylon with bell atop it rang on Sunday mornings and reminded Doc of the hanging water tower in Las Vegas, New Mexico). On he went, amassing minutiae, fingering the texture of events, the woof of lies and prevarications, like some immovable Ancient of Days gathering up the facts so as to have complete command on the Day of Judgment. The returning coach, *Grand Central*, brought back two men in their death shoes. There had been eight passengers. Bob Paul had changed horses at the usual place. It was crossing a big arroyo. The outlaw who did the talking said, Whoa, boys! or Halt! Bob Paul was a brave man among the brave, one of Wells, Fargo's best. So that Bud Philpot could warm his hands, they swapped places briefly. They slowed down for the grade at about ten o'clock. Philpot, shot in the heart, fell forward onto the hooves of his two-wheelers. The horses bolted as a volley of rifle fire came out of the mesquite. One bandit reeled away as if hit. To secure the trailing reins, Bob Paul had to abandon the fighting; the very idea of shooting back died. Bob Paul scrambled down on to the heaving wagon tongue to get the reins. The unraveled rope fibers of the disguises had been sewn to black cloth. Could this have been the work of the Earp women, who sewed awnings? The outlaws' trail led to the Redfield ranch, where two horses were gone, two worn-out ones replacing them. They beat Len Redfield within an inch of his life, knocking his quick temper clean out of him and threatening him with a lynching. The convention had always been that, if your horse was tired, you stopped at a ranch and left it until you came back that way, then took a fresh one from their herd, or you left a note saying what you'd done. Len knocked down one of the posse members, then they worked on him with terrible fervor. Next they found Luther King hiding on the ranch, and he confessed: he had held the horses during the holdup, and the outlaws were, as Wyatt suspected, Bill Leonard, the jeweler, Harry Head, and Jim Crane. Some twenty shots had been fired, or so someone said. What had Bob Paul answered? "I hold for no one." Peter Roerig, native of Kenosha, Wisconsin, was a miner. Doc made a mental note to examine the bullets when Wyatt had them. Clum the mayor and Parsons the Tombstone diarist, almost on the point of joining a second posse, went instead to a prayer meeting and then played chess. The posse, now divided into two that did not ride together, took Luther King to the home of Undersheriff Harry Woods, who allowed him to escape. Actually, it was the home of Woods's wife, except that he never married until 1886. Wyatt had no authority over King, his offense being a local not a federal one. Was Wyatt ever a deputy marshal? If not, why had he gone out there into the Arizona desert wilderness for seventeen days, during which Virgil's horse dropped dead beneath him? For one period of forty-eight hours, they had neither food nor water. For another, they had no food for five days. Yet Sheriff Behan claimed that Buckskin Frank Leslie, famous Indian tracker, was the life of the party, sang in sturdy voice, told engrossing stories, was never weary and always ready to ride on.

On his return, Wyatt marched in and demanded the newspapers, not even greeting Mattie. Luckily for her, she had saved them for him, so he pored over them while she boiled and ironed his best shirt. He was aching to see his fancy-woman in the Oriental.

Then he told Allie to prepare a bath for Virgil, but was told to can it, she took orders from no man save her husband. "Go home then," Virge said, "I want a bath." That clinched it. Surely Wyatt was not reading the Tucson *Weekly Star* to see if he had gotten away with something nefarious, but only, in true narcissistic vanity, to see what figure he had cut in accounts of the holdup. The horse that Doc had rented was Dunbar, the noted racehorse he and Wyatt had entered in the Christmas or Yuletide stakes. It was a blaze-face roan, a mount of unusual strength and stamina. So why could it not manage the nine-mile ride between Charleston and Tombstone? What had exhausted it?

Brooding on his haul of data, after being arrested on April 13 for making threats against life, and indicted by grand jury on May 30 for his part in a shooting affray, Doc began to wonder if his checkered life was working to its end. Accused of double murder by the crooked Sheriff Behan, he floated in and out of jail on a five-thousand-dollar bond posted by Wyatt, who got Virgil to lock Big Nose Kate in a hotel room to sober her up. Doc, she raved, had been beating her, in a foul mood because the bullion was lost. At the hearing, she fumbled and muddled, claiming she had signed a paper that contained she knew not what, perhaps an account of fearful battery inflicted on her by the mystery holdup man. On testifying, Wyatt said he had indeed asked Doc to join his posse, which was why Doc had had a fresh horse waiting after his ride back from the Charleston poker game.

"He may not remember," Wyatt said. "But I showed him Bob Paul's telegram, describing the holdup. In the excitement, I never sent for him, so he spent the night gambling." It was a gallant attempt, a little poem of corroboration, and Doc was glad of it. When Old Man Fuller told *his* story, he said that he and Doc had arrived in Tombstone about six o'clock.

"Eating dinner and gambling at the Alhambra," Doc said. "Wyatt Earp saw me there. Faro." There was some mix-up about times, however, with Wyatt saying he had seen Doc in the restaurant about six-thirty and some gamblers saying Doc had been bucking the bank for hours when Wyatt came in and showed him

the telegram. Those who were being helpful were being too much
so, but Doc was discharged to return to the riotous monotony he
liked, yet not without pondering his way of life, half-marveling at
the hedonistic willfulness of it all, and the deadly patterns it inter-
sected with. Off a man rode to a poker game in a nearby town,
only to find it over, so he rode back through the area of a holdup
to take dinner and gamble the evening away. Soon after, he was
charged with murder. Somebody, he was sure, kept trying too
hard, as Wyatt had out in the desert with his posse, north and
west along the Tangue Verde, Rincon, and Santa Catalinas, then
through the Oracles and Canada del Oro, eastward through the
Santa Cruz, across the San Pedro and back again to the Dragoons,
where, at Helm's Ranch, Behan and Breakenridge his loyal stool
pigeon joined up with the posse for a second time, adding the
aforesaid Buckskin Frank Leslie to the force. By then, Luther
King had already escaped, but none of the new arrivals mentioned
this fact to Wyatt Earp. So there he was, riding in circles to catch
somebody the sheriff was bound to let go anyway, mainly because
an election had been faked, and they did all this without supplies,
bedrolls, tents, mules, chuck wagon or maps. It was not as if they
were cowboys habituated to long cattle drives in the most arduous
conditions, Texas to Dodge, say. Surely, Doc thought, on reviewing the heap of evidence and guess, Wyatt must be someone in
disguise, a Wells, Fargo detective. It figured and justified the disguises in the suitcase.

Obsessed now to the point of craziness, with Big Nose Kate
gone and his very name derided, Doc went over and over what he
knew of the stagecoach affair, imagining how the horses at last
gave out, so that the posse had to double up on the last few rid-
able ones. After they all reached a desert waterhole on the brink
of the San Simon Valley, Behan and his crew split off, certain that
Wyatt and his eight or nine men were no longer in pursuit of the
outlaws. Pressing hard all through the night, Behan's group made
Joe Hill's ranch, some forty miles away, at dawn, Hill being a
Clanton supporter and a pal of Behan's. No help went out to the
Earps. Of course. Late the next night, Behan and his two deputies

reached the San Simon ranch, where they reported the Earps' emergency. Off went cowboys with supplies and fresh horses. Wyatt, Virgil, Morgan and Bob Paul had been without food for five days. *Five days*, Doc mused. I should have been with them; a thin man would have fit in well. Then they set off again behind Behan.

Or did Behan's men hunt the outlaws down near Cloverdale, New Mexico, close to the Mexican border? Where was Cloverdale? They asked, only to be misdirected, eventually reaching a deserted ranch house called the double 'dobe forty miles from Cienaga. Leaving there, they made a circular tour of a huge plain devoid of trees or water and returned at noon to the double 'dobe. Their horses grazed, then on the next day they made it as far as San Simon Cienaga with the urgent news about the Earp party and hired a cowboy to take them some provisions in a hurry, who met them en route and, oh, were they relieved to see him, almost devouring him along with the food, so little able were they to tell where it left off and he began. As for Crane, Head and Leonard, they had gone into New Mexico and that following summer were killed at Huachita by some cowboys intent on the reward. Was it possible that Virgil not Wyatt Earp was the leader of the posse, because he had the legal clout whereas Wyatt was only an undercover detective?

Doc sighed, swigged some bourbon and wished he could sleep it all away, this grotesque tapestry of lies, rumor and accusation, which wound around his brain, a winding sheet from hell, at which he kept on plucking like an invalid in bed pulling threads from the coverlet to clean his teeth with. Who had bashed Big Nose Kate about if not he? It could have been any of her tricks, to whom she was never polite, with whom she was never leisurely. She was a lubricious abacus of increasing mental vagueness, sopping with liquor and bad food. She could no more be trusted to say who had blacked her eyes than she could to give correct change to a customer. Virgil had arrested her for being drunk and disorderly, which was bad enough, fining her $12.50, a sum she apprehended so little she literally threw money at it, unable to count. Virgil handed her her change, lamenting that she was not the whore she used to be, with a neat unwrinkled eye, bulbous lips unmarred by cold sores, chin clear and free of baby eczema.

When Doc at last walked out of custody, almost into Wyatt's bear hug, he offered to get out of the way, having caused enough trouble: "Say the word, Wyatt, and I'll leave Tombstone, I really will." In reply Wyatt told him, "You send that fool woman away and I'll be satisfied, Doc." That very evening, Big Nose Kate left town, seen by neither of them again, except for one bizarre moment in Doc's remaining life.

"I'll go too," Doc whispered, hoarse and coughing.

"You'll stay put, buddy," Wyatt said. "I need you."

"Gittin you a bad name," Doc told him.

"Protectin my back, mister. You stay put. You ain't the personification of law and order, you're the friendly force behind the guns."

Nonplussed, Doc could only recall that he had gone to Charleston that day armed with shotgun and six-guns because certain men hung out there who detested him and, given half a chance, would blow him away. When had it become a crime to go armed into enemy terrain? Was he always supposed to stay put, among friends? Were there consolations? A few: Bill Leonard and Harry Head had tried to hold up that store in Huachita and had been killed for their trouble. Scratch one friend, but that was the way of the West. Old Man Fuller had come through with a useful hunk of truth, but his son Wes was a Clanton bandit through and through and could not be trusted. Off Kate had gone with a thousand dollars in her pocket, as glad to have it, it seemed, as to have had their entire relationship, and eager to get away with it before he changed his mind and snatched it back.

"It's yours," he told her. "Bon voyage."

"Still trying to talk Hungarian!" She snarled and let him have it about once saving his life back in Fort Griffin.

"It's all I can spare," he told her. "Buy a whorehouse and settle in before the maggots drag you down."

His sarcasm usually worsted her lusty anatomical abuse, and this time was no exception. Weeping with operatic rage, she went away, once again slipping into the state of mind that had enabled her to become the promiscuous wanderer she was, somehow shelving Doc until boredom and satiety drove her back the worse for wear, with always the faint putrefying smell of rampage upon her as if she had been with animals rather than with men: a sulfur sting in the nostrils, an aroma of singed bristle as if some overused handkerchief, dried out again and again without being laundered, had come to liquid life again in undisclosed flames and finally gone up in smoke, its caches of green phlegm disappearing last. On the way down, and slowing up, Big Nose Kate moved geographically onward to more of the same, far from propelled by her lover, but having committed the cardinal sin called treachery. With her, for a while, went Doc's finesse; he drank more, got into incessant rows even while trying to avoid them, and walked in the frightful shadow of the suspicion that he had become a chronic, lewd embarrassment to Wyatt Earp, his hero if he ever had one.

The intolerable temptation, Doc decided, was to sit back and let rumor live your life for you; in other words, grow a spine of wet bread. If they wanted him a villain, then he would play the villain with Southern ingenuity. In any case, the Tombstone climate was one of guilt and crime; whatever you did would sooner or later acquire a patina of disrepute, mainly because, where nobody thought the best of anyone, no one ended up guiltless. It was as if the original sin of which Mattie sometimes wrote to him had come to life in their twisted lives, urging them toward things even worse, from the unintended, casual peccadillo to the monstrous deed that earned you a length of rope. Who on earth cared what they thought of you in Tombstone? Just as well to worry about your reputation in hell. There were those, like the Tombstone diarist George Parsons, who made no secret of his scribbling habit, who emerged in the center of the road as decent, honest men, intent only on the facts as one observant sensibility found them. Then there was everybody else, some of them actually saying Wyatt played second fiddle to Virgil, that Wyatt—barkeep, cardsharp, gunslinger, bigamist and viveur, church deacon, private detective, bunco artist and real-estate con man, among other roles—was nothing more than a gifted exhibitionist. That was bad enough: the god with a sculptured nose had feet of manure. Then there was all sorts of other stuff, including Doc Holliday the stagecoach bandit. How could you believe anything, with the faculty of belief falling into disuse? Some exquisite and once-to-be-hallowed picture of glory had broken apart like a dropped jigsaw puzzle and would never fit together again. Wyatt found seventeen rifle shells. Morgan Earp had run down Luther King on the Redfield ranch. Wyatt had shown Doc the bullet that killed Bud Philpot, a hideous-looking .45 caliber. The horse known as

Dunbar, which Wyatt and Doc had entered in the Yuletide, had the same name as the intended recipient of the horse that Luther King was selling to—John Dunbar. Doc thought he was dreaming, subject to an intrusive daytime spell that blurred everything. Had Allie really said that she wanted to go on over to Wyatt and Mattie's place on Fremont and First, to see if Wyatt's disguises were still there in the suitcase? What did she suspect him of? Had he Doc ever given Kate a black eye, a busted lip, a swollen ear? Recently? Could it truly be that Allie and Virge had never married, and what was this propensity among them all to pretend to be married to one woman or another, or *and* another, and yet one further, just to sound respectable while retaining the right to abandon any of them in the interests of private gratification? What did it mean that a stagecoach was *en bonanza* or *en borusca*? Who in his cups had uttered such phrases? Loaded with ore or empty? He would have to guess unless he asked, and he never asked. Surely, Doc went on in nightmare scrutiny of truths told, Bob Paul, that huge and sturdy man, pillar of the community, was no bandit; had he been so, the cleverest accomplice of all, he would have been able to stop the horses, if he was at the reins. It would not have cost him a mile and his accomplices the bullion. Had Doc Holliday asked Wyatt Earp for one thousand dollars to hand over to the departing Kate, to make sure she went, to make sure she would stay away until she'd spent it? No, it had been his own money kept in a roll Doc stashed in the safe of Lou Rickabaugh, half-owner of the Oriental.

Disorganized honesty, like malign reporting, fouls up everything around it, including even the words of the wise. Doc's confusion, and inability to fuse the facts, was his own private map of the region's disgrace, with murderers flouting the law, outlaws rigging elections, and the very governor of the state fomenting crime while in absentia. If there had ever been a moral breakdown in ancient Greece, a failure of the country's nerve, something Doc had distantly heard about as a contemporary event but geographically far away, then surely there had been one in Tombstone too, in a town founded on greed and silver, on dog-eat-dog. With outlawry riding high, meditating vendettas against those who had notably failed to bring it to book for flagrant crimes, a lawman had little standing, was a castrato not allowed to sing.

Everybody's taking sides, Doc thought. It'll soon not be a matter of who you are, but of what flag you're under. We'll all be cannon fodder. Law had broken down, and so had even the conventional, strained goodwill that could still happen during a chance encounter with a Clanton or a McLowery during a morning stroll to the Oriental's humidor. Civility would fray away like paint under a hot desert sun, and the only means of communication would be the six-gun, promoted from one third of human exchange to almost one hundred percent. They were in for a range war confined in a small town, and the only way to prepare for it was to brush up on vocabulary and idioms. At once he took to riding out into the desert with a bag of bottles, there to shoot hell out of them while specifying vulnerable parts of Kate's body, then the names of those others who had lied about him, killing them in effigy. Purged by all this gunplay, and the concomitant verbal chuntering, he rode back to Tombstone with his head full of Latin, vowing to write Mattie a series of letters, which, since he was now at a watershed or climacteric of history, he would give titles to, the only problem being what to name them. After they're written, he decided, I'm bound to know. Nonetheless, he shuffled a few semi-pertinent phrases as he rode, wetting his throat from a bottle of bourbon, and mouthing the words at the empty, azure sky, surely the cap of a civilized, noble landscape: The Stagecoach Letter, The First Numbered Tombstone Letter, The Agua Prieta Letter or The Letter of Swarthy Water, ah that was it, a town in Mexico, even if only just! The Spanish would appeal to her perhaps, though not as much as would a title with a saint's name included. He composed as he rode, slowing up as inspiration came, speeding as it vanished, until he suddenly realized he was out in the open with scarcely a care, in the middle of enemy territory, an area almost as dangerous for him as that between Tombstone and Charleston, into which to reach the poker game he had gone heavily armed. Then headed east (and west on his return), he had been been aimed at the Huachucas, today northeast (and southwest), at the Dragoons. Now it all fell into place; Tombstone, a town on the brink of apoplexy, sat equidistant from four mountain ranges, and it was for these he would name his four letters, beginning with the Dragoons (now behind him). Captious as this decision was, it brought order and proportion into his bewildered mind, which was just as well. He had realized that today, no more than any other day, he had left behind him a trail of blood-flecked foam spat from the back of a horse, the only man in the terrain to do any such thing. They could track him thus and grind him into the desert, even conferring upon him the epitaph *Whatever doesn't kill you makes you stronger.* Not meat for Mattie; he tried to come up with more wholesome thoughts, all of a sudden ravished to the point of tears by his own frailty.

Dearest Mattie, Things are really beginning to hum around here, which is not to say they don't hum usually, or elsewhere. I just have this feeling of climax. The good fellows (us) have been doing things in the wrong way, setting ourselves up as the local military police or whatever, and they all resent it. We moved into their town with our own ideas of law and order (I guess, an almost Eastern-Southern concept of it) and disrupted them. We are, as the French say, "de trop," and they sort of discourage us from asserting ourselves. It's too bad, because I think we were genuinely doing some good. Now, a bunch of outlaws has held up a stagecoach, killed the driver and one other, and there is nobody to convict as all of them have got themselves killed south of the border or as near as makes no difference. The problem is, are we to look for scapegoats anyway, or let the whole matter slide? There are too few of us, too many Indians. I mean, they are not Indians but desperadoes.

How are you? I have not heard from you in a blue moon, although I have been here, and quiet, for quite a while now, pursuing my dismal round. The woman I used to mention to you has left town, but not before I was able to provide her with some funds for the new life she will doubtless embark on as soon as she finds a fresh town. It would be well for all of us to get out of Tombstone, I think we have used up our welcome. I wonder if we ever had one. The townspeople are affable enough, but the "cowboys" in the outlying areas, the ranches, tend to give trouble, previ-

ously having had the whole show to themselves, you see. Here, by the way, we tend to use the term "cowboy" to mean an unruly sort of outlaw who links up with other desperadoes and continues to pretend to be no more than a cowpuncher when in fact he is a people-puncher. They loot and steal whenever they want to, and the local constabulary, as one might call them, are in cahoots with them, thanks to the almost universal local practice of corrupt elections to public office.

How tedious I am, reciting all this, when what I truly wanted to return to, in a letter, was your idea, not so much of prayer as of God's presence, like a huge leg dangling like one coming over the side of a bath (someone getting comfy in a tub) and wriggling His toes. What a weird thought. So, you say, we look outside, at the mesquite (my version) or the flowers (it is still summer for us both), 1881, I am getting older whereas you remain the same, and we see the leg of God dangling into things, oh at least the size of a Florida just overhanging everything as if it has been there all along and might need attention. Mattie: Does God need attention?

Somewhile back, you said yes, God likes to have His presence documented to Himself, not that he needs it, He just prefers it that way, which is very much as I feel about Tombstone. I often think, What am I doing here? Does God think that too? Does God ever wonder what on earth He is doing in the universe when, so to speak, He might be elsewhere doing something superior? It sounds ridiculous, yet not altogether, and I suppose it makes most sense when we around here are behaving at our most godlike, if you will pardon the metaphor. It is a god's role to pardon metaphor, I suppose, since without gods we would not rise or sink to metaphor. No sirree, we would not, though I sometimes think nuns have no business pardoning metaphor since, fixed as they are, they need all the metaphor they can get, at least until the huge lightning storm of inspiration strikes, and then metaphor or simile is just a prop.

That may have been tactless, my six-gun way of putting things. Shoot first and catechize afterwards. I am quite serious about that big foot dangling over the side of the tub and am trying to think of it seriously too. In some ways I think of nothing else, which is like saying God is everywhere; so that big foot is all I can think about, whatever else is around, even when I am riding alone in the desert as only recently, in a distinct empti-

ness full of potential, of course, the Tombstone of the future, if it has any future. Once you have let that big leg into your life, you think of nothing else. Would I become a monk? Besides, how do you pray to it? Would you? Maybe not, just being aware of it is a form of prayer. Thank you, leg, for my being alive, even here, in this dryasdust emptiness. There is one good thing about this place: beyond the town, small enough as it is, there is little to distract you from what you really need to think about. It is a good place to come and have a reconciliation with yourself. There are limits, but I have come to recognitions here I would have found impossible in Dodge City, thanks to the hard burning light, the steady presence of mountains, like beings that crawl toward you when you were not looking but stop suddenly when you turn around to look at them, and, oh, the Earps, those venturesome, original, sometimes puzzling modern-day heroes. An odd back-to-front letter, this. I wanted to salute you as if I were riding toward the Dragoon Mountains, so now I do.

This is Dragoon letter number one.

Each time I write, instead of skulking here in the Oriental, which I won't call my favorite dive as that will give the wrong impression, I should head out into the desert and squat on a rock to scratch away on my writing pad, on this heavy cream overlay paper, or whatever the watermark says it is (can't decipher it inside here in the O.). I am well enough, still have a cough and have found a peppermint swill at the barbershop to get, pardon, the long familiar taste of blood out of my mouth—that dusty, metallic, rotting taste you will never know unless kissed on the lips by God's leg, which can never happen. It was just one of my more cactusy thoughts since I miss you and your scrutiny of my predicament. I am here for my health, just imagine, after all that dawdling, and if I don't eat silverdust, I might survive.

He made a mental note to pack an overweek bag when he returned to his lodgings, something to keep by him in case of sudden flight (a not unfamiliar event in his frontier life). He would need disguises too, he thought, as well as hard tack, beef jerky, coffee, flour and lard. One day soon, he imagined, he and the Earps would have to do a midnight flit, driven to it by the rustler gangs who ruled the Tombstone roost. What he could not understand was why they had not done so already. And it would be very different from the parting he had had from Big Nose Kate, that vociferous trollop.

She, at the door: "Give us a big wet kiss, then."

He, inert on the bed: "Which end do you want it from?"

There would be no more of that kind of thing, no more paid-up worn-out old bags from Buda, aromatic as cow slop. One tale that plucked at him was how Wyatt's exquisite Josephine, the Jewish one, had made the long journey (like Doc) from New York to Dodge and so to Tombstone with a full bladder, and, being unaccustomed to train travel, had been too embarrassed to go and relieve herself. Surely not, he thought: let's leave it at Tucson to Tombstone, she would have burst on that other journey, long before Dodge. I know how she felt. Then he attended to his letter again, picturing the secessive Mattie in her dun robes, wimple and breastplate (he imagined armor where she wore starched linen):

I think of your few possessions and wish they were more plentiful; you have severed yourself from so much. There is your cake of hardly lathering soap, the comb made of bone, the toothbrush filched from the dark ages with soot at the roots of its bristles. Black boot polish smelling of locomotives. For painkilling powders you have to ask, as for tooth powder and nail scissors. Perhaps you even have to ask for a nail file, matches, a smear of grease for a burn. I am presuming, which is the position of one who does not know but yearns for knowledge. You are not even allowed to tell us these things. There are so many secrets you have been sworn to. Are there any you can divulge, or is yours a secret society like some of the outlaw gangs in Arizona?

Tell me all you can, I need a picture of your world.

I know nuns have been photographed, but can we see their features? I picture you behind grilles, shutters, birdcages, stained-glass windows, mouthing at heaven the prayers no one can hear. Apropos of our prayers, did you say tall star or wide star? I thought about that star and wonder if, say, heavy, giant, broad, interminable or incessant might do. Clearly one should not waste time fobbing off God with attributes, for God has none. Correct? God has no name but irresistible power. If only this were a tutorial, with me in the easy chair and you in the hard one, if that is correct. A giant, poring over the land of Arizona, could set his finger into the Grand Canyon and lose it quite, such is the hugeness and the depth. Out riding, I often feel I am in a stage set among tastefully painted scenery, and I always end up thinking (after Blake) did he who made the lamb make thee? Not you, the topography, of course. I think I may make it to Colorado after all, although some have told me that here is friendly to the lungs, while others have told me to head for Yuma or Mexico. Here, on a hot day, you can go sit in the shade of a tree, and feel cold, so weak is the power of the dried-out air to contain the warmth. I could make a metaphor from that, I know, it is like the universe retaining no trace of us after we are gone. I do not mean the hall of records (your Doc for instance always makes a point of registering to vote wherever he goes, so he will always be on record as having been in a certain place). I mean, I do it so as to vote, not to leave spoor, but spoor I do leave, like a tracked animal.

I am wrong about the universe, am I not? Of course it retains traces of us, but we humans are too thick to recognize them, too unqualified, too unbelieving. We go out into a whole transmutation and that is our lot, and though we might endure as angel septums or star powder we will never be able to celebrate the fact. When you are gone, you cannot cele- brate what you have turned into.

In his pocket, mangled and smudged, one of her letters, the most telling of all, tempted and teased him; he had never been able to answer it, since it asked of him things he could not fathom. Did he believe? If so, in what? Did he love her in Christ, whatever that meant? If only she had asked him tenses. But then, why should she ask him about anything? Locked away where she was, she had no option but to become studious, feeding her mind while her body withered—or so he assumed. He wondered if, as she read what he wrote, she could ever see the interruptions, the joins, obviously having no idea when a gunshot had rung out or some drunk had pitched headlong into the table he was writing at, or some taunting song had disturbed the roots of his being sung too fast and too loud, or the call of nature had intervened and off he had gone like a bridesmaid clutching his wafer of paper lest it disappear forever. She never saw the seams in his letters, but he did and began to wish for wholly uninterrupted writing, available only back in a crib or in the stuffy fastness of a hotel room (when the gambling went well and he could afford a little splurge). He was a hotel creature anyway, whether living there or not, a man wholly incapable of looking after such folderol as bedding, laundry, trash, as willing to live in a cocoon of leftovers as to tidy up after himself. He wondered if he should incorporate interruptions into the letters, thus introducing Mattie to the tempo and tumult of Tombstone life, night or day; but he decided against it, preferring to cultivate a smoothness of prose as against an epistle altogether symptomatic and uncontrolled. His writing entered a nunnery sooner or later, and the last thing he wanted was to present some harum-scarum image of himself and the life he led. Lady Luck had been kind to him, as he savagely said to those who asked, so he was now living in the Oriental like a turbulent infant swimming in the font it had been baptized in. There he was, scribbling, a fixture at the writing tables as at the gaming ones, in either case a statue of introversion, his mind on matters distant and abstruse. Don't bother Doc, they whispered, he's planning a letter (this at the faro and poker tables). Don't bother Doc, he's working out a new way to win (this at the writing tables). He used all the facilities of the hotel, a thorough guest, it might be said, sometimes realizing that Mattie made her own bed, collected her own trash (little of that) and sometimes made her own snacks. His mode was never to do anything for himself.

Then came a messenger, oddly bearing a six-gun rather than a tray on which Doc might have deposited a coin as tip. In the Oriental it would have been kosher to put a bullet on the tray, only to hear it fired moments later. There was a package for him at the main desk, that bulwark of mahogany, imported from Belgium. Why Belgium? No, that was the rug. Surely the mahogany had come from some deep, murmuring, steamy forest. This was not the era of bombs, disguised as pagodas or books, and as he approached he could see something huge and fawn dominating the bench it sat on. Was this his? It was. Someone unknown had sent him a flower, a giant stapelia (as he was later to find out), otherwise known as a carrion flower, notorious for its evil smell, if sniffed too close. He saw a raw and menacing cactus, one star-shaped flower near the base of the stems, its segments heavily rippled with purple-crimson striations. A gorgeous, enormous flower, at least a foot across, unadmired by anyone save the attendant, who had kept a strict distance from it and was urging Doc to get it out of there as soon as he could. Thus began the march upstairs, up two flights, the plant making a polite swish as it rocked to and fro, and his nostrils rebelling as he got an occasional whiff of some nourishing process gone completely awry. No, he rebuked himself, this was the way it was, the carrion cactus, and he now smelled into what some of his thousand dollars had gone. Big Nose Kate had made her statement from somewhere in the territory, invisible and vengeful, aching to do him damage, and he would retaliate, he knew, by adopting the plant and taking it with him, installing it on the gaming tables, or even the writing ones, cautioning the unwary to keep their distance. Here was something else to write to Mattie about, for all the world as if he lived in a civilized place and people sent flowers as an act of grace and tenderness. This one, however, she had aimed at his bad behavior, hoping to wound and disgust. He would show her a trick or two, converting the carrion flower into an altarpiece worthy of devoutest horticulture.

Why was he so certain who had sent the flower? There had been no card. No dread message had been carved into the finger-like stems. Why Big Nose Kate? Because it was her style of doing things: impetuous, heavy-handed, coarse—the carrion touch. Well, he could toss it out into the contained trash compound behind the hotel, but that was not Doc's own style. He was an economizer, a make-doer, a snapper up of disregarded trifles; he relished the torrent of minutiae that the world was, which included him, and made him, to the eye of God's leg dangling out of the Milky Way, someone quite negligible. So, he would keep it and attribute it to her, making of it something glorious and lyrical to write Mattie about, the stench omitted of course, this being the very season to appreciate it in: late summer, as he saw it, June being late only to a Southerner or Easterner because it had the torrid heat of August elsewhere. Those watching Doc demurely mount the stairs bearing his potted plant made the usual erotic remarks, but he ignored them all, careful to march evenly and straight, not favoring the side he held it on. This was really living; his room lacked books, pictures, tapestries, mementoes, photographs (apart from one of Mattie in her teens and another of the Valdosta swimming hole), and a flower was going to provide a focus: fire, sundial, talking point, and who knew what else? Doc, who had made a new career out of the bacillus, who had redevised his life in grievous terms, now took the gift of a carrion flower to heart and began to regard it as another life offered him in tender esteem, accepting potluck as divine intervention. What a thing to write Mattie about, who would be lucky to have even a carrion cactus delivered to her crib, surely an essential part of God's armamentarium yet, because floral and seductive, too much of a decoration to be allowed into a nunnery.

He didn't get it: if the All was God's and nobody else's, how could her Church exclude any part of it as too beguiling? If God's stuff all represented some aspect of God, then how could they exclude any of it? Nothing could fall out of the universe. He could hardly wait to pop open the sloppy mechanism that opened and closed his door; he wanted to be asking her these religious questions that had begun to plague him like a new disease. What he did not know when he re-entered his room was that, in no time at all, he was going to feel so much at home with this randomly arrived flower that he would do things with it never before achieved by human agency. That night, choking, he coughed blood into the dry soil that held the bloom in place, wondering if he was poisoning or fertilizing the root, and in the most absent-minded way resituated the plant in its rude earthenware pot to his bedside, there to provide him with both sputum space and solace, a bit of himself to be beside himself with.

Next letter, which would go into the same envelope as yesterday's, he began to tell her about the cactus, at least about its arrival: the sort of event you might expect in a suave hotel in the deep South, with lackeys running to and fro and busboys in satin turbans waiting for a tip or a promise to goose. It stirred his memory, he knew, brought his childhood back, but he said nothing of the carrion aspect or of the plant's status as a spittoon. How firmly embedded it already was into his erratic life; he was amazed at himself, so readily converting a spear to the heart into a muff, say, or a hot water bottle for his toes. Whatever Big Nose Kate had intended by it had misfired, and this revealed how little she knew of his predispositions, his openness; she had always wondered why he handled a six-gun in such a loving way, assuming he doted on death, quite ignorant of his fetishistic feel for the rotundities, the ribbing, the springiness of trigger and hammer, the sense that in pulling back on the trigger he was holding on to a world of huge structure bound to keep him safe. The hammer reminded him of the narrow cone of flesh that dangled in the mouth from the roof of the soft palate toward the back of the tongue: uvula, of course, soft stalactite of the gag reflex, kin to the oiled, strokeable hammer whose rapid motion defeated the eye and mimicked an insect's barb. She never realized he lived in all worlds, not just in two or three: the mouth, say; Dodge; and that of spat-up blood. Oh no, he lived in a hundred more than those, linking them together with jubilant analogies. Not that he had ever talked to her of these, or schooled her in them, any more than she had schooled him in basic Hungarian; his response to the world remained private, and he doubted if he had even gotten it through to Mattie, surely of all confidants the sweetest subtlest one. It was enough for him to feel the vast web of being on his senses, knowing full well, though he could never prove it, that a man drilled through the heart in Tombstone affects a nun teaching apodictics in a Savannah convent. Simply, the ponderousness of a weapon in his hand made him feel pulled toward the center of things, maybe the core of the planet, and steadied him for a minute or two until, having fired, or set the cocked hammer down again, he relented, relaxed, and prepared to resume unoffensive life anew. He strove hard not to be premature in anything, yet was willing to make a mistake, shooting first if in doubt, although making every effort to wing the offender without giving up the supplement of blowing his brains out a minute or two later. It was useless to think while shooting; indeed, shooting was more a self-administered jolt than it was a conscious act.

A plant, however, was something always to think about, even if like stinking rafflesia, say, it smelled worse than the carrion cactus. Perhaps blood would make it mellow, rising to the level of old and faded patchouli, much as the sweat glands of some animals yielded up a scent to drive the ladies wild. He was familiar with morning mouth, as a dentist would have to be, and he had encountered in his studies the phenomenon of the jailed prisoner falling in love with his own body odors, so much so as to live out his sentence in a cocoon of self-administered vapor. Had there been fewer spines, he might have taken the plant to himself and hugged it, quite forgetting whom it came from, setting aside the possibility that it had come from Mattie after all (or her aunts) and had been an error in transcription, meant to be an Easter cactus, a coal to Newcastle, with weak bristles and starry scarlet flowers. Why would not a nun or her devout aunts (unless letter-shuffling was an index to slight misbehavior among the pieties) send an Easter cactus? How much more religious than that could a cactus get? No matter, he doted on the thing, assigning it to Kate so fast he had no time even to proffer nominal thanks to her putrefying shade.

It was here, a shower of green gramophone needles.

With a low-hung bloom like a bulbous nose waiting to nuzzle.

Not a nose, but a face, ruddy and furry, hardly a flower at all, but somehow on the way to becoming flushed flesh.

O.K.: The Corral, the Earps, and Doc Holliday

Doc decided to name it, but had nothing in mind; nothing came to him, and the words lingering in his memory from other use did not fit—Dragoon, Mule Pass, Huachuca, Whetstone, all inappropriate and vacant. He wondered and wondered, uninclined to dub it Mattie, or even Sister Mattie, Sister Mary Melanie, or even St. Vincent. The name would come, he knew, no doubt suggested by Mattie herself, who might take to this essential christening of nature's force.

Spine? No. Too obvious, and misleading.

Spike? Facetious, but not bad.

Arrow? Off the point.

Bristle? As of a toothbrush?

Nettle? Misleading again.

He gave up. Thistle was no good either. He was on the wrong track, fixing on the wrong element when he should have looked hard at the flower, that sullen almost bronze mouth with its five bulbous lips curling away from his gaze in revulsion, craning backward for the comfort of the spines. He decided to ask her, providing only the needed information and making up a little tale about the plant's origin so as not to offend.

Dear Mattie: The strangest thing happened. A cactus nobody wanted because it smelled bad has appeared at the Oriental, looking lonely on a bench by the desk, so after a while I appropriated same and carted it off to my room, where it now reigns supreme, all spikes and one flower, a brown one. Trouble is, I have no idea what to call it, not that a flower has to have a name; it's only that flowers are so rare with me that I want to mark the occasion somehow. Would St. Vincent be sacrilegious? I am no judge of such things. Please suggest another name I can feel at home with.

Otherwise, life here goes on in its humdrum way. Some days you notice its nature, others not. One day I notice as if for the first time how doors never really close; there are always chinks and the door trembles in the opening as if unsure of its destiny. Most of the doors have warped, being thin, so you get odd effects of light and wind, and the only time you think a door can be truly closed is when it's wide open and you have briefly forgotten how awkward the thing is and never quite does what it is supposed to do.

Paul West

Vignettes of life in hot, hot Tombstone, where fans bring little relief. We all go around in a cloud of baking heat, humans as loaves. The trains seem only just balanced on the rails, wobbling and heaving; why they don't come off I never know. The whole place has this temporary, half-hatched quality, thrown together so as to make the mark of some kind of civilization at this point on the map. Like somebody strewing a few eggshells around. When the filles de joie quarrel, the barkeep rings what he calls the Order bell, and they usually stop it within seconds. It is like being at a boxing match. Many of them have British accents, you never know why, but it shows what a country exports. All the shirts (I presume) have too-long sleeves because the men here, without jackets, which is common, like to wear armbands above the elbow enabling them to pluck up the excess length and stow it upstairs, maybe to suggest muscle. It looks as if they are wearing garters on their arms, both a frilly feminine and a severe cigar-chomping look, y'know.

You would not like any of this, it being too coarse, methinks. It is after all the frontier, the very edge of something drastic, such as Mexico, or near enough the Pacific to count as a hinterland. I am disposed to like it, although the denuded primitive quality of life here reminds me of too much I have left behind. When will I ever hear the languid, biased South again? The sound here is raw, tumultuous, and urgent. People are no great respecters of persons. There is constant violent death, rustling, swindling, crookery of all kinds. Yet the air, supposedly, does me good. After a while you meet the magic curve of your life and say, it used to be downward and now it is flatter, the prelude to its climbing upward again, from bottom left to upper right.

He wanted to write something about the tonic effect of Tombstone, but he shrank from the alliteration, which made him sound too glib (so, was there some permitted degree of glibness?). He was trying both to tell a truth and sanitize as well, but something new had begun to nag at him. If Catholics, or even Christians in a lump, had a religion that transcended all the horrors of life, why then did they avoid the horrors and cultivate an almost milquetoast view of life, as if history or depravity were something they needed to be protected against? It was a real question. He had never understood this; surely the people who needed to be pro-

214

tected were those who had no faith at all. The hard part was asking her in a polite way that would not end their correspondence. He tried.

Mattie, if a religion transcends, then it transcends all, doesn't it? There is no need to save people from depravity in that case. It is only when religion has failed that people have to be protected. True?

No, that was no way to do it, but he let the question stand as an example of good intentions gone awry, risking it, trusting in her goodwill and her tolerance of heathen insolence. Surely those with faith would put up with much that unbelievers had to say. If he had known more of the Inquisition, he might not have been so sanguine, poking around in areas where hot irons, squassation and the rack had settled thorny questions in the old days.

Perhaps he was feeling the influence of Mexico, that Sargasso Sea of morbid piety to the immediate south, where death's-heads, skeletons and rotting dogs occupied the popular imagination, where death was always a fellow diner, where life was a figure set against the ground of death rather than the other way around. Mexico, like some blue-black ocean, was pulling on him, informing him that what, in his mind, he ducked away from was always there, fangs ready, appetite stoked, will resonant as a buzzard's cry. Eyes in skulls, he thought; that's Mexico, and once more he addressed himself to the half-handsome way of his letters, popping a toe into the slough of despond although spurning it on her behalf; but that ambivalence in the Christian attitude continued to bother him, even as he raised his inelegant pen.

We are close to Mexico here. The Pacific too. Yet I feel Mexico much more than I do the Pacific, no doubt because Mexico has beliefs whereas the Pacific, well, we haven't yet been able to catch her with an idea in mind! I doubt if we ever will or, if we do, it will be a subtle one beyond the level of Let waves form. The drooping leg of God is very apparent in Mexico, I think; it dangles and bleeds, it rots away, it recalls venison, it seems to get bigger with time, high over Oaxaca, low over Guerrero. Take your pick! I see the haunch of God over an infinite pond of blue-black ink. At least I do now.

He paused to inhale the flower, not so much trying to nauseate himself as seeking resistance to what he felt was flowing all too well. He liked it when things got hard to say. One touch of Mexico and he was off, as if he had been there all his life without ever learning the language, not much of it anyway. He had not realized it yet, the carrion flower was what had prompted the pipe dream (if that) of Mexico; when he did, he might call the flower "Mexico," obvious as that was. Exhaling, he knew he had a clearer idea of what the flower smelled like: private parts, unkempt mouths, armpits, civet, not a wholesome smell by far, but sickeningly seductive, a smell to send you cringingly forward—into the next paragraph.

So much for Mexico. I wanted to tell you more of what goes on here, but I may be repeating myself. I look at the same object and always come away with a different impression, a new account of it, so life will never wear out on me. One thing remains in mind as the folkway of the region, elegant enough as a preliminary. I mean how the gunman's hand peels back the bottom corner of his coat and gets it out of the way, with a nervous, hesitant gesture partly holding it in place, but only a little as the full flexure of the hand has other work to do, or will in seconds. That's how. You see them again and again, those hands that might be shielding the spout of a teapot, or seeking relief by opening the top button of a jacket or shirt, just that touch of preparatory movement, then the hand hovering over the butt with the little finger keeping the corner of the coat out of harm's way. I have stared at that, in flagrante, scores of times, actually beginning to think There, that is just about this poor devil's last fidget on earth, little that he knows. You see, that is how the winner feels, not that he is not at some time going to lose, but I wonder if the opponent ever looks at my hand doing the same thing and asks himself what I am doing, whether I am thinking or not.

Reverie of a gunslinger over. Sorry about that, but I leave it in as a sideshow, an index to what life around here has sunk to. Even stripped of our weaponry, as we had to be in Dodge City, we find our hands going through the same motions, forever palping the vacancy, the holster, the coat's corner, the cool alien butt. I think we all rehearse, especially those with a reputation to lose, those with notches on their six-gun (I do no such thing, of course, and have committed far less mayhem than I get credit for).

It was impossible to be having the life and to keep it all under wraps; it leaked out, perhaps irking her because she imagined all the other details he suppressed, but he found himself unable to talk Tombstone without letting through some of its least benign qualities. He would never tell her, though, how the shot man's becoming an instant puppet, rag doll, burned in his mind: that ghastly sudden change, all muscular integrity flopped, all slack. The West, crowded scene that it was, belonged more to those who idealized it at a distance than to those caught up in it. Mattie at a distance had no view of it at all, but received news of it, thanking God for convents. She had concluded long ago that Doc had found his way there to put his soul through torment, in that way to become a better human; talk of the bacillus she discounted as a mild excuse. The soul came first, even though she was pragmatic, cerebral and earthy, and she paid Doc the ultimate compliment that he had arranged things in the right order. Did she know of whorehouse birthdays for young whippersnappers, with two girls working betimes on the lower body while a third swung a golden shower onto the virginal stomach beneath, or heard whores saying, as they liked to, there were two things they could not do: make love to a woman and piss up a wall. The first one wasn't always true anyway, they said it out of conspiratorial bravado.

After a slump, he wrote, *you know, you just* know *you'll soon be shooting again.*

He stopped, sensing dangerous territory he must steer away from, instead segueing to something pretty. So he wrote *But you don't have to.*

An unthinkable distance away, she wrote him a reply on his exact choice of word there.

Why have to?

He could not answer, but wrote *Kismet or something.*

Now he knew she was scratching away at a complex reply beginning with the words *God is not kismet. You choose.*

It was going badly, this telepathic duet, bound sooner or later to lead into a discussion of free will, the *Zeitgeist*, and God's words to Jesus on the Cross. He was just going to add to this fruitless exchange the phrase *Scores to settle* when a voice and a familiar step entered his room and the language changed altogether.

"Well, Doc, that shit-eatin woman has leff, I'll be dogged" (pronounced dogd). "You done well to send her packin."

"Look what she sent me, Wyatt."

Wyatt agreed as how the carrion flower stank. "Yew could git yourself a piece of year-old round meat and have the same effect. Yew ain't goin to sleep at all in here from now on."

Doc agreed, but could hardly convince Wyatt, who produced from behind him, up to now screened by his bulk, a familiar suitcase. "Brought yew a prisint, Doc. You doin well with two."

Now Doc would own the masks and other gear, ready for when he held up stagecoaches or beat up women behind the hotel. Or when he loitered, detecting for whoever wanted him, Wells, Fargo or somebody else. "Thank you," he sighed.

"Don't menshun it," Wyatt said. "Ah've had mah moneysworth out of this bagful, Ah'm getting ready for real business now. The war is going to start, mah friend. We ain't wanted."

"What war?" Doc stared at him. "We nivver was."

Wyatt had come to tell him there was something he didn't want to tell him, Wyatt who had caused most of the brain damage in Tombstone (and elsewhere) by slamming men over the head with a six-gun barrel. "I had made an arrangement with Ike Clanton," he began, "to have him hand over the stage robbers, who are now dead. He would set them up in a place I could arrest them in, and he would get the reward, without the rest of his gang ever knowin. Not a bad plan, but now those guys have bit the dust and Ike is goin around afeared for his life. If they figure him for the traitor, that will be the end for him. You can see the problem."

Doc could see it all right, but he also saw that Wyatt had schemed to entrap his old friend Leonard the ex-jeweler, along with Head and Crane. Whenever the three desperadoes got themselves mentioned that way, as a trio, Doc had flinched, loyal to the last even to a badman who, as the story came out in dribs and drabs, had been shot in the groin at the holdup by Bob Paul's shotgun, and this wound had gone on festering. Leonard's dying confession had implicated King, already dead, Crane and Head; no one else. Crane had fired the shot that killed Bud Philpot, but who had killed Roerig he couldn't say as they had all banged away at the retreating stage with the runaway horses. The Hasletts had killed the Benson stage outlaws, and now Curly Bill and John Ringo had killed the Hasletts in revenge. There would soon be nobody left but Earps.

Doc said so, but Wyatt disagreed, explaining that the gangs didn't like him and Doc, on the personal level, anyway. That would have been enough. Then there was Ike Clanton with his secret, desperately afraid that he would suddenly appear as a turn-coat along with a couple of others, one who had been willing to sell out for a mess of pottage, some two thousand dollars offered by Wells, Fargo, and now high and dry as the abstract villain in a plot that could not hatch. His fellow outlaws would kill him for even having thought of it. And then there was the hypocritical Behan, the anti-sheriff, in cahoots with the outlaws and making a handsome income from his percentage of their loot. Not only that: marauding had reached a new height, Curly Bill and some others had rustled a herd of Mexican steers to the Clanton Ranch at Cloverdale, but Mexican vaqueros had chased them and regained their stock, after which Curly Bill, John Ringo and others had ambushed them in the San Luis Pass and shot fourteen of them, eventually torturing and mutilating, Apache fashion, eight who had not died. The only losses sustained by the Clantons were Old Man Clanton and four of his men, killed in a feud that resolved itself in a Guadaloupe Cañon ambush, which cleared the way for Curly Bill to take over as titular head of the Cochise County badmen.

"What you now got," Wyatt insisted, "is a lousy situation in which the gang steals the cowboys' payrolls and their cows as well. With a corrupt sheriff and corrupt deputies, you then get a system of negotiation: you dicker with the rustlers through the sheriff's office. It's foolproof, it's like the ground had frozen over solid. Now there have been confrontations in the street, right here, not just the old abuse with foul language, but actual threats to kill, and that includes you as part of *my* so-called gang. These guys want to kill for the sake of killing anyway, not that they doesn't have their own good reasons. Frank Stilwell held up the Tombstone-Bisbee stage while you was writing letters and sniffing away at your unwholesome plant. What ails you, Doc? Sorry, I kind of know. Can you believe that somebody as bent and crooked as Frank Stilwell is Behan's deputy? I can swear out federal warrants to hold these men, but I have no local power. No local say. Like Frank McLowery, he says, If you ever lay hands on a McLowery, I'll kill you. It ain't just talk anymore, these boys is feelin their oats and I guess they want a showdown. What do I tell em? Doc is now busy with horticulture and penmanship? It ain't your affair anyway, Doc. Ah'm jest ribbin.'"

Doc was entertaining in his mind's eye the image of the dapper little bandy-legged sheriff, Johnny Behan, sleek and shrewd and utterly corrupt, who fancied himself as the most eligible man-about-town in Tombstone, now a settlement of some fifteen thousand. He had even taken time off from swindling and outlawing to take dancing lessons in San Francisco. Wyatt of course had displaced him in Josephine's affections, even changing her name to Sadie, which only made Sheriff Behan a more ostentatious ladies' man forever fawning and bowing, tripping and feinting, airing his graces and ceremoniously putting a glib front on everything he did, he the main victim always of the Earps and their roughhouse self-righteous gang. The main obstacle to peace in Tombstone was the fancy-man who orchestrated the Clantons and the McLowerys in a sustained fit of rage. Because Josephine-Sadie had jilted him for Wyatt, the criminal side of his nature burned all the more and firmly installed him among the gangs without in the least coarsening his phony demeanor. It was an interesting phenomenon, Wyatt thought, wishing he had more time for the oddities of human perversity, wishing also that he could buffalo the sheriff in a quiet back street with his revolver barrel. There was a pattern, he thought, a more delicate one moving among the harsher ones of killing and revenge, made up of unmarried men who pretended to be married but hid their women away, doomed men like Doc who put their best energy into letters to nuns and cleared the whores out of their lives, and dainty sheriffs of unthinkable depravity whose manners were quaint. Something was trying to reach the surface, a truant nobility, perhaps, a patch of the otherwordly, but it had no chance among the grudge matches and the senseless killings, the loudmouth threats and the general tolerance for corpses at breakfast time, the night's detritus as Doc had once contemptuously called it.

"So we're coming to it," Doc said, with lenient finality.

"I guess. Some of us anyway. The Earps."

"Include the Hollidays too. I been here all along."

Wyatt included him with a sweep of his hand, then brushed at his royal mustache as if it had sunk too low on either side, urging it upward into something straighter that went across in a thick woolly line and suggested a unique stiffness in his bristles, a springiness that responded to the stiff fiber in his soul. Was Wyatt's mustache not only his badge but an index to his state of mind? Doc found himself attending to such thoughts rather than fixing on the showdown bound to come, in which, to be candid with himself, he wanted to do some of the killing; he had a *right* to wipe out some of the Clanton-McLowery axis. After all, who was it who had cleaned up Dodge? Who had been the first law-enforcing man the new arrival saw? Wyatt cracked heads, but Doc put lead where it belonged. Only the dying, he thought further, have this right or, if not that, this privilege. Slandered, accused, threatened, he felt very much on his high horse, with scores to settle, on the side of the angels (he made a note to work this into his ongoing letter). "Wyatt," he burst out, "I am on the side of the angels!"

"That's O.K.," Wyatt told him, "just so long as them angels can shoot straight and fast. Where they come from, they doesn't get much practice I guess." Was he Wyatt vain enough to kill Behan for romantic reasons? Another way, less romantic, more altruistic, was to snip the body off from the head, removing both Clantons and McLowerys, so the finicky bastard had nothing to work with. It was fortunate, Wyatt thought, that the best way of cleaning up the town was also an amorous triumph too; he didn't want Sadie weakening and looking longingly back at Behan after he Wyatt had won her: Behan the ladies' man, whom the other ladies could have. It was a matter of pride as well as of justice. Partly delighted with himself to be working on so many levels, Wyatt kept reassuring Doc, who saw loopholes in the whole arrangement.

"This reward money," Doc asked. "Alive or dead?"

"Either way," Wyatt told him. "There was a wire from San Francisco head office. There still is. I know it by heart. *Yes*, it said, *we will pay rewards for them dead or alive. L. F. Rowell. Signed By.* I still got it. It was sent to Marshall Williams, who gave it to me. He's a useful man to have on your side. Sounds like a marshal, don't he? He ain't."

"How much was it?" Doc felt dazed and soon began to cough, obliging Wyatt to withhold his answer; Doc felt the blood vessels in his temples begin to swell and throb. Maybe they would explode. His eyes poured, his throat twisted out of control.

"You poor bastard," Wyatt said. "What good is Arizona to you?"

Breathing deep and slow to calm his vocal cords, Doc told him in bald, deliberate, isolated words. "I would be better off the planet altogether, Wyatt. I am going nowhere fast."

"Well, it was two thousand per head of Crane, Head and your old sidekick, Leonard. Six thousand dollars all told. That's what I offered Ike."

"He must have been mighty short," Doc whispered. "Hell, he could make more than that in a good bullion robbery."

"And will 'less we stop him and his associates."

"I'm with you," Doc said. "I'll drown him in blood."

"He says I told everybody, you included."

"I never heard a syllable, Wyatt, I was coughin my guts up."

Then Doc had to see a doctor in Tucson, who merely told him to rest and give up drink, smoke and sex, so Doc told him he was thinking of getting circumcised as he now had a Jewish girl on his plate, with a ghoulish taste in flowers. He also stayed on in Tucson for some high-class faro, arriving back at the Wells, Fargo office only to run into Wyatt and Ike Clanton.

"Ike says I told you about a deal of ours." Wyatt said it deadpan, drawing zeroes with his boot toe in the dirt.

"What deal could that have been, Ike?" Ike told him then and there, transfixing several bystanders with the news. Clearly he was out of control. Doc wondered, a bit slow-witted from too much stagecoach travel, if Wyatt was trying to provoke him into a gun-fight right there, one that Ike would lose.

"You were going to sell out Bill Leonard?" Doc felt an old fury pump through him, agitating not his gun hand but his mouth. "You shit-sucking, prickless, brainless asshole, you couldn't pour piss from a cowboy boot if the instructions was printed on the heel! Who the hell are you to decide who lives or dies? Bill Leonard was my friend, whatever he did bad. He's still my friend in death. Don't you ever care about anybody? I got good reason to git you now, Clanton. Don't you turn your back or it'll be the last time, you lousy latrine of a man." Doc raved on for a good quar-ter-hour, uninterrupted; Clanton had touched a nerve; had he kept quiet, Doc would have gone away grumbling, but now he had announced to the world what a louse he really was, and what a poor friend he had been to Bill Leonard, whom essentially Doc had lost to Clanton. As Doc walked away, Clanton yelled obscen-ities after him, then "The next man who links my name to Wyatt Earp will get a bullet right through him."

Once more, Sheriff Behan let some prisoners go and they and their allies sauntered up and down Allen Street bragging and howling. Wyatt Earp, they said, would be dead in forty-eight hours, and anyone who sided with him. The Citizens' Safety Committee then deputized Wyatt and Morgan Earp and Doc as marshals of Tombstone under Virgil.

Thus the waiting began, inspired by Wyatt, who argued that the Clantons and McLowerys were back of all the activity in the streets: a technique known elsewhere as evidence of presence through hectic dispersion. The longer they waited, he said, the more fidgety Ike and Tom would get, and then they would come hell-for-leather into town. They did, in the late afternoon of October 25, unaware that the town's water hydrants had been tested all along the south side of Fremont Street, and people had been tripping ever since over the apparatus left behind, drunks and madmen most of all. Making a big show of handing in their rifles and six-guns at the Grand Hotel, as required, they went their separate ways, Tom to a poker game at the Occidental Saloon, a favored haunt of cowboys, where Sheriff Beautiful Behan was also playing, and Ike to the first stop of a monumental pub crawl that seemed to have only suicide at its far end. Ike, Wyatt told his marshals, would sooner gab than fight, and indeed Ike gabbed with everyone in sight, except the milling cowboys, who for some reason had quit town. Word came to Wyatt that, in Charlestown not far away, Frank McLowery, Billy Clanton and Billy Claiborne were in J. B. Ayers's saloon, apparently awaiting a signal of some kind, or a time, no doubt intending to join Ike and Tom in Tombstone. The dogs were gathering, Wyatt decided, and the only thing to do was wait. He may have been wrong in this: the fewer against them the better. He also said as how he thought there was going to be no fight. So perhaps his wrong conclusion about the impending fight also decided him on doing nothing but wait. At that time he was the only lawman in the game of prophecy; the others were inclined to go along with him, whatever he decided, and they could only marvel as reports came in about Ike's progress from watering hole to watering hole, with six more to go at. About midnight he went into the Alhambra for a meal, only to have Doc arrive and begin to revile him in the most educated, allusive, dismissory way imaginable in a long harangue culminating in the phrase "sweat-nurse of beshitten mongrels." Doc was drunk, and Ike, who on last meeting him, at the Wells, Fargo depot, had abused and threatened him, now tried to calm him down, but Doc was out for blood. "Would I blab?" Doc yelled. "No, I would not. Would you betray your friends, you sure would, you filth-swilling polecat." At last, Morgan Earp persuaded the pair to step outside, where Virgil threatened to arrest them. At last, exhausted, Doc left and Ike moved on to find Wyatt at his faro game in the Eagle Brewery, where Ike boasted, "I'll have man for man in the morning."

"Aw, Ike," Wyatt said, "give it up, there's no money in gunfighting. You ought to know that. Or feuding, for that. Now, you go home, Ike, you talk too much for a fighting man. Go home and kill yourself to prove how brave you are." Wyatt's money went into the safe, and then he and Doc strolled up Fourth and west on Fremont Street to Fly's, where Doc was rooming. Wyatt then went home too while Ike ended up in a boozy all-night poker game at the Occidental. By dawn he was stalking the streets with his Winchester at the ready, his six-gun back in its holster, strutting up and down in the leaky snow-sobered sun, seen by few save three miners crossing the road behind him on their way to the Vizina Hoisting Works. At eight he was at the telegraph office, summoning the clan, thence at Kelly's Wine House, carping and grousing at large. By noon he started making trouble in Hafford's saloon and left there only to head for Fly's, hoping to roust out the sleeping Doc. Then he could be found in front of Doc's cherished post office, being interrogated and vexed by editor John Clum. With the long rod of steel that was the barrel of his six-gun, Virgil buffaloed Ike in the alley between Fremont and Allen on Fourth, subduing the drunkard in him if not the hellraiser, then hauling him into court. Next Ike attended Dr. Gillingham's surgery in the post office building, emerging bandaged and dizzy, entering Spangenberg's gun shop where he tried to buy a further gun, only to walk like a scalded cat past the assembled and silent Earps at Hafford's corner. Back to the Occidental he went, then to the Dexter corral to meet his brother and the McLowerys. They then crossed Allen, passing through the O.K. Corral and so to Fremont, all set for a Tombstone war even as Doc considered breakfast amid the unholy fumes of his carrion plant and decided it would have been a morning for caviar, had there been any. He would settle for eggs with grits and maybe a Genuine English Ale on draft at Kelly's.

·20·

Dear John, All over again that sweet ever made precise. Forgive this fancy way of celebrating your deliverance from death by gunfire. You were in a gun battle with outlaws and, after this one, for the first time, you wept uncontrollably. You must understand that to weep was not unmanly but a form of prayer. The vulnerable soul, adrift in the huge universe, feels a need to collapse and go with the stream, which it hopes will bear it up unbidden. Unbidden means unprayed to, I think. But, if we pray at the same time, the stream can probably not resist us. We flow away, but with dignity.

I shudder to think of so much deadly gunfire in the space of just a few seconds, especially of your own role of spectator in the beginning, watching so many terrible things but unable to help anyone. How despicable of certain people to say you started the whole thing, agitating for gunplay of the fiercest sort. It is astounding that you have come through unscathed apart from the bullet that struck your holster and then skidded along your back, cutting a swath. How can such things be, only yards from people eating a quiet meal or playing cards? Of course, I pray for you in the act of repining and recovering, and hope you will never again have to endure any such thing. Ultimately, in this life, one of the severest challenges must be to turn the other cheek, but not to bullets. What restraint it must take not to retaliate, and I wonder at your Mr. Wyatt, who instead of firing at the young hysterical man charging him merely shoved him away and aside, acceding to the man's plea not to kill him, he himself was not shooting. To be able to say, as he did, "This fight's begun, get to fighting or get out," argues a charitable control in his nature. Exit Claiborne, exit after him Isaac Clanton. You see, I take in everything, distill it, then restage it in my mind, recovering all that has evaporated. I am sorry, my metaphors mix as in a broth, but I will never poison you, dear John. That is your least worry.

The part of your account, now with the guns all cold for a long time, that still captures me is your initial passivity, stationed on the flank of the duel so that you might forestall any attempt to come at you all sideways (if I have it right). From where you stood, you missed nothing. There were the fatal five, lined up, with one disappearing as he thought the better of it. All at the west end of the lot. Just imagine what would happen if I told any such thing to my sisters in Christ. They would blanch and faint, but I, having shared a childhood and adolescence with the likes of you, am made of sterner stuff. Imagine: I read about the gunfight in a smuggled-in newspaper, then hear from you afterward the direct version of a participant! What a peepshow life has become, like looking into the ear of God.

You said they looked rather flashy, ranging in age from nineteen to thirty, burly and almost dressed up for the occasion, as if they knew it would be their last chance to shine, if that's the word. They might have been handsome, you say, but you were looking at their guns and hands, plain to see, whereas the guns of your confederates (oops, hardly a correct word) were all hidden away inside coats and pockets. It was the men with hidden guns going up against the men with visible guns, not the wisest course, though I am no gunfighter, just an illicit correspondent, though of no newspaper. As you like to say, you were on the side of the marshal's angels; and angels, as I now learn to say, hide their guns behind their wings.

I can almost see the young Billy with a gun in each holster, slung rather low, his belt, I mean. Billy Claiborne, that was, who fired twice and missed, then fired again and missed again, disappearing into Fly's Gallery when Sheriff Behan opened the door to let him in. What a way to go. I am trying to keep it all straight, and I am jumping ahead.

So: there they stood, a bit flashy and Mexican in their attire, with narrow mustaches, big sandy-colored sombreros, gaudy silk neckerchiefs tucked into their shirts or tied in a knot around the neck, expensive halfboots, those woollen shirts that keep the warmth in because they have little breathing-holes, and tight doeskin pants with tucked-in cuffs, the style you call the Curly Bill look. It was almost a uniform, you say, whereas what you and the Earps were wearing was austere. Two of them wore short, rough-textured coats and the others, three, wore ornate vests without sleeves. Their good taste if any was not in evidence that day.

I can see you now, as you say, doing a quiet whistle, one of your tuneless ones from long ago, to keep your spirits up, rather shorter in stature than the Earps, wearing a black sombrero and your favorite black flapping overcoat, for which you have become famous. You and Wyatt Earp seem to have the same blond mustache. As you advanced down Fremont Street, you gradually spread out, jutted your jaws, stretched your legs with each step inside the dark trousers that encased your black high-heeled boots. I would have fled at the sight of those long-skirted coats advancing with who knew what weapons concealed within them! White shirts and black string-ties. Why, those clothes have swept the nation. There's a new fashion, the O.K., high-priced. The worldliest nun in the world is telling you this, her own version of the important news.

Then the do-nothing, hypocritical sheriff tells you he has disarmed the other crew; but he failed to arrest them although he now promised he would. Fat hope. He then as sheriff-politico ordered you all four to desist and you continued to march forward even as he cried out to you that you would all be killed. If I were ever going to have grandchildren, I would tell them this by the fire, glad I never saw any such thing. Virgil, the man in command, walked first, in the lead, followed by Wyatt and Morgan. You yourself, "the wise Dr. Holliday" they call you in the press, halted because you had a splendid view of Fremont Street while the others went left into the Corral. I set the scene in my depraved mind's eye: Fly's gallery door bangs. Sheriff Behan appears at a window looking onto the corral yard. A side door opens up. On the other side of the lot, the five rustlers stand almost at attention, their backs against the assay office wall. Myself, I would have opened fire out of sheer nerves.

The bad hombres had even situated two ponies to block any fire from the assay office. I can think of gentler uses; who uses a cow pony as a barricade, I ask you, each with a Winchester rifle tucked into the saddle boot. I can see it now, with trembling eyes.

By the way, whatever became of the next letters in your series-to-be of titled ones? I liked the idea, but see you have reverted to customary practice. Talking of titles, I was glad to see you referred to, almost without fail, in the press as Doctor Holliday. Only right and proper; it was not as if you were some mere cowboy prancing about for effect.

The newspapers said that you uttered one unprintable word as you took your position, referring to that fraudulent sheriff, no doubt calling him after a portion of his own body. I remember the coarse side of your verbal nature and am thankful for newspaper discretion. Now, Wyatt Earp, that sagacious man, had decided there would only be gunplay if the outlaws began it. But it was Virgil, the nominal leader, who cried out, "You men are under arrest. Throw up your hands." Frank McLowery then dropped his hand to his gun and muttered something filthy. The rest of them set their hands on their weapons without a word, getting ready. "Hold on!" That cry came from Virgil Earp as he flung his right hand upward, bearing aloft your cane, which he had taken from you when he handed you the shotgun. "We don't want that," he added. These words, telegraphed around the nation, which seems to have been waiting for just such a gunfight to happen, remain in my brain, etched and moving. You had no end of spectators. Wyatt said that the entire fight occupied only half a minute, but it happened so fast that time melted, dragged out almost to infinity. There was a man who kept record of his doings. It is no use living impulsively, without plan, letting the fire of the moment always be your guide.

So the firing began, with Frank McLowery and Billy Clanton both shooting at Wyatt Earp and making the adobe walls clatter. I am so glad I was not there. Their guns were half-drawn already, but Wyatt was faster, he always was. The McLowery bullet ripped through the skirt of Wyatt's coat on his right and the other one tore his sleeve, and before either could shoot again Wyatt had shot McLowery in the stomach, right above his belt buckle. He staggered forward and ran like a wounded deer (not you, but the newspapers). His left hand clasped over the wound as if to suck the bullet out. He was the most dangerous of the five, so Wyatt had done well to immobilize him, much as the two of them who fired first, who opened the firing, had marked out Wyatt as the most dangerous of their opponents. There, doesn't that make you feel better?

It did not. Doc, who had suddenly realized how few places he was ever actually in (saloon bar, his room, the Oriental's writing lounge), felt hemmed in, not least by his newfound reputation. In the old days he was a superb gunfighter and now he was an arch-criminal, the *cause* of the set-to at the O.K. Corral or near it. It was too much to bear, as was Mattie's aghast semi-pleasure at the newspaper accounts, full and florid, as distinct from his own concise epistolary versions, all restraint and modesty. To have lived so intensely for so short a time wounded a man in his mind, most of all if he began with a decided deficit, as he did. He was a dying man who walked the plank and then, though blindfolded, turned around at the right instant and walked back, confounding his executioners. Well, he told himself while inhaling his carrion flower like an addict, if you can dodge one executioner, you might be able to dodge another. There is hope in chance. What was it I used to say to myself at dental college, amazing myself with the fourth word? "Blood, sweat and campus." Not very brilliant, but what do people expect of a dentist? He resolved to keep his accounts of the shoot-out to a minimum, feeding her nothing but trivia—yes, Mattie, out here the gunfighter keeps only five bullets in his six-gun as a safety device since there's no "safety" on the gun. What an unusual thought, for her anyway; why, she was going to ask, don't they call it a five-gun then? He looked forward to writing to her, on the bed or in the Oriental's lounge, but he dreaded her praise, cobbled together from rumor, newspapers, and his own letters. Doc had the weird sense that his life had been written for him and that he would never regain his previous reputation, such as it was, nor the Earps theirs. This was why he lingered on the preamble to the showdown, hardly able to believe in causation itself, wondering if he had really told Ike Clanton, "I hear you're going to kill me. Get out your gun and commence." Had he ever said "commence" to anyone? How French, how pompous. Why had he not said, "Then let's begin"? Then, he asked himself if John Clum, the mayor, had actually seen Ike standing at the corner of Fifth and Allen armed with revolver and rifle and inquired of him where was the war? Facetious? No doubt, but on target, so the newspaper editor's intuition was working well that night. Yes, he had heard it said, while hell was bubbling over downtown, Doc Holliday was having a good sleep in his rented room, getting ready—for what?

Wyatt had told Doc not to get involved in this local war. "This isn't your fight, Doc," he said, and Doc had answered, "That's a hell of a thing for you to say to me," a bit piqued as if his name no longer counted in Tombstone, as if he were not worth a gun battle with. The buildup had been bizarre, Virgil slapping the side of Clanton's head with his gun barrel, Wyatt slapping Tom McLowery outside the courtroom and buffaloing him, while Doc, the unretiring Doctor H., what did he do? He waltzed up to Billy Clanton and shook his hand, perhaps to simulate the executioner's good cheer and plea for forgiveness. At Hafford's Saloon, finally admitted among the elect, Doc deferred to Virgil Earp, who offered him the shotgun and took his cane instead. Since Doc was in no way a peace officer or lawman, he had to be schooled in procedure, and this Morgan did; Doc felt taken over, conscripted out of charity. Let Virge do the talking, Morgan instructed him, and cover our right flank. "If anybody so much as moves," Morgan added, "let them have it." Doc was more than willing, unable to forget that the Clantons and McLowerys had already been looking for him where he lived, milling around in the front yard. He had every reason to shoot them down where they stood, so, while he waited with Morgan a little apart from the other two, right in the center of Allen and Fourth streets, Doc was impatient. What happened then? Virgil shoved his gun into his waistband, way back against his left hip, and Wyatt slid his into his coat pocket. Slivers of Act One came back to him as they always would until he died: Tom McLowery's shirt not tucked in, the serious cerebral quality of their inaugural march toward the outlaws, the formality of the start, then those first two shots, Wes Fuller arriving too late to be a part of anything or to interfere, yet not too late to scoot around afterward, picking up debris and a gun; and he himself, everyone's Doc, obliviously thinking (was it correct?) *Et ego in Arcadia fui,* another way of saying then I scrammed. Would this be the last one? How could he feel so cool? Was the Wells, Fargo shotgun any good? When had it last been used? Against those who attacked the Benson stage? He hated shotguns. If only God will let me live long enough, he thought, they *will* see me. They will get me. They will get the benefit of me. They will see how I do things. They will see how I shoot them down. They will get an eyeful and a bellyful. They will wish they had never seen me or shaken my poxed hand. They will wish to be home with their mothers. They will know who they have dealt with. They will learn that it is not only the Earps that run Tombstone and the next world. If God will let me live long enough, I will return to my carrion cactus and thank it for waiting. What had they said about us? They were waiting for those sons of bitches. Just as soon as those damned Earps appear, the shooting will start. Today I have become an Earp. I am climbing socially, I guess, downward. From dentist to assassin. Not bad. What I want is never again to find them in the Alhambra when I want to eat, or in the Oriental when I need to write a letter, or in Kelly's when I want a cigar, or in Colonel Hafford's when my gullet craves what stills it. I am going to be nobody's. His mind flicked to Officer Andy Bronk, who lived catty-corner from Wyatt, and came to see him for some commitment papers concerning a prisoner, incidentally saying there was liable to be hell to pay. "You had better get up." Virgil went to get the papers and then went back to bed in spite of Bronk's saying, "Ike Clanton has threatened to kill Doc as soon as he wakes." Then Bronk arrived again, saying Ike was hunting an Earp with his Winchester, and Virgil thought that worth getting dressed for. Ike Clanton was looking for everybody until he found them, and then he lost interest.

Now Tom McLowery rushed behind Frank's horse, pulling his six-gun and firing beneath the neck at Morgan Earp, slicing through Morgan's coat. A second and a third time, Billy Clanton shot at Wyatt, missing even as Morgan fired back, aiming at Billy's stomach but finding his gun hand. Doc had seen this in a trance, wondering why he was exempt from the action, why he was where he was bound to be exempt. Deep down, he knew he could have done better than any of them, even with the cumbersome sawn-off shotgun. Meanwhile, with Doc like a man underwater, Wyatt aimed again at Tom McLowery even as *he* fired at Morg and caught him in the shoulder with a slug that touched bone, then tore across the bottom of the neck into the other shoulder, leaving a big gash, about which no one knew at the time,

Morgan feeling as if he had been branded, steerwise, across the top of his back.

"I got it," he managed to grunt as he almost keeled over.

"Get behind me, Morg, and keep quiet," was all Wyatt said, intent on his front. He had fired at the withers of the pony behind which Tom McLowery was hiding; the pony leaped forward and ran for the street, drawing the other horse with it and exposing Tom, who grabbed at his rifle in the saddle boot but missed. Yes, Doc was thinking, it has nothing to do with me, I could be one of those bounty hunters with tied holster, just standing here waiting my chance, ready to parley. I could be made of steel, fresh from a long sleep, in as little danger as a telegraph pole, the one invulnerable observer; he almost wanted to be hit, giving him an excuse to go away, tell the story, be bandaged up before resuming his sleep. He was doing what he had been told to do in the Earps' master plan for exterminating the two gangs, and he was not going to renege on that. Almost put upon his mettle, he wondered if he would remember it more vividly than he saw it. It was clear to him, at least from this position, that the Earps were shooting better than the others, taking their time and aiming with zealous calm.

Not far away, at the other end of the lot, Virgil was still holding Doc's cane, like a bandmaster, when Billy Claiborne shot at him twice, at which point Claiborne began a run that took him across the corral toward the side door of Fly's gallery, already opened by Johnny Behan, who wafted into and out of view like a hoped-for target. Claiborne shot again at Virgil while in the act of disappearing, and now Ike Clanton without having fired a shot charged at Wyatt Earp, yelling incomprehensibly. The battle ground on, with Virgil firing his first shot, which broke Billy Clanton's arm held protectively in front of him, but deterred him not at all as he passed his gun to the other hand and went on shooting, except that Morgan, told to be quiet and still, shot Billy in the chest as Virgil put a bullet through Billy's twelfth rib. Now Ike Clanton was pleading with Wyatt, grabbing at his left arm.

"Don't kill me, Wyatt! Don't kill me! I'm not even shooting."

Unmoved, Wyatt mustered all his calm to say his famous line about getting to fighting or get out. Put up or shut up. Boozed to the eyelids, Doc thought. Was *I* ever that way? No, he said as Ike Clanton ran for the same door Billy Claiborne had gone through. It was almost operatic, with characters exiting the stage at given moments through arranged gaps in the action. Two had gone already, which evened the odds a little. Tom McLowery had actually fired at Wyatt as Ike Clanton tugged at his arm, pleading and groveling, at which point Doc had had enough, firing with impatient accuracy both barrels of his shotgun at Tom McLowery, who recoiled, then ran around the corner like escapee number three toward Third Street, only to fall dead a few paces farther on, doubly buckshot in the stomach and plugged through the ribs by Wyatt even as he ran. Disgusted with a weapon that apparently did not work, Doc hurled the shotgun down with yet another unprintable curse on which his imagination had worked too little and hauled out his nickel-plated Colt, finally at home with his weapon.

What then? Doc shook his head to clear it. He could tell her none of this; he need not, it had all been in the newspapers, pasted together from the accounts of a dozen satisfied witnesses, who all had seen the battle differently. Was it over? Doc noticed how, during gunfights, lulls could seem terminal, like accidental good shots; then the whole fracas resumed and could go on forever until ammunition ran out.

What next?

Frank McLowery was on the move, shot through the abdomen, shooting even as he staggered forward.

Billy Clanton, arm broken, shot through the chest, came wobbling after him. Where were they headed in their respective mists?

Now Frank, weaving and swaying, fired in vain at Wyatt and Morg, each time shooting short. Glass crashed behind Wyatt and a new burst of gunfire came from Claiborne and Sheriff Behan through the smashed window of Fly's Gallery.

"Look out, boys!" Wyatt yelled. "You're getting it in the back."
At once Morgan spun around, tripped and fell, and Doc's next
moment came; he put two bullets through the window and
stopped the firing from that quarter. He now saw Ike Clanton
sprint from the back door across the alleyway and into the stalls of
the now-famous O.K. Corral, hurling his still unfired gun into a
corner of the yard. Doc shot after him twice, but too late, murmuring to himself, Why doesn't the bastard run again, just to
please me? I wouldn't miss again, I'm letting the team down. He
would have pursued that thought into remorse and perhaps even
into Arcadia, but Frank McLowery, now in the street after some
slow-motion exercises, was aiming at him, trying to stand erect
and steady his gun arm, wasting energy on abuse.

"I've got you now, you blood-sucking asshole," he said with
languorous contempt. "This is it."

Doc laughed at the poverty of invention on show. "Think so?" he
said, waiting to see what would happen next. Falling Morgan had
managed to convert the energy of his fall into a roll that brought him
up short facing Doc and McLowery, at whom he fired in the very
same instant as Doc at McLowery and McLowery at Doc. All
flinched, McLowery most of all, both hands flung high as if
acknowledging an ovation, spinning slow because shot through the
head by Morg's exquisite aim upward. Morg got up, noting the hole
right behind McLowery's ear, then Doc's shot through the heart:
Frank McLowery double-killed with professional accuracy on top
of being gunshot by Wyatt. Frank's final shot was the one that struck
Doc's hip holster, spun away and shaved skin off his upper back, little as he felt it at the time. Doc still felt disgusted: this savage free-
for-all lacked the symmetry and formality of a true gunfight, a duel,
and was like removing teeth with a sledgehammer. Doc liked the
neat, the paced, the almost-even. So was it over yet? Did it have to
grind on?

Overcome with disgust and moderate horror, Doc seized the
pen with which he had toyed throughout his long, incredulous
reverie and began to write to Mattie about there being only five
seconds more to the gunfight. It had been a tornado, blowing up

out of nowhere, involving everyone and ending several lives. What sickened him was the speed of it, but also his delayed-action role, then the comparative paucity of what he did, his job having been mainly to watch, like a schoolboy getting a reward. Was he trying to pass muster, like those Cherokees who, after marching on the Trail of Tears, had tried to look like George Washington by dressing in military jackets? Was he that fraudulent, that subdued? Was there not—

No, he cautioned himself, don't waste such a thought. So he wrote it down:

Dearest Mattie (trespassing into the realm of hyperbole):

Is there not, in the universe, a returned spirituality such as we might have tried to assign to the Deity, which, not being needed, returns to us in time? I mean, seeking to aggrandize the role of God, in order to worship God the more, we send our souls' intensity His way, but he does not need it and reflects it back as light? Am I making sense of any kind, to a religious woman? It might be worth thinking about, especially as I look back on the O.K. Corral with distinct loathing. It was bad enough to have been involved in it, but worse to be blamed for it, as if it were something I had planned and desired. No such thing. My getting into it with Wyatt was the merest chance. Over and over I rehearse it, for what it was and what it was worth, and I find it was a nothing and worthless, demonstrating the power of the bullet: no more than that. I find especially significant and moving the amount of running-away that took place, and the amount of running-to. Quite a few of the participants wanted not to be involved, not after the first few shots; they shrank from the remorseless, mechanical nature of the feud, suddenly awakened to the mundane beauties of the street, by which I do not intend filles de joie.

Bless you for understanding how I became implicated in the whole business, and what has happened to me since. Those who pretend to administer the law are usually the ones to break it, and Sheriff Behan, the dainty quickstepper, is no exception. He was the one we should all have shot, until he was a mess of pottage. In the end, as I look back on all that slaughter, I keep score, just to steady my mind. It went, goes, thus:

O.K.: The Corral, the Earps, and Doc Holliday

Gone:
Tom McLowery
Frank McLowery
Billy Claiborne
Billy Clanton . . .

Runaway:
Ike Clanton.

Of course, a list would not, except in some muted twisted form, bring back the clouds of noxious black powder billowing or the almost incessant scream medley of horses and people, nor the bangs crowded up on top of one another followed by the flimsy click-click of triggers on empty chambers. Doc would smell and hear all this until he died, remember the horses weaving and swerving down the street. He remembered wondering if Frank McLowery, in trying to retreat, shoving past him, was trying to go to earth in the house of a woman he was courting. Near an adobe building opposite the lot, he halted and looked Doc in the eye, wobbling with pistol rested on his arm, right on left, spitting out a few hostile words, the same ones ever: "Got you now," even as Doc the emaciated turned suddenly exposing only his right side, as one should, before answering, "Well, suck my Rebel dick. You're a daisy if you do." How many times would he see Morgan Earp, like some muscle heap rising from the ocean, rear up, sit and take aim at Frank McLowery, putting a slug below, or behind his right ear (Doc could not tell which). Brooding on Frank as he sat in front of the Oriental's huge front window, looking out at Allen Street, a mere cup of coffee in front of him, and somewhat glazed by so much light through too much glass, Doc began to ponder what might have happened if they had not disposed of Frank so readily; he had already hit Morgan in the shoulder, Virgil in the right calf, Doc in the holster and Wyatt in the coat. With luck he might have killed all four of them in short order. Oddly, he thought of Wyatt's skill with a pool ball hurled and tried to gauge how much use a fast-traveling ball might have been at a vital juncture, smashing a nose or knocking an Adam's apple back deep into the throat. Every little bit would have helped. As Wyatt and Morgan trudged out of the lot into Fremont Street, where Doc had been throughout the battle, Doc tried to force his way through the turmoil of the crowd, yelling, "The sonofabitch has shot me, and I'm going to kill him." Had it ended? Had he forgotten anything? Had staring at some street sign effaced his ability to take things in? A slug had whizzed right through the pants of a visitor from the East, who had been looking for local color; finding it, he took the next train out, ready to dine on the experience, having as the French say "assisted at" the making of history. Camilius S. Fly, distinguished photographer, ran out of his store and snatched the six-gun from the hand of Billy Clanton, shocked by Billy's dying request for more cartridges: "Just a few, buddy." As if a sporting event had ended, the Vizina Mine whistle blew denoting an emergency, but the milling crowd sensed something vital and hedonistic in the sound and began to smile even as armed men come into Fremont Street to discipline the leftovers. Doc gave Wyatt an anxious look: Who were these men and why were they armed? "You threw us Johnny," Wyatt said to Behan, now busily officious again after having, by accident, figured in the initial line-up, between Billy Claiborne and Virgil Earp, a vacillating, deceitful protester, one eye on the Clantons, the other on the McLowerys.

"No," Behan said. "You did your worst, Wyatt. I am going to take you in, all of you."

"In that, you're wrong, Johnny," Wyatt answered. "We are not going to be arrested this afternoon. You may want to see us, but we don't want to see you. Take a good look. You see before you some men with new careers in mind." The Earps' wounds were dressed uptown, and Doc's as well, Virgil and Morgan being ferried home in the town hack hauled by hand in some weirdly submissive tenderness that said wounded men had to be dealt with by hand, like parcels. The dead went to the Dexter Corral, which Doc had always thought of as the right-handed one, the endless darkness in their eyes meeting the darkness of the back room where the undertaker lurked and plied his trade, plugging holes and mopping blood away. It was a last delicacy for the slaughtered, whose legend among the cowboys and outlaws was going to be that only two of them, Billy Clanton and Frank McLowery, had been armed and that the Earps fired the first five shots to make sure of the outcome. They lifted their hands when commanded to do so by Virgil, and were massacred where they stood. Next day the Tombstone brass band led the funeral down Allen through a heaving throng and eight passengers left town by stage.

·21·

The whole trouble with letters, Doc decided, was that you wanted the reply as soon as you finished your last page, so that you would be answering that answer before your letter even went off. He wanted to add that, of the dead, only Billy Clanton retained in his face the pain of dying; the other two had a peaceful, fulfilled look. He would have added that, but not now as he had gone through all the formalities of farewell, wishing to live in a quicker world. What worried him was losing interest in what you had said, so that when the answer came you cared little what it said in response, and you had to make a new start, forging into untried material, and in the end repeating yourself, confessing that you went up to the bar and drank from others' glasses, bequeathing them a bacillus they had only too much in mind, actually used the phrase Old Mister Death, fired your six-gun into the sky whenever fireworks were let off, to his face called Bat Masterson by his correct name of Bartholomew, criticized Mrs. Wyatt's laudanum and openly boasted of his lady friend in Savannah without ever declaring her true vocation, promising that she might come to Tombstone to join him (thus, he thought, saving face). The planet was going well, complete with a naive star.

Even in the blood-spattered and legalistic aftermath of the fight, his mind, under too much pressure of having come even closer to the premature death promised him, he found himself contemplating the fondness of American men for secreting a common-law wife, hiding her (or them) away, sometimes, as the press had made well known, murdering them and chopping up the corpse. The practice, no doubt primitive in origin, must have had something to do with the hunt for perfection and the strain of committing to one woman, a Kate or a Wyatt's Mattie, for the rest of your days. Why did men like having a harem of women locked away or otherwise disposed of? To ensure sexual freshness every day? It could not be that crude a problem, having to do more with the fun of secrecy, spying, subterfuge and counterfeit; in other lands, men hid their women in tents and behind veils, so perhaps this was the frontier version, with one ostensible Missus hidden behind another, with the real woman in possession out in the open, yet unmarried, prey to snigger and lewd overture. Doc regarded himself as essentially dead, yet he longed for the problems of the living, who predicted for themselves not only longevity but complexity too. Now he knew: Wyatt not only had a suitcase of disguises, he also owned a brothel full of ancient "wives," some of them his, whom he allowed other men to use for free. That was how he kept so cool in hell. Nothing detained him for too long.

Doc was suffering from melodrama hangover; the event was done, but he was still experiencing it, and bits of it kept haunting him, not just for an instant, but for days. The shots that spun through the air and into people at the O.K. Corral, so-called, were as nothing to the small concerns that punctured his thinking and his nerves, making him wonder, not if he had imagined the whole thing, but if he would ever recall it aright, free of prejudice and loathing, shame and guilt. Up to now, Doc had fared quite well as a man without overt conscience, under sentence of death; now he found himself backsliding, blamed by many for the whole atrocity, and likely to be jailed. In fact, he and Wyatt *were* arrested and jailed, taciturn siblings in sin, while Morgan and Virgil were allowed home to heal. Why could Doc never achieve that trueblue symmetry of Wyatt, a man who knew the right and abided by it, no matter who said what, steering a manly course through personal disaster and professional tribulation? Somehow Wyatt continued to chart a tight ship on a reliable course, as if arrest and accusation were mere flickers in the matrix of duty. Doc, the more efficient gunman of the two, was less stable; but then, he told himself, when you spend half your life coughing you cannot always expect the best of yourself. Had Doc really fired twice at Billy Clanton and missed? He had, whereas Wyatt had not wasted a single shot of his five, confirming him as some kind of paragon. Billy Clanton, for example, had fired six times and hit nobody at all, a disaster of a marksman, qualified only to fire for sound effect like a man in a circus act. So, had Doc actually shot and killed Frank McLowery? He was willing to pay the freight for that, as for shooting Tom McLowery in the chest. He had been of that much use, more perhaps than Wyatt could have asked of a man recently roused from sleep, from the innumerable waking contemplations of a man whose closest associate (if that word were valid) was a distant, cerebral nun—Wyatt apart, that is. In that context of the corral, even a door slamming, as when Wyatt fired back toward the gallery behind Fly's against whoever had shot from the landing, had instant effect. The entire episode had been so fast, faster almost than thought, faster perhaps than emotion even, which was why his feelings were coming through belatedly. Tempted to give up gunplay and devote himself to horticulture, Doc said no, what else would he have? He was no longer a dentist, and what he should be, if in his right mind, was a patient in a Colorado sanitarium, as Wyatt kept saying, yet without enough zeal to propel Doc into the move. Had there been the prospect of a gun battle in Colorado, Doc would have gone, toot sweet, ready to serve, as during the railroad skirmish when he shipped out from Dodge on behalf of the Sanny Fay.

Morgan had not missed even once.

Virgil had missed just once (his first shot at Frank McLowery).

At the very thought of newspaper people taking notes and drawing diagrams, Doc allowed himself a leaky smile, knowing that history took care of its own, and that little-known forces— such as hopeful fudging and vengeful embellishment—looked after their own, swiftly transforming events into episodes, so much so that those who had seen and remembered trusted themselves no longer, but allowed articles and books to interfere with empirical certainty. Myth gobbled away at the certitudes of gunman and spectator alike, revamping the dead above all as supremely eligible for the favor of makeover, almost as if a combined force of taxidermist, undertaker and color commentator had inherited history, determined to make it mutate into something not merely rich and strange, which was acceptable enough, Doc thought, but drastic and ineffaceable. He saw how, suddenly, distinct from rumor and gossip, popular metamorphosis had seized hold of him and would never let go; he had crossed over from an already not fully known personage of renown into other terrain, where he did not ever have to do anything further but simply watch the tide of reputation coming in, warts and amours and all, lathering and shaving him afresh each day, in one sense a goner as an identity, in another a revenant who had hardly shed his own blood, whereas others had lost a sight of it. How easily tempted the mind was: for instance, he always remembered how Wyatt had told him about his first and only marriage, to Urilla Sutherland (a fine old Scottish name, the second), who died in childbirth. It had been an unpopular marriage for both families to begin with, and her death sent her two brothers into a paroxysm that took them into a street brawl with the Earps, Wyatt, Virge and Morgan and James against Fred and Bert and three others, Granville, Lloyd and Garden: a twenty-minute street fight because Urilla's family blamed Wyatt for her death. Yet all that Doc could think of, in his heartless enterprising way, was that Urilla rhymed with Gorilla, and Wyatt should have listened to the language and abstained. Distraught and angered, he had then fallen in with a rough crew and was soon indicted in Arkansas for stealing horses. It was loss, though, that bound Doc to Wyatt, that gave him his own bleak hinterland of chances wasted, lives subtracted, hope denied, all the miserable variety of striving. And loss went on, as Doc had seen, Wyatt's Mattie to laudanum, his own Mattie to the convent whose name he sometimes could not remember. You pushed forward even while pieces of you were falling away ravaged and bleeding, and you did not bother signing your name to your life, other agencies (forces) than you having had the decisive say from the first. Doc felt his life had been lived for him by the bacillus, and all else had been compensatory sideshow while other lives around him glowed and flamed.

Once again he was hurrying down Allen Street, almost pushing himself along with his cane, eager to find out what the Earps had decided to do. He caught them leaving Hafford's Saloon, their headquarters; the saloon owned by a man who doubled as an undercover agent for Wells, Fargo, just like Wyatt. They took him on, shifting their intentions from avoiding a street brawl to beefing up their team. He withdrew an arm from its sleeve and fitted the sawed-off shotgun into place. Once he was in position he saw, in a corresponding position on the far side of the two confronting lines of gunmen, Wes Fuller, who, without being involved, was prepared to keep an eye on their flank. They should have cut him down before he got anywhere near; fighter or not, he was a tyro outlaw, committed to their wretched cause, and Doc would have shot him if he hadn't thought Virgil was going to. Doc was remembering too fast, as always, how Johnny Behan had intended to become the town's hero, staving off disaster by persuading the outlaws not to fight. What had someone called him, Morgan maybe? "The outlaws' best friend." From where he stood, Doc could not fire a shotgun lest he spray his own side with slugs. He remembered all the waiting, then Billy Claiborne's three careless shots before he bolted to join Behan in Fly's studio, at whose window Doc would aim two shots of his own to keep the heads of the drygulchers down. He had forgotten to reload, indeed there was no opportunity for such an act, so when he tried to shoot Clairborne he pulled the trigger and heard only a spring-loaded détente. Of all nine men involved in the fight, only he and Wyatt had been in a condition to continue, Wyatt protesting to Behan, "I'll answer for what I've done," Doc saying nothing.

When the charge came, it was for abuse of police power in an attempt to wipe out two families of cowboys, the only snag in the charge being that Wyatt, in the middle of things with bullets whizzing around, had refrained from shooting the unarmed Ike, in other words demonstrating the most scrupulous concern for what was just. The case against Wyatt and Doc collapsed, as it had to, but not before, divided from each other by widely spaced bars, they had this jailhouse exchange, ever to stir in Doc's retreating memory.

"Always my job, I'll do that," Wyatt said, "even in hell."

"You's not goin to hell, Wyatt. Hell's full of Clantons and McLowerys."

"It is now, I guess. That Clanton kid, Billy, he had promised his mother not to die with his boots on. Damn me if with his last breath he didn't ask for his boots to be taken off. If I'da known, I'd have asked a few favors too." Wyatt scowled and tweaked his mustache. "Doc, I feel just about as sociable these days as an ulcerated whore."

"Be my guest. I don't insist on courtesy."

"Well, Doc," Wyatt murmured with an almost hangdog look extraordinary in one so strict-demeanored, "you should. Don't you go accepting the manners of just anybody because you happen to be in the calaboose with them."

"No sir. Hey, Wyatt! Is it true you wore a bullet-proof vest, do you always? Is that why they never wing you? Even Doc Holliday takes his lumps now and then. Why, I got holster-shot in your fight, the one you said I needn't get involved in." Doc felt that, left to their own rhetorical devices for a few months, right here in jail, he and Wyatt would evolve a whole new lifestyle for peace officers, guaranteed to see them through the worst showdowns; it was all a matter of soldierly bearing, concise English, and the right ice cream—on their way to the gunfight, he and Wyatt had passed Banning and Shaw's, Fourth Street above Fremont, where Wyatt had favored the huckleberry and the candios.

"Bullet-proof? Anybody who asks," Wyatt joshed, "has not been living in Arizona. You'd die of suffocation or apoplexy if you wore one of those. No, I nivver wore an extra thang." Again he had reverted to their mutual twang, making them more redneck than they were, but founding them in the unreconstructed race of humble men afraid of a language that had bitten many.

"They are guardin us well," Doc said. "This here hoosegow is no bigger than the O.K. Corral, eighteen feet square if you ask me."

"We could touch." Wyatt yawned. "Gittin cold at night, they sez it's been a-snowin."

"Yair," Doc told him. "They say Parsons the diarist and foremost letter-writer in Tombstone saving one other has been bathing in ice-cold creeks to keep his codpiece down. He should try the bacillus, then he would think he had a drunken eel."

"You would know. Sixteen days."

"It's called celibacy," Doc said with a leer. "Them monasteries ain't that bad, I guess. Three meals found and a dry bed, with the best company in the world. I haven't felt this jolly since dental college." His mind had flicked lovingly back to Big Nose Kate and her uncanny habit of oiling and starching his two holsters with her genital mucosa, giving them an acrid aroma but also a crisp interior that the six-guns barely seemed to rest upon; they almost floated there in sensual dark.

Wyatt just stared ahead and put his hands together, mock-praying, ever the pack leader with the piercing eyes. "They sez Frank McLowery shaved off his chin whiskers before he came to fight—his imperial I guess you'd call it."

"Then he come to do or die."

"He did the other then," Wyatt whispered, almost reverent. "You won't be shaken *his* hand again."

"Lily-livered bucket of puma piss," Doc said in his remote, diagnostic way. "I'm a bit worried about my cactus."

"Cactus is always fine, not like humans."

Doc told him, "I never shot a cactus."

"You must, Doc," Wyatt said. "I kin see it in yore eyes."

Next night they were out and Wyatt, showing off, snuffed the light in his office with a revolver, just to show willing. He could, he boasted, have done it with a bullet too, even as Doc fondled and inhaled his carrion plant, weary of what he called "empty yeller talk," and anxious to clear the air around his name. They might have been exonerated, but they were still popularly accused. The entire nation was still convulsed about the assassination of President Garfield back in September, but the new President, Arthur, warned the citizens of Cochise County to curb the lawlessness there or he would impose martial law. Doc's comment on the death of Garfield was predictable: "There went a man who could write Latin with one hand and Greek with the other. No man was better qualified for high office, not even Johnny Ringo." In December, Doc received a box done up in tissue paper and tied with a pink ribbon, inside wrapped in soft white cotton a .45 caliber bullet and a little card saying, "I've got another one just like this that I'm going to give you someday—in the neck. Well Wisher." Doc placed it on the skimpy soil of his cactus plant and hoped for thorns. He had mailed all the letters he wrote while in jail, but had received only answers to letters much previous, most of her comments based on newspapers. He could not wait for the blaze of publicity to abate and Mattie to attend again to what *he* wrote.

· 22 ·

Little matter that the bodies of the dead from the O.K. Corral had been cleaned up a little and then put on display in open boxes in the window of the Tombstone hardware store. What bothered Doc like an incubus, sitting in his mind and daunting him, was the image of short, stocky Ike Clanton, who, having run up to Wyatt and grabbed his left arm, had been repulsed, thereupon mustering to his own purposes the energy in Wyatt's left-handed shove and bolting away into the lodging house, then through the rear door to the back landing, past Sheriff Johnny Behan skulking there with six-gun at the ready for who knew what, over the top of Billy Claiborne also skulking there, low and prudent, into the famous photography gallery itself, after which he sped down the hallway, thence to the back, right around the gallery corner, over the intervening fence, between the dismal, worn-out outhouses, clean across Allen Street, beneath a freight wagon like a collapsing greyhound, around the card tables, right through the active, astounded fiddle player, through the rear door, all the way down the unwanted alley and into Alfred Henry Emmanuel's building on Toughnut Street, where while trying to think of how to go into hiding next he ensconced himself behind a barrel of mescal. He behaved like someone trying to create a record of propulsive adaptation, one who, as the current saying goes, talked the talk and did not so much walk the walk as run the run. Always, Doc told himself, Ike Clanton hiring somebody to talk against somebody. How many times had he or Wyatt run into Ike Clanton in the street, only to hear about yet another deal in the wind? If you remembered anything in detail about anybody, such as the peppermint candy that Virgil liked, or the huckleberry ice cream that lured Wyatt, it was the miasma of verbiage that haloed Ike Clanton's face: Ike the survivor, the self-exempted, the floater. No trace of his passage from corral to mescal barrel, Doc lamented, nor of anybody else either, souvenir hunters having collected up both guns and empty shells (or savvy allies trying to help). He would not go so far as to say it was as if the Corral battle had never been, but had taken place out in the desert, say, in a purer form where there was no medical help, no cheering, no spectator, nor, he winced, any gun shop for outlaws to buy bullets at, nor a butcher's such as Bauer's where outlaws could sell their rustled beef. Out on the flank during the gunfight, and therefore a late starter, Doc had not even been called to testify at the trial; he felt one of the unnecessary, deemed so by their eminent lawyer Tom Fitch, a former editor and politico, without whom, Wyatt argued, they would have been sunk. It had been Tom Fitch who, invoking habeas corpus, had gotten them out and paid their bail. If a man needed a Fitch to survive in Tombstone, what would he need in Frisco? Doc, as he miserably recognized, had a bad name, and Fitch had thought it best to bury him as a despised phantom, good when chips were down and trigger fingers itchy, but a liability when people had gotten self-righteous and wanted a necktie party to add to the ongoing circus the town had turned into, with gun battles in its midst, corpses on view, and a huge, elongated trial swallowing both people and time, words and sleep. No one had, yet, said that this had been a showdown between Republicans and Democrats, but the slander was in the air; Wyatt was a self-proclaimed Republican, but did he think of himself in that light when having breakfast, peeling back his no doubt huge and ponderous foreskin, loading his Colt for the day's excitement? Doc saw himself as a freebooter, a man who lived for himself in his own terms, who never apologized. He had no politics save those of a patrician gentility, but he was surely, in his nerves and tendons, an aristocrat, transplanted and grown crooked but still a son of the South. Who or what else would respond gladly to the convent letters of a sequestered Mattie, who entered the nunnery almost as soon as he quit the South?

Wyatt, not one given to intimidating guesswork, had said to Doc that the bullet which struck him in the holster would have smashed his spine had it been an inch farther over. Doc felt it whizz past him, made almost virtuous by luck; it was not he but Albert Bilicke, owner of the Cosmopolitan, who had seen Tom McLowery holding a gun as he came out of a store, and others had seen Ike and Billy Claiborne buying cartridges at Spangenberg's gun shop. Everybody had something to contribute to the horn of plenty of knowledge, even those who had witnessed nothing at all. Nobody wanted to be left out, even to the point of slandering Doc (he liked to kill the healthy, they said), he would slice you from belly to dick for a mispronounced vowel, and he was addicted to the melody of money. He would go any distance, they said, for a five-dollar gold piece. Of course, nobody mentioned his passion for letter-writing, letter-receiving, and his gradually intensifying pagan religiosity fanned by his nun. He was a more private man than they knew, with a noxious flower, a lung-frenzy, and a critical devotion to Wyatt Earp, who seemed to him not quite enough of a gentleman but certainly enough of a lawman. Often enough, Doc's mind was on the most recent sentence he had read in a Mattie letter, or on something else she had sent all the way from sultry Savannah. She had recently confessed to him that she had widened her studies again, had sought to go back to being a poet, at least had begun writing new poems, not quite the poems she herself would have expected from a near-nun, based on readings or meditations that surprised her about herself as, tentatively, she burrowed into ancient literature, fired by some rusty old tome in the convent library (too boring to be censored, apparently) into attempting the monstrously difficult form of old India known as the *ghazal*, no sample of which she had yet sent him ("still slaving at it," she wrote), abandoning for the time being the little prayer she had mentioned earlier, and now, as if having at last found a questionable—*most* questionable—form for her blazing sensitivity, voicing a statue of the poet Ovid in a Rumanian town—something she called "The Poet Ovid's Prayer from the Black Sea." So, she was back to prayer again, but in a most abandoned way that would surely have got her expelled had she circulated the poem.

O.K.: The Corral, the Earps, and Doc Holliday

Please make the huge red hibiscus my dinner plate
All grubby again while I, black bird-limed statue
In a Rumanian square, hunched on a giant plinth
Bearing contemptible insignia while a hesitant boy
Crosses the road, beg for a tent to cover me,
A quotation from the piratic winds wobbling
In the uproar above my skull. I was unsafe to know,
So let me once more wind a tapeworm around
My throat, in homage to treason.

It was the closest Doc had ever seen her to theological suicide, fixing on that rapscallion Ovid, whom he recalled distantly for the spicy *Ars Amatoria*, passed from sticky hand to sticky hand at school. Why she had chosen Ovid she did not say, though any reader could see rebellion stewing in her lines, in the last one especially. Heavens: perhaps she had in mind an entire series about Ovid and his rank behavior, designed to get her crucified, at least to the extent that nuns suffered any such thing. His Mattie was busting out, he could see that, but only within the confines of a letter, a poem. It was as if she had taken up boxing in the chapel. As poems went, her Ovid poem was not half bad, he thought, too garish perhaps (but she often had been) and, depending on how you read it, weighted with a too blatant pathos. Her early poems, which he had read at ease on his back in a Georgian valley, had been less acrid, less historical, more swooning and fertile. So this was what postulation, or whatever they called it, might do for a young woman left to her own devices, still dickering about the devotional life. It did not sound as if she had quite taken to it, not if her Ovid was any indication. Anyway, where were the *female* Roman poets? Had there ever been any? He knew of none. Her dilemma, he sensed, had to do with the faint difference between doing God's work as prescribed by an institution and God's work as permitted to the free-ranging imagination: duty and desire, the pernicious twins. Oh hell, why did he have to go through all this? Why now? Just when he thought he had her in exact focus, she had moved on, or sideways, not so much becoming another woman as turning into a different abstraction. He had really doted on her in their teens, and now she was sea-changing at speed, not even matching up to his notion of the Nun, but behaving more as if she had gone on to some supreme graduate school into which he had the brains to follow, but hardly the impetus, and certainly not from an enormous distance with killings all around him, his friends dead or wounded, his future very much in doubt. He had still not gotten over the white gloves encasing the hands of the three corpses before they were wheeled away for burial. The same town, that put its dead on show in the hardware store window like so many shoes in boxes, offered Paris dresses to those who could afford them, and many could, fortune-hunters who had come good on the silver platform that Tombstone provided. Remnants of events tugged at him, matters he should have been able to dismiss, but which occupied him with all the force of cadavers. W. B. Murray had offered Virgil twenty-five armed men "at a moment's notice. If you want them, say so." Had he and the Earps not needed them, even if only to spread the blame? Had Virge really answered that it was all right for the outlaws to be armed in the O.K. Corral because it was not illegal to carry arms in a livery stable? Why had they had any part of the right on their side? The horse with its head in the window of Spangenberg's bothered him, especially when Wyatt as deputy city marshal, if that, decided to pull the offending animal off the sidewalk. As he seized the bit to back the horse, Frank McLowery charged outside and grabbed the reins. Virgil came to help and he and Wyatt both watched the cowboys slotting bullets into their gunbelts, as if nothing were going to happen. What part had the crowd in front of Hafford's played in the shootout, egging on the Earps? Would we not have done it, Doc wondered, without popular support? Were we putting on a show for the rabble? Did we really need to do what we did? Yes. The town was rife with feuds, between town and country cowboys, between cowboys and miners, maybe even, if you could track it down, between poets and consumptives, bards and lungers. They should all have settled for a five-cent bottle of iced beer to blur their prejudices, although the effect of beer on the likes of Ike Clanton was extraordinary: no help. Yet Ike Clanton had remained unarmed. Maybe there was a connection between beer and helplessness. What had he said, the worst among all the preposterous things he came out with? "Fight is my racket. All I want is four feet of ground." He was lucky not to have found six, buried in the correct cowboy rig for the great last day: stockman style, as they called it, shotgun chaps, Mexican loop holster for the .45, high-heeled boots, vest and dark shirt, wide flat-brimmed hat. A general look of natty, pragmatic splendor, all for the grave. The Earps looked so much alike that Tombstone had weighed them, the differences being minimal, none of them above 158, Virgil the oldest the heaviest, Morgan a touch heavier than Wyatt, each with wavy light-brown hair, periwinkle blue eyes that never twinkled, and copious mustache. Indeed, those firing in the O.K. Corral could not have known who they were shooting at, the point being of course that he Doc was the deadliest marksman, in fact and by repute, yet he had been the last to shoot just because of circumstances. He might not have been there at all but finishing off the last hour of innocent sleep. Had they weighed *him*, he would have come out light on account of all the blood he'd spat over time. Give a horse to Morgan and Wyatt would end up with it even though it properly was Virgil's. Why, Doc mused, even if they had compared penises, the Earps would have been identical, although, come to think of it, could the other two like Morgan that day have vaulted the Alhambra lunch counter to lead him Doc out into the street before he got into worse trouble with the profuse Ike? Out in the street, bickering and yelling, they attracted the attention of City Marshal Virgil Earp, who never kidded about his job, having already arrested Mayor Clum for speeding in a buggy and his own brother Wyatt for brawling. If they refused to quit their indoor and open-air row, Virgil said, he'd calaboose them both, and it would cost them dough. So Doc sidled away and Ike headed for the Eagle Brewery, where Wyatt told him there was no money in fighting. Come to think of it, Wyatt had always been more interested in money than in fighting. Laughing about the 1880 territorial census, they had all joked about what they put down as their Tombstone profession, Wyatt a farmer, later to become saloon-keeper, James Earp also saloon-keeper, Morgan and Warren Earp laborers, Doc a dentist, Virgil correctly as a U.S. deputy marshal. Therefore, Doc noted, *ergo*, during the O.K. Corral gunfight, Wyatt was a saloon-keeper deputized as a deputy town marshal by Virgil expressly for shooting duties and he, Doc, the deadly dentist also roped in and deputized. He would have loved to wear the star just once—the shield, the badge, whatever it was known as in the profession. Doc dreamed about U.S. Marshal Crawley P. Dake, officially blamed for not keeping order in Cochise County, arriving in Tombstone with a trunkful of badges to pin on all brave and willing men, Doc among them. It could all have been more glamorous, and perhaps it would be again, once the corpses had cooled.

·23·

Landladies he had had here and there, best of all in Atlanta where a Mrs. Pomeroy had ministered to him, red-cheeked and insultably polite, never quite certain if he was being sarcastic or sentimental (she never knew him quite well). This landlady had a booby trap called Miss Amelia, her sister, some dozen years older, and Miss Amelia liked to explain the fire drill in case the house went up in flames. She showed all guests the long, coarse rope, thicker than her wrist, and told them to tug it three times for her to come and guide them (she was almost blind), and to slide down it as far as possible while she was coming up. Doc could only imagine the bedlam on the stairs if the fire drill ever went into operation. His worst/best experience with Miss Amelia had been in his first week, when, sleeping late, he had been in bed when she came upstairs on her sleepwalking household chores. Making his bed with him still in it, and wholly unaware of his presence, so numb her hands were, she covered him over with a winding sheet of her own devising. That clinched it. He could not let go such a novel incessant interlude, shocking him with humdrum surprises daily, so much so that he longed to be in Miss Amelia's inchoate neighborhood, ready to escape conflagration with her as they slid down the rope together toward its soaped noose. That kind of company, of gifted unself-conscious eccentrics, he had always needed and would go far to get, never dreaming of course that it would take him as far as Tombstone and into such real peril as distinct from the mythic kind.

In the meantime he owed Mattie a poetry-sensitive letter on the occasion of Ovid's prayer and his statue in unthinkably far-off Rumania. Then he would tell her more, much more. After the Bird Cage Variety Theater opened on December 21, 1881, providing Tombstone with something new to gawk at, the town did not quieten, but filled with threats and rumor: some undelivered horror stood ready.

The same old Tombstone, Doc thought: it was always like this, except that the talk included not only the Earps and Doc, but Marshall Williams of Wells, Fargo; Mayor Clum; Judge Spicer (who had dismissed the lawsuit) and Thomas Fitch. It was as if the gun battle had confirmed the town in its ways, proving that blood could always be shed with the merest effort, no matter what quasi-civilized behavior provided a background for it. December 28, a Wednesday eight weeks to the day after the O.K. set-to, with the election for city marshal only a week away, Virgil Earp drifted from the Oriental Saloon to his inelegant little room at the Cosmopolitan Hotel, half an hour before midnight, ready to call it a day, thanking his stars for a few hours of comparative quiet. His limp had abated, but it still characterized his gait, and he would always favor that leg after the calf wound. As he neared Fifth Street, going slow, a series of shots rang out from a construction site on the southeastern corner, hitting him twice. He did not go down and obstinately resumed his walk, now a lurching totter, aiming for the Oriental, where Wyatt still would be. He was at once helped to his room at the Cosmopolitan, mainly for privacy, and Doctors Matthews and Goodfellow were called, the latter soon to make a golden reputation in San Francisco. Virgil's left arm had suffered most, above the elbow, the damage being a longitudinal fracture of the humerus. Four shots, diarist George Parsons recalled, from "very heavily charged guns, making a terrible noise," so loud he thought they had come from right under his window, so he dropped behind the adobe wall until the firing stopped. Sent for, Doc soon arrived and made a routine inspection that was quite unneeded. Guards took position outside the hotel and Virgil's room even as he was saying, with excruciated laughter, "It's hell isn't it?" He still had one arm left to hug his wife with, he said, when she was in the mood.

To soothe himself after the commotion, George Parsons, the scribbler Doc envied more than he did anyone in Tombstone, stopped by Mr. Massey's and had a game of euchre with Messrs. Morehouse and White. As for Doc, he was wondering when his turn would come, but decided to walk boldly wherever he went, shrinking from no bushwhacker, no assassin. Mayor Clum decided not to run and within months had sold his interests in Tombstone and gone to a less violent place more in accord with President Arthur's edict. When George Hearst, the mining baron, visited the town in 1882, amid rumors of his being imminently kidnapped, Wyatt served as his bodyguard, showing him the "Dead House," the morgue, with the remains of two fellows blown up by dynamite only days before: boots, bones, and flesh in no discernible order, matted with hair and cloth. "You never know," Wyatt said.

"I'd rather not," quipped the mining magnate. "This town has a bad name. Even its accidents have a peculiar intended quality." Squabbling in the street with the admittedly superior classical scholar Johnny Ringo, abuse flying on the back of earlier abuse and guaranteed never to cease until either was dead, Doc began to wonder if any of them would survive the aftermath of the gunfight. The rhetoric of blood filled the afternoon street; people bumped into one another with improvised impatience, scowling and muttering. There on Allen Street the Earps waited for trouble to explode yet again and eventually disarmed both Ringo and Doc, urging them to go their separate ways, Wyatt making a mental note to get a posse out after Ringo, the outlaw leader. When the posse eventually left town, it stayed out a week, only to return and find Ringo had given himself up to Johnny Behan and was awaiting trial. George Parsons, wondering how much longer he could last in a town of such swirling, malign momentum, told his diary he was so agitated when he was out walking that he removed his gauntlet so as to maneuver his pistol freely. A week later he was writing, "Yesterday Earps taken to Contention to be tried for killing of Clanton. We saw Earps on one side of the street, Clantons on the other. Watching each other. Blood will surely come. Hope no innocent innocents will be killed." Three days later he recorded a killing by Indians at Antelope Springs, but managed to soothe himself with thoughts of railroad steam and singing coyotes. He got himself vaccinated as well.

The worst thing happened on March 18, 1882, not just the work of swindlers and outlaws, but of scheming murderers, the context of the whole facetious and zany. At the Schieffelin Hall, the Lingard Troupe was performing "Stolen Kisses" for Tombstone, an artifact of immeasurable wholesomeness attended by Wyatt and Morgan, who then repaired to Campbell and Hatch's Saloon for a game of pool, at which Morgan excelled through long practice. As he craned forward to execute a particularly difficult shot almost out of his reach, the upper window in the rear door exploded behind him. There were two shots, one of which bored into the wall above Wyatt's head (heeding the unwritten obligation that required all and sundry to miss him), while the other took Morgan in the small of his back, crashing through his spine and out the other side. It was a fatal shot, but only for Morgan, not for George Berry into whose thigh it burrowed while he stood by a stove in the front of the pool hall. Dying, Morgan whispered something to Wyatt and then expired, to lie surrounded by flowers in the Cosmopolitan while the bells of Tombstone tolled again. It was by no means unusual in Tombstone to hear shots after eleven at night; indeed, some residents had been known to get fidgety if the customary premidnight bangs did not take place. To his diary, George Parsons whispered that it must have been Frank Stilwell, the notorious outlaw, then added, "Morg lived about forty minutes after being shot and died without a murmur. Bad times ahead now. Attended church, morning."

The only certain thing in Tombstone now was what Parsons and others called absentee reckoning: only the dead had not done it; there was no telling which bandit had or had not come to terms with the Clanton and McLowery gangs for which insensate deed. All that was certain was that the same names came up in reported threats, with a decreasing number remaining, especially after Wyatt sent the Earp wives to California by train, Morgan's body having gone off a day earlier. To Tucson with him he took a small posse, Doc included, all of them heavily armed, to guard the family as they got off the train to take dinner and then to reboard. When Wyatt saw Frank Stilwell, there ostensibly to meet another train bringing a grand jury witness to town, Wyatt gave chase, caught up with Stilwell as the westbound prepared to depart, and accosted him about twenty yards in front of the engine, thrusting the barrel of his shotgun toward him even as Stilwell grabbed it. They wrestled each other to the ground, Wyatt levering the barrel lower and lower until it sat opposite Stilwell's heart and then went off. The person accompanying Stilwell to Tucson, and with him in the train station, was Ike Clanton, incessant talker at the O.K., blathering accuser at the first trial, and drunk who rambled all over town the night before the gunfight, the impotent loudmouth ever recruiting to the Clanton gang men who would shoot to preserve it. But after the death of Stilwell, Ike vanished, and Wyatt and his men spent hours searching for him, now in the mood to wipe out as many Clantons as they could, justice or no justice.

It was at this point in his august career that Wyatt went beyond the law, having no authority to kill Stilwell, although bearing in his pocket warrants for others, a permit from U.S. Marshal Crawley Dake, and some two and a half thousand dollars in posse money. While Doc was mouthing off about skinny piles of pus, yellow-belly threats and counterthreats mired in ordure and washed in slime, Wyatt was busy preparing a personal vendetta or, as a more modern idiom would say, losing it. "It all ends now," he would say in a seething rage, though nobody was clear what he meant, maybe his own life and Doc's, or the lives of all Clantons, women, children, distant relatives in Bohemia and Dublin included. His favorite brother had been murdered, and the absence of Morg's affable, sturdy, bluff countenance had turned him askew. Wanted for murder, he had to leave Tombstone, with Sheriff Behan on his track instructed by wire from Tucson; but the telegraph operator happened to be a friend, who delayed the wire an hour to give Wyatt a head start. He liquidated his assets, said goodbye, and cleared out of town at the gallop, still with a posse, now enlarged, and still muttering, "It all ends now." Hearing him, Doc remembered something Morgan said before the O.K. gunfight. "Kill them all. Let them have it." To which Doc responded, "Morg, Wyatt is my friend, but I am beginning to *love you.*"

·24·

Under constant pressure and accusation, severed from humanity except by a tenuous lifeline to Savannah, Doc tended his nasty plant devotedly, not that a cactus needed much. It was never until he left his condign little hovel for the bright lights of the saloons and card rooms that Doc recognized how little padding there was in his days, that the miscellaneous noise of the rabble—shots fired into oil lamps, horses ridden into stores, fireworks let off like exclamation marks in the midst of the general outcry, screams of affront and howls of pain, long slithery sounds of throwing up, undisguised groans of disgust as hangovers bit home—all this kept him chipper, out of himself, away from the sullen recognition that most of his life he had lived against the odds, delighted usually to wake each morning, not much afraid to go to sleep, never in much need of company so long as he heard the racket of the mob, the untuned pianos, the strident fiddle, the click of gambling chips, the diminutive clatter of cup on saucer, the tiny suffocated ping of fork on plate, and could, with Wyatt say, stride out along Allen Street munching one of Pucette Romany's redhot morning buns known to the local gentry as earps (or early acting roasted pussy). Where her name came from, what book of half-hatched handles, he did not know, but to eat the things was a juggling act as, too hot to handle, they bounced from one hand to the other, a crumb of civilization although not of the South.

My dear Mattie,

It is so long since I have seen one of your poems, this one as startling as I have seen, arriving in this turbulent town like a well-trained dove from an order of being, a dimension, of sweet deliverance. As you know only too well, Tombstone has been in the news in the worst possible light, and people are leaving town. More will have gone by the time this reaches you. Those of us remaining feel as if a spell has broken; not only do we feel like survivors, as survivors should, if indeed we still are that, but we feel both elect and doomed at the same time. Wyatt is still in Arizona, thank goodness, out and about on various missions, and I may soon join him. If he is not prospecting, he is looking people up or tracking the missing.

I had never realized you had a fondness for Ovid, whom I remember from grammar school for some risqué things about love. I find, now, that addressing a nun is no different from addressing Gosper, the acting governor of Arizona with whom I once roomed. I do not have to be delicate or abstemious: just tell the truth. After all, as I understand the veil, at least as well as I do the cloth and silk, nuns exist to assist people in dealing with their own abominations. So it is not a matter of protecting people from the bad things in life, but of helping them to deal with them. The nun, out in practice in everyday life, dips her hands in the dreadful without becoming contaminated. Unless, of course, we are dealing with nuns who devote themselves to things metaphysical and never go out. I sometimes do not know which type you intend to be.

Back to your poem. It has gorgeous images, as always, and some arresting shifts of voice. I like that hesitant boy crossing the road—he might be the young Ovid or an epitome of the young braveling, a foretaste of the rotten things that could happen to an outspoken poet.

He paused as some clatter began on the stairs, no doubt a new arrival carelessly lugging his belongings alongside him, heedless of others' repose or of those intent on attempting an appreciative letter to a gifted nun with a poetic gift.

In the end, the strongest image I find is that of the tapeworm around the throat, a gross metaphor for all outspoken people. It might have been around almost anything else, but where it is makes you gag as being throttled along with him. This takes me back to the huge dinner plate in the first line, one an image of plenty, the other one of strangulation. I love the notion of the big flower (they are a foot wide, aren't they, some of them?) being a dinner plate: you eat the perishable off the perishable. My own flower, mate or buddy, is the carrion cactus, not easy to sniff at, but, once you get used to it, cordially encouraging. This is how we were taught to read poetry in the old days, quite instructive I used to think, and now it stands me in good stead. Your poem is not one to puzzle over, however, unless you get lost in speculation, say about how the petal plate got grubby again, perhaps from a second helping? You never know. Nivver, we used to say around here. I sit here at the end of an era, telling myself, oddly enough, I am on my own again with my own disease, as one is when reading poems. I like Ovid for wanting a tent over him; I know that feeling, Mattie (nun-like?), and I relish his thought about being unsafe to know, which has been true of yours truly.

Now the battery from the stairs became another noise, mobile, more aimed, a clomping shuffle that preceded a knock on his door, then two more, followed by a series of impatient increasingly fast ones, in the humiliating vocative: *"Doc?"* He did not answer, but, sucking inspiration from defiance, cocked both pistols and arranged himself against the pillows to face the door, which was not locked (it did not lock, it was a door that had seen better days and more rambunctious knockers). On he wrote, hectic, nervous, piqued, managing to get a sentence further before it all became too much and he bellowed a response.

I wanted to tell you how I responded to the piratic winds, so [he left a space for the mot juste, now feeling too harassed to decide on it] *and I had to think about that one, it is almost more rich than I can bear. Someone at the door, sorry, I will resume.*

"What? Who the hell?" He bellowed, but his throat was dry, his vocal cords had tightened from the sheer concentration of writing the letter, and what he yelled was hardly audible even to him—unneeded, however, as the door burst in, with almost the intemperate speed of someone drawing on him, and Parsons the diarist appeared in the doorway, lucky to miss the bullet that hummed past his neck and buried itself in the wall across the corridor. In his hand, perhaps drawn in panic like a six-gun, reposed his latest toy, the newfangled Waterman fountain pen, huge and chubby, almost too big for him to manage (the first model, arriving from back East). With this weapon in hand, Parsons appeared tinier than ever.

"Jesus, Doc, you didn't have to shoot!" Parsons's life was a series of near-misses, all dutifully recorded in his little book. Panicked as he was, he marveled to see Doc clearly interrupted in the act of writing, yet with a gun in either hand, one emitting a haze-blue curl of smoke.

"You almost got me that time," Parsons said, unoffended but austere. Doc might have seemed to have been cheating at poker (Parsons loved games, discerning in them perhaps a model of Tombstone itself: life as a gamble, a prank, an exercise in mindless distraction). "Please don't."

"You sure got better at ducking, you old fart," Doc told him. "I wouldn't go around knocking on doors and then barging in. Wyatt will buffalo you, but some of the surviving badmen will drill you for sure."

"I came to tell you," Parsons began, mustering a broken smile, but Doc interrupted.

"I don't want to hear. You write your diary and I write my letters. Would you care to exchange roles for a week? What do you know of Ovid the Roman poet?"

"Smutty," Parsons told him with an almost disdaining leer. "Your Latin is better than mine."

"*Tot homines, quot sententiae.*" Doc was getting into the mood.

"Misquoting again," Parsons bluffed. "All we need is Johnny Ringo and we'll have a triumvirate of classical scholars. God forbid." Parsons palped between finger and thumb his recently healed broken nose, an injury sustained by accident in one of Tombstone's swarming crowds; an elbow had caught him and laid him low, back into his diary, where he had written, "Hurts like the devil. Can't blow it."

"You're a messenger, I take it?" Doc had suddenly realized this was not a social call on Parsons's part, gregarious as he was, especially toward people in power. By now, however, Parsons had thought fast about the messenger's being killed in the old Greek tradition and was almost on the point of not delivering. Yet, in tough times of heavy lifting from office to office—heavy ledgers and boxes of carbon copies—his colleagues had called him a Trojan, so it was as a doughty Trojan that, clear of all involvement with Latin, he said what he had come to say. As he did so, he wished he could have done it in Latin, thus creating an aura of doubt as to the exact message.

"They want you down in Bisbee."

"No, they don't," Doc quipped, suddenly aware of why this man irritated him: not with his incessant diary, about which he talked all the time like an invalid discoursing on an irreversible disease, but with his use of the sobriquet "Doc" to indicate Dr. Goodfellow, Tombstone's best. This purloining of his own local copyright had always bothered Doc, and right now he was not in specially genial humor. "No they don't," he snapped, "and they can't have me anyway. I have to be leaving town." He already had in mind Silver City, Rincon, New Mexico and Colorado, along with Wyatt and whoever else wanted to come along, leaving the George Parsonses behind.

"You're wanted for sure," Parsons told him. "There was an accident. A shooting."

"None of my work," Doc said. "I'm retired, you know."

"What is that stench?" Momentarily distracted, Parsons had succumbed to the carrion cactus, backing into the doorway that now framed him, the very personification of a man about to depart or deliquesce, perched on the very edge of being temporary, wrinkling his almost-healed nose. Laconic in his diary entries, often to the point of omitting verbs, Parsons was becoming that way in conversation too, almost a fugitive from Dickens, *The Pickwick Papers*, say, which he had read and allowed to form his prose style, wishing he did not live in Arizona and could emulate Dickens in his apparently simpleminded relish of such English things as roaring fires, slipping on ice, a haunch of roast beef at Christmas, and elementary love affairs. Samuel Weller the pithy cockney bootblack who was his progenitor might have found a richer vocation in Tombstone. Again Parsons tried to deliver his message. Now he gave Doc the wire that had arrived downstairs in the lobby.

Puzzled by the scrawl, Doc got up, walked to the window and winced at the disappearing soreness in his back. Mildly injured, he felt the wound's traces still. He was wanted in Bisbee to assist in an investigation of a death: Big Nose Kate was no more. He felt no grief, but an almost arithmetical pang for the woman who, in the end, in a drunken fit, had tried to frame him as an outlaw. She had taken her thousand dollars and gone, and he had never expected to see her again. Now they wanted him to come and view her remains, with the gift of her cactus still prickling his nostrils. He would rather go the other way, northward, out of the whole damned area, but something from an old honorable Southern tradition nagged at him; she had not died, she had been killed, but by whom? Pestered by Parsons, who was always keen on gossip, he at length got himself dressed under those deliberate eyes and invited the diarist along for the twenty-mile ride to Bisbee, where Kate had died in infamous Brewery Gulch, a victim of ill-fortune, far too young for this.

After a brisk series of gallops without conversation, Doc and Parsons were in Brewery Gulch by noon and conducted to the squalid little shed in which she lay in state naked on a wooden slab, bosomy and buttocked as ever, hardly the worse for wear, with no sign of a wound. It seemed that some hothead drunk had entered the saloon, shooting at random as cowboys often did, an event that Doc had often witnessed without even looking up from faro. It had always struck him as the loudest form of crude conversation. Those in the know, Kate included, had gone for the floor while bullets whirled until the cowboy ran out of ammunition and his little paddy was over. They all arose save Kate, who had remained there on the floor in her ungainly sprawl, inert and unblemished, dead perhaps of a heart attack. Or so the locals thought, lacking any kind of a doctor to check her out. Now they had a former dentist, far from ideal, but many of them would have let a veterinarian examine them, none too fussy about the dividing line between animal and human.

"Look," Doc said to the aghast diarist, already making notes he would later write up without the verbs. "Nothing." He looked again, turning Kate over onto her front, trying not to hear gurgles from within or notice an aroma not that of carrion cactus, but akin. Then he saw what nobody else had seen in their cursory first and final look: a tiny fleck of blood on one buttock, a dab, a bloblet, congealed of course but firmly attached almost like a blister. They brought him the razor he asked for, and as best he could he performed partial autopsy, confirming that, when the shootist drunk had entered the saloon, Kate had dived for the floor with her butt toward him and taken an invisible hit in the rectum, an area of little or no resistance. The bullet had traveled all the way up to her heart, rending her entrails as it went. Doc removed the bullet with an agonized sigh and patted the remains in bewildered pain. He felt distorted, called upon to perform on his old beloved an act so gross it shocked even Parsons the diarist, and Doc depending on medical knowledge long rusty had gone right only through a series of mistakes. It was grotesque to be paddling around in the penumbra of the parts that had given him so much pleasure not that long ago. He felt sickened by the sheer meatish quality of human life and he agonized, right there in the presence of her remains, about the lyricism that celebrated the private parts of women, what dear old Milton had called the "zone," adored, revered, coveted, fondled, licked, buffeted, hymned, only to come to this last favor. Who could tell now what bliss her parts had given, even to him alone, or what jealousy they had provoked, what lust, what hatred? He could not bear to think about it, even in one who had betrayed him. Why had she behaved so badly toward him after behaving fairly well? Now she was—nowhere. She still had seepages, of course, and an almost peaceful contemplative look with closed eyes, as if old Buda had come to mind one last time and she was thinking of trying life once again from scratch, from a different starting point, heading into Russia instead of the United States (a term that immigrants dreaming of America never used).

"Accidental death," Parsons suggested, licking his pencil's point. "Misadventure."

"All of that," Doc told him. "They used to say that, if you found yourself among bullets, the best thing was to hoist your rear end into the line of fire and trust to luck. It was the least lethal place to be hit. So much for maxims. Poor Kate, buggered by a bullet."

"Bulgarian?"

"Hungarian, actually."

"Oh," whispered Parsons, disappointed, having hoped for a structural pun of some kind. How little we knew of those eastern countries, some of them only just created out of a loose amalgam that united states, provinces, areas, principalities and puppet monarchies. Kate had come from there to an ignominious end, raw material for the diarist, the autopsy man, the peerer and leerer, ripe for a dirty joke in the saloon. In later years, the rumors would begin, bringing her back to life, hailing her origin (this time in Pest), and a host of impostors would surface, claiming to have known Doc and seen him at the O.K. Corral on that accursed day. No doubt the very gun that killed her would reach antique stores with a ticket dangling from its butt, worth a fortune even while the sublime meat of her body had almost completely rotted away. By then, though, they would be saying that Doc suffered from syphilis; indeed, he did not put it past Parsons to do just that, ever alive to something picturesque and scandalous.

What happened to Big Nose Kate, though, was more than Parsons could stomach: one side of him, the sensationalist, doted on the approach to her the slug had made, almost like fate retaliating, whereas the other side winced and looked away, unhappy that any human could suffer a destiny so gross. He was no killer or shootist, that was plain, unaccustomed to seeing men in extremis, and less able to handle the gruesome spectacle than your average nun. Armed with the slug that finished his Kate, Doc left Bisbee in short order, having seen to her burial and arranged for a suitable cross. How would Mattie have handled this? He did it just so, trusting in his divination of her tact. Whatever Kate had done, whatever she had taken her wages for, she had done with it all now and her name must be left in peace and honored—honored for what, he wondered. For the dignity of having been used and idealized. He instantly regretted all the times he had yelled at her, called her names and otherwise abused her (just as he deplored, and then forgave, her own version of the same thing). He fixed on the romantic interludes, most of them conducted in a vaporous glow from a red light, when he persuaded himself she never went off whoring to pay the rent. It took some effort to achieve that degree of oblivion, but at times he had risen to it, sharply sealing off their situation from any outside event. He had almost learned, from Napoleon perhaps, how to make his mind a chest of drawers; when a drawer was closed, he did not think of its contents. So there were hours when his cough did not plague him, and her promiscuity did not wound him. Try not to think of God, he would tell himself, and he almost managed it, at least until he recognized that God was in everything, at the heart of Kate's misbehavior even. That stopped him, at least until he saw that the universe accommodated everything without the least ripple; it left moral judgments to human beings, who of course were part of the universe in any case.

Back in Tombstone, he set the death slug in the pot that held his carrion cactus and bowed it welcome, wondering what would join it next. He asked the diarist if he might read about various events, most of all the gunfight at the O.K., but Parsons refused, saying he might let Doc look at his entry on going to Bisbee to see the end of Big Nose Kate, an entry that as far as Doc could tell he never made, out of dithering shock or an all-enveloping fastidiousness.

When he got back, Doc found a letter for him in which Mattie described the convent, drawn into it by a reference to their orchard, which doubled as a cemetery, with the obvious implication that dead sisters nourished the fruit, if such a thing could be. There were pews for visiting nuns, a hospice, an almonry, a bakehouse for guests (with a better menu), a kiln or drying house, a special room for the preparation of sacramental elements, a refectory, a bath, a *latrina* as she termed it, a cloister garth, an old room once consecrated to leeching and now an infirmary, a barn with a threshing floor, a guest house (he smiled), a school and what tempted him most: a scriptorium and library. What premises, he thought, worldlier by far than where he had lived and spluttered in Dodge, Las Vegas, Prescott and Tombstone. *He* was the deprived one, eking out a living in restricted quarters. He looked again, hard, having missed one item because his eyes had skipped, eluding the penmanship imperative of her bold, announcing hand: *calefactory*, he read. Ask her what a calefactory is. Something to do with heat, where things are warmed up, perhaps? She went into the practice of painting frescoes into wet plaster—while it was still "fresh," and he loved the idea. What on earth would they have done with Big Nose Kate impaled on a bullet? Would the resident doctor have quailed? Not a bit of it; she would have rendered back unto God God's own creature without the least sentimental obfuscation. And what was an almonry? He would have to ask, perhaps mentioning his journey to Bisbee, just to see what she would say. Maybe the soul of Kate had arisen in a flash, like the corposant that showed sometim in a ship's rigging. He had not been there, and if such a thing happened it took place in the first few seconds after death, did it not? Could a pure soul have ascended from Big Nose Kate, the depraved courtesan? He did not doubt it, sensing she had gone to a celibate Tombstone worth idolizing, gunless and cardless and whiskeyless. Not a bad start.

Already I am not here, he thought; I have not been wholly here for months. No wonder they bump into me in Allen Street and challenge me; they do not see me—bits of me are dangling in the wind like spider webbing laced with dew, no longer me but some intermediate material you cannot shoot through, nor eat, nor pull down and roll into a pretty ball. You are less yourself than you used to be, just when they slander you as an outlaw and hold-up man, the real badman, you have floated off to the calefactory and the almonry, never to be bothered again by censorious gossips. What had she told him, in a footnote intended to make him marvel? In old Toledo, the Visigoths permitted Christians to worship in their own way, referring to them as false Arabs or Mozarabians.

·25·

Newly haunted by events at Bisbee, he now found himself scrutinizing saloons for modes of evasion during gunplay. How many crouched low, backside in the air, as Kate had, no doubt offering a juicy target? Did these insane cowboys actually look for a comely ass to puncture? Or did they fire off rounds at utter random, hoping to miss but not going to break their hearts if they hit someone? Was this what the new President of the United States meant when he spoke of the depraved goings-on in Cochise County? Doc had always prided himself that his own shooting was pragmatic and diagrammatic, which was to say useful and instructive. Sometimes he lost his temper and shot somebody out of pique, but he had always tried not to, and he had never like Wyatt resorted to buffaloing men with the barrel of his gun. Kill them or wound them, he said, or walk away. People stayed away from Doc unless they had made their peace with the Almighty and drafted a will, whereas to an extent they allowed themselves to be administered or bashed about by Wyatt. As for Kate, Doc had already lost her when she died; she was remoter than any Mother Superior, he thought, and his memories of her were garish, savage, the tender touches fading first. Wyatt's famous line (said without a bridging *if*)—"I see a red sash. I kill the man wearing it"—sounded more like Doc than like Wyatt, but Wyatt was political. Only since the murder of Morgan had he become the raving avenger, galloping hither and yon to bring somebody to book.

Once again, Doc had surrendered his time to Wyatt who, gallivanting all over the desert with a pocketful of warrants for outlaws and rustlers, had become very much a man with a mission, cleaning up the neighborhood before quitting a town with a price on his head. Truly, both he and Doc were on both sides of the law, charged by Sheriff Behan with murder and lesser crimes, always being discharged when they showed up in court. Doc wondered if all the reasons touted for feuding were valid and if the real reason for it was not just plain dislike. What was the expression he had sometimes heard in the South, something nautical? One man did not like the cut of another man's jib, and that was that. It could be argued that Wyatt had tried to bribe Ike Clanton to squeal on the stage robbers only so that he Wyatt could claim the glory of their capture and so win the election, or any other election. But there was something else pushing him, a hunger for neatness, a passion for social hygiene, a yearning to have only friends and admirers about him. In the old days, Doc never hesitated to back him up, but now he witnessed a Wyatt intent on settling private scores— the murder of Morgan uppermost. Of course, but these vendettas kept him in Arizona until he had killed Stilwell, Florentino Cruz, Curly Bill and others. Wyatt had wiping them out much on his mind, and he certainly knew how to do it, first interrogating the villain under duress, then finishing him off out of sight as if taking a dump behind a bush. The sanitive in Wyatt bothered Doc, who had a strong yearning to be elsewhere, and this showed on March 24 when Wyatt killed Curly Bill Brocius at Mescal Springs, Wyatt having ridden ahead of the posse, creating the impression (as he got it) that they had hung back, leaving him to it. So, Doc had seemed hold off back with them, Texas Jack having had his horse shot out from under him. When Wyatt came back, Doc greeted him amiably: "Here, Wyatt, you must be shot to pieces. Let me help you off your horse." Wyatt felt bad about Doc's not having kept up with him, but he kept quiet; he had stumbled upon Curly Bill and Pony Deal while on foot, shotgun at the ready, only to be shot at by Curly Bill, the double charge of buckshot tearing through the skirt of his flapping coat. Curly Bill had used the Wells, Fargo shotgun he had stolen from the held-up Bisbee stage. Wyatt's double discharge blew a big hole in Curly Bill, virtually halving him, even as seven others all of them named in Wyatt's warrants broke for cover, and like the good businessman he was he checked them off, saying each name aloud as if casting a spell. Wyatt had a restive mount and was having trouble fishing his rifle from the saddle boot only to have more difficulty finding his six-gun, whose holster had slid down his leg and twisted to the back. All this time he was under fire from Pony Deal and the rest, with Doc and the others galloping out of range. Now, with his gunbelt around his thighs, he could not open his legs to mount, so he kept on shooting into the cottonwoods where the gang had hidden until he was able to hitch his belt higher, replace his empty six-gun with its twin, and grasp the saddle horn, aware suddenly of a potent aroma of rotten egg. Had Wyatt Earp befouled himself in anger? Once remounted, he backed away from the woods, keeping them covered with his Winchester. He saw Texas Jack removing all his tackle from the dead mount, and then making a run for it; it had taken him awhile to disentangle himself from the stirrups, and now Doc came to his aid, spurring out from cover and helping him to safety. Now Wyatt arrived behind the shoulder of rock where his posse waited, eyeing them skeptically; gunshots had followed him and his left leg was numb.

"That was a great fight you put up, Wyatt." Doc seemed unaware of Wyatt's indignation. "How bad are you hit?"

"Just my left leg, I guess."

Wyatt counted up, enumerating impacts as he had enumerated the wanted outlaws he had seen. Saddle horn shattered. Three holes in his pants legs. Five holes in the crown of his sombrero. Coat in rags. Yet no wound in that numb leg. Lifting his foot, he found a bullet stuck in the heel. His horse had three scrapes or nicks, nothing to fret about. Now Doc said, as he might have said earlier, "Let's go in and get them," but Wyatt demurred, saying they wouldn't get ten yards across the sand flat in between posse and gang. "They know what they're doing, Doc. They've gotten over their panic." Off they rode to water their horses and find Warren, Wyatt brooding on the first occasion that Doc had not supported him. The posse had seen no tracks because Curly Bill and his crew had come in by an abandoned trail, and Wyatt had been half-asleep in the saddle. His posse had been too far behind to do him any good. Or so he persuaded himself, arguing that they were good, brave men and simply did the wiser thing, being behind him and behind the bend in the trail—they had not seen anything. Wyatt had contested his own sense of disillusion before, usually managing to convince himself since he believed mainly in the decency of his associates as distinct from the depravity of others. He would never know. Had Doc and the others dawdled because they suspected some ambush, into which he himself had led his horse, or had they genuinely not known what was going on until they heard gunfire? Nobody trusts a man who trusts nobody, he told himself. Stop gnawing away at it. You came out lucky, but you might not have. Get these guys to stay closer and not let you get ahead so far, playing point.

They made camp some four miles from Tombstone, where Wyatt wrote and sent urgent letters to Wells, Fargo and *The Epitaph*, reporting his activities so far and the death of Curly Bill. Texas Jack rode off into town and came back with a vigilante who said Behan's deputies were on the prowl again. Now Wyatt wanted Ringo and Ike Clanton, except that Ike had gone to ground in Mexico. Wyatt decided, on advice, to stay where he was and await news of rustlers, reasoning that Curly Brocius's death would encourage the folk of Tombstone to report rustler doings to the right quarter. One way or another, working from intelligence received or stumbling into wanted men in the bush, he would get them all, wipe the slate clean, and head out never to return. He had had enough, but would not leave, he thought, until all of his jobs were done. The new, better Tombstone would be someone else's baby, which was pretty much what Doc felt, though he had a keener vision of the future: more camels, more cockfights, louder *mariachi* bands accentuating the Mexican flavor, more outdoor parties with bourgeois wives and children, not so many cribs in which lone wolves such as he could sleep and rage, awaiting the next showdown with nervous avidity. Yes, he might just as well have won Big Nose Kate in a card game; had it ever been subtler, more gracious than that? When he told Wyatt of her death, Wyatt merely nodded and murmured something about blood brothers and women always disappearing when they got bored. Only Josephine had kept his interest, to the disgust of

Johnny Behan, whose pursuit of Wyatt surely had an erotic basis; he hated Wyatt the pretend married man because Wyatt had cuckolded him, the divorcé. One day, Doc reasoned, Josie would link up with Wyatt anew; for now, Behan had his chance again, for what it was worth, reluctant to leave town because Josie was there unguarded, reluctant to stay because Wyatt was off in the hills, rampaging and vulnerable, as Curly Bill had initially found out. A lucky bushwhack could end Wyatt Earp forever.

Doc yawned. If Wyatt could write letters, so could he, it would be like the old days when they crossed the Jornada together and came down by way of Rincon. He could not, however, use Wyatt's semi-military messengers to send them off; he did not trust them and, in any event, his letters were not ready. He was wondering again about Mattie's Ovid poem. Surely that statue of Ovid was imaginary; it was what the town of his exile should have had years ago, and they didn't have it yet. Perhaps the poem's point was that Ovid was giving in to wishful thinking, hoping for a statue and so pretending to be one, even though statues could not speak. Was that it? Statueless dead poet craves yet another mode of non-speech? He smiled at her covert ingenuity and told himself not to be so sloppy in his letters, or indeed so reticent. Tell her the complete truth about the revenge killings: Indian Charlie (Florentino Cruz), Curly Bill, Stilwell and the rest. Such was the nature of life in Tombstone. So he began during the lull, taking heart from the rural setting and making a mental note to tell her about the landscape here, but first of all writing Mattie about H. Solomon, Aitch as he liked to be called, he who had once raised bail for Doc and now stood in the doorway of his bank as the Earp posse began to leave and, because they looked so miserably underequipped for what they intended to do, went straightaway indoors and emerged with a sawed-off shotgun and a belt of buckshot shells which he thrust on Doc, saying "Take it, Doc, with a banker's blessing."

That poem about Ovid kept troubling him, not because it was obscure, but because it seemed to imply something about himself, was a whispered hint about his own performance hardly as a lover, but as a confidant, an ally. As he now saw it, had grown to see it, Ovid the exiled scatologist who never saw his wife again was some version of John Holliday the exiled dentist who never saw his nun again. Oh, he kept getting the times and phases of things mixed up, as he did when trying to reconcile one letter with another, the lost ones sent with the one ready to go, the ones received with the one that just arrived. Could it be that she was hinting at something in their own lives? Had he become a mere statue to himself, to her? When a woman converted into a nun, did she become a statue too? When you were a statue, you longed to become flesh and blood. He felt this all the more, having, as a doctor, proved himself at an autopsy on Big Nose Kate. He would only ever be allowed to operate on the dead. Gone the days when, in a fit of rage back in the South, he had put Lucius Terrapin out with laughing gas and removed all his teeth, not so much out of vengeance as to see what would happen. It changed Terrapin's life; he left town and eventually drank himself to death in Biloxi. Doc had never regarded that feat as a victory, but he wished he could have done a like favor for the Clantons and McLowerys. So much of his expertise and his tenderness had gone to waste, never to return. And now this damned poem had come to haunt him, to remind him what an exile he was, what a severed person in his so-called prime. She meant to tell him something by way of dumb show or gesture, making a model rather than crafting an explanation. Her drift was obvious: they were never going to get together again, and her only concern was with his soul, that shred of agitated plasma he had almost forgotten existed. Trying to think so exultedly for so long made him long for something, someone, more banal, like George Parsons the indefatigable although untrustworthy diarist, with his gaping teeth growing outward at a curable angle, his short bandy legs, the constant speckle of perspiration across his brow, his shiny pomaded red ears, his general demeanor that of an overpromoted parrot, head jutting forward, heels raised as if ready to topple, craning over into his raw material, people. How Doc missed that bumptious, inquisitive little man who, when he got upset, which was often, went the color of permanganate. He would rather have Parsons develop another life for him, never mind how lowly, than have Mattie converse with him obliquely about exile and last things. He had never thought about it before, but he preferred the rough-and-tumble of his present mediocrity to the high steeples of pure distinction. He had eased off, even from gunfighting, and was not going to go back unless, God forbid, Wyatt were to challenge him and almost certainly lose. Wyatt would never be the quicker of the two of them, practice as he might; that abrupt, timeless contraction of the nervous fibers was not in his blood, whereas so much else was. It was a toss-up whether or not he would see Wyatt again, ever, which was weird considering how much extreme time they had spent together, not merely as wanted, accused, acquitted men in Arizona and, as he was to discover, elsewhere, but as fornicating friends, big gamblers and bigger spenders, dandies of the mauve twilight, as marooned in Tombstone as if they were on the moon. It was not in either of them to sag into nostalgia, looking back on the old days when they shone; it was more like them to bump into each other again after twenty more years and resume carousing as if nothing had intervened. Success in friendships with men, Doc had learned, had much to do with oblivion, with not seeming to care too much, always able to retreat to the position listed under ships that pass in the night. Men, American men, men of the West, Doc thought, did not have much gift for friendship, but for killing, yes, for piratical escapading, yes, for getting away from it all to some secret tree house in Avalon, of course. His dedication to Wyatt was a temporary thing, as both must have recognized, and would not outlast their time in Tombstone. They were hardly going to open up a saloon in Denver or a gun shop in San Francisco. Men lived in their private, synthetic dream, misers of aloneness, besotted with silver, blood and sperm. All else to them was alien pissantery.

Once having caught the sulk of disapproval in Wyatt's eyes as he returned to the posse after killing Curly Bill, Doc never forgot it, not that he felt ashamed about hanging back; after all, it was he who had ridden out into the open, fired at, to rescue Texas Jack Vermilion from his horse. If Wyatt had thought they were backward in coming forward, he was entitled to think it, but you had to judge men by the general tenor of their intentions, not by every little snippet of behavior. There was a way of putting up with the George Parsonses of the world, provided you judged them evenly, never letting any particular word, gesture or stunt put you off too much. An habitual extremist, Doc sometimes recommended mellow behavior to himself, but never became as mellow as Wyatt, whose disapproval was never eloquent, whereas Doc's came blazing out, guns behind it. He had a temper that some of the time he kept civil, and to worry about Wyatt's disappointment only made Doc more of a firebrand. In Wyatt the impression persisted that the posse, Doc included, had thought about their own skins first, and he let that sleeping dog lie; but he would never again expect heroic support from the men with him, never again say certain uninhibited words, make certain benign assumptions. This says that Wyatt had an old-fashioned, absolute view of friendship and honor, that he might have been an exemplary Knight Templar, while Doc was only working his way toward such an idea, and right now not at all, too busy keeping his balance in the saddle during arduous weeks and hundreds of miles of rough riding over difficult country. He never stopped coughing, but he stuck the course, sometimes fixing his mind on a distant subject—Mattie, Ovid, the swimming hole, his carrion cactus, the bullet that killed Kate—to distract him from the hardships of the ride. He did his share of firing too, killing several of the rustlers who had plagued the area for years. In fact, the posse did rather well, a good many of the surviving outlaws moving on to more hospitable pastures. Behan's light infantry, as some called his gangs, suffered major setbacks and became a phantom army, spread far and wide, just so long as they did not have to reckon with Earp the scourge and his violent small platoon. Supposedly, Johnny Ringo and Ike Clanton hung on in Mexico, waiting for Wyatt to lose interest and move on, which he did when he realized that no amount of vengeance was going to heal his heart. The accommodation had to come from within, not from scouring rough country for malefactors of old. It was said that more than a dozen rustlers had bitten the dust, which no doubt included the three dead from the O.K. Corral. Yet Behan, daunted enough to break up his own posse, nonetheless got back at them by arranging to put them on the wanted list in both Cochise and Pima counties, all of them, whether deputy United States marshals or not. Returning from his pursuit of the Earp-Holliday gang as he chose to think of it, he submitted an account for expenses of thirteen thousand dollars, one of his ways of staying wealthy, and waited for things to happen, caressing his enmity, dwelling in his authority.

What looked like a godsend was an invitation from Pitkin the governor of Colorado, indirectly saying the Earp posse would be welcome there, all the work of Governor Tritle of Arizona, who understood the situation. So away they rode, vindicated and predictably safe from the Behan machine, on the lam again but honorably self-discharged. It was a move that worked for Wyatt, but not for Doc, who chatted finally with him as they disposed of their horses in Silver City, New Mexico, and embarked by train for Pueblo, Colorado.

"You let me know," Doc told him, "if you need me."

"Yip."

"You sure ain't the talkin kind today, Wyatt."

"I'll be all right. I usually am when I'm lookin after mysel'."

"You're a daisy or a huckleberry then."

"Could be. You take care of that cough."

"Ah, Wyatt, it will take care of me, and soon."

"The train it is," Wyatt sighed. "Back to trains. Boy, have I seen trains."

"It will be restful," Doc answered with fake buoyancy. "It must." Then the posse climbed aboard.

All save Doc, who decided to lie low in Denver, headed for the boom town of Gunnison, and Doc on arrival checked in with the Arapahoe County sheriff's office on May 15, making the acquaintance of Charles T. Linton, a deputy who at once steered in his direction a so-called journalist from Arizona. So much for safety in numbers and any consequent anonymity. Having set eyes on Doc, the journalist pulled a couple of guns and announced that he was making an arrest. So there Doc was, high and dry, without his constituency of more or less like-minded territorial knights, in the custody of one Perry Mallen. Unarmed, Doc had only sarcasm to defend himself with, and Mallen, vastly impressed with himself and the newspaper noise he made, seemed impervious. Denver was fascinated, knowing enough about Doc to misspell his name as "Holladay" when reporting (the *Rocky Mountain News*) that Sheriff Perry Mallen had arrested "the notorious Doc Holladay, leader of the famous Earp gang of thugs, murderers, and desperadoes, who have made their headquarters in Arizona and who have committed murders by the dozen." Nobody knew who this Mallen was, or where he held the badge of sheriff. It was enough that like a water beetle he skimmed along on the meniscus of Doc's appalling reputation, waiting to make his arrest until Doc was comfortably unarmed. The Arizona reward due to him, if he got Doc back to Tombstone alive, was five thousand dollars, but the newspapers predicted that Doc would never make it. Johnny Behan's long arm of pseudo-law was reaching all over the country and succeeding only because he was well-connected and had had a good deal of practice in hounding innocent men. The *Denver Republican* got things wrong, identifying Mallen as a Los Angeles cop, and it also said that, compared to Billy the Kid, Doc was the more fiendish desperado. Indeed, it claimed that Doc had been the leader of the infamous "cowboys," thus supplanting the now defunct Curly Bill. The newspapers argued it out, the *News* going so far as to state that Doc was not without friends and proponents in Denver, which cheered Doc enormously; even the Wyatt Earp of Colorado, General D. J. Cook, who had tamed the wild men of his state, came out on Doc's side, perhaps because Doc thrived in Wyatt's shadow and Cook revered Wyatt. Besides, both Cook and Wyatt happened to be undercover men for the Wells, Fargo Company. Had Mallen not appeared, Colorado would have left Doc in the same peace as it left Wyatt, with Cook and Pitkin both endorsing their presence. It was to his advantage that those who cherished Earp would have to protect Holliday too. All would have gone well had Mallen in his intrusive greed not stirred the pot. Bob Paul, their old comrade in arms, was obliged to begin extradition proceedings, but now Bat Masterson, then deputy sheriff of Las Animas County, Colorado, where Doc had once figured in the census, came to his aid, denouncing Mallen as a fraud and a pawn of the Cochise County gangs. On went the maneuvering to keep Doc out of Arizona, he having left behind him in Tombstone, donated to the Oriental saloon, both the carrion cactus and the bullets, hardly his good-luck pieces, but indices to what in life he took gravely: the birth of life and the taking of it. He had always liked the idea that your fate was propelled by some outside force of enigmatic severity, a force you could dominate if you tried hard enough, and thus you emerged a victor, somebody self-satisfied because self-defined.

It was a poor idea of individuality, perhaps, revealing his assertive, climactic nature and his relative indifference to quality of life. It seemed enough to him to have struck the right attitudes, as so often in the South and in Southerners. Style was all, that perilous, chromatic emanation from the personality, something almost God-given but Satan-oriented, something the puritanical efficient North could never understand. To have arrived at the correct demeanor mattered more than almost anything; after all, a sophisticated person, he told himself, is one who is surprised by nothing, nothing at all, and so may be said to have lived it already. Something superstitious was gaining the ascendant in his personality; he not only liked the right social manner to be also the perfect private embodiment of a true aristocrat, he adored the thought that old souls, such as his, could rise to almost any situation without flinching, and to that of death most of all. If he had lived before, he had done it sagely. Nothing panicked him, though much provoked him. When he got angry, it was an anger five hundred years old, and he was a werewolf, a vampire, one of the undead, and he often wondered if the inviolable Wyatt had not somehow infused him with something of the same safety. Through all their battles they had come virtually unscathed, though skinned a bit in his own case. Surely this was enough to base a faith upon; famous generals have done no less, striding about amid the bullets, confident of never being hit. Perhaps, Doc thought, some other gift came with this one of being invulnerable, something not promised or striven for, something that promised a tremendous service to humanity: John Holliday, boon to humanity, sought out by millions, but for the time being jailed on a trumped-up charge which, improperly handled, could get him hanged. By the skin of such teeth did he establish his uniqueness, knowing he was going to make his predicted rendezvous with the undertaker and not be snatched away prematurely by some marauding band of outlaws, local sheriff doubling as hangman, lynch mob destroying the cheese box Tucson used as a jail. Perhaps he had never been superstitious enough, leaving complex presences to the whims of others, creating for himself a straight and narrow that only a monomaniac could accomplish. He was a good man in a bear pit, awaiting rescue by millionaire or altruist.

Above all, he sensed in himself a tendency to no longer need the things he used to transcend. He had transcended so much, in both Tombstone and Dodge, that he had come free in an autonomous zone devoid of provocative particulars. Was this the first onset of faith in himself or the eternal sign of universal steadiness? It was such a weird change he did not know what to call it, concluding it should not have a name at all. Beside the point, now, that people had assumed he was called Doctor because he had been good at caring for gunshot wounds, or that Wyatt had boastfully owned a string of racehorses or that when he saw Mattie off at the Tucson train depot it was the last time Wyatt set eyes on her, or that fifteen bandits had been hanged on the same tree at the same moment. The vast and slewed omnium gatherum of stuff he had crammed his head with suited him no longer. An odd innocence had come upon him based on ignorance. It was, God forgive me, he whispered, loving *his* Mattie without needing to see her and without needing to hear from her ever again. There she was, radiant and complete, needing nothing of him, tooled and gilded, there in the empyrean like an immigrant, heedless of human history. If this was the result of his lungs' decay, almost taking him to the point of ectoplasm each time he coughed, then the bacillus had made a useful point. He was matter. He had been matter. He was going to be more glorious, he thought, beautiful as an empty test tube in a rack.

·26·

May 22, 1882
    Dear Mattie,
    A jail is no place to write from, though perhaps none better to write in. They have manufactured yet another charge against me, and you must really be having second thoughts about your correspondent languishing in a Denver calaboose after committing once again the dastardly crime of being himself. Don't do it. Or they will latch on to you.
    The good side is that the other day a newspaper man came here to interview me. The last person to offer himself as a newspaperman was a bounty hunter in disguise who started this whole ball of—dirt rolling. All they want is the reward. Anyway, I told this reporter as best I could what had been going on, that a bent sheriff in cahoots with outlaws had been after me from the start. There I was, doing my best in front of everyone in Denver who could read. I was the martyr who would rather kill himself than be lynched by Sheriff Behan and his gangs.
    He has been the terror of the lawless element in Arizona, they wrote, and with the Earps was the only man brave enough to face the blood-thirsty crowd which has made the name of Arizona stink. Perhaps you will feel a small flicker of pride to find me presented thus. He saw me as slender, no more than five feet six inches (he got that wrong unless this whole business has shrunk me), with soft small hands, weight 150, about right, and determined-looking eyes. Hands like a woman's, he said. With a slender, dainty trigger finger and a slender wrist—he could have left that out, it needs no emphasis. I wore black, with a colored linen shirt, as now. I have, he noted, a quiet voice and gentlemanly manners. Hardly your basic impression of a thug? People will always see what they want to see, won't they?
    So I told him the old truth, about the so-called cowboys, who are murderers really, stage robbers and thieves, many of them fugitives from

284

Eastern justice. The proper name for them, I said, was Rustlers. They ran, run, things down in Arizona, and the big trouble began, I reckoned, with the killing of Marshal White by Curly Bill. I arrested Curly Bill. Marshal White fell into my arms.

They then asked if I expected trouble, being sent back to Arizona to face charges there. I told them after a moment's thought, and they watched me as I stared out at the rain enclosing Jailer Lambert's room. Taken back, that would be the last of Holliday. Once Sheriff Behan, whom we have tormented from the first, has me in his hoosegow, I am done. It was he who instigated the murder of Morgan Earp, whom he hated. They then asked me about Sheriff Paul of Tucson, not exactly a friend, but trustworthy, whose job it would be to take me back. His hands would be tied, I explained. Rather than go back to Tombstone, I would try to escape here and get shot by a decent man. Rather that than be hung by robbers down there. That shook them a bit. Paul is a good man, I said, but he cannot protect me. The jail there is a little tumble-down affair, which a few men could shove over on its side, and then a few cans of oil would burn it up in a flash and either burn a prisoner to death or drive him out to be shot down.

Did I not have friends there? Yes, I said, but the respectable element would stand by me, the trouble being that they were unorganized and intimidated. People leave rather than do anything. Until some respected citizen gets shot down, I mean another, nobody will do anything to clean the town up. They'll never do what they did out at Fort Griffin, where twenty-four men were hung on one tree when I was there. The Tombstone rustlers are part of the Fort Griffin gang.

They said I was charged with killing Frank Stilwell. I denied the charge and still do. I know he robbed a stage as he gave the money to a friend of mine to hold for him, and I know he was involved in the murder of Morgan Earp. He was seen running away. And Pete Spence. Sheriff Behan was behind these things. He hated me ever since I stopped him from quarreling over a faro game I was running. I refused to let him play anymore. Why, he has five rustlers under him as deputies. Imagine that. I told them all this and their eyes widened like those big hibiscus dinner plates you wrote about. Not long ago, three weeks ago, one of them, John Ringo, who fancies himself a scholar of Greek and

Latin, jumped up on the stage of the variety theater in Tombstone and grabbed all the jewels from the proprietor's wife in full view of the audience. This is the kind of country I will be going back to for my health.

His eyes teared with indignation and he ceased folding and refolding his copy of that day's *Denver Republican*, from which he had been refreshing his memory, snatching at marked phrases to brighten things up, at the same time trying to keep his recollection from being too shocking (he had forgotten, in the turmoil of being charged and arrested and jailed, that he had decided he need not shield her from anything anymore since the newspapers told all, and then some, and nuns were born transcenders anyway). Was he cutting a sorry or an heroic figure in the eyes of Denver and Mattie, or what? He almost did not go on, but he thought she should have the interview firsthand, at least addressed to her in a special version. On he wrote, laboring to compress, ending up with what resembled irony: *It's a nice, sociable country, I told them. They blinked. Then they asked who was this Mallen who came to arrest me, having already accosted me in a variety theater here (see, I did get out and about a bit, cheering myself up in a strange place). He exclaimed he wanted to thank me for saving his life in Torrance once, but I said I did not recall any such thing. I said I had never been in Torrance, but I now recall I was there briefly. It was a short stay. Then he told me he had come up on the train with Josh Stilwell, brother to Frank, whom I was supposed to have killed. The brother is going to shoot me on sight. You see what kind of a zoo I live in. It is all promissory bullets. If you give me away, this Mallen said, I will kill you. Who the ―― are you, I said, to threaten the likes of me? I ran into him in a saloon days later and asked the barkeep who he was, and the barman said he was a rancher who had sold out and was relocating in Colorado, had maybe come from Arizona, and had borrowed eight dollars, then ten, neither debt paid off. I knew then this Mallen was a total liar, one of the many I had run into in my short career. Next time I saw him was in Denver and he dropped his guns on me, had me arrested. Sheriff Paul does not know him and considers him a crank. He sure acted like one at Pueblo when he took down his clothes and showed a mark he said was a bullet wound, but which was the healed-up purulent sore of some disease. I laughed in his face, I couldn't help it. This Mallen claimed to have been with Curly Bill when he was killed, but he's lying again. I was more or less there when Wyatt did it, the killing, about three o'clock on a warm day after a long and dry ride from the San Pedro river, and we approached a spring situated in a hollow. As we did, eight rustlers appeared from behind the bank and sprayed us with gunshot, some thirty-five to forty bullets, cutting our clothes and saddles, killing one of our horses, but hitting none of us. A miracle, but we scampered out of there real fast, I can tell you, except for Wyatt who had ridden on ahead as he often did. I think we would all have been killed in that ambush if God had not been on our side. Wyatt Earp turned loose with his shotgun and killed Curly Bill. Each of those outlaws had a big price on his head, but none of them was Mallen. Wyatt said the name of each one aloud, having recognized them all, and he had warrants in his pocket for all of them dead or alive. Spence, Pony Deal, the usual trash. All wanted by the Wells, Fargo Company, whose stages they had robbed repeatedly. Deal, I was told, died a few days later, killed on the railroad by soldiers. Then I said the Earps were over in Gunnison, that we'd had a little misunderstanding about where to stay in Colorado, but we got that settled and I came here. Sorry, Mattie, I went on too long. That newspaperman really yanked my string.*

Hand-weary, Doc flexed his writing muscles, fished around for extra paper and prepared to say more, wondering why he was not writing her about Ovid and her almost enigmatic poem. Now they were both in nunneries, actually, and a word came to him he had never used with her. She was an anchorite, an anchoress. How had the word *anchor* gotten into *that?* Rock of ages? A weight that kept you steady? He went on, telling her how the Earps could not help him in Arizona without getting into new trouble themselves. He explained how he had told the interviewer that he owed his safety to the masses of red tape attending his incarceration. He owed something, he said, to Sheriff Bob Paul, of the frank open countenance and large physique, and hoped for similarly neutral treatment from peace officers everywhere. Bob Paul had referred to Doc as "decently peaceable," which was not a bad tribute, though, Paul had added, he was a holy terror to the criminals of Arizona.

The day after Doc wrote his letter to Mattie, Mallen confessed that his yarn of a seven-year hunt for Doc was a mere fabrication, anxious to claim a dwindling reward that had gone down from five thousand to five hundred (at what point did you cease trying?). A trumped-up arrest merited a trumped-up charge, and Bat Masterson, prompted by Wyatt Earp, now dreamed up a bunco charge that would keep Doc in Denver and go forever unheard. Doc paid his bond of three hundred dollars and emerged a free man, living on amid rumors that he had killed over fifty men and that Jesse James was a saint compared to him. The biggest lump of twaddle appeared in *The Cincinnati Enquirer* and gave Doc many a smile as he contemplated liberty in Denver. Perry Mallen vanished in possession of $161 and a revolver not his own, and was eventually arrested in Pittsburgh. Back to gambling and theatergoing, Doc kept on having minor squabbles with the law, as any opinionated full-tilt personality might; but his various cases were always the same case and his continuances stretched out to infinity. He had hit on a new form of permanence: ever accused, never called to appear; his sometimes tortured mind lingered on memories of the tassels on the train's window blinds when he left Arizona and how, in the darkness, men with shotguns at the ready among the steam and smoke looked like insects with short probosces.

Ah, freedom [he wrote to Mattie], *for a while there I thought the leaden doll was going to fall into the chasm and never be seen again, but now I feel game for anything. No more bounty hunters, no more threats from Arizona. I have become a Denver man, knowing nobody well enough to discuss my nonexistent private life with. I never talked about such things with Wyatt, even. There was no need; we both had mysteries we wanted kept that way, and each understood the other's need.*

> *Once I was in Denver jail;*
> *My head was thick, my eyes were pale.*

O.K.: The Corral, the Earps, and Doc Holliday

And when at last they let me out
I trumpeted like an elephant without mahout.

Coughing hard into the sun,
I gave in to more than one temptation,
Talked huckleberry and daisy, gave my word
Never to shoot when my senses were blurred.

Dear Mattie, it will improve, this doggerel of mine in response
to your graceful Ovid, who makes me think harder than ever. What is
she up to? Did she invent the whole thing? Maybe she invented Ovid
even as a theme for an exiled man. It makes sense. I used to be so feckless,
especially in my teens. Now, what do you think a feck is? No prize for
guessing.

·27·

So, in a sense, his life returned to normal, to a norm of gambling anyway, as he made the rounds of gaming establishments, riding on Colorado's narrow-gauge trains, a ghost peering idly at crevasses, crags and gigantic overhangs. Was he not now in the landscape always recommended to him for his health? As he sat there in the convulsive, rattletrap train, did his health improve fraction by fraction? Where did it start, in the feet or the head, or, more dramatic, in the lungs themselves? In Arizona, most of all when out in the wilds with Wyatt's posse, he had been living an imitation of the healthy life, countering long hours at the faro table by saffron lamplight with hectic riding that, while not the perfect exercise for someone such as himself, seemed to keep him fit, breathing restorative mountain air and active at least in the mount and dismount. Here, in Colorado, though, he had a sense of consummated mission, finally believing that picturesque mountains were bad for his bacillus; people here seemed to like being among their mountains, whereas in Arizona they liked the flatland, enjoying the hilly peaks as a mere backdrop. Now it was trains, then it was horses. He was grateful for the difference, amusedly wondering if you got a worse hardening of the seat from riding the train than from sitting on a horse. Either way, he found himself, once on board, squirming about, perching first on one buttock, then on the other, trying to find an equilibrium that perhaps never existed, doing his damnedest not to become one of the hard-assed courtesy of Colorado trains. One day in the future, he mused, train travel would be less of a torment, especially on the hindquarters. Meanwhile, grateful to be out of jail though never out of jeopardy, he rode the rails, for once taking time to savor and envy the occasional fisherman stranded there among the rubble, his rod jutting out like some attenuated bill as he tested the mumbling waters, and trains with two locomotives chugged by behind him. On he went, en route to Silverton or Pueblo, through the sheer Animas Canyon in the mineral heart of the San Juan range, a sufferer come home to roost among the peaks and hoping to try his luck once again, although without the huge greed that had informed his gambling since he could remember. Now he gambled in a diffident, experimental way, interested in whatever happened, almost resigned to losing all the time, which is what happened, as if the hex he'd been able to impose on games had withered away after being shaken to death by the Rio Grande Railroad. In his head, wherever else he went, he carried the image of the Palace Theatre in Denver, supposed by some to be a death trap for young men, a wen of vice and corruption. Bat Masterson had met his wife Emma there. The gambling room had twenty-five dealers, accommodated some two hundred players, and sported an immense gas chandelier in its ballroom, place that Doc longed to inhabit more than he dared enter it, blinding hoofers with the light from half a thousand prisms. The Palace, Doc thought, was more the land of heart's delight than any of the Tombstone or Dodge establishments had been. It gleamed, though its outside looked rickety and needed paint, especially when assembled patrons no longer stood in front of it at ground level or up on the low-fronted balcony, inmates allowed at last to go home, revealing the building in all its run-down aspiration, with what seemed two sentry boxes flanking the entrance (but these were public conveniences and known as such, called that out of bureaucratic euphemism). Doc even liked the name up high, *Theatre* with an *re*, which struck him as classier than *er*, more Southern don't you know, and he liked within the impression that depravity was always hovering, ready to descend on all those amateur debauchees who had come here in half-conviction only, looking for fun but also seeking some kind of social distinction that precluded the vilest forms of sin.

After a while, Doc took a job in Leadville as a faro dealer, an old vocation of his, at the Monarch Saloon, 320 Harrison Avenue, too easily provoked, however, especially by the presence of old Tombstone adversary Johnny Tyler, who had always known how to jerk Doc's chain, and did so repeatedly in Leadville, at last provoking him into an outburst so vehement and histrionic it got Doc fired. Doc-watchers of old would have noted the abbreviated shortness of his temper, his now almost total inability to regain his breath after a rhetorical outburst invoking orifices and secretions. Could it be that Doc was running down? The next stage was predictable: broke, poorer in health than ever, and liquored up when he could afford it, Doc managed to talk Mannie Hyman, owner of a saloon on rubble-strewn Harrison, into giving him a room. Then he had some wins at poker and was able to move to more rural quarters at 219 West Third. His only mistake during this miserable clamber back into respectability (which he sometimes took a fancy to) came about when he borrowed five dollars from an old Tomb-stonian called Bill Allen, a notorious troublemaker and pedantic settler of old scores whom Doc, responding to his insistent public duns, shot at with a Colt single-action .44, the bullet going high. Twirling around in the shock of being fired upon, Bill Allen slipped and fell, this time taking a slug in the right arm from a thoroughly enraged Doc, whom Captain Bradbury of the City Police promptly apprehended and disarmed. His bill paid by friends, to the tune of eight thousand dollars, Doc walked free into a winning streak at poker which enabled him to get his pocket watch and meager jewelry out of hock. When his trial came up, he explained what pains in the neck both Tyler and Allen had always been, was acquitted but told to get out of Leadville, which eventually he did, but not before making a final effort, by using his wits and his near-choreographic sense of human drama, to make ends meet again.

With Montague Baker, a sophisticated but unprincipled off-shoot of a reputable family, Doc concocted a swindle that depended on so-called golden bricks which, his story went, he had acquired in spite of their being stamped property of the United States government. Finding a well-heeled but gullible banker in Leadville, they persuaded him that he could have the bricks at the mark-down price of twenty thousand dollars. Tests followed, in which Doc substituted filings of pure gold for the metal his pigeon filed from the fake gold bars. The bargain was struck and with Baker the banker set off by train for Chicago. Strange to relate, before the pair of them arrived, self-styled marshals arrested the banker and his escort for receiving stolen property that also belonged to the government. Only by paying a fifteen-thousand-dollar bribe did the banker manage to buy his way out. Later on, he realized whose accomplices the marshals had been, and by then his money had been gambled away. That banker never visited the two-mile-high town of Leadville again, though Doc remained there, on and off, until 1887, but not before managing one final killing, of one of Bill Allen's men, an oaf named Kelly, who had taken it into his head to make a reputation by challenging the Doc as he faded and waned. Doc had always been able to muster an ornery mood when cantankerous deputies were in the vicinity, but he mostly did not shoot them, resorting mainly to verbal humiliation; yet, in his declining years, he did tend to shoot and heap his abuse on the corpse. None of this changed his reputation much; people always pointed him out, and he received many an example of what he came to call the dinosaur stare from those who, being ignorant, envied him, or, being wrongly informed, hated him on sight.

When faint of heart, he would look up at Mount Massive towering over Leadville and tell himself he was high enough to cure his lungs. Small moves he made, from Denver west to Leadville, then southwest to Silverton, east to Trinidad, then north back to Denver, executing a sloppy rhomboid he never noticed. He was, he liked to think, occupying his time, sometimes meeting Wyatt in Gunnison on the way from Leadville to Silverton, and vice versa, or going with him to the Tabor Opera House, an unlikely structure to have appeared in a town that in 1876 did not exist except as a broken and disfigured streambed. Three years later there was opera in Leadville and a civilization predicated on silver from lead carbonate. Doc had always responded warmly to the notion of wealth, gold or silver spurting from the earth: just his sort of acquisitive magic, but he also enjoyed removing money from other people by cards, bunco or con. You had to look out for the little (five feet ten to five feet six) peripatetic hermit of Leadville whose trigger finger was as soft as a dandelion stem, unlike his heart.

Jittery because he now needed a cane to walk with, not just to flourish as in the old days, Doc had decided that Denver, full of anti-gambling sentiment, was no place to be. The city was having one of its periodic outbursts of moral fervor, and once again he would be the target, an honest swindler among hypocrites. He had always felt a covert, illicit affection for the scapegrace Doc, maybe because, while training as a dentist, he had run the full gamut of respectability, even if later on he actually shoved his six-gun into the mouths of the anesthetized or removed all their teeth while they slept in the chair. This tolerance for himself amounted, he thought, to self-esteem, self-respect, helping him extend himself beyond customary limits; it had helped him turn gunslinger and bunco expert, rough rider and unofficial peace officer. Would it help him now as, with whitening hair, a bit of a wobble when he walked and an unfamiliar itch all over his body, he tried to find places to go to, to settle in for a while as Denver went through its latest bout of moral turpitude. Watching himself in storefront windows, he saw a frail, slender, stooping man almost like the Doc of long ago crouched at the draw, ready to blast the opposition with searing speed. Arrested for vagrancy, though it was less vagrancy than indecision about which street to take next, he began to review places to go, not necessarily to live in, but where he could go dawdling around, inhaling the good air and sometimes tucking into a bottle or a sturdy meal. Having tried Pueblo yet again, and dismissed it as a done, dead ville, empty as a bone orchard, he went and sat in Pap Wyman's little cabin that occupied the middle of Harrison Avenue, blocking all traffic and defying anyone who tried to plan the town. There he sat, on the step, as if evicted, next to a crude irregular sign that said "Doc Holliday Friend to Wyatt Earp of Tombstone."

It was a remarkable little kennel, defiant and rickety, but it had been there longer than it had any right to be, flanked by tall aspens that reinforced its synthetic look. Doc thought it was like sitting in a stage set, squatting in the doorway of Pap's cabin and looking out at the street while he thought and thought, counting the buckboards, horses, and covered wagons. Where should he go? The name surely had something to do with it. Battered map in hand, from frequent folding and refolding during his journeys by train as he matched the map's dot to the depot's actual appearance, or tried to match the steep relief surrounding him with the bland blanks of a map that showed relief only in the merest, sketchiest way, he reviewed the names he knew by heart, not all of them on the railroad, but reachable: Como, Gypsum, Glenwood Springs, Vance Jo (he liked that), Ouray (hurrah?), Dolores, Durango, Alamosa, Nepesta, Antonito, Waldenburg (he flinched a little at this dollop of the Germanic), Cripple Creek (he warmed at once to revisiting though he had right now no image of the place), Manitou and No Agua (he loved a place that explained itself). He could not decide.

High altitude was making him vague with not enough oxygen going into lungs that knew not how to use it anyway (and not enough nitrogen either, he noted with irritable learning), and only a couple of drinks made him blurrier than ever. Nor did he write letters as often as he should, no longer responding, answering, but being pungently allusive to something he no longer kept the text for, or had allowed to float away from him on a high wind, as if in some caricature of a broken old man prey to the elements, doddering, shuffling, clasping uselessly at minor tourbillons of mountain wind. What the hell am I doing here, he wondered. It should be making me better. They all said it would, but it strings me out, making me falter, ruining my aim, impeding my vision— I don't see the cards in correct focus. Now, what if I were to become a dentist all over again? I'd soon make them a bunch of plug-uglies and I'd have all their teeth in a leather sack, for sale in California.

Once again, for lack of a cogent reason not to, he opened up the rolled sheaf of cousin Mattie's letters: contraband from a nun, he thought, my old childhood sweetheart; I was jilted for Jesus. No, not fair: she went to him because I left Georgia for my health.

Where are you? [she had written to him] *Why do you never answer? There is a hiatus in our mail. Are you sick? Are you dead? Have you wearied of writing to a woman virtually bodiless? You said you were going to Colorado and I applauded, and you had left the carrion cactus and the bullets behind you, which was at least symbolically good. Perhaps the move has gone all wrong, they sometimes do, and you want to reverse direction, repack, and take it all back with you, but you can never get it the way it was, distributed through a house or crammed into a room. I wonder about you.*

I was going to send you the second and third Ovid poems (it's becoming a miserable little series, John), but this is more in the nature of an urgent letter inquiring about your well-being. Do write and say. Nobody takes half as much interest here in my poetry as you do. You were right in thinking that I had you in mind when choosing Ovid, who never saw his wife again; she stayed on in Rome, doing all she could to ensure his release from exile, and died in the attempt. He never left the Black Sea.

Urgently, from a spirited anxious heart,

Mattie

Previously, tears had formed when he read such fervent appeals, but nowadays the tears were there to begin with, thanks to the wind and the slicing sunlight. Something stirred his mind, some echo, Ovidian no doubt, of an old Roman verb that meant an eye tearing. It had been the verb for what an eye does when it runs. Nothing stayed put in that stagnant lake called his memory. He had to say things several times to his inner ear before voicing them at all. What had Oscar Wilde said in Denver on his visit back in April? "We can have archaic and eat it too." Doc, and just maybe Johnny Ringo, had been the only ones who laughed. Odd, because the pun had been in English. They were just a bit slow up Denver way, he thought, as at Tombstone and Dodge. This was not the country for literate humor. It felt as if he had dreamed all that. Had Oscar Wilde, locally known as Scar, really been there to talk about Benvenuto Cellini and the ethics of art? Sure, he said to himself derisively, ensconced like a permanent waxwork in Pap Wyman's obtrusive cabin, don't you remember what he said when they asked him why he hadn't brought Cellini along with him? If he was that good and worth quoting at such length, then where the hell was he? *Dead for some while*, Scar had answered. *"Who shot him?"* Nothing typified the Denver audience more than that; it was a Tombstone question shouted in the Dodge City manner. Ignorant as pig tracks, all of them. And what had Scar replied? *Had* he replied? Yes, stealing from Pap Wyman's saloon, where above the Bible in the entrance it said, "Please do not shoot the piano player. He is doing his best." No, the sign saying that was over the piano. Above the intimidating Bible it said, "Don't Swear." Scar had brought the house down with his reply. Benvenuto Cellini had always been doing his best. Nobody had shot him. He had shot his bolt. He had shot himself, maybe in a comfy little cabin obstructing the road, checking the flow of commerce. For a moment, Doc felt tempted, happy to have heard Scar as a final reward. Maybe that man too had been a dentist who hit the skids. Then Scar went to Leadville, dressed in a rubber suit, to descend into the Matchless mine in an ore bucket, bottle of whiskey in hand, which he shared with the miners, who survived the whiskey diet less well than he, revering him for this fact alone.

Then Doc remembered. He had been in jail when Oscar Wilde came into town, and his fervent memories had based themselves on a newspaper account, on several, in fact. He knew all about Scar's train being late, from Leadville back to Denver (a common enough occurrence), and how Eugene Field the newspaper reporter had dressed up in wide-brimmed hat, overcoat and wig, and had ridden through Denver lisping and waving a white handkerchief at the crowds lining the streets merely to rewelcome the venerable Scar, who hastened away from such gaucherie early that evening. Yes, Doc thought, but had he received his check? He probably had, or he would have hung around. No imitator, Doc had decided, could do justice to the shoulder-length hair, the cutaway and dark velvet knee breeches, the diamonds that dazzled like the opera house's gas chandelier. Here was a shiny young man indeed, allowed to go away unshot, something that he might not have managed to do in Tombstone or Dodge. Yes, Doc told himself, had I not been in the calaboose on a trumped-up charge, I'd have stood up, skinned my guns and offered him one to take away with him: the most dangerous gunman in the West giving a six-gun to Scar himself to kill the critics with, Doc Holliday to Scar Wilde, as the headlines might have had it. The trouble was, Doc's daydreams, perfected in jail, had taken on a mesmerizing quality he could no longer resist.

A lost word came back to him, evoking fabulous scenes of chivalrous conduct and elaborate social finesse. *Gracegentry*, he murmured. Now what the hell was that? Was it even a word back then? Who said it, used it? Did it mean a true aristocrat reserved the right to shoot at anybody who appealed to him as a target? *Droit de seigneur* applied to last things? The answer would not come, but the word remained to torment and beguile him as he wondered at its sudden appearance, its aroma of excess. Somewhere still, he thought, they use it, somewhere in Georgia or Alabama, where I will never go again, never see that greensward abounding. He would never be a mountain man, nor a seafarer, a rustler, an Indian scout, a tracker, a shoesmith, an aviarist, a *cavaliere servente*, a balloonist, a governor or senator, a painter, a poet, a lawyer or a dentist. It was a matter now of gathering up the various remnants of his being, even as his lungs turned to sludge, so as to have an entity with firm edges while awaiting the end, promised him long ago and not to be denied him. He was almost grateful, sad to have never settled certain questions: Wyatt's disguises, for example, a trivial example, but something that nagged at him. He would ask him outright next time they met with Bat and Emma at the Palace. Whatever happened to Wyatt's Mattie, addicted as she was? Why, Wyatt could have shot her on the quiet after seeing her off on the train from Tucson. There were other questions about Wyatt he no longer had the patience or energy to ask, mainly about the real estate Wyatt kept transferring to his father in California. He longed for the salty, awkward details of convent life from Mattie: the toilets, the washrooms, the insects in the bedrooms, the lack of speech or profanity, the true nature of professed faith (meaning how much of it was mumbo-jumbo and guess-work). The important thing in relationships, he decided, was loy-alty: you had to be true, you had to keep your bargains. If you had made a promise, keep it even if it killed you, and the same went for standing by a friend, right or wrong; this was why the incident of his seeming not to back Wyatt up on that one occasion bothered him so much (and Wyatt too, who clearly maintained the same code of behavior). You went to your end with so many things unresolved, he said; you died in tatters and doubt, raving for yet another day in which to tidy up loose ends, begin a new project that might save you.

Instead, this, as desperation and pain curtailed what might have been a long voluntary, neither of them able to reply to the other with sufficient speed, so that their ostensible exchanges became a mode of palmistry, hand to hand clasped, their ideas askew, their feelings laid bare on the surface for the other to see before it was too late, she on the moon, he underground, inspired by the ghost of Scar Wilde:

She: *There is no subject matter save how you are. Tell, for pity's sake. Do not hide from me.*

He: *Free again, but I dislike Pueblo now. I have thought about other places, maybe Glenwood Springs, which they call a sanitarium. We shall see.*

She: *As before, what is happening? Are you unfit to write?*

He: *The whiskey helps less. I am breathing more shallowly, like a frog in the dry.*

She (they sometimes seemed to achieve reciprocity, but it was an illusion): *Are you gasping then?*

He: *Not in iambic pentameter, but something less predictable, see, maybe closer to patterns of speech.*

She: *I could stand even a joke, anything, so long as I knew the truth about you. I am not a traveling woman anymore, you must appreciate that.*

He: *I sometimes forget who I am addressing, even in daily inter-course. I start out O.K., then lose it.*

She: *I could ask the police to find out.*

He: *Gracegentry—is that a word you ever heard in your childhood in the South?*

She: *So you still have not gone to Glenwood Springs, as promised. I wrote you there, not Denver.*

He (on a particularly woozy day): *Women with huge breasts feel possessed by them and that is what attracts men like flies to syrup. They sense themselves in the presence of the automatic and the lewd. Sooner or later the bosoms overpower the women. Don't answer, this is just a meditation.*

She: *May send the next two Ovids if you promise to take the train out to Glenwood Springs, G'wd Spr, as you write it, obsessed as you have become by code.*

He: *Can you believe it, when I got off the train I had to be helped. Legs seized up. Yep, I'm helping in the bar, doing faro again. Nice place, sort of purgatory. Don't comment on that, please.*

She (outraged by something else draws a line across the page to make him wonder what she might have written had she been using words): ————

He: *The Glenwood Hotel. I scare the room service boy s——less, always drawing my six-guns when he waltzes in, shouting stickem up, son, or be blasted. Once he dropped the whole ——— tray.*

She: *I think you were trying to offend me, but I defer to your request. No comment from this anchorite in training. You know better.*

He: *They have hot springs that will cure the dead, at least the cure is so extreme and caustic you know nothing bad can survive it. Every day I feel the springs of life recoil from such remedies.*

·28·

Ironic for Doc the pastmaster con man that the Glenwood Springs turned out to be sham, offering cures when in fact it extinguished many hopefuls, smothering them with the fumes of sulfuric acid, which in his case chewed through the tissue of his lungs, shredding them so much that there was no way of stopping the fluid from rising and choking him. He went into intermittent delirium like a broken homing angel, hooked on a daily tumbler of whiskey whose effects were both lethal and benign. He had always claimed the bugs would get him before the worms did. Bedridden and incoherent, with his gunbelt abandoned, looped around the brass ball of the bedstead, Doc was covered in sores and had now advanced from pulmonary tuberculosis into the so-called miliary kind, which invades everything, not just the lungs, like some fanatic general wiping out France to make sure of Paris. In a final con, while he was minimally alert, Doc had told Father Ed Downey, the priest, he was already baptized a Catholic and the Presbyterian minister, W. S. Rudolph, that he had been baptized (and raised) a Protestant. All he wanted to do, really, was keep his promise to Mattie to die in the faith, whatever that was. He was as vague about religion as the press corps about the sores on his body, which they claimed were healed-up wounds from a career of gunfighting. The only genuine scar had been inflicted at the O.K. by Frank McLowery the outlaw, killed only instants later.

Doc would have ingratiated himself with Hindus and Shintoists if he had had a chance, all religions for him approximating the same imagistic response to a baleful sense of the ridiculousness of human life, whose quantity he had never shirked reducing. All men were killers, he used to think; just a few were good at it. People who die in hotels get short shrift from the management, even if their bill has been paid. Sensing the damnable moment was

301

at hand, Doc exclaimed to himself that he felt such euphoria, having already swigged his daily bourbon. The day before, Wyatt had come and brought him a marshal's badge and kissed his brow, so he was free to travel now, as open as he had ever felt. "I'll be damned," he whispered, "this is funny." Dead by ten in the morning, he was put under by four, buried at the foot of the mesa until the bad winter weather abated and he could be moved up the steep mountain road to Linwood Cemetery, which they forgot to do. Up on the mountain, an empty chamber with his name on it awaited his lost corpse year after year, replete with simplicity and requiring one last boast: "In all my life I was never killed."

Paul West is the author of eighteen previous novels and the recipient of many prestigious awards, including a Lannan Literary Award for fiction and the Award in Literature from the American Academy and Institute of Arts and Letters. In 1996, the French government decorated him Chevalier of the Order of Arts and Letters.